Praise for

A DEEPER SHADE OF BLUE

'A sensual portrait of modern Greece, as well as a great page-turner: taste the salt, feel the heat as you follow the dramatic story . . . offers much more than the crime fiction genre usually encompasses: a rich and intelligent story, with fascinating characters'

Scotland on Sunday

'The very best crime novels are those in which location, character and story combine in a single, powerful whole. With *A Deeper Shade of Blue*, Paul Johnston stakes his persuasive claim for a place in that pantheon'

John Connolly

'A perfect setting for a tense thriller . . . This is an intelligent and satisfying book, part contemporary thriller, part the dark sister of *Captain Corelli's Mandolin*'

Scotsman

D0696360

A DEEPER SHADE OF BLUE

'A new departure for an immensely talented author, and the change of scene from the Scotland of the earlier books to the author's new home of Greece pays great dividends'

Barry Forshaw, *Publishing News*

'Clear your diary, take your phone off the hook and ignore the doorbell. The new Paul Johnston thriller is here . . . Once again, Johnston provides evidence of his talent for spinning an involving, sophisticated yarn, while his love for his setting, his many colourful characters and the Greek culture is infectious'

The List

'Has a fine sense of place, a brooding atmosphere of menace and a cast of exceedingly sinister characters'

Sunday Mercury

'Excellent'

Philip Kerr

THE HOUSE OF DUST

'In a series of highly original books set a couple of decades in the future, Paul Johnston has created a portrait of the post-Enlightenment city-state of Edinburgh ... the books are always entertaining, in part because of the unsquashably rebellious personality of Johnston's maverick sleuth, Quint Dalrymple, and the sardonic humour which enlivens the narrative ... another fine example of great storytelling'

Sunday Telegraph

'Johnston's plotting is consummate and his characterisation deft. He is also a very funny political satirist so that although *The House of Dust* is set in the future he is, of course, commenting on Scotland and England today. Very enjoyable'

Observer

THE BLOOD TREE

'Johnston introduces some welcome new characters and a change of scenery by sending his quirky investigator, Quintilian Dalrymple, outside the city state of post-Enlightenment Edinburgh to its hated rival, Glasgow ... this futuristic series is still refreshingly original and entertaining'

Sunday Telegraph

'Quint Dalrymple [is] a testy, tenacious detective ... a smart move to shift much of the novel to Glasgow'

The Sunday Times

WATER OF DEATH

'An acclaimed crime series . . . Johnston brings an intelligent perspective to the dark excitement of the thriller'

Nicholas Blincoe, *Observer*

'Both prescient and illuminating'

Ian Rankin, *Daily Telegraph*

THE BONE YARD

'A sly satire and gruesome thriller'

Mike Ripley, *Daily Telegraph*

'An ingenious and chilling thriller that has the added bonus of being a sardonic political satire'

The Sunday Times

BODY POLITIC

'A hugely entertaining fantasy . . . engagingly imagined'

The Times

'Imaginative . . . remarkable . . . shows that crime fiction can be not only thrilling but intellectually exciting as well'

The Economist

Also by Paul Johnston

Body Politic
The Bone Yard
Water of Death
The Blood Tree
The House of Dust

About the author

Paul Johnston was born in 1957 in Edinburgh, where he lived before going to Oxford University to study Greek. He made his home on a small Greek island for several years. He now divides his time between the UK and Greece. He is the author of five highly acclaimed previous novels, *Body Politic*, winner of the John Creasey Memorial Dagger for the best first crime novel, *The Bone Yard*, *Water of Death*, *The Blood Tree* and *The House of Dust*.

PAUL JOHNSTON

A Deeper Shade
of Blue

NEW ENGLISH LIBRARY
Hodder & Stoughton

Copyright © 2002 by Paul Johnston

First published in Great Britain in 2002 by Hodder and Stoughton
A division of Hodder Headline

The right of Paul Johnston to be identified as the Author of the
Work has been asserted by him in accordance with the Copyright,
Designs and Patents Act 1988.

2 4 6 8 10 9 7 5 3 1

All rights reserved. No part of this publication may be reproduced,
stored in a retrieval system, or transmitted, in any form or by any
means without the prior written permission of the publisher, nor
be otherwise circulated in any form of binding or cover other than
that in which it is published and without a similar condition being
imposed on the subsequent purchaser.

All characters in this publication are fictitious and any resemblance
to real persons, living or dead, is purely coincidental.

A CIP catalogue record for this title is available
from the British Library

A New English Library paperback

ISBN 0 340 76615 8

Typeset in Plantin Light by Palimpsest Book Production Limited,
Polmont, Stirlingshire

Printed and bound in Great Britain by
Clays Ltd, St Ives plc

Hodder and Stoughton
A division of Hodder Headline
338 Euston Road
London NW1 3BH

For Silje,
eventually

ACKNOWLEDGEMENTS

This book benefited greatly from the attentions of my excellent editor Philippa Pride, who fashioned a sleek tiger from the original woolly mammoth.

I'd also like to thank Karen Geary for brilliant publicity work; Sheila Crowley for running the most dynamic sales and marketing group in the business; and Briar Silich, whose department has skilfully handled rights.

AUTHOR'S NOTE

Readers should be aware of the following:

1) Greek masculine names ending in -os, -is, and -as lose the final -s in the vocative case: 'Panos, Lefteris and Nondas are raising their glasses.' But, 'Raise your glasses, Pano, Lefteri and Nonda.'

2) Feminine surnames differ from their masculine counterparts: Alex Mavros, but Anna Mavrou; Panos Theocharis, but Dhimitra Theochari. (Also note that the first two letters of Dhimitra are pronounced 'th' as in English 'these'.)

1

Outside, the half-moon, tilted on its back, was rising low over the eastern islands, casting a shimmering path on the grey-blue sea. A light breeze was blowing over the ridge, and on it came the creak of cicadas and the clang of goat bells from the upper slopes. The drag of water over the fractured feet of the cliffs below was a regular pattern, as soft and insistent as a lullaby.

Inside, the woman choked back a scream and drew fetid air into her lungs. She closed her eyes and counted to ten, but the darkness was still there when she opened them again. She pulled hard against her bonds. The ropes on her wrists and ankles bit into the raw skin, making her gasp, but she persisted with the movements, trying to understand what was happening. Her mind was spongy, unfocused, and there was a dull buzzing in the background. Was she drunk? She jerked back and forward again, tears spurting as pain shot up her arms and legs. For a moment she thought she was going to be sick, but nothing came. Her throat was too dry and her stomach was empty.

Then she heard the voices. They were low and hard to distinguish, coming from some point in the outer darkness. She swallowed hard and tried to control her breathing. The voices seemed to be familiar. There were two of them, one lower than the other, but her wandering mind couldn't locate the faces that went with the sounds. All she could tell was that the speakers were having a fevered discussion. Something told her that calling out to them wasn't advisable. She raised her bound wrists to her face and touched the broken surface of one cheekbone. Had she already made a noise? Had they hit her? She felt her stomach turn over.

The voices in the darkness were less tense now, the argument apparently over. The woman moved her back against the wall – it was much rougher than the wall of a house – and realised with a spasm of shock that she was naked. There was gritty sand on the skin of her backside and she drew her tied wrists up over uncovered breasts. She started panting as the nature of her predicament overtook her like a tidal wave. And then a light came on.

It was bright, blinding, and directed at her face. She tried to look away as it moved closer and felt another frisson of horror as she saw a loose assembly of bones in the far corner, plumes of skin and tattered tendons trailing away from it across the floor. Then the light was up close and a heavy hand took hold of her chin, forcing it up.

It was the laugh that broke her spirit, an explosion of inhumanity that the softer intonation of her other captor's voice did nothing to dilute. Without resisting she allowed herself to be pushed forward, rough hands on her breasts and between her legs, until she was crouching on all fours, her eyes clouded by tears. The light was withdrawn and she caught a glimpse of a tripod, heard the whirl of a video camera. Then she was caught by a driving agony. She had already sunk into the lowest depths of fear and desolation. The knowledge that a recording was being made of what she was enduring meant little to her.

It ended in a series of grunts. The woman was knocked against the wall and a heavy hand rained blows on her head and shoulders, as if she had failed the man who had assaulted her. The camera's sibilant clicking stopped and she opened her eyes. She saw boots, shoes, the tripod, but she kept her gaze away from the decaying body on her left.

And then, in the seconds before the light went out, a bottle thudded against her bare thigh, followed by a hunk of what smelled like bread in the sand by her face. The low voices faded and the woman stayed motionless. She understood that the screw had been tightened. She was not to be set free, she was not even to be slaughtered like a captive animal. She was to be kept in this stinking hole, she was to stay alive so that the bastards could continue violating and filming her whenever they wanted.

She tried to hold her breath until she passed out, tried to resist the temptation to open the bottle, but she soon gave in. She drank brackish, inert water and swallowed coarse bread. How long had she been here? When had she last eaten? She had no sense of time, no clear idea of where she was. A cellar? A deserted hut? A cave? In the distance she heard the sound of a vehicle start up and move off.

The enclosed space around her was sable, black as the most starless of nights, and she became aware of the flutter of scaly wings over her head. She wondered if they were bats, but whatever they were, the creatures didn't frighten her. They were nothing compared with the realisation that had crept over her.

She had no idea who she was.

2

Walking down Vrysakiou at the eastern boundary of the ancient marketplace, Alex Mavros spotted the shoplifter immediately. It was a little after ten and the sun was high in the sky, burning through the pollution cloud and suffocating central Athens. Tourists, thinner on the ground than they had been a few weeks ago during the high season, were picking their way in baseball caps and shorts through the shattered pediments and statues of the *agora*, their sights set on the Acropolis which was wreathed in scaffolding to the south.

As he watched the young man in the stained denim jacket and crumpled cream trousers, Mavros wondered why none of the shopkeepers had noticed the intruder. It was obvious that he didn't have much to spend, but he was running his hands through the oversize worry beads and picking up green metal replicas of ancient statues as if he were a genuine tourist. Then Mavros saw a group of men on the road and realised that the souvenir sellers were engaged in animated conversation, their attention slack in late September after months of good business. He could have identified the shoplifter to them – the guy had just slipped a reproduction of a figurine in poor-quality marble into the inside pocket of his jacket – but he decided to start the day with a test of his professional skills.

The young man, his thin face and dirty hair suggesting he was one of the large Albanian underclass that scraped a living in the city, moved quickly away down Adhrianou towards the Temple of Hephaistos, his eyes averted from the shopmen, who were now shouting at each other. Mavros went after him, keeping about ten metres between them. It was easy enough to find cover by weaving between the foreign visitors, some of them carrying heavy backpacks. After a few minutes, he realised that the shoplifter knew what he was doing. The young man ignored every shop, kiosk and stall until he was well away from the one he had hit, only showing interest again after he had turned right towards Ifaistou, the Flea Market's main thoroughfare. On it there were clothes shops and jewellers as well as stores selling tourist junk. He headed for a place festooned with watches and raised his eyes to the goods.

Mavros approached him slowly from the rear. This time the shopkeeper was alert, his gaze levelled immediately on the badly dressed individual in his doorway. Mavros thought about it. Either he could wait to see how desperate the guy was – how much he needed something to trade for food or drugs – or he could intervene before things got nasty; shop owners had been known to beat the hell out of thieves, especially if they were Albanian. The young man raised his hand towards a fake silver watch that probably wasn't worth more than a few thousand drachmas and Mavros decided to act.

'Don't touch it,' he said in a low voice, standing close behind the shoplifter. 'You understand Greek?'

Dropping his hand, the man turned to Mavros. His eyes took in the sunglasses, the shoulder-length black hair and the unshaven face, then were lowered to the white T-shirt and faded blue jeans. The alarm that had initially tightened the sallow skin on his cheeks was replaced by a look of incomprehension.

'Who are you?' he asked in heavily accented Greek. Although undercover police patrols operated in the Monastiraki area, they didn't make a habit of smiling at their prey.

Mavros beckoned him away from the shop to a neighbouring doorway. 'Don't worry, I'm not a *batsos*.' He used the colloquial term of opprobrium for the forces of law and order that equated them with physical punishment.

'Fuck off then,' said the Albanian, making to walk away.

Mavros caught his arm and looked into his open jacket. 'I think you'd better give me that,' he said, nodding at the blank, angled head of the stone figure that protruded from the shoplifter's pocket.

'So you can keep it for yourself?' the young man asked bitterly, displaying uneven stained teeth.

'No,' Mavros replied. 'So I can give it back to its owner.' He opened his eyes wide, hand extended. 'Please?'

The Albanian looked surprised by the politeness of the appeal. After a few moments' thought, eyes flicking up and down the crowded street, he decided against further resistance.

'Thank you,' Mavros said, taking the replica. 'Here,' he added as the shoplifter turned away. 'Get yourself something to eat.' He gave the young man a five-thousand note.

The Albanian stood speechless, his lips apart. Then his mouth formed into an incredulous smile. 'Are you a madman?' he asked, tapping his head.

Mavros laughed. 'Maybe. Go to the good, friend.' He was pretty sure that the shoplifter wouldn't take the words literally.

Back at the shop where he'd first seen the Albanian, Mavros waved the owner over from the heated debate about the latest foreign coach of the Olympiakos football team.

'Good morning, Alex,' the bald souvenir seller said, his eyes falling on the off-white stone sculpture. 'What are you doing with that?' He looked towards the shop. 'Is it one of mine?'

Mavros nodded as he handed the figure to him. 'You should be ashamed of selling rubbish like this, Kosta. The original Cycladic pieces take people's breath away. This just makes me want to throw up on your shoes.'

The tourist shark raised his shoulders, unconcerned by the quality of his wares. Then his eyes narrowed. 'Did you let another thief go? Mother of God, Alex, why didn't you hand him over? How are we supposed to make a—'

'Bye, Kosta,' Mavros said with a wave, heading off down the street again. The sharks made so much money from the tourists that they all had German cars and holiday homes with swimming pools on the coast of Attiki. What good would another Albanian in the cells do them or anyone else?

★   ★   ★

Mavros turned up an alleyway off Adhrianou towards a door wreathed with honeysuckle. Although the plant was well watered, the entrance to the small *kafeneion* was distinctly unwelcoming. The green paint had been in need of a new coat for years and the sign – Tou Chondrou, The Fat Man's Place – was hanging at an angle from the lintel. It was all part of the plan, as was the narrow passage beyond the door filled with cardboard boxes and empty bottles. The owner didn't want tourists cluttering up his café. He didn't really want anyone cluttering up the place – a year in prison during the dictatorship hadn't done much for his sociability – but he made a few exceptions.

'Good morning, Fat Man,' Mavros said as he went through the main room with its back-wrenching wicker chairs and out into the shaded courtyard.

The sole occupant didn't look up from the book propped against the chill cabinet with its meagre selection of cheese and vegetables. 'Morning, Alex.' Although the standard diminutives of Alexandhros were Alexis or Alekos, Mavros had always been known by the foreign form. Cynics like the Fat Man reckoned he stuck with it because he wanted to be different.

The courtyard, confined by the high walls of the surrounding buildings, was given shade by a wooden pergola that supported a spreading vine. As it was late summer, the branches were hung with bunches of dusky green grapes. The wasps and other insects they attracted were being enticed through short lengths of bamboo into plastic bottles containing sugared water; once in, they never found their way out and eventually drowned.

'When are you going to pick those grapes, Fat Man?' Mavros shouted as he sat on the canvas-backed chair he always used. 'It's like a zoo in here with all these creatures. Or a slaughterhouse, more like.'

The café owner – Yiorgos Pandazopoulos by name, but never addressed as such except by the hygiene inspectors, tax officials and policemen he despised – peered out into the yard. 'I like watching them die slowly,' he said, a slack grin appearing on his heavy features. 'You should get into it, Alex. Just imagine they're right-wing politicians.'

Mavros groaned. 'For God's sake, give it a rest. And bring me my *sketo*, if it isn't too much trouble.'

'Right away, sir,' the Fat Man replied with mock servility.

Mavros shook his head. 'You're living in the past, my friend. The old ideologies are dead and buried. No one cares about them any more.' He looked up at the drowsy wasps in the bottles above and breathed in the scent of grapes that were beginning to rot. 'Everyone in Greece is too busy making money these days.'

Shortly afterwards the Fat Man shuffled out, a stained white apron stretched over his swollen midriff, and placed a minute cup and a glass of water on the metal table with incongruous delicacy. 'Go to the devil, Alex,' he said, staring belligerently at his only customer. 'What do you know about this country? You're not even a real Greek.'

'Don't start that again,' Mavros said, taking off his sunglasses and running a hand through the swathes of thick hair that had swung down and obscured his vision. Then he picked up the cup and breathed in the dark, unsweetened liquid's sublime aroma. Whatever else anyone said about the Fat Man, he made the best coffee in the city.

'Don't start what again?' the café owner said, planting his thick legs apart on the gravel floor. 'Are you or are you not half Greek, half *Anglos*?'

'Wrong!' Mavros shouted. 'I'm half Greek but not half *Anglos*. How many times do I have to tell you? *Anglos* means English. My mother is Scottish.'

The Fat Man had raised his eyes to what was visible of the fume-choked sky. 'Screw you, Alex. You know well enough that *Anglos* means British in the common tongue.'

'Well, it shouldn't,' Mavros replied, blowing over his cup. '*Anglos* is English and *Skotsezos* is Scottish. You know which blood I've got in my veins.'

'Anyway, who cares about that half?' the Fat Man said. 'They're all capitalists on that rain-soaked island. Your father was Greek, you've lived in Greece most of your life, you did your national service here.' His brow furrowed. 'You've no right to give up the struggle, you traitor. Your father won't be resting in the grave, he'll rise again as a vampire . . .'

'Come on, my friend, give me some peace,' Mavros said, glaring at the imposing figure. It always amazed him how difficult it was for even committed communists to free themselves from the superstitions of the Orthodox Church that they had imbibed as children. 'Vampires? What kind of shit is that?'

'And what kind of shit is that job you do?' the Fat Man demanded, changing his angle of attack. 'Private detective? Private nose in other people's business, I say.' He leaned over his customer. 'You're no better than an underwear-sniffing cop.'

Mavros had his hand over his eyes. He had woken up with his head throbbing and it was worsening by the minute. 'Go away, will you, Fat Man? I've spent the last week looking for a fifteen-year-old junkie who went walkabout. The parents – remember those boutique owners from Kolonaki? – won't pay me the balance of my fee because they say he was on his way home anyway. I don't need this from you, not this morning.'

The Fat Man was nodding his head. 'See? What do you expect if you work for bourgeois wankers from the arsehole of Athens.' Kolonaki, 'Little Column', the area to the north-east of the parliament building, was the most upmarket district in the city. By coincidence, and to the delight of people on the left, *kolos* also meant 'arse'. 'Oh well,' the café owner said, his tone softening, 'everyone has to work, I suppose. Do you want some *galaktoboureko*?'

Mavros looked up. 'Have you got any left?' The Fat Man's mother made a tray of the custard-filled filo pastry every morning, but it had usually been devoured by the early-morning trade and his interlocutor by this time.

'For you, Alex, anything,' the Fat Man said, the irony less sharp than it could have been.

'Bring me a couple of aspirins as well,' Mavros called, glancing at the ponderous form in the kitchen and flicking the pale blue worry beads he'd been using to distract himself since he'd given up smoking a year ago. He'd known Yiorgos since he'd roamed the backstreets around the hill of Strefi in central Athens as a kid. The Fat Man was eighteen years older than Alex, making him fifty-seven, but he'd always had a soft spot for the boy. Mavros was sure that Yiorgos had initially befriended him because his father, Spyros Mavros, was a high-ranking member of the Communist Party. But a deeper friendship had developed over the years, one based on their mutual antipathy towards authority in any shape or form. Except Mavros had taken that a lot farther than his friend by steadfastly refusing to join the Party. He had seen too much of the damage caused by strongly held beliefs. What Yiorgos said about everyone having to work was a bad joke. His mother, now in her early eighties, kept the café going with her cooking and cleaning, but only just. The Fat Man survived by running illicit card tables late at night. If pressed, he justified himself by giving a sly smile and characterising Marx and Lenin as political gamblers.

The pastry and pills arrived, Mavros washing down the latter with the unchilled tap water the Fat Man had brought. He took a forkful of the *galaktoboureko* and closed his eyes as the glorious flavour of the filling flooded his taste buds. 'Aaach,' he moaned. 'How does she do it? It gets better all the time.'

The café owner nodded, his jowls wobbling. 'The crazy old woman won't tell me the trick, you know.' He shrugged. 'So when she goes . . .'

'Come on, Fat Man,' Mavros complained. 'I'm eating my breakfast and you're talking about dying?'

'What's the point of keeping quiet about it? We're all going to die some time.'

Mavros looked at his watch and waved him away. Any minute now a potential client would be arriving. He took his note-book from the pocket of his jeans and reminded himself of the name. Deniz Ozal. Turkish, but the accent on the telephone was American. He said he'd been given Mavros's name by Nikos Kriaras, a police commander the US embassy had contacted on his behalf. Apparently his sister had gone missing. So Mavros had told him to come to the Fat Man's. That was his version of the café owner's test. Any clients who turned tail at the sight of the run-down dive weren't serious enough for him. The Kolonaki boutique owners, dressed up in the latest outfits from Paris, had probably been turned on by the sensation of slumming; and by the smell of the *galaktoboureko*, which the husband had paid substantially over the odds to sample.

Mavros sat back to enjoy the remaining mouthfuls of his portion.

The door to the main room opened not long after he had finished eating. He looked up and watched as a middle-aged man of medium height with a thin moustache walked in with an assured air. He glanced at the Fat Man, twitched his head dismissively then turned towards the yard. He took in Mavros with a piercing look, running his eyes all the way up from the dark blue espadrilles to the mane of hair, concentrating finally on the firm, stubbled jaw, the aquiline nose and the dark blue eyes.

'You the private dick?' he said in English.

'I'm the dick,' Mavros confirmed with a loose smile. 'And you're Deniz Ozal.' He pointed to a chair with a wicker base.

The man was wearing a pair of tailored olive-green trousers with a matching short-sleeved shirt that he hadn't tucked in. The bulge of his stomach was still obvious. He rested his heavy briefcase on the floor, looked over his shoulder to establish that no one else was in the vicinity, and sat down opposite Mavros.

'Jesus Christ,' he said, wincing. 'How do you people sit on these chairs all day?' He peered at what Mavros was sitting on. 'Oh, I get it. The torture gear's for the tourists.'

Mavros glanced at his canvas chair and shrugged. 'You can have this one if you want.'

'Nah, forget it,' Ozal said. 'Do me good to remember the shit my ancestors went through.' He laughed, displaying straight white teeth. 'After all, Turks and Greeks are basically the same, aren't they?'

Mavros raised his eyebrows. 'I wouldn't recommend that as an ice-breaker at social gatherings around here.'

Deniz Ozal nodded. 'Tell me about it. I'm as bad as it gets as far as most Greeks are concerned – Turkish blood plus American nationality. That's probably why I get screwed so much every time I come to the so-called cradle of democracy.'

Mavros nodded. Ozal had a point. The historical enmity between Turks and Greeks had survived into the twenty-first century despite the moves of a few well-meaning politicians and the occasional outburst of fraternal aid after earthquakes; while American military involvement in the civil war that followed the Second World War and the CIA's machinations during the dictatorship of 1967–1974 had not been forgotten or forgiven by many Greeks.

'What are you then?' Ozal demanded, his eyes locked on Mavros.

'I told you, I'm the dick.'

'Yeah, yeah,' the Turkish-American said irritably. 'You know what I mean. Are you Greek or what? Your English is perfect.'

Mavros raised his shoulders. 'My father was Greek, my mother is Scottish. But I've lived here all my life, apart from four years of university in Edinburgh.'

'Edinburgh, Scotland, huh? Cool city. I went to an antiques auction there about five years back.' Deniz Ozal leaned forward and cocked an ear as his seat creaked. 'So how good a dick are you, Alex? It's okay if I call you that? What have you got that I should buy?' He turned towards the Fat Man, who was deep in his book of card games. 'Hey, can I get a cup of coffee here? What'd'ya call it? *Varyglyko*?'

Mavros nodded. Strong and extra sweet. 'What have I got? Didn't Kriaras tell you?' He'd known the police commander for ten years. When something came up that the official police didn't fancy, it would often be shunted in his direction.

The Turkish-American opened his arms. 'Sure he did, but you and him could be best buddies running a scam for all I know. You give me a sales pitch and I'll tell you if I like it, okay?' He leaned forward again. 'I'll tell you one thing. You don't look like any private dick I've ever seen. Haven't you got a set of decent clothes? Haven't you got an office? And what kind of hairstyle do you call that?'

Mavros blinked and put his hand to his forehead. If he was going to offload this guy, now was the best time, before he found out what the job entailed. He'd made the mistake in the past of sticking with a client he couldn't get on with for the sake of what seemed on first impressions to be an interesting case.

'Well?' Ozal said impatiently. 'What have you got, Alex?'

Mavros watched as the Fat Man lumbered across the gravel with the coffee and a glass of water.

'Thanks, pal,' Ozal said. '*Efcharisto*.' His accent and intonation were good. 'Hey, anything to eat?' He looked at Mavros's plate. 'What did you have?'

The Fat Man was already on his way back to the kitchen. Mavros knew for sure that, even if there was any *galaktoboureko* left, Ozal wouldn't get it. The café owner was even more anti-American than the Party's Central Committee.

'I wouldn't bother,' Mavros said. 'You don't want to eat in here.' He moved his eyes around the yard and up to the wasp traps dangling from the pergola.

Ozal followed his line of gaze. 'Jesus, I see what you mean. Look at those poor suckers.'

Maybe it was because he'd left his potential client hungry, maybe it was because at least this one wasn't an Athenian snob, but Mavros decided to go along with him. 'All right, Mr Ozal—'

'You can call me Deniz, Alex,' the Turkish-American said with a wink of complicity.

'All right, Deniz. What have I got? I studied law at university in Scotland, specialising in criminology. After my military service back here I worked in the Justice Ministry, implementing legislation, liaising with the police, that kind of thing. Then I got involved in a special study of the private investigation sector in this country. This was about ten years back when it was really taking off. People didn't have much faith in the police – they still don't – and there were plenty of cowboy operators . . . you know what I mean?'

'Very funny,' Ozal said with a grunt.

Mavros smiled. 'Who were no better than the criminals who were preying on their clients. That was when I realised I could do the job as well as any of the competition. Plus, it got me out of the office, as well as the barber's shop. It also allowed me to wear whatever I liked and it made me responsible only to myself.' He smiled again. 'And to my clients, of course.' That was Mavros's usual sales pitch. What it didn't include was any reference to the intense frustration he'd felt when he worked as a civil servant – frustration caused by political interference, bureaucratic incompetence and the gradual realisation that his conception of justice, which was based on the individual's rights and needs rather than those of the faceless state, wasn't shared by anyone else in the ministry's echoing marble halls. But he didn't think many of the people who wanted to employ him would be too interested in that.

Deniz Ozal sipped the coffee, his look of suspicion turning to one of beatific joy. 'Shit, this is great coffee.' He turned round. 'Hey, big guy. Excellent coffee. *Poly kalos kafes.*' The Fat Man looked up blankly then went back to his book.

'You speak Greek?' Mavros asked.

Ozal shook his head. 'Nah, just a few words I've picked up on visits. Anyway, keep going, Alex. You haven't told me about the cases you've cracked.'

Mavros shook his head slowly. 'And I'm not going to. You've heard of client confidentiality?'

'Good answer,' Ozal said, grinning. 'But you've got experience of tracing missing persons?'

'Kriaras must have told you that,' Mavros replied impassively, concealing the curiosity that had suddenly gripped him. Finding people who'd disappeared was his speciality – more than that, it was his *raison d'être*.

'Yeah, yeah. Give me some idea of what you can do, Alex. I don't wanna go into this blind.'

Mavros studied him then nodded. 'All right. For a start, I'm completely independent. I've got contacts where I need them and I know how the various systems work, but I only use them when I have to. Meaning I can avoid the bureaucratic snarl-ups that this country's famous for.' He paused as Ozal nodded approvingly. 'Second, I know the press and the other media, and I know how they work. I make sure they don't know anything about me and what I'm doing unless I want them to.' Ozal gave another nod. 'Third – and maybe most important for you – I have a hundred per cent success rate.' Mavros tried to ignore the customary stab of guilt. He really had succeeded in every case he'd taken on, apart from the one that meant most to him. But that wasn't business, that was family.

The Turkish-American looked sceptical. 'Is that right?'

Mavros nodded. 'It is. You know how I've managed that?'

Ozal laughed, an unpleasant grating sound. ''Cos you're the fuckin' Greek version of the Continental Op?'

'There's that,' Mavros replied, his expression intent. Obviously the man was a fan of Dashiell Hammett's stories. 'And there's the fact that I only take on cases I have a feeling for.'

Ozal took out a packet of unfiltered cigarettes from his shirt pocket and used a heavy gold lighter on one. 'What does that mean, have a feeling for? Have a feeling that you'll be able to handle them without screwing up?' He held out the packet.

Mavros shook his head and moved his hand to clear the smoke. 'Not exactly. I have to feel interested in the case or I won't take it.' He smiled and opened his eyes wide, then flicked his worry beads across the back of his hand. 'Now it's your turn to make a pitch.'

The Turkish-American blew out another cloud of acrid smoke, this time in the direction of the nearest humming wasp trap. 'All right, smart guy. See what you think.'

Deniz Ozal began to speak in a low voice and gradually the sound of traffic and the cries of the souvenir hawkers faded from Mavros's ears. Soon he was hooked.

★   ★   ★

Island of Trigono, 1500 hours, September 27th

The sun was glinting so brightly from the flat surface of the water in the harbour that Navsika had difficulty seeing the surrounding boats, let alone the mountainous bulk of the island across the straits.

'Let's go!' At the rudder Yiangos was smiling, but there was tension in his voice. 'It's time.' He gunned the engine and waited as she loosed the forward mooring rope. When she sat down next to the pile of dark red net, he steered away from the quay and headed for the far end of the breakwater's line of boulders.

The *trata* named *Sotiria* was a nine-metre-long, diesel-powered fishing boat with high bow and stern, and a squat wheelhouse amidships. Although the official season for operating with seine nets didn't begin for another couple of days, several of Trigono's fishermen had been out testing their engines and winches in advance of the deadline. Yiangos was hoping that people would assume his father had sent word for him to get ready and that he was doing the same thing.

'Look, Yiango,' Navsika called, her arm extended to her right. 'It's the beast.' She laughed, the wind flicking her raven hair across her chestnut eyes.

The helmsman glanced to the side and took in the blue hull of the large *kaïki* owned by Aris Theocharis. The bald, fleshy figure coiling a rope on the foredeck was following the *Sotiria*'s progress. The eyes under the green sun visor that he habitually wore were fixed on Navsika and his tongue was playing along his thick lips.

'Go to hell, rich man's son,' Yiangos said under his breath, spitting over the side and increasing the engine revs. He knew that Aris had been watching Navsika for years, openly staring at her as she changed from pretty teenager to stunning woman.

Yiangos looked ahead, making as if he were judging when to steer hard to port beyond the light but in reality watching his girlfriend. Navsika was sitting with her legs open at the top and crossed at the ankles, the material of her purple bikini bottom taut across her crotch. Christ, what a woman she'd become. Her firm, full breasts were hard to ignore, as the beast had just proved. He twitched his head. That fat bastard. He should keep his eyes to himself.

'Turn, Yiango, turn!' Navsika was staring at him, a wide smile extending across her face. 'What's the matter? Seen something you like?' She stretched her arms and pushed her bosom forward, then laughed. 'Not yet, my friend. Not yet.'

Yiangos completed the manoeuvre and lifted his weight from the tiller, his cheeks burning. Although they'd been a couple since they were fifteen, Navsika still had the power to turn him to jelly. He often felt like a little boy beside her; he couldn't understand why she stayed with him or what she saw in him. But that would all change when his father gave him the money that was due to him. This trip would show how useful he could be to his family and to hers.

Suddenly Navsika was beside him, her arm round his back. 'Isn't it beautiful?' she said, pointing to the island's eastern flank. The afternoon sun was still on the slopes of the southern massif, giving the dusty ground a deep brown glow. 'Aren't we lucky to have such a place for our home?' She laughed, her eyes bright. 'Think of all the tourists who come from far away to see Trigono.'

Yiangos grunted. He didn't like the foreigners, the loudmouths who crowded the bars and kept the local people awake till morning, but they had their uses – after all, they poured money into the island. What he was doing now was mostly for the foreigners. He felt a twinge of uneasiness, less because he feared he might mess up than because he didn't know how Navsika would react.

'Come on, misery,' she said, nudging him in the ribs. 'I said not yet.' She smiled seductively. 'But soon, all right?'

Yiangos felt her hand brush across his groin. He wasn't sure if they would have time before the delivery, but afterwards she would definitely see what a man he was.

'So let me get this straight.' Mavros moved the plastic ashtray off the table. 'You lost touch with your sister Rosa in the early summer after she came on holiday to Greece and Turkey.' He looked at the photographs Ozal had produced from his briefcase again. Rosa Ozal was a dark-haired beauty with a bright smile and a figure that looked good in a bikini. 'Until now the last contact your family had was a postcard from Istanbul in July and you've spent the last six weeks trying unsuccessfully to get the Turkish authorities interested in locating her.'

'Like I told you,' Ozal said, 'they don't give a shit about a foreign woman, even if she has got a Turkish background. At least not unless there's a body involved. To tell you the truth, the State Department people didn't get off their butts until recently either.'

Mavros held up the postcard showing an Istanbul street scene. '"I've met someone,"' he read. '"See you when I see you. Love, Rosa."'

'Yeah,' Ozal said, shaking his head. 'You can imagine how that went down with my mother. She's going crazy, thinking Rosa's been hijacked by white slavers and forced to do unspeakable things.'

'Your sister's twenty-nine,' Mavros said. 'Can she look after herself?'

'Sure she can,' the Turkish-American replied with a nod. 'She's a New Yorker, for Christ's sake.'

'Husband, boyfriend, partner?'

Ozal lifted his shoulders. 'Nah. Rosa dates guys but she isn't into long-term relationships.'

'And she was travelling on her own?'

'Yeah.'

'Has she stayed away beyond her scheduled return date before?'

Ozal shook his head vigorously. 'No way. She's really into her work in the gallery back in Manhattan. That's what worries me most. She'd never have given that up, even if she'd met the hottest date in the universe.'

Mavros put down the card and picked up a second, this one sheathed in a transparent cover. 'And now – out of the blue – comes a postcard from the Greek islands, dated six weeks before the Istanbul one.'

'Yeah. Like I said, it arrived back home a week ago.' Ozal looked at the transparent plastic envelope. 'I told my brother to put it in this before he couriered it to me. Not that there'll be any forensics on it after all this time, I suppose.'

'Too much forensic – the postman's fingerprints and your family's, for a start.' Mavros reached over and took the envelope. The postcard was a typical tourist shot of an island square, a blue-domed church sheltering behind a large tree and, beyond, a street lined with two-storey houses. An 'X' had been placed above a house with a distinctive blue-and-yellow door.

'"*Nisos Trigono, Kykladon. Ieros Naos Ayias Triadhas,*"' he read. 'Island of Trigono, the Cyclades. Church of the Holy Trinity.'

'Yeah, yeah.' Ozal lit another cigarette.

'And the handwriting is definitely your sister's?'

'Definitely.'

'No sign of nerves or compulsion?'

'I don't think so.'

'"This is more like it,"' Mavros read. '"Hardly any tourists, beautiful scenery, even an archaeological dig! X marks the house where I'm staying. See you all soon! (Sorry, Mama, the handsome men are already married . . .) Love, Rosa." Postmarked June . . .' He squinted at the blurred stamp. '. . . June third.'

'Fucking Greek postal service,' Ozal said, spitting strands of tobacco on to the gravel. 'It must have sat in a bag they forgot about until recently.'

Mavros compared the writing on the two cards. It was similar, although the Istanbul one was in capitals. 'And you want me to go down to Trigono to look for Rosa? See if she went back there?'

'Yeah. Maybe she met some guy after all.'

'I take it the Greek police aren't interested?'

Ozal stubbed out his cigarette. 'Your guy Kriaras got his sidekicks to call the police department on Trigono, but they didn't have a clue. That's why he put me on to you.'

Mavros was studying the Turkish-American. 'Why don't you take a trip down there yourself?'

'I haven't got any free time right now,' Ozal replied. 'I've got a shitload of meetings here and in Istanbul over the next week. Anyway, what's the use of me going down there? You're the local expert.'

'Not in the islands.'

'You want this job or not?' the Turkish-American asked. 'What's your problem, Alex? An all-expenses-paid trip to a holiday island? Sounds like a great deal to me.'

So why are you paying me to enjoy myself? Mavros wondered. Why is your business more important than your family? He looked at the Turkish-American. 'You're in the antiques trade.'

Ozal returned the look curiously. 'Yeah. How d'you know that?' He stared into Mavros's eyes, a puzzled expression spreading across his face.

'You mentioned earlier that you went to Edinburgh for an auction.' Mavros looked away, aware that Ozal had noticed the brown marking in his left eye. It was usually women who spotted it.

The Turkish-American's expression lightened. 'Oh, right. Smart guy. You pay attention. I like that.'

'I need to think about it,' Mavros said, closing his notebook. 'Don't worry, that won't take long. Can I ring you tonight?'

'Jesus, you're a hard man to convince,' Ozal complained. 'All right, call me at the Intercontinental at ten.' He got to his feet, one hand massaging his backside, and picked up the photos and postcards. He started to put them back in his case then changed his mind. 'Here, you keep these. You can drop them off at the hotel if you don't go for it. Maybe they'll help you make the right decision.'

Mavros nodded. 'Maybe they will.' He watched as Ozal moved towards the Fat Man, tossed him a couple of thousand drachmas – provoking no response – and left.

And maybe they won't, he thought. The idea of leaving the city for a barren rock inhabited by tourist-fleecers, fishermen and goats wasn't very enticing, even if Rosa Ozal definitely was.

The Fat Man raised his eyes from the book as Mavros came up to the counter a few minutes later. 'Alex,' he said, looking concerned, 'do you realise that you look like shit? You've lost weight, your fingernails are bitten to hell and your face is all pasty.'

'Thanks, you mountain of flesh.' Mavros handed over some notes. 'You look wonderful yourself.'

'No, seriously. You need a holiday.'

'Not you as well,' Mavros said with a groan.

The Fat Man shrugged. 'Only trying to look out for you, my friend. If you go on like this, that women of yours is going to take fright. What's her name again?'

'Niki,' Mavros said. 'Don't talk to me about Niki,' he went on over his shoulder as he headed for the door. 'I'm the one who's taking fright.'

The Fat Man laughed. 'You really know how to pick them, don't you, Alex? You're too handsome for your own good, my boy.'

'Not a problem you have to stay awake at night over.'

'Very funny. No, seriously, it's that weird eye of yours that attracts them. Like flies to—'

'It's a mark of my mixed heritage,' Mavros said in an elevated tone. 'How dare you equate it to a display of sexual power? It's a metaphor, a poetic marriage of—'

'It's a nasty brown stain on what would otherwise be a pair of beautiful blue eyes,' the Fat Man interrupted with a guffaw. 'Good health, my friend.'

Mavros smiled. 'Go to the good, comrade.'

The café owner watched the door close and shook his head before stuffing the money he'd been left into his back pocket.

3

Mavros went out of the Fat Man's and into the sunlight that was broiling the city. Ahead of him the Erectheion and the Parthenon were riding the tainted air above the rocky plug of the Acropolis. He took his sunglasses from his belt where they'd been hooked by one leg and put them on. Turning quickly to the left, he strode up the street towards the enclosing wall of Hadrian's Library. If he was lucky Deniz Ozal wouldn't have got too far ahead.

He caught sight of the Turkish-American in the crush around the engineering works in Monastiraki Square. Although the city council had been trying to clean up Athens in advance of the Olympic Games that were only three years away, it wasn't getting very far with the Flea Market. The bottom line was that tourists liked the dusty, overpriced souvenir, clothing and junk shops, and they liked the coconut and dried-fruit sellers. The coins and small-denomination notes they left in the begging bowls proved that they were even sympathetic to the gypsy women in bright chiffon veils, their pathetically deformed children spread out on the pavements like exhibits in a medical museum. So, as it was in no one's interest to change things, the council let the traditional local colour remain despite the revulsion it induced in many upwardly mobile elected members.

Mavros closed on Ozal as he moved up Ploutonos, making sure he was obscured by a group of French women who were haggling over the price of an ugly red-figure vase. He rarely accepted jobs before he'd obtained some background on his potential clients – he had once narrowly avoided conspiracy charges when a Piraeus gangster hired him via an intermediary to trace a guy who subsequently turned up attached to a cement block in the harbour. Deniz Ozal had piqued his interest more than most. He'd never yet come across an employer who told him the whole story at the first meeting. The Turkish-American seemed curiously at home in Greece. Mavros wasn't convinced that the Greek he knew came straight from a tourist manual. He was also wondering about the business dealings Ozal had apparently been pursuing in the weeks since his sister disappeared, dealings which seemed to mean more to him than Rosa did.

Stepping sharply to the right, Mavros positioned himself behind a stand of postcards – the ubiquitous fertility god Priapus with his giant, bent erection to the fore – as Ozal rang a bell on the other side of the street. This was interesting. The door opened and a shadowy figure in a bright red shirt ushered the Turkish-American in. Although the door closed quickly, Mavros had time to recognise the host and, anyway, he knew the premises. Tryfon Roufos of Hellas History SA was one of the most notorious – meaning corrupt – antiquities dealers in Athens. He was able to find his customers anything from Bronze Age figurines to the rarest of Byzantine icons, as long as they were able to pay his grossly inflated prices and live with forged certificates of provenance. Ozal had confirmed that he was in the antiques trade. It looked like he might not be restricting himself to the clearings from Scottish country homes these days.

Mavros waited where he was for a few minutes, scaring off a solicitous male shop assistant with a glare, before he walked on up the street. He hadn't found out anything concrete about Ozal, but at least he had a better idea of the person he was dealing with. Anyone who did business with Tryfon Roufos was well endowed both with funds, as the Turkish-American's clothes and briefcase had already suggested, and with dubious commercial intentions. Neither of these was necessarily a deal-breaker as far as Mavros was concerned, but he would have to watch his back. The most interesting cases usually gave him a frisson of illicit excitement, unlike the work he used to do in the ministry.

Heading through Mitropoleos Square, Mavros caught sight of

an advertising hoarding that had been erected in front of the ugly grey cathedral where the nation's politicians gathered like sheep on important feast days. The city centre had been plastered with this poster for weeks. Above and below an ancient lekythos, a flask that contained oil for offerings to the dead, were the words

Panos Theocharis Museum of Funerary Art
– Special Exhibition –
'Life and Death in Classical Athens'

Mavros stopped to examine the image of the lekythos. He'd always found the white jars, the graceful tapered base and thin body leading up to a curved handle and black-rimmed spout, compelling. This one was decorated with a painting of a male figure in a rough cloak, his face bearded, standing on the deck of a boat. Small letters picked out his name in the space above his triangular cap. He was Charon, the boatman who ferried the souls of the dead across the infernal river. Although recently it had happened to him less often than in the past, Mavros couldn't prevent the shadowy features of his lost brother Andonis flashing up before him. Andonis was his one failure, the missing person he'd never managed to find. He took a deep breath and blinked to dispel the face, still familiar though he hadn't seen it in the flesh for nearly thirty years, then turned off towards Ermou. He wanted to pick the brains of Bitsos, the crime reporter on the country's most respected independent daily newspaper, who was usually to be found eating *peïnirli* – hot cheese bread in the Asia Minor style – around midday in his favourite backstreet café.

Before Mavros got there, his mobile phone rang.

'Alex, *esí*?'

'Yes, it's me, Anna. What's up?' Since she'd married a Cretan, Mavros's sister always started off speaking Greek to him, but he would respond in English. Even when their father was alive, the children had spoken English in the house at their mother's insistence.

'Not what's up.' Anna's voice was tense. 'Who's up. Or rather, down.' In the background there was a less animated but equally insistent voice. 'Mother's slipped and fallen again.'

Mavros found that he was leaning against a shopfront full of women's undergarments. He shook his head and swore silently. 'How bad is she?'

'I don't know,' Anna said, a hint of panic in her tone. 'She says her knee's only bruised, but I think she might have twisted a ligament or done something to a cartilage. The doctor's on his way.' There was a pause. 'She wants to talk to you.'

'Alex?' Dorothy Cochrane-Mavrou sounded more in control than her daughter. 'Don't worry, I'm fine. I didn't want Anna to bother you. It's the marble floors, you know. I've never really got used to them.' She'd never lost the burr of her Scots accent either. 'Alex?'

'Yes, Mother.' Mavros knew what was coming.

'Are you very busy?' Dorothy's voice was less assured now. 'Only it would be lovely to see you. It's been a while . . .'

Mavros was shaking his head again, trying to ignore the pair of high-cut black knickers at eye level behind the glass. It was precisely three days since he'd seen his mother. Then again, if he was going to take the Ozal case and hightail off to the Cyclades maybe he should build up some reserves of maternal goodwill. For all her Scottish blood Dorothy was as clinging as any Greek mama. He glanced at his watch – a stainless-steel Gucci number that Anna had given him on his thirty-eighth birthday and which the Fat Man had designated an insult to the working classes. The reporter Bitsos would be back in his office soon. He'd have to catch him later.

'All right, Mother,' he said, 'I'm on my way. You listen to what the doctor says.'

'Yes, dear, of course.' Dorothy's voice was lively again now that she'd got her way. 'See you soon.'

Mavros walked on, skirting a huge motorbike that had been chained to a metal post and was blocking the pavement. As he put a foot on to the road a Honda 50 brushed past at speed, the adolescent rider shouting abuse. Bastard bikers. Mavros loved the city, it was his territory. Ever since he was a kid he'd felt at home in the uneven, ankle-shattering streets and the smog-filled squares with their incongruous classical names. He knew it was crazy, but he'd learned to accept both his curious obsession with the city and its numerous failings – apart from the motorbikes and scooters. Despite the regulations that allowed only half of the cars registered by Athenians into the centre each day, and gave priority to the yellow trolleybuses and their blue-and-white diesel counterparts, the avenues and streets were clogged from not long after dawn until well into the evening. So the locals, apart from investing in a second car, made sure they also had some form of two-wheeled transport, which was immune to the restrictions. Mavros hated motorbikes like the plague and regarded their riders as self-centred, dangerous fools. He walked everywhere he could.

As he began to scale the slope of Pindharou that led towards the bald, green-fringed summit of Lykavittos, the city's highest central point, the crowds thinned. The area of Dhexameni around the reservoir built by the Romans was residential, only the throw of an anarchist's grenade from the centre of the exclusive Kolonaki Square. Mavros stopped and looked down the narrow spaces between the apartment blocks towards the glistening blue of the Aegean east of Piraeus. The suburbs stretched down towards the sea in a pungent haze, and his ears rang with the blast of horns and the revving of engines. As he turned to go, an old woman bumped into him. Her face was heavily made up, her yellow linen suit from a high-class boutique.

'Well?' she said in a voice drenched in vitriol. 'Let me past. What are you waiting for?'

Mavros stepped into the road and watched her move carefully down the steep pavement, almost hoping she'd take a tumble. He twitched his head at the unworthy thought. But her words struck him again as he walked towards his mother's block on Kleomenous, the spectacular stretch of water glinting up at him invitingly. Trigono lay basking out there, free of crowds, motorbikes and sharp-tongued harridans.

What was he waiting for?

Trigono, 1715 hours

The *trata Sotiria* rounded Cape Oura at the south-eastern corner of the island and headed westwards. Yiangos was standing with an arm on the rudder and a foot on the long rod attached to the throttle, a cigarette between his teeth. Although his curly brown hair was short, the breeze and the momentum of the boat were ruffling it. He cut the engine revs and let the boat bob along on the swell. The southerly wind wasn't more than Force 4, but they were now beam on to it so he couldn't afford to let his concentration drop. He was early, but he didn't want to take any chances. Perhaps the others would be too.

'Look!' he cried. His left arm was over his eyes, the right pointing towards the outermost of the chain of islets ahead. 'Look, Navsika!'

The young woman was lying beside the winch wheels on the forward deck. She sat up, drawing her long, tanned legs beneath her. The purple bikini top stretched as she raised her arm to shade her eyes. 'What is it, Yiango?' she said, looking over the glare of the waves.

'Eschati,' he shouted. 'The last island before Santorini. There's good fishing on the western side.'

'Good fishing,' Navsika said to herself. 'Is that all you can think about?' She ran her eye all around. There was empty sea on three sides and only the bare, near-vertical cliffs running down from the summit of Profitis Ilias, Trigono's highest point, to the north. Beyond the forbidding rock face was the great ridge that linked Profitis Ilias with Vigla, the other main peak. Seeing that they were alone, she undid the clasp of her bikini and released her breasts. Maybe that would take Yiangos's mind off the fishing. She looked sternwards and groaned. Now he was bending over and doing something with the nets. She lay down again and let her thoughts drift away, feeling the white skin on her chest tighten in the breeze. If her mother could see her now . . .

What were they doing? she wondered. Yiangos's father Lefteris would go crazy if he discovered the boat had been used when he was away at the court on Syros. The *trates* weren't allowed to fish with the heavy nets until the season began on October 1st, and if the coastguard caught them things would be even worse. Ach, shit on them all. You're only young once and Yiangos was a beautiful boy, she'd known him all her life. Not that she intended to marry him – they weren't even engaged. She had other ideas about her future. She'd learned a lot from Eleni the archaeologist. Eleni said she was smart enough to do the university entrance exams again, smart enough to study in Athens. And Eleni's foreign friend Liz had told her the colleges in England were desperate for foreign students. It was a pity Liz had left so suddenly, without even saying goodbye.

'Wooo!' Yiangos was upright at the stern, his eyes wide open. 'You'll make me hit the rocks, Navsika. Put them away.' He grinned at her uncertainly. She'd recently started doing things like that, pushing beyond what the island's young women were permitted. 'Do you want me to help you with that suntan oil?'

'Wait till we're on the beach, idiot,' Navsika replied, laughing. 'I don't want to have to swim back to Trigono.'

Yiangos shrugged. He wasn't intending to jump her on the foredeck when they were under way – his father's boat was far too precious to take risks with – but it did no harm to show that he was interested. If he wasn't careful she'd be after a smarter boy. He was sure the archaeologist and her crazy friends had been encouraging her to dump him. But today he would impress her, today she'd finally see how important he was.

'Your loss,' he said. 'I'm going to be too busy with the winches to lie around.' Busy with the ship's gear – that cover story wouldn't last much longer. His stomach clenched again as he asked himself how Navsika would take it when the other boat arrived.

Yiangos put another Marlboro in his mouth and scratched a match down the worn grip of the tiller. He knew Navsika was drifting away from him, he knew he wasn't good enough for her. But some of the stuff she'd picked up from the women who weren't from the island wasn't so bad. He took a surreptitious look at her open legs and bare chest. That made him remember what she'd let him do on the beach beyond the cemetery a couple of nights ago. He felt a stiffening in his groin and turned his head to the right, taking in the cliffs and the caves hollowed out by the sea at the shoreline These waters were dangerous even when the wind was light. He looked back out to sea, but there was no sign of the speedboat.

Soon the islet of Eschati drew close, the summit of its low brown hill marked by a light on a metal frame. Yiangos remembered his grandfather telling him that during the war the Italians had disabled the lamp in order to make the passage harder for the *kaïkia* that carried Allied soldiers and agents between the mainland and the bases in the Middle East. Old Manolis knew plenty of stories about those times, but he rarely opened up. When he was a little kid Yiangos had heard the old man talking to his father Lefteris late at night when the *tsikoudhia* they made from the fermented skins of the family's grapes had loosened their tongues, but his attempts at eavesdropping had been unsuccessful – in the house they always spoke in a low mumble, as if everything they had to say was top secret.

On the starboard beam now were the solid forms of Aspronisi and Mavronisi – White Island and Black Island – the first and smaller of pale rock, the second of darker volcanic stone. The pair guarded the entrance to Vathy inlet, the only safe anchorage on the south coast. The narrow bay was over half a kilometre long but access for vessels was difficult, restricted to a ten-metre channel between Mavronisi and the main island. In the old days they'd loaded ore and lignite from Trigono's mines on to boats at Vathy. When the seams ran out before the war, the settlement in the inlet was abandoned. Yiangos had only been down it once when there was a festival at the derelict church of Ayii Anargyri. Virtually the whole population of the island had gone by boat, people spreading out after the service to eat their picnics on the pebble beach. But the priest was old now and he only observed saints' days in churches that were accessible to his son's four-wheel-drive Nissan.

'Eh, Navsika! Get up!' Yiangos shouted. 'We'll be dropping the forward anchor in a minute.' He steered to port, rounding the low promontory at the north of Eschati. The island was shaped like a teardrop, the raised ground with the light on the wider southern part. 'I need your help.'

Navsika sat up and reached for her bikini top. For some reason she felt uncomfortable acting the deckhand with bare breasts. Then she put it down again. If she didn't hold Yiangos's attention now, he'd get straight into testing the winches. She looked round at the narrow beach on Eschati. She'd heard from her cousin who ran tourist trips in his *kaïki* during the high season that the sand was soft, and today there was no one else anywhere near the islet.

She knew what she wanted as she glanced across at Yiangos and smiled. Judging by the way he returned her gaze, his eyes focusing on her chest, she was sure that at last he'd come round to her way of thinking – even if he did keep looking over his shoulder to the south.

As soon as she'd dropped the anchor into the rippling, translucent water, she stepped out of her bikini bottom and plunged overboard.

Yiangos wasn't too far behind.

Mavros turned the key and pushed open the glass street door. The hall of the apartment block was cool and his nostrils filled with the pungent smell of the cleaning fluid used by the janitor. Although his mother's flat was on the sixth floor, he ignored the lift and started up the stairs. As he passed the second landing an elderly man with thin hair and a tightly knotted tie looked at him suspiciously from a half-open door.

'*Kali mera*, Mr Theo,' Mavros said jauntily. He was addressing Theodoros Ioannidis, a retired senior civil servant and fervent nationalist who despised people he'd once misguidedly described to Dorothy as 'long-haired layabouts'. He'd also given her to understand that he disliked being addressed by the diminutive form of his first name, a piece of information she'd immediately passed on to her long-haired son.

Mavros went on towards the sixth floor, his pace slowing as the breath began to catch in his throat. Not for the first time he regretted his commitment to using his feet whenever possible, as well as his mother's decision to move out of the family's run-down neo-classical house on the other side of Lykavittos after his father's death. He'd loved his early childhood in the Neapolis district with its haphazard mixture of elegant nineteenth-century buildings and modern blocks. He'd also been very fond of the musty house, originally built by a currant exporter, that was such an unlikely dwelling for a senior communist official. It had long been in the Mavros family, the men having been lawyers rather than ideologues until Spyros combined the two, and he was as devoted to it as anyone. He squared it with the Party by putting up penurious students and visitors – often on the run from other countries – which meant that life in the old mansion was never dull. But Dorothy had never felt at home there, despite her adoration of Spyros, so it came as no real surprise when she used her own money to buy a modern flat. The house Mavros spent his formative years in was now an official Party hostel. He reckoned that was as good a use for it as any.

'It's all right, Alex.' Anna was in the hall of the flat as soon as he opened the door. 'It's only a heavy bruise.'

'I told you it was nothing to worry about,' came a triumphant voice from the lounge.

Anna Mavrou-Chaniotaki raised her brown eyes to the ceiling and mouthed imprecations.

Mavros put his hands on her shoulders and kissed her lightly on both cheeks. 'Calm down,' he said, shaking her slender frame gently and hearing the material of her pale pink blouse rustle. As usual his sister was dressed in the best that the designer outlets of Athens could offer, her short skirt displaying perfectly tanned and exercised legs. Her stockbroker husband Nondas liked her to look her best at all times. 'So the doctor's been?'

'And gone,' Anna said, the nodding of her head making her gold earrings rattle; her jet-black hair, drawn back in a clasp, didn't make any false moves. She was five years older than Alex and had two teenage children, as well as columns in several of the capital's fashion and gossip magazines. Organisation and method were her watchwords, much to her husband's approval.

'Nondas all right?' Mavros asked as they moved towards the *saloni*. Despite his brother-in-law's dedication to the money markets and his behind-the-scenes involvement with the conservative Nea Dhimokratia Party, Mavros couldn't find it in him to dislike Nondas Chaniotakis. He was a lively, well-educated Cretan who liked to eat in neighbourhood *tavernes* and who regarded his rich man's toys – the BMW, the motor launch, the home cinema – with only passing interest. He loved his wife and his children too much to be engaged by the status symbols required by his profession and his party.

'Mmm,' Anna said distractedly. 'I really ought to be getting over to the *Ena* office, I've got a piece to outline to them.' But she followed Mavros into the spacious room where their mother was sitting in an armchair, the older woman's left leg bandaged and stretched out straight. 'Honestly, Mother, you were lucky I happened to drop in. You must be more careful, you'll—'

Dorothy Cochrane-Mavrou raised an arm. 'Leave me be, Anna. I can manage perfectly well on my own.' Her dark brown eyes flashed as she turned towards her children, the pure white hair with its natural waves catching the light filtered through the half-closed blinds. 'When I *break* my leg, then you can be worried.'

Anna stepped to the window impatiently, her dark red lips set in a tight line.

Mavros bent over Dorothy and kissed her. 'She's right, Mother. You should be more careful. These floors are—'

'Stop it, Alex,' the old woman interrupted. 'You know she only does it to annoy me.' Dorothy and Anna had spent years perfecting the ultimate mother–daughter routine. They were devoted to each other, but were incapable of exchanging more than a few sentences without irritation flaring.

'I'm not getting involved,' Mavros said, assuming the neutral position he'd established when he was at primary school – he'd had the examples of his father and his brother Andonis to follow. 'Anna's only trying to be the dutiful daughter. You know that's the way in this country.'

His mother made a dismissive sound. 'They're far too obsessed with family here,' she said firmly. 'People should learn to cope as individuals.'

Mavros took in her long, spare form, then found his eyes drawn irresistibly to the black-and-white photographs in matching plain wood frames that were the only ornament on the waist-high bookcase beside Dorothy's chair. Individuals and families, they made up the dual heritage that Mavros lived with. His Scottish mother was self-reliant and had never been able to come fully to terms with the priority Greeks gave to family. The individuals in the family, especially his father and his brother, were strong characters, leaders, but they had taken their strength from the family that nurtured them. Mavros had always felt split between the demands and duties of family and a burning need to be alone, to find his own way in the world. But whatever he did, Spyros and Andonis were never far from his mind – and he was glad they weren't, for all the pain he had from his memories of them.

He looked at the photos. Spyros had been in his fifties when the picture was taken. Five years later, his heart gave out a few months before the Colonels started persecuting the leaders of the left. His thick black hair was combed back from his handsome face, the hooked nose both his sons had inherited dominant. Above the open-necked shirt the skin on his throat was heavily wrinkled, giving him the look of a much older man. The years he'd spent in detention camps on remote islands after the Second World War and the subsequent civil war had taken a heavy toll. The old communist's mouth, surmounted by a heavy moustache, rose at the corners to form a tentative smile, hinting that, despite the terrible weight of his suffering, he had somehow retained his faith in humanity. His eyes, dark blue in life but glossy black in the photograph, seemed to have witnessed great happiness.

Dorothy took in the direction of Mavros's gaze but kept her own eyes to the front. 'Let them be, Alex,' she said in a lower voice. 'They were with us and now they have gone. Will you never learn to accept that?'

Mavros was only dimly aware of her words. He was staring into the flat pools of Andonis's eyes. The photo didn't do them any kind of justice. Although Andonis was eleven years older than his little brother and had disappeared when Alex was only ten, the bright blue of his eyes was what people still remembered about him. Alex's were darker, the brown flecks in the left one the result of a rare genetic mutation that made him stick out from the crowd. But Andonis had also been prominent since he was a small child, the burning blue of his eyes joining with the force of his personality to cast a spell on everyone he met. Boys listened to him and laughed with him, girls fell head over heels in love, both at school and later at the polytechnic. He had been one of the most daring of student anti-dictatorship leaders, even though he was younger than many activists. He was his father's son, resourceful and inspiring, possessing few of his mother's analytical powers and never for a moment in doubt of his abilities. There were a few people who had found him arrogant and overbearing.

And then, one night in December 1972, he had failed to return to the family home in Neapolis where he still slept. He had been at a meeting of an underground cell in the nearby town of Paiania and his comrades took him to the bus stop. But no one had seen him since.

Mavros sometimes wished that he could lose sight of his vanished sibling, even though the sudden flash he'd had of Andonis today when he was looking at the lekythos on the museum poster had been more vivid than the image in the photograph. He suspected that things would be easier if he could move on. But he'd been haunted by his brother for so long that he couldn't imagine life without him. It was Andonis who lay beneath his work, it was his love of Andonis that drove him to search for strangers – as if by finding them he was keeping some faint glimmer of his brother alive in the family.

'Alex,' Dorothy said quietly, 'you have to stop chasing shadows and ghosts. You've tried everything. You've spoken to witnesses, you've been through all the public and secret records you or anyone else can find. Please' – she took his hand – 'let Andonis go.'

'Where have you been looking this week, *adherfouli*?' Anna said from behind him, her use of the affectionate diminutive at odds with her stern tone. 'Eh, little brother? Where have you been wasting your time since I last saw you?'

Mavros straightened up. 'I traced a taxi-driver in Glyfadha. I heard about him from a new contact. The guy had supposedly been in the security forces during the dictatorship.' He looked away from the bookcase. 'It turned out to be a case of mistaken identity. He spent the winter of '72 to '73 building a hotel in Limnos.'

'Mother's right, Alex,' Anna said, grasping his arm. 'You have to leave Andonis in peace.'

Mavros shook his sister off gently, not wanting to fall out with her. He was attached to her, even though he rarely made that obvious, but he didn't much like her gossip-fuelled life or her ultra-modern house in the rich suburb of Kifissia. The poster he'd seen for the Theocharis Museum came up before him again, the image of the white flask with the sepulchral boatman. Ancient Greek myth had it that the souls of the unburied dead roamed for ever, denied access to Charon's bark and the shadowy underworld ruled by Hades. That was how he'd thought of Andonis since he was a boy. His elder brother was a lost spirit wandering the earth, haunting him by day and by night, often appearing as a blurred face in which only the bright blue eyes were real. The reality was that Andonis was a permanent part of the structure of Mavros's life. Because of his dual nationality he'd always felt different from other Greeks, and the mystery over his brother's disappearance during the country's most recent experience of totalitarian rule had made the sense of alienation, of living on the margins, even more pronounced. The fact that he had a flawed eye seemed like confirmation of that.

'Yes?' Anna asked, touching his arm again.

Mavros nodded haltingly, loath for her to know that he resented the way she'd built a life that had little or no room for Andonis.

The truth was that he used Anna's intimate knowledge of Athenian society in his work; as long as he disguised any requests that were to do with their brother, she never refused him. He wasn't proud of the way he manipulated his sister, but he didn't want to lose that precious resource.

Dorothy struggled to her feet, waving away their offers of assistance. 'I'm going to make us some lunch,' she said, limping towards the kitchen.

'No, no,' Anna declined hurriedly. 'I really must go.' She bustled away after kissing them both. She knew that the meal would take time to prepare and consume.

Mavros remained, allowing his mother to limp around, fussing over him and feeding him the smoked salmon she'd started ordering on the Internet from a supplier in the Highlands of her homeland. He'd never felt comfortable in the flat. He didn't like the heaps of books and papers relating to the publishing business Dorothy had run single-handedly for years. He felt that the clutter had given her a way to block out those she had lost, though he knew she remembered Spyros and Andonis in her own way. Over the years she'd filled a niche in the book trade for philhellenic publications, the scribblings of the numerous British visitors over the centuries who'd succumbed to Greece's charms. Mavros was with the majority of Greeks on that issue. He couldn't stand the pseudo-lyrical bullshit, twisted history and shallow, updated mythology that professional Greece-lovers spewed out. A famously crude critic had once called them 'Greek landscape fuckers' and he could see what the guy was getting at – sexually repressed Northerners were often inspired by the mute terrain rather than by its human occupants who might answer back. Dorothy took an opposing view and, as the numbers of British tourists had increased, so had the profits of her company, Persephoné and Hecate Publications.

Despite those feelings Mavros stayed in the flat all afternoon. He was tired. The week he'd spent asking low-life dope dealers if they'd seen the boutique owners' spotty kid had taken it out of him. It was easier to let time roll by rather than bother about

Deniz Ozal and his missing sister. There would be time enough
for the Turkish-Americans later.

Before he knew it, the private eye had nodded off in his mother's
chair, worry beads entwined in his fingers.

Trigono, 1845 hours

The sun was in the far west now, casting an orange light tinged
with purple through a low layer of cotton-wool clouds over Sifnos
and Milos. The southern cliffs of Trigono were in the shade, but
the teardrop form of Eschati was still lit up. The wind from the
south had stiffened, the waves running in harder from Ios and the
faint mass of Santorini's shattered volcano.

The *trata Sotiria* was no longer riding off the sandy beach. Its
anchor had been pulled up and its bow was now pointed towards
Mavronisi and the narrow entrance to Vathy inlet. As it rocked in
the swell, a metre-long scrape on the waterline amidships showed
beneath the second of the three old tyres that acted as fenders.
Seagulls hovered above the boat, their barking call ringing out in
the clear evening air. They took it in turns to swoop down and
inspect the nets that were trailing from the stern, soaring back up
on the air currents to begin their cry again.

Two metres below the surface, Navsika and Yiangos were in
a tight embrace, their naked limbs wrapped around each other.
Strands of the girl's hair were being washed through the dark red
skein of the net. Their eyes were wide open, their lips drawn back,
but no bubbles were being expelled into the chill salt water from
the couple's lungs.

As the *Sotiria* drifted towards the teeth of the rocks another
sound, high pitched and playful, could be heard. The notes of a
herdsman's pipe were fluting out over the ridge that ran between
the flanks of Mount Vigla and the whitewashed chapel marking
the peak of Profitis Ilias. Almost immediately they were scattered
and lost on the breeze.

4

Mavros finally tracked the journalist Bitsos down to an *ouzeri* in a backstreet near Omonia Square. Although it was evening – the garish lights of the shops around the city's hub of commerce burning the eyes and dubious deals of all kinds coming into their own – there was no reduction in the crush of humanity. Athenians worked late, shopped late, ate late and played late. The air was heavy with nostril-stinging exhaust gases, the odour of grilled meat from the *souvlaki* joints and the smoke from thousands of cut-price cigarettes. The district was sleazy and encrusted with decades of filth, but Mavros harboured an abiding affection for it. He smiled as he crossed the narrow street towards To Kazani, The Cauldron, then jerked back as a long-haired young woman without a helmet roared past on a powerful motorbike and almost took his toes off.

'Idiot!' he yelled after her.

'Wanker!' came the shrill response.

Inside the ouzo-house every table was taken, the surfaces covered with glasses, small carafes and plates of *mezedhes*. Mavros spotted his contact in a corner, the chair next to him piled with papers and folders.

'Still hungry, Lambi?' he asked.

The crime reporter was cramming octopus salad into his mouth, soaking up the olive oil and vinegar dressing with chunks of bread. He was in his late forties, bald and surprisingly slim considering how much time he spent eating. A pair of gold-framed glasses hung round his neck on a cord, and his short-sleeved shirt was spotted with traces of the day's meals.

'What are you after, Alex?' he asked suspiciously. 'I don't suppose you want to buy me a drink out of friendship.'

Mavros smiled as he transferred Bitsos's papers to the floor and sat down.

'Eh, careful with those,' the journalist complained.

'Leave off, Lambi. Got your dirty magazines in there?'

Bitsos gave him a long-suffering look. 'My dirty magazines are under here.' He lifted his backside to reveal a cushion of glossy editions, the cover of the top one showing a pair of half-naked, bottle-blonde women in a clinch.

Mavros shook his head. Lambis Bitsos was divorced, his three daughters grown up, and he visited the hard-core kiosks in Omonia at least once a week. 'Give it a rest, Lambi,' he said. 'It'll come off in your hand.'

Bitsos took a sip of ouzo and replenished his glass. 'What do you mean? I'm doing a story on the porn industry.'

'I believe you,' Mavros said ironically. 'How many years' research have you put in now? Thirty? And still no results.'

The journalist laughed. 'I wouldn't say that, Alex.'

A waiter appeared, his head inclined. Mavros ordered more ouzo and a prawn *saganaki*. He wasn't hungry after his mother's lunch and – unlike many Greeks – he could drink without eating, but he knew the melted cheese delicacy was one of Bitsos's favourites.

After a run-through of the latest crime stories – the government minister who'd had his son's dangerous driving charge pulled, the ship-owner whose illegal weekend villa had suddenly become legal after the investigating official took an all-expenses-paid trip to Bangkok – Mavros asked Bitsos about Tryfon Roufos, the antiquities dealer in the red shirt he'd seen Deniz Ozal visit.

'Roufos?' the reporter said in a low voice. 'That greedy, fuck-anything-that-moves vulture? Every night you can find him in the shittiest bouzouki clubs groping creatures plastered in make-up, most of them Greek-Russian immigrants whose papers are as fake as the mayor's hair colour.' Bitsos's expression was suddenly avid. 'Shall we go?'

'No thanks,' Mavros replied. 'I don't go to those dumps. That music's an insult to animals, never mind human beings. Anyway, I know where to find Tryfon Roufos. He isn't going to tell me what I want to know.'

The journalist dribbled water into his ouzo glass and took a sip of the cloudy mixture. 'And what exactly is it that you want to know, Alex?'

'What's he up to these days?' Mavros leaned closer, breathing in the savoury aroma of the *saganaki*. 'In particular, is he up to something with a Turkish-American by the name of Deniz Ozal?'

Bitsos looked at him thoughtfully. 'Deniz Ozal?' he repeated. 'Can't say the name means anything to me.' He dipped another piece of bread into the metal dish. 'No, definitely not.'

Mavros sat back. 'Oh well,' he said. 'That's good. Probably.' He swallowed ouzo and glanced away, taking in the hubbub in the *ouzeri*. In the far corner a shapely middle-aged woman with long black hair was fiddling with a guitar and an amplifier.

The reporter was looking disappointed. 'Don't you want to hear the word on Roufos, then?'

'Why not?' Mavros raised a hand to the waiter and pointed to the empty carafe.

'Right,' Bitsos said, licking his lips. 'The Antiquities Squad are about to nail him, or at least try to nail him, for trafficking in fifth-century Corinthian coins. Apparently a private collection was stolen six months ago from a house in Vouliagmeni. There's also talk that he sold one of those Cycladic figurines – you know, the ones with their arms under their tits and the vacant expressions on their faces – to a German collector for a mound of money. And at the weekend one of his people was caught on the ferry to Italy with an icon that went walkabout from Mount Athos last . . .'

Mavros let the journalist rattle on, not paying much attention. The singer had started off on one of his favourite songs – Chatzidhakis's '*Odhos Oneiron*', 'Street of Dreams' – and he felt himself float away on a wave of melancholy. For a moment he saw Andonis's face again then, to his surprise, it was replaced by the soft features of Rosa Ozal from the photos her brother Deniz had given him. He came back to himself when the crowd started clapping and looked at his watch. 'I've got to go,' he said, getting to his feet and throwing down a couple of five-thousand notes. 'Have something else, Lambi,' he said. 'To eat, not to play with yourself over.'

Bitsos laughed. 'Thanks, Alex. Anyway, I don't need any more magazines. Not today. We'll talk, my friend.'

'Yes, we'll talk,' Mavros said, raising his hand.

On the street he headed towards the nearest kiosk to call Nikos Kriaras. The police commander had left a message on Mavros's mobile with a number and time to call after Mavros had tried to reach him earlier. Kriaras was paranoid about being bugged, with good reason – the most muck-raking of the newspapers had invested in surveillance equipment which they often pointed in the direction of senior establishment figures.

'Yes?' The voice was sharp, no identification given.

Mavros leaned up against the yellow wooden side of the *periptero*, the day's newspapers fastened to a string with clothes pegs above him, his hand over his free ear. 'This is Mavros.'

'Are you on a land line?' The tone was still brusque.

'Yes. On the street. Happy?'

'Not very. What do you want? Be quick about it.' Nikos Kriaras tolerated Mavros because the police needed someone to do the jobs they either couldn't or wouldn't take on, often to do with foreigners who didn't appreciate the Greek way of handling things. The fact that Mavros wasn't interested in playing politics had helped to keep the unofficial conduit open.

'Deniz Ozal.'

'Ah. He came to you?' There was a hint of apology in the commander's voice. 'I should have warned—'

'Doesn't matter, Niko,' Mavros interrupted. He'd deliberately used Kriaras's first name to put him even more on the back foot.

'No names, wanker,' came the angry response.

Mavros smiled, remembering the girl on the motorbike. He'd

been characterised that way twice in an hour now. One more time and maybe it would come true. 'What kind of language is that for a—'

This time it was Kriaras who cut in. 'Stop it. This is foolish. What do you want from me?'

'The individual in question,' Mavros said, going along with the policeman's demand to avoid names for the time being. 'Is he on the level?'

'As far as I know.'

Mavros gave a hollow laugh. 'Are *you* on the level?'

There was a pause. 'As far as I know he's clean. You can go ahead with him. That's why you're asking, isn't it?'

'Of course. I hope you're right.'

'Trust me.'

'Oh, I do.' Mavros pressed his head closer against the *periptero*. A man in a leather jacket was perusing the papers behind him. 'Did you know he's an acquaintance of Tryfon Roufos?' he asked as quietly as he could above the noise of the cars.

There was another pause, this one longer. 'Is he really?' Nikos Kriaras was trying to sound unconcerned, but Mavros thought he'd caught a bum note.

'Yes, really. Are you sure you didn't know?'

'Certainly. Why would I?'

Mavros glanced over his shoulder. The guy in leather had gone. 'You know plenty about our friend TR, though. What about the Corinthian coins? What about the icon from—'

'All right, all right.' The policeman was animated enough now. 'How do you know about those?'

'No comment,' Mavros said with a laugh.

'Stupid question. You have evidence linking the Turk to "our friend", as you call him?'

'Turkish-American,' Mavros corrected. 'And no, I haven't. Not yet, at least. But do you still think he's on the level?'

There was silence on the line. Mavros peered through the small side window of the kiosk, taking in the stacks of chewing gum, cigarettes, condoms, batteries and biscuits. The elderly man inside caught the look and raised an eyebrow. Mavros opened his eyes wide in a gesture of indifference.

'If what you say is the case,' said Kriaras, 'if he has dealings with our Greek friend, then I'd be reluctant to put any faith in him.'

'I don't want to start a religious cult,' Mavros said in irritation. 'I just want to do a quick job.'

The commander laughed, a dry, grating sound. 'Come on,' he said sardonically. 'Surely you don't need me to vet your clients for you.'

'No, I don't. But I also don't need you to set me up with an international criminal.'

'Very well,' Kriaras said, businesslike now. 'I'll check and let you know if I find anything you should be aware of.'

'Thanks a lot,' Mavros said sharply. 'Be sure you do.'

The policeman laughed again. 'Calm down. You look after our foreign visitor and I'll look after you. If you don't hear from me, assume there's nothing on him.' There was a click and the phone went dead.

'Fuck it,' Mavros cursed, moving round to pay.

A wizened old woman in a crumpled housecoat and slippers glared at him. 'What are you saying, sir?' she asked in a scandalised voice.

Mavros watched as she wandered off towards the rear entrance of one of Omonia's filthiest pay-by-the-hour hotels. What was her problem? He turned up Stadhiou towards the more upmarket square of Syndagma, heading for home.

The wailing started just after dark.

At first the villagers thought it was kids chasing each other through the narrow streets. Then the noise moved closer to the square and the words became clearer. The words and the names.

'Navsika! Navsika!' The final syllable was a long scream of agony.

'Yiango! My son, my sweet son, oh Yiango . . .'

There was a cascade of feet on the paving stones, questioning voices in between the screeches.

'What's happened?'

'Who is it?'

Another desolate wail. 'My girl, my beautiful girl, what happened to you? What happened to you?' The woman's words trailed away in a bitter groan. 'What evil fate . . .'

'It's Navsika, Christos's and Marigoula's daughter . . .'

'Navsika? What's happened to her?'

Another scream. 'Drowned! The sea has taken them from us . . .'

'Taken them? Navsika and Yiangos? Oh my God! How?'

Ear to the door of her house in the wall of the Venetian castle, old Maro listened, trying to make sense of what was going on. Navsika? Yiangos? Drowned? No, it couldn't be. Not Navsika and Yiangos. She was related to both of them, not closely to Navsika but Yiangos was her great-nephew, her brother Manolis's grandson. My God, how could you do this to us? Her hands were trembling, her eyes filled with salty tears. Haven't we suffered enough?

She felt pressure on the door and stepped unsteadily back.

'Are you there, Kyra Maro? It's me, Rena.' The woman, in her late thirties and wearing black blouse, skirt and knee-length stockings, bustled in and took the old woman's arm. 'Come, sit down and I'll tell you what's happened.'

Maro allowed herself to be led to the table, her eyes blurred. In the bright glow of the gaslight she could make out that Rena's expression was kindly but excited. Death always roused passions on Trigono.

'Is it true?' Maro asked. 'Is Yiangos really—' She broke off and tried to visualise the boy, tried to remember his face. Since her eyes began to darken a few years back, she hadn't been able to see people unless they were as close to her as Rena was now. It had been a long time since any of her family had been that close. The dead boy had never even been in her house. She recalled a handsome face, a cheeky grin and a sturdy frame that had seemed to grow in great spurts. But then she'd only seen him occasionally; across the square at Easter, or down at the harbour for the Epiphany celebration when he and the other village boys would dive into the freezing January waters to retrieve the cross.

'Kyra Maro? Are you hearing me?' Rena's hand was on hers. She always addressed the older woman respectfully as Mrs Maro. 'Don't cry.' Then the younger woman let out a sob herself. 'Oh, why shouldn't you cry? Everyone on Trigono is crying tonight.' Outside, the screams were louder than ever as all the island women joined in the grieving.

Maro pulled her hand away and tried to cover her ears. That sound, the sound of desperate keening, was killing her. She'd done it herself when loved ones died and she couldn't bear to hear it again. Until her eyes betrayed her, she'd gone to her fields on the slopes above the Kambos whenever there was a death in the village. Stayed out there with her donkey tethered to the ridge wall till the funeral had taken place and the *miroloyia*, the ritual lamentations, were over.

'What . . . what happened?' she said, staggering to her feet and moving towards the door.

Rena was quickly by her side. 'Oh no, Kyra Maro, don't go outside. They won't . . . they won't like it. Yiangos's mother Popi is in a terrible state, what with her husband Lefteris in Syros . . . the other women are rallying round her and Navsika's mother, but it's not . . . it's not a good time to go out, Kyra Maro . . .'

She felt herself being taken back to the table, Rena's arm around her back. 'Thank you, my girl,' she said, the words making her eyes flood again. My girl, my daughter. Maro had no daughter, no one to look after her in her decrepitude as was the custom. Her own family hated her, refused to have anything to do with her. Only Rena cared for her, came in every day to check that she had enough to eat and to refill her drinking-water bottle at the public tap; did her laundry, even swept the floor of her tiny two-roomed home in the metre-thick walls of the old fortress. Rena, who'd come from Serifos to marry a local builder and been left a widow, childless and barely tolerated in the village because she had refused to move out of the house her husband's family wanted back after his death. She'd defied them, insisted on what was legally hers, and people hated her, said terrible things about her. But she was a good woman, she still wore the black of mourning and refused to return to her own island. She said she'd put down roots on Trigono and enjoyed renting her spare rooms out to tourists in the summer.

'They were in the nets, Kyra Maro,' Rena said haltingly. 'It seems that Yiangos had taken his father's *trata* to check the equipment or maybe to do some illegal fishing, and Navsika went with him. Oh God, who knows what they were doing?' She leaned closer. 'They were both naked, clinging together. And the boat was drifting towards the rocks off Vathy inlet. Some fishermen from Paros came round the western end of the island and managed to get a rope on the *trata* before it was smashed to pieces on the rocks.'

Maro looked up and blinked, her vision more blurred than usual. 'They were naked?' she repeated.

'Naked and caught in the nets,' Rena said, nodding. 'They were being dragged through the water.'

'Drowned,' Maro said softly. 'My God, drowned. Not more victims of the sea. What happened? The wind isn't so strong, is it?'

Rena shook her head. 'Not very. And Yiangos knew how to handle a boat. Kyra Maro?' She watched as the old woman's head dropped forward till it was almost touching the embroidered tablecloth. 'Are you all right, Kyra Maro?' She lowered her own head and tried to see Maro's face. The eyes were half open and there was a faint groaning coming from her mouth. Maro often sank into a reverie. She could remain in such a state for hours.

'Ach, old age,' Rena said quietly. 'Yes, Kyra Maro, you go off into your own world. It can only be better than the one the rest of us have to live in.' She got up and moved towards the door, cocking an ear. The wails were less strident now; the women would have moved to the houses of the bereaved. She was going to join them. Even an outsider like her could be of some use at a time like this.

A few minutes after the door closed behind her old Maro raised her head slowly and looked around. She ran her arm across her eyes, the sleeve of her ragged cardigan soaking up the tears. Then she walked carefully to the door and locked it. Now she was truly alone. No one could reach her except the ones she wanted.

Going into the small, musty bedroom with its single iron bedstead, she slid her hand into the pocket of her old lace apron and took out a box of matches. She lit two candles in the hollow in the wall that was used for icons in other homes. Her holy place contained a single framed black-and-white photograph. It was of a young man in military uniform, cap on his head and leather strap running diagonally across his chest. He was looking into the lens with a restrained smile.

Maro stared at the photograph from close range then stepped back. 'My love,' she said. 'My sweet love. Come back to me now.'

She bent down and pulled a tin box out from under her bed. 'Come back to me,' she repeated as she opened the battered lid and lovingly lifted out a misshapen, blackened skull.

Mavros walked up the slope from Monastiraki, trying to ignore the blast of bouzoukia and the cheers of tourist groups as they took their turn at performing Zorba's dance in the rip-off joints. That was the problem with living so close to the Acropolis. He glanced up at the great crag, the columns of the temples red in the floodlights of the *son et lumière*. Obviously the narrator was describing one of the great battles, Marathon or Salamis.

He lifted his eyes and took in the velvet of the night sky, the pinpricks of stars glinting through the pollution cloud. A breeze had got up so at least he'd be able to sleep easier. He inhaled deeply as he reached the corner of Pikilis. Even though he was only a couple of hundred metres from the snarls of traffic on the central boulevards, the air was already sweeter. The scents of bougainvillaea and hibiscus floated up from the ancient marketplace, mixing with the underlying aroma of pine needles dampened by the early autumn dew. Mavros felt his spirits lift. For all the clamour and the press of sweaty bodies, the city retained an irresistible hold on him. Then he saw the graffiti some moronic kid had sprayed on the wall – 'Athens, I fuck the whole of you'.

He turned the key in the wooden door of number 18 and hit the stairwell light. Nothing. He swore under his breath. He'd replaced the bulb only last week. There was no light under his ground-floor neighbour's door so Mavros had to feel his way up to the first floor. It was a pity he didn't smoke; matches or a lighter would have been useful. Then, as he reached out for his door, he realised that his feet were catching in something sticky.

He cursed again, kneeling down in the darkness and tentatively putting a finger to the marble surface. The smell was familiar, a faint odour of thyme. He wondered what the cleaner had been playing at.

He managed to get the key in, the metal scraping the paint of the door, and fumbled for the switch. No light here either. He could see the glow of the streetlamp through the shutters that he'd left closed in the morning, so there hadn't been a sudden power cut. His own fuses must have blown. He stepped inside then remembered his feet, bending over to pull off his espadrilles. The fuse box was in the kitchen. Moving in that direction, he blundered into something hard.

'Shit!' he exclaimed, clutching his right shin.

It was then that he heard stifled laughter from the armchair in the corner of the main room. A match flared and was applied to the thick candle on the coffee table.

'Niki!' he groaned. 'What the hell are you doing?' He moved the heavily laden magazine rack aside.

'Didn't you like my offering outside?' Another throaty laugh. 'I thought it was perfect. Sweet honey for my sweet man.' The irony in the voice was lacerating.

Mavros swallowed hard and went into the kitchen to re-engage the switch of the main circuit. The lights came on in the sitting room and he focused on the form curled up in his black leather chair. Andhroniki Glezou's long legs, bare under a loose orange skirt, were drawn up beneath her, her arms crossed under the

shapely breasts that her tight T-shirt emphasised. Her pale face
with its delicate features and small straight nose was composed,
but her dark eyes were as restless as ever beneath the crown of
tousled, highlighted hair.

'Well,' Niki said, her tone softening. 'Aren't you pleased to see
me, Alex?' She caught his eye. 'Why didn't you call me? I left you
a message.'

'Did you? I never got it,' Mavros lied. He'd turned his phone
off when he was at his mother's and hadn't felt like returning the
message after he left there. The truth was that Niki had begun
to get him down. 'I've been busy and . . .' He let the words trail
away, knowing that, whatever he said, he was in her sights.

'Sweet man,' she said lightly, smiling at him. 'Of course you've
been busy.' Her eyes flashed. 'Busy offering your arse to people
who are rich enough to pay for it.'

'Niki, I—' He broke off when he realised that she was still
talking.

'Haven't you realised, Alex?' she said, unravelling her legs and
standing up, right arm raised and left foot forward like an Amazon
about to cast a spear. 'You're a whore, nothing more. All you care
about is that your clients hand over the cash.'

He shrugged, knowing that any comment would only make the
onslaught worse.

'Because you only work for rich people, don't you?' Niki continued. 'You only work for thieving businessmen and foreigners
who've more money than Croesus.' She held her position, the arm
still up. 'Well, you do, don't you? How many poor people have
you ever helped? Have you ever taken on a case for free, out of
the goodness of your heart?'

Mavros was leaning against the door jamb, his eyes lowered.
He'd worked without a fee on more than one occasion, but Niki
wouldn't believe that. She was a social worker and she spent her
days with immigrants from the former Soviet Union who'd come
to the home country with nothing to their name except their Greek
blood-line. After six months with her, he had realised that she
resented every evening she had to spend on her own. She was

an orphan and had rejected her foster parents, though not until after they'd paid for her to go to university in London.

'Leave it, Niki,' he said, turning away and taking a bucket and sponge out of the cupboard. His upstairs neighbour was a ballet dancer and he knew she was performing these evenings. If she came back and dragged her precious feet through the honey Niki had smeared on the landing, he'd be in even deeper trouble.

'No, I won't leave it!' she shouted, her voice breaking. 'You're a freak, Alex, with your two-tone eye and that brother you're forever hero-worshipping. Why can't you pay attention to someone who's alive for a change?'

Mavros froze.

She came over to him quickly and clutched his arm. 'I'm sorry, Alex, I'm sorry,' she said, tears welling up. 'Let me clean up, I was only . . . I was only trying to make a point.' She pulled the sponge from his hand and went out into the stairwell.

Mavros took a deep breath then filled the bucket and followed her. 'Bit of a sticky situation,' he said in English as he squatted down on the marble. He knew there was no point in arguing with Niki. She would only become more hysterical and, besides, she was right – he was a freak. The worst thing was that, most of the time, it suited him.

Niki let out a sobbing laugh and brushed the hair back from her face with a forearm. 'Oh Alex,' she said. 'What are we going to do?'

He smiled at her, then left her kneeling on the floor as he went to screw the stair light back in. He didn't have any thoughts about what they were going to do as a couple. Although he found Niki sexually exciting – she was a wild woman between the sheets or anywhere else – he struggled to handle her mood swings. He knew what was going to happen tonight. As she was hopeless in the kitchen he'd cook something for her and they'd go to bed, but they'd got to the stage where that wasn't enough. Niki wanted him to share the large flat in the coastal suburb of Palaio Faliron that she'd been left by her long-suffering foster parents. The one thing he was sure about was that he was staying in Pikilis.

As Mavros balanced himself on the ladder he was gripped by panic. If she shook the legs now, he'd go head first down the stairs. He lowered his eyes and was confronted by Niki's raised backside. Shaking his head at the injustice he'd done her, he climbed slowly down. It was time he sorted himself out.

Then he remembered Deniz Ozal and his missing sister. An island in the Aegean. Trigono came at him out of the shimmering blue with a whispered promise of sanctuary.

In that second he made the decision.

The old man in the tower on Trigono ran a trembling hand through his sculpted white beard. It was time. He'd been sitting in front of the tattered leather-bound volume for hours, but he hadn't been able to open it. Yes, it was time to lay the ghost once and for all. But he still couldn't bring himself to touch the book, as if it were infected with some deadly virus.

Running his eyes around the sumptuously decorated room with its circular walls in an attempt to distract himself, he rested them on the framed poster by the door. Larger versions of it were all over Athens, advertising the museum's latest exhibition. The lekythos with its exquisite lines, the painted figure of Charon on his boat, the icons of death that had haunted him for as long as he could remember and had inspired him to establish the museum – now they seemed to be mocking him. 'What do you know about death?' they were asking. 'What do you really know?'

Panos Theocharis forced himself to look at the book that was in front of him on the antique mahogany desk. What he knew about death, what he had experienced, was largely contained in this compact volume. But not in his words. These were the words of the man he'd tried to destroy. How bitter would the story they told be to him? Did he have any right to read another man's private confessions?

He turned his head towards the high window and took in the lights of the village that lay beyond the expanse of cultivated fields. He'd been told about the deaths, the drowned boy and girl, but even that news had failed to distract him from the diary. No, he couldn't put it off any more. He had to do it now.

Taking a deep breath that rattled in his lungs, Theocharis put his fingers on the soft, dark leather and opened the book. The man he had forgotten for decades flew out like an avenger from the lines of faded blue ink and seized him by the throat.

5

'Yeah? Who is it?' Deniz Ozal was breathless.
'This is Mavros.'

'What the fuck happened to you, bud?' He grunted. 'Get off me, you—'

'Is this a bad time?'

'You were meant to call me at ten, weren't you?' Ozal had raised his voice. 'I said get off me. Jesus.'

Mavros was on his balcony with the mobile. Niki had stayed and he'd waited until she was asleep before phoning. He didn't want her to hear that he was about to leave the city. 'I can call again in the morning if you've got company.'

There was a rustle followed by a high-pitched giggle. 'Nah,' Ozal said. 'It's just a hooker who's bitten off more than she can chew, if you get my meaning.' He gave a humourless laugh. 'Anyway, how d'you know I didn't give the job to the competition?'

Mavros raised his eyes to the night sky. 'Because there isn't any competition worth the name, Deniz.'

'Is that right?' There was a heavy slap. 'I told you to wait, goddammit. So, d'you want the job or not, Alex?'

'If you promise to stop hitting the woman. The Intercontinental's pretty strict on visitors in guest rooms at this time of night.'

Ozal grunted. 'You think I didn't square it with the desk? Hey,' he said, his tone hardening, 'you threatening me?'

'Of course,' Mavros replied. 'I always threaten potential employers.'

The irony silenced Deniz Ozal for a few moments, then he

laughed again. 'Funny guy. But can you use that mouth of yours to find my sister?'

Mavros took the plunge. 'I'll give it a go. My rate's a hundred thousand Greek a day plus expenses. In this case, as there's travel involved, minimum five days, up front. Okay?'

'Jeez, that's pretty fuckin' steep, my friend.'

'Take it or leave it, Deniz.'

There was a long pause.

'Okay, done. You got a mobile phone?'

'No, I prefer to use carrier pigeons.' Mavros gave the number.

'I'll be travelling so I'll call you when it suits me. Since I can't rely on you to call me when I want you to. And give me your bank details. I'll transfer half a million tomorrow, okay?'

Mavros passed on the information, letting the jibe go unanswered. 'Let me talk to your guest.'

'What?'

'You heard me.'

There was rustle of sheets.

'Yes? What can I do for you?' The voice was young, female and brash, the English smooth. She probably thought he wanted to arrange a rendezvous.

'The name's Alex Mavros,' he replied in Greek. 'I'm the only one in the phone book. If he hurts you, call me.'

There was silence for a while. 'All right.' The girl sounded less sure of herself. 'Thanks.'

The connection was cut.

Mavros got on to Olympic Airways and booked a seat on the morning flight to Paros, the nearest island to Trigono with an airport. Then he went back to bed, lowering himself carefully on to the mattress to prevent the bed frame creaking. Niki stirred, her arm moving against his thigh. Apparently comforted by making physical contact, she sank back into her usual deep sleep. Before he went the same way, Mavros wondered about what he was doing – not just the Ozal job, but the fact that he wasn't going to tell Niki where he was headed. He knew it was wrong, knew that he should have had the nerve to face her and say that he didn't want to see her any more, but he shrank from the inevitable confrontation. It wasn't a question of gutlessness, he told himself. He didn't want to hurt her, but he didn't know how to avoid it. Being in a relationship was hell, he thought as his eyes closed. And then you started another one.

Before the first tinges of dawn had crept down the street from the ruins of the Roman marketplace to his windows, Mavros got up and, keeping one eye on Niki's lightly breathing form, put some clothes in a leather satchel. He reckoned his usual outfit of T-shirt, jeans and espadrilles, supplemented by a pair of shorts that could double as swimming trunks and a pair of trainers, would do for the Cyclades. Not that he had much recent experience of the islands. He rarely took holidays and his last trip off the mainland had been to find an Austrian woman on Zakynthos a couple of years back; her local husband had decided that she would benefit from an enforced stay in a hut in the hills. Mavros also had a major dislike of travelling with anything other than hand luggage. Deniz Ozal could pay for anything else he needed on Trigono.

Padding noiselessly into the kitchen, he wrote a note for Niki:

Urgent job – probably away for a week. I'll be in touch.

A.

He knew she'd immediately notice the lack of 'with love' or the like, but he couldn't bring himself to do anything about it. He propped the piece of paper against the coffee jar – Niki couldn't function in the mornings without a substantial caffeine shot – and let himself out of the flat. As he went down the stairs he felt a weight come off his shoulders and shook his head. That was his problem. He was cold-blooded enough to walk away, but not callous enough to avoid the remorse.

He found a taxi at Monastiraki and asked for the airport. At least the driver wasn't a talkative one. That turned out to be a mixed blessing. The swarthy, unshaven type must have seen *Bullitt* recently. He raced up the central avenues, cutting through the sparse traffic flow with rapid movements of his head and hands.

Mavros spent the journey with his lips pressed together, his legs braced and one hand clamped on the door rest, but he didn't risk putting on his seat belt. That insult to the driver's abilities could have been fatal. By the time they arrived at the gleaming new terminal beyond the ring of the city's mountains, his white T-shirt was sodden.

After he'd collected his ticket and checked in – the Olympic staff as supercilious as usual – he glanced at his watch. Ten to six. His mother would be up already. She was the opposite of Niki, a sleeper so light that even earplugs were no use to her, and she usually started work editing typescripts or writing letters to aspiring authors before the nightclubs had emptied. He highlighted her entry in the phone's directory.

'Morning, Mother.'

'Alex, good morning,' she said, her voice conveying alarm. 'So early. What's the matter?'

'Nothing,' he replied hastily. 'Just to say that I'll be away for a few days. I'm at the airport.'

'Oh. Are you taking my advice and having a holiday?'

'Uh-uh. Work.'

Dorothy let out an impatient sigh. 'Really, Alex, you need a rest. Where is it you're going?'

'Trigono.'

'In the Cyclades? How lovely. Those islands are wonderful, so full of history. Remember what Byron said about—'

'Sorry, Mother, I've got to go,' Mavros interrupted. A blast of philhellenic zeal was not what he needed right now. 'Oh, and Mother? If Niki calls, don't tell her where I am.'

'Whyever not? I don't know how that girl puts up with—'

'Talk to you soon. Bye.' Mavros flinched as guilt buried its teeth in him again. The screens were showing his departure gate, so he called his sister as he walked towards the security checkpoint. She was another early riser, because of kids and the pressure of work rather than any particular love of the morning sun.

'Trigono?' Anna said. 'I suppose it makes a change from lurking behind cars in the suburbs. Did you see the island was on the news last night?'

'No.' Mavros got his intelligence from the midday papers rather than the overdressed TV newsreaders. 'Why? What happened?'

'There was a terrible tragedy.' She broke off. 'Hurry up, Evridhiki! Have you got your ballet bag? Sorry, Alex. Yes, a tragedy. A local couple, teenagers, were drowned.'

'Bloody hell,' Mavros said under his breath, wondering how his investigation would be affected by an outpouring of grief on the small island.

'You know who lives there?' Anna continued smoothly. She often gave her brother information before he asked for it. 'Panos Theocharis, the mining tycoon.'

The oil flask from the hoarding with the image of Charon on his boat flashed up in front of Mavros. 'The guy with the museum?'

'Mmm. Laki, if you don't drink that milk you're not playing basketball after school, do you hear? Yes, the Museum of Funerary Art. He's sunk billions into it and—'

'Got to go, Anna,' Mavros said, looking at his watch. 'Say hello to the kids.'

He broke the connection and put his bag through the X-ray machine. A double drowning and the founder of a museum that celebrated death on the same island. This case looked like it was going to be full of laughs.

Then he looked out of the tinted glass and saw the small aircraft on the tarmac outside. Holy shit. So far he'd managed to suppress his fear of flying, but not any more.

October 11th, 1942, Beirut

I've decided to take the risk. The keeping of diaries is, of course, strictly against regulations but this is too good an opportunity to miss. I will have plenty of time to myself in the coming months and will take every precaution to hide these writings in places where even the most scrupulous Italian intelligence officer will never think to look. Besides, as numerous masters and tutors have pointed out, my handwriting is minuscule enough to put even the most avid of readers off. No, this is the great adventure of my life and I must record it. I spoke to Larry Durrell before I left Cairo and he told me how much he envied me. Not as much as I envy him. He showed me some of the stuff he's written about Corfu. God, what wouldn't I give to have lived in that paradise before the war?

But now I am to have my own Greek island to experience and describe. There will be a book in it, maybe a series of books. George Lawrence's Trigono Days, *a masterly evocation of wartime life on a Greek island.* Farmers, Fishermen and Fables, *the finest description of island society this reviewer has ever come across. Come on, man, control yourself. The books have yet to be written. The important thing is that I will have my own material and experiences to work on.*

Tomorrow we set sail in a battered but apparently seaworthy kaïki. *I won't put down her name in case she runs into difficulties later. The point is that in a few days I'll be in the Aegean! My God, I've been waiting so long to see the shores where Western civilisation began. It's as if my whole life has been a preparation for this moment; the years learning Greek at prep school and Big College, the courses of literature and archaeology at Cambridge. Even the modern Greek I picked up from my fellow student Aristotelis T. now seems part of some hitherto unfathomable design. And what used to be the frustration of never visiting Greece in the long vacations because of poor Pater's straitened circumstances is now something I'm grateful for. Because the wait has made my appetite for the land and sea of the Greeks even keener. They are about to become my closest companions. At last!*

October 15th, 1942

The navy boys who run the flotilla are wonderful seamen, but this voyage has turned into a test of everyone's endurance. The wind has been from the north since we set out, strong enough to prevent writing until we finally took shelter in this cove on the island of A. Even now it's blasting over the hills, making the boat rock and pull against the mooring ropes. The crew erected spreader poles and hung camouflage sheets over them so, in theory, we blend into the cliff side and are invisible to any passing peasant. Apparently the nearest garrison is fifteen miles away. Having been unable to keep anything except water down for over two days, I'm now looking forward to the corned beef and hard biscuits that are being broken out. There's rum as well, though I don't know if I'll be able to trust my stomach with that. It'll be dark in a couple of hours. I wanted to get out and have a look at the surrounding countryside, but the skipper wouldn't allow it. So frustration mounts again! It looks like Trig will be the first Greek soil, or rock, that I touch after all. I'd better check my radio and my weapons before the light goes. If the wind drops we'll be on our way again tonight. I'm almost there.

October 16th, 1942, Trig

We have arrived! We were lucky with the wind and the skipper brought us into the long, narrow inlet on the south coast of the island an hour before dawn. Then we spent the day under the shrouds again. The longing I felt to jump into the clear blue water and strike out for land was almost overwhelming. I managed to restrain myself and wait till nightfall. I even managed to get some sleep, my face crushed up against the timbers of the hull. The old kaïki did a fine job. I only hope she gets the boys back in one piece. As soon as it was dark, the Greek liaison chap, a sour-faced veteran of the Albanian campaign and the German invasion who worked in the mines here before the war, headed off to check that the hills were clear and to let the local resistance leader know I've arrived. When we got the signal from the ridge, the crew and I lugged my gear up. I didn't have time to rejoice over finally touching sacred soil. We were too busy scrambling up the steep slope from Vathy. I managed much better than the Jack Tars, the training I was put through in the desert standing me in good stead. Fortunately my map-reading skills survived the voyage as well. I located the herdsman's hut below the ridge between Profitis

*Ilias and Vigla without difficulty and we dumped everything there.
My first job will be to find a more secure hiding place for it. Then,
under a brilliantly starlit night, with the Milky Way curving across
the velvety dome like a royal road, I said my farewells to the sailors.
They'll lay up at the mooring till nightfall waiting for the liaison
chap then set off again, so I'll be alone until the others arrive in the
near future. Now all I have to do is glory in the evocative code-name
I talked the brass hats into assigning me – Achilles, greatest of Greek
warriors before the walls of Troy – and wait for the dawn.*

October 17th, 1942, 11 p.m.

*I'm still reeling. I've been busy since twilight, scouting around for a
safer spot to stow the gear (I found some out-of-the-way caves that
might do the trick) and my feet are aching from the rocky ground.
But all I can think about is the first real view that I had of Greece
in the morning light. I crawled up to the ridge before sunrise and
waited there, my heart pounding. At last the peaks of the mountains
on the eastern islands began to appear, nothing more than faint lines
hovering in the darkness. Then there was a sudden red smudge and
before I could fully take stock of what was happening, the sun's upper
edge appeared over the highest peak and a great burst of red shone
out, so bright that I had to shield my eyes. I felt them dampen, not
just because of the light's intensity, and turned to take in my island.
Trigono lay in front of me, the coastlines converging in an almost
perfect triangle to the patch of white that marked the main village,
Faros, at the northern point. In the space between, the slopes of Vigla
and Profitis Ilias ran down steeply to the flatter expanse of Kambos
with its strips of arable land, the dark brown earth dotted with mills
and houses. And beyond it all was the sea, the brave blue Aegean
dancing away towards Paros and Andiparos, flecked with dusty islets
and a few hardy fishing boats. The gods themselves could not have
constructed a more glorious panorama. I lay on the rocky ground for
hours to absorb it all, only moving when I heard the distant notes
of a goatherd's pipe and the clang of his animals' bells on the clear
air. Now I must try to come back to earth and concentrate on why*

I am here. Tomorrow night I meet Kapetan M., code-name Ajax, who, according to the departed liaison officer, can be an awkward customer. As long as it's the Italians' lives he plans to make difficult I don't care how tough he is.

Ah, Greece, ah, Trigono. What a day this has been!

Mavros spent as much as he could of the flight with his eyes closed, clutching his worry beads. The nineteen-seater twin-prop Dornier was only half full, so he managed to keep some distance from a foursome of garrulous Scandinavians. They spent the trip gasping and squealing in delight as the aircraft steered south-east across the steadily brightening sea and the islands that had been scorched rust brown in the long summer. Mavros hated all kinds of flying, but he was especially uncomfortable in propeller planes that flew low enough for the occupants to make out the deserted buildings on the islands' terraced slopes and the dismembered remains of ships that had been wrecked on their indented coastlines. Crushed in the narrow seat, head bowed, he almost missed a first glimpse of his destination. But he'd opened his eyes as the pilots lined up their approach to the airport on Paros, the runway looking far too short given the speed they were doing, and Trigono reared up in the middle distance. The village in the north, only five kilometres from the end of Paros, was dwarfed by a mass of mountains to the south, the ridge between them bare and scarred by rockfalls that were visible even at this range.

'Jesus,' Mavros said, his voice drowned in the blast from the engines. 'What am I doing here?' He swallowed hard as the plane yawed alarmingly. The pilots, who had been gossiping about stewardesses they were chasing, stiffened and started to concentrate.

Then the wheels touched with a loud thud and the engine noise became even more aggressive as reverse thrust was applied. Mavros had his thighs clenched until the plane had swung into the turning circle in front of the terminal building and the engines were cut. Only then did he manage to get his breathing under control. Even though the ferries took much longer, he'd have to give serious consideration to returning by sea.

Walking unsteadily down the steps, he took in his surroundings. The airport building wasn't much more than a medium-sized house, whitewashed in the Cycladic way but topped by incongruous aerials and discs. The airport certainly had better scenery than most. The low lines of Andiparos to the west were countered by Paros's central massif containing the seams of marble that had made the island's name over the centuries. And ahead of him lay Trigono, too insignificant to merit a landing strip of its own but as imposing a sight as any of the islands.

If you were into that kind of thing, Mavros thought. The open spaces and gusting southerly breeze were already getting to him. He'd rather have been in a sheltered city square, protected by the pollution cloud from the blinding rays that were making a joke of his expensive sunglasses.

It was as he went through the gate and into the car park that Mavros took the step that he'd been considering on the flight. It had worked on Zakynthos, so why not here?

'Taxi? Taxi, *kyrie*?' The driver, a middle-aged man with quick eyes and huge hands, had picked up Mavros's body language and summed him up as a Greek.

'Yes,' he replied in English. He stuffed the worry beads into his pocket and let his limbs go loose, trying to dispel the aura of self-confidence that Greeks habitually exude. 'Yes, taxi, please. I want the ferry for Trigono. All right?'

The taxi-driver grinned, scenting easy prey. 'All right, my friend,' he replied in heavily accented English. 'I take you right away.' He looked at his watch. 'Boat go in one half hour.' He wrested Mavros's bag from him and put it in the boot of a large silver Mercedes. He turned to the other passengers. 'Trigono! Who want Trigono?'

The tourists looked at him blankly, while the few Greeks who'd been on the plane raised their chins in the gesture that signified 'no'. It looked like Mavros was on his own. That would give him a chance to bring his non-Greek side completely to the surface.

He'd discovered when he was on Zakynthos that he could learn a lot more by feigning ignorance of the local language and culture. Overhearing and eavesdropping were useful investigative tools. There were two problems, though: you had to make sure you didn't give the game away by suddenly being seen to understand Greek; and there was an underhand element to it that he wasn't happy with. Too bad, he thought as he got into the car. This is business, not pleasure.

He was dropped off on the waterfront at Alyki. The taxi-driver, who hadn't bothered to turn on the meter, tried to extract five thousand from him for the short trip but settled for two when he saw the sudden hard look on Mavros's face.

The small port on the south-western corner of Paros was the ferry terminal for Trigono. According to the guidebook in English that Mavros bought from a kiosk, the large boats from Piraeus called at Trigono's harbour of Faros twice a week in the high season and ignored the island for the rest of the year. He watched as a turquoise-and-white bus pulled up and disgorged passengers. There were a few tourists in skimpy shorts and baseball caps, but the majority were islanders. The men were in heavy trousers that made little concession to the heat, the women in knee-length skirts, a few wearing straw hats but most leaving their faces and scalps uncovered.

Mavros moved closer to the crowd of locals on the quay as a small ferry rounded the cape to the east. Their heads were bowed and they were speaking in low voices that he struggled to pick up while pretending to be engrossed in his book. None of them gave him a second glance. The talk was all about the young people who had drowned. It quickly became clear that most of the speakers were related to them and were on their way to console the families.

'Navsika and Yiangos, God forgive them, what were they doing on the boat on their own?'

'Yiangos should have known better. Lefteris wouldn't have let him out if he'd been here.'

'Why was Lefteris in Syros anyway?'

'He had to go to court, remember? That tourist he beat up. They'll have postponed the trial after this, of course.'

'But what happened, in the name of God? The wind wasn't so strong. And Yiangos knew what he was doing, he—'

'Yiangos knew nothing!' exclaimed an old man with a thick moustache that was heavily stained by tobacco. 'He was a kid. The sea's always tricky around Eschati. He shouldn't have been there, especially with no one to help him. What good would a girl have been?'

'Come on, Maki,' a plump woman put in. 'Navsika was a good girl.'

'Yes, Navsika was a good girl,' admitted the old man, 'but she didn't know anything about boats.'

The group drew closer together and Mavros couldn't make out much more. He watched as the ferry came in, its forward door lowering as it approached the concrete ramp. The young men on the mooring ropes looked like they'd been in a battle, their bodies slack and their heads down. Friends of the dead boy, he surmised. He waited till the small group of departing passengers left, a gypsy watermelon seller in a pick-up truck that looked like it was about to fall apart giving them an impatient blast of his horn. That attracted hostile glares.

'Show some respect,' muttered the deckhand at the ticket desk.

Mavros paid and climbed the steps to the upper deck. The ferry – the *Loxandra* according to a plaque under the funnel – was pulling away from the quay when a large green four-by-four vehicle came across the port area at speed, its horn blaring and headlights flashing.

'Fuck it!' the captain cursed from the wheelhouse. 'It's Aris. We'll have to go back.' He moved the throttle and headed towards the ramp, lowering the door again.

The top-of-the-range Jeep drove on board quickly, missing a motorbike by centimetres. The driver swung his door open and jumped down, his bald head bisected horizontally by a green sun visor. He walked across the garage deck with his chest out, keeping his eyes off everyone around him, a slack smile on his lips.

The captain swore again. 'Don't worry about my bike, you big buffoon,' he said, glancing at Mavros as he put the engines into reverse and swung round towards the strait.

Mavros felt the wind stiffen as they moved away from Paros, tugging at his hair and making his T-shirt flap around his sides. The ferry began to roll as the swell took it, provoking cheerful complaints from the few tourists. The islanders had already taken refuge in the smoky cabin, a couple of the men joining the captain on the bridge.

'Have you seen Lefteris?' the wrinkled sailor was asked.

He nodded and leaned back from the wheel to spit into an empty plant pot. 'Iason went to get him from Syros in his *kaïki*. They got back about five this morning.'

'How's he taking it?'

The skipper muttered something and gave Mavros another look; he'd moved closer to the wheelhouse door, his arms resting on the wooden rail and his eyes on the island ahead. The English guidebook was under his arm and this seemed to dispel the sailor's suspicions.

'You know Lefteris,' he said. 'He's made of stone. Who can say what he's thinking? But I'm sure he's been badly hit by their loss, especially with Yiangos being an only child.' He lit a cigarette, the acrid smoke gusting past Mavros. 'I'll tell you something interesting, boys.'

The others looked at him expectantly.

'I heard the sailors from Paros who found the boat talking to the Port Police on the VHF.' The captain inhaled again.

'Come on, Louka, let's have it.'

'All right,' the sailor replied, rubbing the stubble on his chin. 'They found a deep scrape on the *Sotiria*'s hull, along the waterline.'

'So? She hit a rock. There's plenty of them off Vathy.'

Kapetan Loukas was shaking his head. 'No, no, my friends. The *trata* didn't hit a rock. They were certain of that. She'd collided with something made of wood or metal. They could see blue paint in the abrasion.' He dropped the cigarette butt into the pot. 'And what colour is the *Sotiria*'s hull?'

His interlocutors looked at each other, their eyes widening.

'White,' one of them replied in a low voice. 'I saw Yiangos and the girl leave port. He didn't hit anything then, I'm sure of it. Christ, what happened down there?'

Mavros, his book now open at the pages showing a map of Trigono and the surrounding islets, screwed his eyes up in the dazzling sun. It looked like Rosa Ozal's disappearance might not be the only mystery to be cleared up in this windswept quadrant of the Cyclades.

Panos Theocharis leaned against the wall of the terrace that ran all round his tower and looked towards Paros. Picking up the U-boat commander's binoculars that he'd bought on the cheap in Hamburg after the war, he trained them on the distant white object in the straits. It was the ferry all right. He hoped to God that his son was on it. Aris had been on Paros overnight. God knows what chaos he'd caused in the bars. At least there hadn't been any phone calls from the family's tame policemen over there.

The old man glanced at the supine form stretched out on the recliner behind him, the woman's large breasts glistening with tanning oil, and shook his head. What a sight Dhimitra was, her legs splayed and the three Alsatians she adored resting their chins on the edge of the mattress. It had been some time since he'd been able to gain any comfort from her.

Theocharis gripped his stick and moved out of the sun, his yachting shoes dragging on the tiled floor. He sat down at the table by the pool and ran his hand down the smooth flank of the foot-high sculpture by his wineglass. It wasn't an original. He had very few Cycladic pieces in the museum and even fewer in his private collection. He'd commissioned this copy from a sculptor on Naxos so he could have physical contact with the island's history whenever and wherever he wanted, not that he travelled much any more. *The Huntsman*, it was called.

The figure of a Bronze Age warrior, baldric incised into his chest and hand gripping the broken haft of what the experts took to be a sword, was the first Cycladic piece to be unearthed on Trigono. Unfortunately the mining engineer employed by the family who came across it in the 1920s sold it illicitly to a German museum and, despite all Theocharis's efforts, no other figures had been located on the island. Until recently. At last Eleni Trypani, the archaeologist he'd been subsidising for years, had found some stunning figurines, and her excavation reports were optimistic about locating more. He shook his head. He wasn't sure that Eleni Trypani was trustworthy. She wasn't submissive like others who worked for him, and she was becoming distinctly difficult to handle.

The old man leaned back in his chair and ran his fingers through the pure white strands of his shaped beard. He lowered his head, desperately trying to find other subjects to distract him. Now there had been the deaths of the two young people, the island would be sunk in sorrow for weeks. He asked himself if there would ever be an end to the young dying before their time, but he knew the answer well enough. There was no point in hiding from it. It was intrinsic to the place. Trigono was the final destination on the passage the island's inhabitants worked to death, and many of them arrived prematurely. It had always been the nature of the place. He of all people knew that. He'd realised it since the time he spent on Trigono during the Second World War. The island was a sanctuary of death. The diary he'd started reading only emphasised that.

The face he'd managed to forget for almost half a century appeared before him again, the face of Lieutenant George Lawrence. Theocharis had fooled himself into believing that the Englishman's shade had long ago been confined to the underworld like that of Achilles, the great warrior whose name Lawrence had appropriated and whose soul, according to Homer, had been reduced to a status lower than that of the commonest serf. But now the pale ghost had risen, brought back to life by

the young woman's questions. That accursed woman. What
irreparable damage had she done him?

Panos Theocharis twitched his head, trying vainly to dispel the
image of a fresh-faced, excitable young man in ill-fitting peasant
clothes, and let out a long, low groan that made the trio of dogs
prick up their ears.

Would the things he had done in the war never leave him
in peace?

6

The ferry-boat *Loxandra* rounded a prong of low rock on the northern tip of the island. According to Mavros's guidebook its name was Cape Fonias, The Murderer – it must have been the graveyard of many ships. The outcrop was topped by a large light on metal columns that had been built next to a crumbling pile of masonry. The straits between Paros and Trigono were said to be very unpredictable, and there had been a beacon on the cape for centuries. That was why the whitewashed village was called Faros, Lighthouse, rather than the standard Aegean name of Chora, chief village.

Mavros watched as the compact capital swung into view, some fishing boats riding at anchor in the shallow bay and others moored at the gently curving quay. The buildings were reflecting the morning sun, making it difficult to take in their contours. They rose up a gentle slope, crowned by the blue dome of what he assumed was the main church, the flat rooftops a jumble of TV aerials, chimneys and washing lines festooned with clothes. The only other area that wasn't brilliant white was a line of brown stonework beside the church. He presumed this was the wall of the Venetian *kastro*, the fortified centre that had been impregnable until a gang of pirates in the seventeenth century bribed a merchant to let them in – they had subsequently massacred the inhabitants, including the traitor. The guidebook made the most of the island's violent history.

'Room? Room?' a boy offered eagerly as Mavrós stepped off the boat.

He shook his head. He'd been expecting a pack of hawkers to surround the ferry, but most of the downcast people on the quayside had congregated around the Greek passengers. A loud groaning broke out, interspersed by tearful kisses and embraces. The tourists wandered off, pursued by children who'd been delegated the job normally done by their elders. There was one woman dressed in black, probably in her mid-thirties, who was hanging back, her pleasant face directed shyly towards Mavros for a few seconds. He passed by her, needing a caffeine hit before he did anything else, and headed for the first of two cafés. He was hoping that the general mourning hadn't closed them. There were no customers sitting outside.

Inside O Glaros, The Seagull, the two tables farthest from the door were occupied. A doleful youth looked up from the bar and pointed to another table at the rear.

'Coffee?' Mavros asked in English, maintaining his foreign guise. 'Greek coffee? *Sketo?*' There was no way he was willingly going the full tourist route and drinking the foul instant 'Nes'. Fortunately there were plenty of foreigners who liked to show off their knowledge of Greek culture by ordering the traditional version, so no eyebrows would be raised.

He glanced around the place. It was decorated in what someone who'd never been beyond Athens imagined was South Sea Island style. There were plastic palm fronds and coconuts hanging from the ceiling and the walls were decorated with posters of perfect beaches that were beginning to peel at the edges. The table to the right behind him was taken by two couples displaying their nationality with a three-day-old copy of the *Sun* and numerous empty beer bottles. One of the men was wearing a faded Union Jack T-shirt.

'Christ Almighty,' the Englishman said, his arms glowing red even in the dim light of the café. 'How long's this going to go on? Not much bleeding fun sitting around in the dark, is it?'

'Shut up, Norm,' the younger of the women said, glaring at him. Her blonde hair was held back in a clip. 'You heard what Thanasi said.' Her voice dropped to a loud whisper. 'Two of his cousins were drowned.'

'Yeah, that's right, Jane,' the other woman said, applying mauve lipstick. Her ample breasts were unsupported beneath her top. 'Thanasi's doing us a favour. The bars are supposed to stay closed as a mark of respect until after the funerals.'

'When's that going to be then, Trace?' the second man asked, lifting his head from a paperback copy of *The Guns of Navarone* and grabbing a bottle. His eyes were heavily ringed and his clippered head was criss-crossed by a network of scars. 'I came here for the booze and the discos, not the local colour.'

'Oh for God's sake, Roy,' said the blonde woman.

'What do you expect, Jane?' Roy said with a grin. 'I'm not smart like you. I dig ditches for a living.'

'You do not!' Trace said, looking to Norm for support. 'Installing cables is a highly skilled job. You two have done very well for yourselves.'

Mavros nodded to the waiter as he brought the coffee and a glass of water. Behind him to the left he could hear the other two occupants of the place carrying on a muttered conversation.

'They're frightening, those people,' said the woman, her American accent cultured but her tone sharp. 'No wonder Britain's finished as a world power.'

'Give them a break,' the man said in long-suffering voice. 'They're on holiday.' His fair hair was uncombed, the stubble on his face several days old.

'They're morons,' said the woman, her face fleshless and pale. 'You know, Lance, this has turned out beautifully. Trigono is the most unspoiled island we've been to and now there's to be a double funeral. I couldn't have asked for more.'

'Yes, you have been lucky, haven't you, Gretchen?' the man said, the irony in his voice faint but unmistakable. 'Think of the material you'll get out of that.' He leaned closer to her. 'We'll have to be careful about taking photographs, though. Maybe I should go up on the walls of the *kastro* and . . .' He lowered his voice and the rest of his words were inaudible.

Mavros finished his coffee and headed for the door after paying. Putting on his sunglasses, he took in the harbour scene. The boats were bobbing jauntily in front of the beacon, the imposing bulk of Paros in the background. The scene was enough to raise the spirits even of a committed city-dweller. Then he saw a group of old men gathered in the shade of an awning. Their heads were down and their limbs loose. Mavros dismissed the faint feeling of guilt that eavesdropping always gave him and sauntered past them, one ear cocked.

'Eh, Manoli?' one was saying. 'What was your grandson doing down at the end of the island?'

The man who'd been addressed was silent. As he turned slowly towards his interlocutor, Mavros saw that he had lost an arm. The stump was protruding from his short-sleeved shirt. There were plenty like him on the islands, fishermen who'd resorted to dynamite in the famine years before and after the Second World War.

'How would I know?' he replied in a gruff voice. 'Yiangos could handle the *trata*, you all know that. What happened to him? Maybe the *gorgona* took him.' According to the folk tales, encountering the mermaid could be fatal. The old man fixed his companion with a rheumy eye. 'Or maybe your granddaughter took his mind off the job.'

Mavros walked past the old men towards the start of the main street, his ears ringing with the voices that had been cracked by years in the salt sea air or on the dusty fields. They were complaining, struggling against the bitter fate that had taken the young people from them, but they were not giving in to it. He was struck by their stoicism.

He headed up the narrow road past a small supermarket's wasp-infested fruit display. There were tourist shops on both sides but their doors were closed. Anyone who wanted to buy garish pots and miniature Cycladic houses was out of luck, the storekeepers presumably involved with the preparations for the funerals or showing their respect. Moving up the slope towards the centre of the village, Mavros took in the atmosphere. If he hadn't known about the tragedy, he'd have found the island's tiny capital a serene and restful place. The road was paved with irregular stones, the mortar between them picked out with *asvesti*, white lime. There were few people around, the houses with their blue wooden balconies and shutters as quiet as if they'd been deserted. There was a slightly high smell about the place, the aroma of hibiscus and other plants cut with sewage gas from the cesspits.

Halfway up the street he came to an open space on his left. Behind a dusty yard surrounded by acacias and pines stood the wide single storey of the island's primary school, a few brightly coloured swings to one side. Through the open windows Mavros could make out the avid faces of small children, eyes fixed on their teachers. He wouldn't have volunteered to go in front of a class today and keep the youngsters' minds off what had happened.

As he passed, a two-metre-high white marble column caught his eye. There were a couple of faded wreaths at the base and he stopped to take a closer look over the wall of the school yard. The tapering stone shaft was square and names had been inscribed on the lower part of the front face, beneath a carved olive branch and the years 1940–44. Several of the surnames were repeated – Glinos, Roussopoulos, Matsos. They were obviously some of the island's main families.

And then he noticed something else. The lowest name on the memorial had been erased, the marble roughly chipped away. But the strange thing was that an attempt had been made to reapply the letters with black paint. The surface of the stone had been scrubbed, recently by the rough look of the marks from a wire brush, but a few of the letters were still visible. Mavros thought he could make out a capital 'T' and, farther to the right, a 'Z'. He gave up trying to decipher the writing where a surname would have been.

Behind him came the sound of a throat being cleared. He turned to find the one-armed old man with the fierce expression he'd seen in the port crossing the road to join him at the wall.

'*Ti thelete?*' he demanded. What do you want? His eyes bored into Mavros's. '*Edho dhen einai yia xenous.*' This place isn't for foreigners.

Mavros was startled by the old man's fierceness and he feigned incomprehension. He moved away from the memorial with a shrug. The islander stood in front of it like a sentry, his gaze still on the intruder. Manolis was his name, Mavros remembered from the conversation he'd overheard. It was his grandson who had drowned. He would have been stricken by the event, but why was he taking it out on a stranger? Maybe he just saw Mavros as an easy target.

Mavros soon reached the *plateia*, the main square. It wasn't very large, no more than twenty metres across, the centre taken up by an ancient mulberry tree with a thick trunk. Its branches hung low over the tables of the *kafeneion*. The village's central café was closed and there were clusters of desolate-looking men in the shade of the tree, their voices low. The southern side of the square was formed by the wall of the *kastro*, small windows set between massive blocks of russet-brown stone. He sat down on the low retaining wall around the base of the mulberry and took the postcard Deniz Ozal had given him from his bag. The church to his left was Ayia Triadha, the one in the picture. He swivelled his head. So the street with the house Rosa Ozal stayed in was the one leading away past the castle wall. It was clearly the main road out of the village to the south. He stood up again and walked in that direction, looking for the blue-and-yellow door the missing woman had marked. He found it in less than a minute.

Knocking at the door and receiving no answer, he thought at first that he was out of luck; the occupants may have been with the bereaved family. Then he noticed a slight movement of the curtain at the front room to his right so he tried again. Again there was no response. Perhaps the owners didn't want to rent rooms at this terrible time. He was about to give up and go back to the shade in the square – the sun was burning down on his head in the treeless street – when there was the sound of a key turning and the blue-and-yellow panelling swung aside.

Mavros recognised the black-clad woman immediately. He'd seen her when he came off the ferry. A shy smile appeared on her lips as she nodded. It looked like she remembered him too. Her dark hair was tied back in a bow.

'You need a room?' she asked, her English accent unexpectedly good.

Mavros nodded. 'Yes, do you have one?'

The woman nodded again. 'I have plenty. The season is finished. There is no one else in my house.' She kept her eyes off him as she ushered him in. Her face was square and fleshy, but the skin was smooth. Even though there wasn't a trace of make-up she looked less worn than the average island woman and her brown eyes shone with intelligence when she summoned up the nerve to raise them.

'This way,' she said, leading him down a dark passageway. 'Your name?'

'Alex,' he said, keeping his surname to himself for the time being. He wouldn't be able to pretend that he was a foreigner if he told her his surname unless he constructed some story about being a second-generation emigrant returning to the fatherland. It would be easier to use his Scottish identity.

'I am Rena,' she said, turning to him as she stepped out of the corridor. 'Welcome to my house.'

Mavros was pleasantly surprised. If he hadn't needed to check out the place where Rosa had been, he'd have avoided staying on a main road. He'd made that mistake in the village he'd visited on Zakynthos and had been woken before dawn every day by the sounds of farm vehicles with unsilenced exhausts and loudly revving motorbikes. But this was something else. The house backed on to a small courtyard that was cool and quiet. It was sheltered by a wide pergola over which had grown vines and bougainvillaea, a whitewashed stone wellhead in the centre.

Rena pointed to a small, single-storey building on the far side. 'Your room is there, with kitchen and bathroom.' She pointed to the wall behind. 'I live on this side. Alone.' She nodded, smiling shyly. 'So no noise, no disturbance. I will show you now.'

Mavros followed her across the spotless flagstones to the outhouse. 'Where did you learn your English?' he asked.

'Why?' Rena looked affronted. 'I say something funny?'

'No, no,' he replied. 'It's very good.'

'I learn English here. There is a *xeni*, a foreign woman, who makes lessons.'

'Ah.' Mavros stopped behind her as she raised a key to the door.

'You will like this, I think,' Rena said, lowering her eyes as she stood to one side and let him move past her into the room.

Mavros felt his upper arm brush against her chest and saw her cheeks redden instantly. He stepped into the rectangular room to give her some space, keeping his eyes off her for a few moments. Although the low building had looked small from outside, the main room was expansive, a double bed in the centre and a wide table under the shuttered windows. The decor was less minimalist than was often the case with rooms for the tourist market, yellow curtains setting off the pale blue paint of the walls and a tastefully framed print of an island scene by the painter Theofilos over the bed. To the right a pair of doors led into a spotless bathroom and a small but well-equipped kitchen.

'Very nice,' Mavros said.

Rena acknowledged the compliment with a smile. 'You will stay?'

'You said you have other rooms,' Mavros countered, wondering where Rosa Ozal had stayed but not wanting to ask the woman before he had her confidence.

'Yes, two,' Rena said, her face falling. 'You don't like this one?'

She looked so upset that Mavros decided to leave further questions till later. Besides, this room served his purpose very well. He would be in the centre of the village and able to come and go without disturbing his landlady.

'I do like this one,' he assured her with a smile. 'It's wonderful.'

Rena's expression lightened and she handed him the keyring. 'How long do you stay?'

Mavros raised his shoulders. 'I'm not sure. A few days at least.'

She nodded. 'That is good. Usually I ask for money in advance, but you have an honest face.' She gave a shy smile, then she became sombre again and turned away.

Mavros was sure that she had just remembered what had happened to the young couple and the fact that their funerals would soon be taking place. He suddenly felt like an intruder in the village. But maybe grief would make people drop their guard and that could be to his advantage. There were times when his profession made him ashamed.

In the late afternoon Mavros woke up in the double bed, wondering for a few moments where he was, and then took a shower. Rena had given him lunch of home-made *fava* – ground yellow peas with onion and paprika – salad and a smoky local white wine that had sent him straight to sleep. Often when he had a siesta he felt terrible afterwards – one of his British friends had dubbed the activity 'death in the afternoon' on a visit to Athens – but not this time. He was ready to start the search for Rosa and he sat down at the table to consider the options. He would obviously have to hang back with direct questions about the missing woman. If her hot date in Istanbul had turned out to be a wet blanket and she'd come back to the island, it was possible that she was involved with a local guy who might not take kindly to someone snooping around. Even if she wasn't hooked up with some bronzed fisherman, it was a fair assumption that she was keeping her head down. He'd need local information to help him locate her, and now was hardly a time when the islanders would open their hearts to a foreigner. Anyway, gathering impressions of places was the way he always worked when he was out of Athens. Initially the best course would be to check things out surreptitiously and see if he could pick up her trail on his own. It was time to do some more eavesdropping.

There was no sign of Rena when Mavros left the house. He pocketed his keys and headed for the square, but it was as dead as it had been earlier. The only people around were a few card players in the *kafeneion*, all of the men looking downcast. He decided to go down to the port. On his way he stopped outside the school again, feeling the eyes of some small children on him from the swings. Stretching his hand across the wall, he managed to touch the abraded area of the memorial column. He ran his fingertips over the space to the right where the surname would have been and felt the faint outline of three more letters – 'PEN', he thought. Continuing down the street, he tried to make sense of it. Why would the people who ran the island have sanctioned the removal of a name that had clearly been approved when the memorial was first erected? And who had tried to write the name on the column again, not very long ago? Twitching his head, he told himself to forget it. He'd always had a tendency to waste time on speculation. It was part of the curse of being an investigator.

When he got down to the port, the last of the sun turning the buildings a deep red, he went over to the café he'd been in earlier. There was only a faint light from the depths of the interior, chairs stacked on the tables outside. He tried the door and found it was open. Even though he didn't want to start showing people the photo of Rosa Ozal yet, he needed to find the village's hot spots. Not everywhere could be closed because of the impending funerals. There were enough tourists around to tempt someone to offer them a good time. Not here, though.

'No, no, closed,' said the waiter, Thanasis, who'd served him in the morning, raising his head from the sink behind the bar. His eyes were heavily ringed and damp.

'Okay,' Mavros said. 'Is there another place open?'

The youth shrugged. 'I don't know.' It was clear he didn't much care.

Mavros sympathised with him. According to the guidebook the population of the island was only around five hundred, so he must have been known the dead boy and girl well. He turned to go.

'Wait,' Thanasis said in a low voice. 'There is bar called Astrapi.'

Mavros looked back at him. *Astrapi* meant 'lightning'. 'Where is it?' he asked.

'Go down Ayia Marina road about one half kilometre.' The young man shook his head. 'All crazy people there.' He lowered his head and didn't speak again.

Mavros went outside again and was about to head back up to the centre when he caught sight of a pair of figures at the near end of the pier. They were engaged in deep conversation, their heads close. One of them was Manolis, the one-armed old man who'd sent him packing from the war memorial; he was clutching the other man's bare forearm. Looking around him and seeing that there was no one else in the port, Mavros walked away from them. They stopped talking and looked at him suspiciously as he went past them into the darkness beyond the last streetlamp. Waiting till he heard the voices start up again, Mavros ducked down behind a bus that was parked at the quayside. He felt his heart suddenly pound in his chest. What he was doing was wrong, but there was something about the fierce old man that puzzled him. Years of watching people at the margins of society – criminals, addicts, people at the end of their tether – had sharpened his senses.

Mavros crept behind the bus's long flank and found that when he'd reached the rear wheel he could make out the voices. The sun had sunk farther, the last of its red stain swallowed up by the waves.

'Life is a whore,' the old man cursed. 'And the sea is a whore and murderer. Do you hear me, Lefteri?'

The other man mumbled in assent.

'I was here when they brought them in. Naked they were, the idiots. What had they been doing? You don't fuck when you're on a boat at sea, for God's sake. Their eyes were as glassy as an octopus's. I've spent most of my life pulling fish from the salt-veined killer and now I pull my own grandson from it.'

The other man wrenched himself away. 'I know, Father,' he said in a sullen voice.

'You know nothing, Lefteri,' the one-armed man raged. 'Where were you? Going on trial for beating a tourist to pulp. And all because he went to sleep in your boat. What do you know? You should have been here, and since you weren't you're going to hear everything about it. Christ, the horror. The young men in the boat from Paros pushed me away – gently, mind – when they took the tarpaulin off them to spare me that sight, but I forced myself forward. There had to be some member of the family present and you weren't even on the island. Besides, I was the oldest.'

'Yes, Father. Now let me—'

'Stay here, you fool. You shouldn't be going shooting rabbits tonight of all nights, but if you must then you'll go with what I have to tell you in your mind.'

There was a silence for a few seconds.

'Very well.' The old man's voice was harsh and he was no longer bothering to control the volume. 'I kneeled on the deck – do you hear me? – and touched my grandson's hand. I felt the flesh that was already cold and lifeless. Their mouths were gaping, as if they'd been crying out as they took their final breaths. Navsika's hair was knotted around the white skin of her shoulders. I saw our boy's limp cock as they cut away the nets and pulled the bodies apart, and I saw the triangle of thick hair beneath the girl's stomach. Then I heard the wailing of the women as your wife and your mother arrived running, their lips spattered with froth. I kept them back as long as I could and then the old women took over. They've been through many deaths. But where were you, you fugitive? You coward?'

There was another, longer pause.

'I'm going now.' Lefteris's voice was deep and resentful.

'Is that all you have to say?' the old man shouted. 'Your only son is dead and you're going hunting? My God, Lefteri, what kind of a man are you?'

Mavros looked round the edge of the bus cautiously and saw the younger man's heavy body and clenched fists.

'I'm the kind of man you were when you were young, Father,' he said slowly. 'All the men of the Gryparis family are hard as stone, aren't they?' He grunted. 'Except my son, it seems.' He leaned closer to the old man. 'Leave me be,' he said. 'My affairs don't concern you, old man. Don't get involved.' Then he stepped away, his heavy boots crunching across the sandy asphalt. Soon afterwards there was the sound of a starter motor and headlights came on. Mavros shrank back against the side of the bus and watched as a gleaming new pick-up with a high suspension came past on the road that skirted Faros towards the south.

The old man stood where he was, his voice only partially audible. He was saying something about Gryparis women being hard too, about the family being cursed in the female line. Then he shuffled away towards the main street, the vigour suddenly gone from his body and his shoulders drooping as if they were carrying a fearful weight.

Mavros watched him move off, trying to get his head round what he'd just heard. Far from grieving for the loss of their male heir, the old man and his son seemed to be locked in their own savage world, one in which normal human feelings were unknown. Mavros felt like a traveller in a previously undiscovered country. How could a father go hunting the night after his son had died without any expression of grief? And how could a grandfather talk about his grandson's shrivelled genitals and the poor girl's nakedness as if they were nothing more than animals?

He shook his head and wished he'd never embarked on the surveillance strategy. But how else would he be able to find the missing woman in this beautiful, brutal place?

Mavros walked towards the square on his way to the bar he'd been told about. The night air was cool. In Athens the evenings at the end of September were still warm, but on Trigono the breeze had cleared away the heat of the day and there was a lot of dampness in the atmosphere. He'd seen the signpost to Ayia Marina earlier. His guidebook told him it was a beach resort six kilometres out of Faros on the eastern leg of the triangle that formed the island. He passed through the square, now even quieter with only a pair of black-clad old women talking in undertones outside the church, then headed past Rena's house down the street that led out of Faros. Apart from the occasional child's cry and the muted sound of televisions, the village could have been under military curfew.

The streetlights were dim and infrequent. Mavros suddenly found himself beyond the last buildings. A dog barked away to his left and a rustling came gradually closer. As he rounded a corner, hand against the stones of a low wall, light flooded out from a single-storey house. It fell on the grey face and ears of a donkey in an enclosure to his right. As he got closer he made out a sign with the bar's name, silver bolts of lightning around the letters. The pounding of rock music became more audible with every step.

Mavros opened the door and immediately felt eyes on him. The lights inside were low, a deep red colour that made it hard to make out faces. Approaching the bar that ran down the right side of the cramped space, he recognised the English foursome, their table covered in beer bottles. Beyond them were the two Americans from the Glaros, the sharp-tongued woman and the laid-back man, a half-empty bottle of wine in front of them. The other tables were occupied by people he hadn't seen before. A tanned, middle-aged couple looked at him curiously.

'What would you like, my friend?' The guy behind the bar spoke English. He was thin and short, his mousy hair gathered into a ponytail that made the heavy earrings he wore even more prominent. 'Beer, whisky, cocktails, I've got everything.' He extended a scrawny hand. 'Rinus is the name.'

'Hello, Rinus,' Mavros said. 'I'm Alex.'

'And I'm Eleni.' English with a Greek accent.

Mavros turned to the woman who'd appeared out of the shadows at the end of the bar. She was of medium height, her black hair spliced with threads of silver. A dark blue shirt and loose-fitting jeans covered a figure that was on the borderline between full and overweight, the skin on her round face burned and creased by the sun. Shaking her hand, he put her age at over forty, maybe as much as fifty.

'So what's it to be, Alex?' Rinus's accent was a mixture of European and American, his manner friendly but also detached, as if working a bar were somehow beneath him. His stained white T-shirt bore the words 'Astrapi – Let The Lightning Blow Your Mind!'

'Beer,' Mavros said. 'Amstel, if you've got it.'

The barman laughed. 'I told you, I've got everything.' He

flipped the cap and handed Mavros the bottle. 'Besides, I was born in Amsterdam. How could I not serve Amstel? The stuff they brew in Greece is a lot better than the Dutch piss too.'

'Is that right?' Mavros said, looking around the place.

'Where are you from, Alex?' Rinus asked, swallowing beer and then pouring a clear liquid into three shot glasses.

'Scotland,' Mavros said.

'You don't look very Scottish,' the woman called Eleni said. 'Or sound very Scottish.'

Mavros shrugged. 'We don't all have red hair and Billy Connolly accents.'

'Who's Billy Connolly?' she asked, leaning forward to take one of the shot glasses.

'Who cares?' said Rinus, handing Mavros one and raising his own. 'Welcome to Trigono, my friend.'

Mavros acknowledged the toast and swallowed neat spirit.

'*Tsikoudhia*,' Rinus said. 'The local ouzo. Clears the throat, doesn't it?'

'Yup.' Mavros washed the oily taste away with beer.

Eleni gave a hollow laugh. 'You picked a good time to come to Trigono, Alex.'

Mavros looked at her through the cloud of smoke that was hanging in the bar. 'It does seem a bit quiet,' he said. 'Apart from in here.' The music – mid-period Van Halen – was making conversation difficult at more than arm's length.

Eleni kicked her bar stool closer. 'Two young people, a boy and a girl, were drowned yesterday. The island is in shock.'

'That's terrible,' Mavros said, playing dumb. 'How did—' He broke off as the door opened with a crash.

A uniformed policeman walked in, followed by the heavily built, bald man Mavros had seen driving his Jeep on to the ferry. Rinus immediately lowered the volume of the music.

'Good evening, Stamati,' the barman said. 'Nothing wrong, I hope. Can I offer you something?' His Greek was fluent but with a strong foreign accent. 'Evening, Ari,' he said to the other man in English. 'The usual?'

'Fuckin' A,' the bald man replied, looking around the room, a slack smile playing across thick lips. 'I'll just help myself.' He leaned across the bar and grabbed a bottle of vodka, then went over to the tanned couple in the corner.

'The music,' said the policeman in a low voice. 'There have been complaints. You shouldn't have opened the night before the funerals.'

Rinus raised his bony shoulders. 'Is there a law against it, Stamati?' He poured a large measure of whisky.

The policeman looked around, his eyes resting only briefly on Mavros. 'No, Rinus,' he said, pronouncing the second syllable of the name as 'nose'. 'But be more careful or I'll close you down.'

The barman smiled nervously. 'You wouldn't do that.' He leaned close to the policeman and whispered in his ear.

Mavros saw the cop grin as he gulped down his whisky. He went over to where the big man was sitting. 'I have to go now, Ari,' he said. 'You won't make any trouble tonight, eh?'

Aris laughed provocatively. 'Me, Stamati?' he said in Greek. 'Trouble?' He gulped vodka from the bottle. 'Go fuck yourself.' His tone was no longer playful.

Eleni shook her head as the policeman left. 'Wanker,' she said after him in Greek. 'You lick his fat arse and like it.'

Mavros kept his face expressionless. He wondered if Stamatis was the officer who had been unable to give any information about Rosa Ozal to the Athens police. After a moment he asked, 'Who's the big man?'

Eleni glanced over her shoulder. 'Aris Theocharis,' she said. 'The beast, you mean, not the big man.' She drank from her glass. 'Don't tell him I said that,' she added, giving Mavros a stern look. 'I work on his father's land. Theocharis the mining tycoon?'

'Theocharis,' he said. 'The name's familiar, I'm not sure why.'

She was studying him thoughtfully. 'Do you know anything about ancient Greek art? Have you heard of the Theocharis Museum of Funerary Art?'

Mavros nodded. 'Of course. I visited it last year when I was in Athens.'

The Greek woman clapped, an ironic smile on her lips. 'Bravo, Alex. We all want foreigners to learn about our wonderful culture.' She drank again and then stood up. 'I'm going now,' she said abruptly. 'I'm an archaeologist, you see, and I have to be at the excavation not long after dawn.' She waved at Rinus. 'Goodnight.'

Mavros watched her walk away, her solid frame moving with surprising grace towards the door.

'Ach, Eleni, don't go,' the bald man bellowed. 'I want you to sit on my knee and tell me about the exciting things you've discovered.' The couple he was sitting with laughed, the woman louder than the man.

The archaeologist stopped as she reached the door, but she didn't turn round. It slammed after her.

'Shit,' Rinus said with a groan. 'I only just got that replaced.' He tilted his head towards the table behind Mavros. 'The big man decided he wanted to take the old one with him one night. He was pissed out of his brains.'

Mavros looked at him. 'You're Dutch, yeah? Where did you learn to speak English?'

The barman laughed, revealing uneven yellow teeth. 'That good, is it?' His expression darkened. 'My father was in the oil business. He sent me to an English public school. Then I made the mistake of marrying an Englishwoman.' He shook his head. 'Bitch left me after we moved here. Took the kids back to Salisbury.'

'Ah.' Mavros moved farther down the bar. He didn't want any more of the Dutchman's *tsikhoudia* or his life story. He was more interested in the museum benefactor's loudmouthed son.

'. . . ruined the island, Ari,' the male half of the couple to the rear was saying. 'There are far too many houses being built and sold to foreigners on the east coast.'

The bald man let out a guffaw. 'Correct me if I'm wrong, Mikkel, but aren't you a foreigner? Didn't you buy a house on the east coast?' His English had a strong American edge to it.

'Yes, but that was ten years ago,' the woman put in. Her

features were well formed, her expression a strange mixture of arrogance and vulnerability. 'Before the hordes came and lowered standards.' The Englishmen were murdering a Gloria Gaynor song and she gave them a withering look.

Aris leaned over and put his arm around her, provoking a nervous smile from Mikkel. 'Ach, Barbara,' he said in a loud voice. 'You Germans are such snobs.'

Norm, the worst of the singers, had just been shamed into stopping by a nudge from his other half, Jane, who looked embarrassed by his performance. He glanced around. 'You got that right, big fella,' he said, raising a bottle in salutation.

The woman called Barbara gave him a vicious look. For a moment Mavros thought she was going to get up and lay into the much larger English male.

Aris grinned and put the vodka to his lips. As he lowered the bottle he winked at the Americans, Gretchen and Lance. They smiled back nervously.

'Anyway, what about these drownings?' Barbara asked. 'They say that Yiangos and Navsika were found naked, in a clench.' Her eyes were wide and her tongue flickered across her lips.

Aris drank again, his eyes back on the English group. The buxom woman Trace was staring at him with drunken interest.

'I can't understand it,' the German Mikkel said. 'I went fishing with Yiangos sometimes. He was a natural seaman. How could he—'

'Fucking shut up, will you?' Aris roared, getting to his feet and swaying over the table. 'This is a bar, not a funeral parlour. I'm going to find some company that knows how to have a good time.'

Mikkel mouthed his embarrassment to Barbara, who shook her head at him fiercely. Mavros watched as Aris Theocharis stumbled towards the English table and swept the bottles away.

'Who wants a party?' he yelled.

'Oh, yes please,' said Trace. 'We'd love a party.'

Jane didn't look so sure, but Norm and Roy gave a cheer when the big man ordered a double round of drinks. The barman seemed unperturbed by the increase in the noise. It was clear to Mavros that he had an arrangement with the policeman, one that no doubt involved more than free drinks.

Suddenly Mavros remembered something that his brother-in-law Nondas had once said about the smaller Greek islands, that they were magnets for all the world's misfits. Bull's-eye. He decided that he'd gathered enough background detail for one night and headed for the calm of his room in Rena's courtyard.

7

Mavros let himself into the house as quietly as he could. A single light had been left on at the far end of the passage that led into the courtyard. He crossed over to the outhouse and opened the door. Turning as he closed it, he caught a slight movement behind the half-open shutters at a window on the first floor. A shadowy figure was visible, remaining there as he looked up at it. Obviously his landlady thought she hadn't been observed. He held his gaze for a time then went into his room. Rena was a strange one, he thought. She was shy and reserved, her black clothes showing that she had been bereaved – a parent? a husband? – but there was deep emotion simmering beneath the surface, he could sense it. What was she doing at her bedroom window? Taking the night air or keeping an eye on her latest tenant? Mavros wasn't sure whether to be irritated or flattered.

He closed the shutters and plugged in the electric anti-mosquito device. The siesta he'd taken meant that he wasn't ready to crash out immediately and, besides, he hadn't checked the room yet. Although he hadn't so far been able to ascertain from Rena whether Rosa Ozal had stayed in it, he wanted to look around anyway. There was the faintest of chances that something had been left behind. An impartial observer would call him a nosy bastard, but he had learned to be thorough – during a case in which a divorced father abducted his twin daughters, he'd come across an incriminating letter behind a rack of vintage Macedonian wine. He started behind the bedstead, immediately discovering that Rena was a scrupulous cleaner. There wasn't a speck of dust.

He sat on the floor and wondered if he was wasting his time. Anything that had been left behind would have been found by the landlady. He glanced around the room. Where might she have missed? His practised eye soon found the only likely place. In the far corner there was a traditional hand-built *tzaki*, the uneven stones of the fireplace rising in a narrowing column to the ceiling. The raised platform where the wood was burned was spotless, the space beneath the chimney almost filled by a bright blue vase containing a fresh spray of magenta bougainvillaea flowers.

Mavros moved the vase on to the varnished stone floor. Before he put his hand up the chimney, he asked himself what he was doing. In such an out-of-the-way place he wasn't just looking for things that had been left, he was after things that had been deliberately hidden. Why would Rosa Ozal, or anyone else, make use of the chimney? He almost gave up, but curiosity had wrapped its coils around him. The only way to shake them off was to get his hand dirty, so he did.

He had to struggle to get the vent flap open. It had been closed to stop insects and dirt coming into the room. Either the chimney badly needed sweeping or there was something on the topside of the metal plate. He finally managed to swivel it upwards and a plastic-covered object slid into the palm of his hand. Feeling a frisson of surprise, Mavros drew it down carefully and put it on the grate. It seemed that the chimney had no need of sweeping after all. The pale blue plastic bag that had descended from it was pretty clean. It was about the size of a paperback book, though not as heavy. The bag had been folded tightly around the contents and secured by a couple of strips of tape.

Mavros picked up his find and took it over to the table. He should have handed it over to Rena without opening it, but he rejected that course of action. After all, he could stick the tape back and give the package to his landlady if there wasn't anything interesting inside. Smoothing the plastic down, he scraped gently at the edge of the tape. Both strips peeled away easily. He slid the straightened fingers of one hand into the bag and pulled out the

contents. Two objects lay on the wooden surface in front of
him, both instantly recognisable. One was a black computer
diskette. It bore a label with an inscription in blue ink. At
the top were the letters 'GL' followed by the number '1' and
at the bottom were the letters 'EC'. The other was a paper
photograph folder.

Mavros sat back. He wondered if he was about to see some
previous tenant's holiday snaps. But why would they have been
put up the chimney along with a diskette? He shook his head
and opened the folder. There were only three photographs in
it. The first showed a flat expanse of stony ground in front
of a steep cliff. At the foot of the cliff was a corrugated plastic roof that protruded a metre or so from the ground. The
arid terrain and windswept bushes on the rocky surface behind
suggested that the scene was in Greece. Was it on Trigono?
Raising the photo to his eyes, Mavros made out a series of
holes in the cliff-face. They looked like the entrances to caves.
After checking that the back was blank apart from a printed
serial number, he put the photo down and picked up the next
one. It showed the Trigono war memorial that he had been
looking at earlier in the day, the list of names clear and legible, apart from the one at the bottom that had been roughly
removed.

Mavros put the second photo down and rubbed his fingers
across the stubble on his chin. Why had someone gone to such
lengths to hide these two images? They were hardly standard
tourist shots, but they didn't seem to show anything very
significant. Then he noticed that the third photo was completely
different. For a start it was in black and white rather than colour,
or rather what had originally been black and white but had now,
with the passage of time, turned brown and cream. The subject
matter was completely different as well. It showed a young
man in military uniform, a peaked cap on his head. Mavros
didn't know much about such garb, but it looked British. He
flipped it over and saw a small stamp on the bottom left corner
that read 'Vafopoulos, Photographer, Alexandria'. Above it was

written the name George Lawrence and the date 1941 with a question mark immediately after it, all this in pencil that looked recent. Turning the photo back round, he looked at the soldier. He must have been in his mid-twenties, the cap and the raised brass insignia on his epaulettes showing that he was an officer and the style of the tunic suggesting the Second World War. He was facing the lens with a weak smile, his boyish features lit by more than the photographer's flash. His eyes were uncertain, though. They were focused away from the camera, the limp lashes giving him the look of a poet rather than a warrior. Who was George Lawrence? And why had his image ended up in a chimney on Trigono?

It was only as he put the third photo down by the others that Mavros realised what he had omitted to check. He picked up the shot of the war memorial again and turned it round. This time he saw a brief inscription in ballpoint above the serial number. It read 'Trigono, June 5th 2001'. This writing was not the same as that on the back of the portrait. He recognised it. Heart racing, he leaned over and opened his satchel to remove the plastic folder with his notes. The postcard Rosa Ozal had sent to her family was at the back. He placed it face down next to the war memorial image. There was no doubt about it. The writing was identical.

Opening her eyes to the darkness, the woman felt a wave of panic. She fought to control her breathing and sat up, the ropes impeding her movements. She let out a long groan then clenched her arms against her bare sides. The blanket she'd found on the ground near her had slipped off her torso and was tangled up with her legs. Her throat was dry, her lips cracked, and she stretched out for the bottle. It was full again. She put it to her lips and swallowed metallic liquid, then jerked it away, spitting and feeling her thighs dampen. Why did she keep passing out and sinking into dreams that wove patterns in her mind, patterns that one minute were seductive, full of glorious colours, and the next were ripped apart by monstrous, clawing hands? What was in the bottle?

She felt around in the impervious black until her hands landed on food – bread, a piece torn from a large round loaf like the last time, and something wrapped in foil. She pulled it open and raised it to her face. Something roasted. She took a tentative bite, tasting skin and strands of meat. Chicken. She ate greedily.

It was as she sat back, having put the blanket between herself and the rough wall, that the hairs on her neck rose. She froze, inclining her head to take in any sound. There wasn't much to go on, the enclosed space seeming to soak up all the traces that her senses were straining to identify. She held her breath for as long as she could but all she heard was a faint susurrus, a continuous high-pitched scratching in the distance. Did it come from some kind of insect? She remembered now. The noise she heard as she walked to the beach, the noise that came back as soon as she shook the water from her ears after swimming. Crickets rubbing away in the burning heat. Yes, now she could picture the beach.

The woman sat still and tried to bring more back, fingers to her forehead. The beach, a line of dusty bushes and in the middle distance a cluster of white houses. The beach and the water that deepened quickly when she stepped into it, tiny fish nibbling at her legs and submerged stones that hurt her feet. But that was all. She could see no people, no one to help her recover who she was or where the seashore was located. Had she been on holiday there?

She tugged at the ropes in frustration, her wrists stinging, and began to sob as she realised that she still had no grasp on her identity. She felt for the bottle and tipped it to her lips again. She no longer cared if there was something narcotic in it. Oblivion was better than struggling in the dark.

Her eyelids twitched and she felt a numbness spread through her limbs. So when the circle of light suddenly appeared on the ground in front of her, she could not move, could only watch as it moved over her legs and up her abdomen to her face. Then she heard a voice, a soft voice that whispered comforting words, wished her a peaceful sleep. She wanted to float away, lose her senses, but the faint rattle of the camera came to her and she tried to scream, felt heavy hands on her midriff again, screamed but knew no sound was coming from her throat.

Screamed as she fell into the abyss, its demons thrusting and prising her apart.

Mavros woke early by his standards. It wasn't yet eight when he became aware of the birdsong in the courtyard and the grid of sunlight shining through the shutters on to his bedroom wall. He sat up in bed and thought about what he had discovered the previous night, flicking his worry beads with his thumb. After spraying himself with cold water in the uncurtained shower, he put on jeans and a clean T-shirt, this time a darker-coloured one, and secreted the beads in his bag. He wanted to pass as a tourist and his way with them was too practised. He opened the door and saw his landlady across the yard.

'*Kali mera*, Mister Alex,' she said, throwing some breadcrumbs to the birds.

'Good morning to you.' Mavros ran his eye over Rena's neat black outfit. Her eyes were ringed and she seemed downcast. He wanted to ask her about the things in the chimney, but this didn't look like the right time.

'You need anything?' she asked. 'Coffee?'

He shook his head. 'I'll go out.'

Rena pursed her lips. 'No shop open this morning,' she said. She seemed to have lost her command of English. 'Everyone going to the church. A boy and a girl—' She broke off, drawing her hand across her eyes.

'Oh yes, the funerals.'

She looked at him. 'You hear about them?'

Mavros nodded. 'It's a terrible thing,' he said, feeling awkward as he stood under the pergola. He intended to follow the funerals – everyone would be there and he would get an insight into how the island functioned – but he didn't want Rena to think he was prying.

'I'm leaving now,' she said. 'I have to help an old lady get

ready. If you need coffee or anything else, please take from my
kitchen.' She gave him a quick smile and then turned away down
the passage that led to the street door.

Mavros raised a hand after her. He felt comfortable with
her restrained hospitality. It was a lot more genuine than the
disguised rapacity he'd experienced on Zakynthos. No doubt
there were plenty of smiling thieves on Trigono too, but he
didn't think Rena was one of them. She was bound to be right
about everywhere being closed, so he went into the kitchen that
led directly off the courtyard. There was a *briki*, a small metal
coffee pot with a long handle, on the gas ring, so he rooted
around in the spotless cupboards for coffee, spoon and cup.
A plastic canister of drinking water was standing on the marble
top. He might as well make the coffee here rather than in his
own place. The kitchen was old-fashioned, without the gadgets
beloved of Athenians, but it was well enough equipped and
stocked. Vegetables and sprays of drying herbs hung from the
walls, their bright colours matched by the chequered plastic table
covers and floral curtains. The open door was hung with muslin
against insects.

He stirred the coffee until it came to the boil and took it out
into the yard. There was a wooden table under the branches that
hung from the pergola, wooden chairs with wicker bases around
it. Although there were houses on either side, only one window
overlooked Rena's courtyard so she had a quiet oasis to herself in
the middle of the village. Mavros glanced up at the upper floor
of her house, the shutters of the window where he'd seen what
he presumed was her shadowy figure still hooked half open. If
he was true to his profession he'd go and have a look upstairs,
but he dismissed the idea. What could Rena have that would
help him? Later on he'd show her the photo of Rosa Ozal and
ask if she'd seen the Turkish-American woman since June.

Mavros finished his coffee and took the cup back into the
kitchen. He noticed the local telephone directory there and took
the opportunity to locate the number of the Olympic Airways
office and that of a travel company, both on Paros. Going back

to his room, he switched on his mobile phone. He'd turned it off the previous evening because the signal on Trigono was variable. It was strong enough now. He wasn't surprised to find that he had a message from Niki.

'Alex? Where are you?' She sounded even more exasperated than he'd anticipated. 'Why haven't you got your phone on? Well, anyway, give me a call.' Her tone hardened. 'Call me, you fugitive. Or I'll do worse than put honey in your hallway.'

Mavros shook his head and wondered what was he going to do about Niki. Then again, she'd called him a fugitive. Maybe she'd already realised that he was trying to break free.

Before he spoke to her, he rang the airline and tried to find out whether Rosa Ozal had flown in or out in the past three months. He wasn't surprised to be told that such information was confidential. He considered taking the boat back across the straits and flashing his investigator's card at the woman who'd brushed him off, but he suspected she'd only laugh at him and demand an official request. The man who answered the phone in the travel agency actually did laugh at him, wondering if he had any idea how many people travelled to and from Paros every day in the summer. When Mavros pointed out that the ferry companies were legally required to record the names of all passengers on their tickets, the connection was cut. He might have been able to bribe the information out of a more compliant clerk, but it looked like a waste of time – passenger names were often omitted, and even if he found confirmation that Rosa had arrived or left at some stage, she might easily have done so again. Collating information on Trigono would be a better bet.

Taking a deep breath, Mavros returned Niki's call.

'There you are at last,' she said hurriedly. 'To hell with you, wanker.'

'What?'

'I'm in the car. Some lunatic just cut me up.'

'Maybe I should call back later.'

'No, I want to talk to you now, Alex. Where are you?'

'Em, on an island.'

'What?' she screamed. 'Which island?'

'A tourist island,' he prevaricated.

'Which island, Alex? Tell me or I swear I'll accuse you of rape.'

'Niki, for God's sake . . .'

'I was joking,' she said with a bitter laugh. 'So, which island?'

Mavros felt bad about what he was about to do, but he didn't want to give Niki the chance to land on him out of the blue. 'Em, Zakynthos,' he said. 'I had a case a couple of years back, a farmer who shut his wife up in a cowshed. It looks like another guy has done the same thing, except this time no one knows where.' The fluency of the lie depressed him.

'That's men for you,' Niki said. 'Come on, Alex, isn't that a job for the police?'

'Yes. But I'm acting for the woman's parents, trying to avoid any mistakes . . . look, Niki, I don't know how long I'll be. I've got to go now, my clients are here. I'll talk to you soon.' He broke the connection before she could remonstrate further.

So much for *his* private life. Now for the private life of Trigono.

October 21st, 1942

At last I'm organised. The last few days have been hard, but now everything is in place. The explosives and the wireless along with its batteries are in a well-hidden cave, and I've taken up residence in a hut on the ridge that even the goatherds have abandoned. I thought I was beginning to turn into a nocturnal creature like a follower of Bela Lugosi in that ridiculous film as all the work had to be done under the light of the moon. There's an Italian post on the southern slopes of Paros and I couldn't take the chance of them spotting me in their binoculars. It's five miles or more, but the visibility here is so good that you can make things out from incredible distances. Now I'm ensconced, I don't need to skulk about so much. I have my peasant clothes and my heavy shepherd's cloak so I shouldn't attract much attention during the day.

And I have finally made contact with the locals, or rather they made contact with me. I was beginning to get concerned and wondered if they'd had second thoughts about working with me. But on the third night Ajax came up to the ridge with a couple of burly companions, relatives judging by the resemblance they bore to the resistance leader.

Things were a bit sticky at first – I think they feared I was going to start ordering them about – but when they heard me speak Greek, they loosened up. We drank some of the local spirit, which made my eyes water but I suppose you can get used to anything, and went over the plans for the base. As I experienced, Vathy inlet is the perfect hidden landing point and the brass in Beirut were right to single it out. As soon as a regular kaïki link is established, we'll be able to stockpile supplies and forward them to underground groups all over the central Aegean and eventually, I hope, to the mainland. That's not all. I mentioned my ideas about sabotage on the neighbouring islands to Ajax. He was keen, telling me he'd already given the Eyeties – makaronadhes, he called them, spaghetti-eaters – a beating on the Albanian front and would enjoy a repeat performance. He didn't seem unduly concerned about the threat of reprisals, unlike some of the Greek officers in Egypt. As long as we did as little as possible to implicate the people on Trigono, he said. That was very encouraging.

Now I have only to wait for the team from base. I've signalled that all is ready here. I'm expecting a small squad of Greeks, members of a Ieros Lochos, one of the so-called Sacred Band units modelled on the Theban warriors who died for each other on the battlefields of the ancient country. They should have been here with me from the beginning but there was some wrangle in Cairo and they've only recently been given the green light by Greek high command. Fortunately I wasn't delayed and here I am, holed up on a ridge in the Aegean like an Olympian god surveying his domain. Ah, this country! The sun-scorched fields, the dun-coloured hillsides mottled with bushes like the flanks of gigantic leopards, the hum of contented bees. And around it all, the endless blue deepening into the distance. If anything is worth fighting for, it's this place.

Now I must sleep. Tomorrow Ajax will be back with bread, olives and wine, the soldier's simple fare. What more could I ask?

The procession moved slowly towards the square, headed by three old women in black carrying the wine that would be poured into the grave and the food that would be distributed to the mourners later. Alongside were three boys bearing a cross and staffs surmounted with round metal representations of cherubim, their eyes flicking from side to side nervously. Behind them came the priest in his round black hat, a decorated golden cape over his robes, and then the coffin borne by male relatives with tear-stained faces. The women around them had their heads bowed, many unable to restrain their wailing.

Mavros was standing in an arched passage that led into the *kastro*, trying to keep out of the way as the multitude moved across the square to the church. Earlier he'd overheard a conversation between two women. The boy Yiangos was to be buried first; the girl Navsika's service would follow in the afternoon. It had been many years since there had been two funerals on the same day in Trigono. Not since the war, they thought, not since the hard years. 'Ach, Yiango, ach, Navsika,' one moaned. 'Say farewell to these streets that you played in only a few years ago.'

As the priest began to chant over the open coffin inside the crammed church, his voice amplified by speakers on the roof, Mavros went into the old castle and climbed worn steps to a vantage point that took in the village and its surroundings. The great massif of the southern hills was shimmering in the haze. Then he saw a large vehicle come down the street at speed past Rena's house. He'd noticed 'No Entry' signs on all the central roads when he arrived, but the locals didn't seem to pay much attention to them. He recognised the car. It was the Jeep that had delayed the ferry yesterday. It pulled into the square and parked outside the *kafeneion*. The bald-headed Aris, his face grim, helped a tall old man with a full white beard get out. Then he went round to the other side and opened the front door for a statuesque woman wearing a dark blue ensemble and wide hat. Eleni the archaeologist stepped out from the rear, her hair pulled back from her face.

'Look at Aris. Do you think he'd rather be somewhere else?'

Mavros looked over the edge and realised that he was standing above a small wooden balcony set into the wall. He stepped back but kept listening.

'Of course he'd rather be somewhere else, Barbara.' The voice was that of the barman Rinus. 'Wouldn't you rather be somewhere else right now?'

'I'd rather be on the beach,' said the tight-faced German woman Mavros had seen in the corner of the bar. 'But I didn't have the nerve to swim this morning. It didn't seem right after the drownings.'

'It's unlike you to lose your nerve,' Rinus said sardonically. 'Why aren't you down in the church if you feel so bad about it?'

'I'm not Orthodox, am I? And anyway, Yiangos, well, Yiangos was a—'

'Never mind what Yiangos was,' interrupted the Dutchman. 'Some more wine?'

'A funeral libation?' Mikkel's voice was more faint. 'Don't worry, I won't pour it on the ground.'

'What's he talking about?' demanded Rinus.

'Don't mind him,' Barbara said derisively. 'He's been reading too many ancient history books. Look. Isn't that a touching scene? Eleni listening obediently to her master's every word.' Her words were harsh but her voice wavered, giving the impression of barely controlled tension.

Mavros watched as the group from the Jeep moved slowly – reluctantly, it seemed – towards the church. He recognised the old man as Panos Theocharis, the museum founder, although he looked much older than he did in newspaper and magazine photos. The pointed beard gave him the look of an ancient god, Zeus or Poseidon, but this effect was marred by the stick that he was leaning on heavily. Eleni was at his side, her head inclined towards him. The woman in the designer clothes – he couldn't make out her face under the brim of her hat – stepped across the flagstones elegantly, shod in high-heeled shoes that made a clicking noise he could hear from the top of the *kastro*. Barbara was right about Aris. He was slouching along behind the others, a look of distaste on his fleshy face. At least he wasn't wearing the green sun visor.

'I thought Eleni said she was going to the excavations today,' Rinus said.

'Her orders were obviously amended,' Barbara said. 'It'll do her good to get out of those holes she spends her time in. And to follow orders. It makes a change from her ordering everybody else about.'

Rinus laughed. 'You're too hard on her. She's an educated Greek woman. They have to impose themselves whenever they can. You know how chauvinist most men are in this country.'

'That doesn't mean she's entitled to treat me like dirt.' Now Barbara's voice was sharp, full of what struck Mavros as extreme loathing. He remembered the way she'd looked at the Englishman in the bar.

'She has a problem with foreigners who inflate the price of land and tempt the locals into selling off their family plots,' the barman said. 'You can't blame her. After all, that's what happened on the east of this island, isn't it?' He laughed. 'Where your house is.' Although Rinus was a foreigner himself, he was being uncomplimentary about his fellow strangers. Mavros was struggling to grasp the dynamics of the barman's relations with the German woman.

'Stop it, Rinus,' Barbara snapped. 'Eleni's a loudmouthed bitch and you know it. Anyway, you used to have a house on the east coast. Until your ex-wife took it away from you.'

'And sold it,' Rinus said bitterly. 'The cow. And now she's making a fortune from her fucking tapestries back in the UK.'

Now Barbara was the one to laugh. 'While you pretend to write the great novel during the day and provide the tourists with whatever they want at night.'

A flock of pigeons soared over the square towards the *kastro*,

the sudden clatter of their wings making Rinus move forward on
the balcony and look up into the sky. Mavros, one eye on the
church, wasn't quick enough to change position.

'Alex!' the Dutchman called. 'Good morning. Watching the
local customs?'

Mavros shook his head. 'I just got here. What's going on?'

'The funeral of the boy who drowned. Come down and have
a drink.' He put his hand over his eyes and smiled. 'It's open
house.'

'No thanks,' Mavros said. He didn't intend to miss the
procession to the cemetery.

'See you in the bar later, then.'

Mavros nodded and stepped back.

Barbara's voice rang out. 'I hope he wasn't listening to what
we were saying, Rinus.'

'Why should you care, darling?' came the sarcastic reply.
'He's not your type, is he? Not exactly a muscle-bound peasant
with a . . .'

Their voices faded as they went inside.

When Mavros got back to the archway, the church service was
finishing. Space had been found for Theocharis and his female
companions inside but Aris had stayed in the square, his hands
in his pockets and a sour look on his face.

The priest was chanting one of the final prayers, inviting the
gathered brethren to kiss the departed farewell, and suddenly
Mavros felt his own losses knife into him. Although as a communist his father had been a dogged atheist, an Orthodox funeral
was the only practical option in 1960s Greece. So the family
had followed the coffin to the vast Proto Nekrotafio, the First
Cemetery of Athens, and let the priests perform the rites. A large
crowd of banned Party members had clapped their comrade to
his final home – a home, as one of them said zealously to the
numbed family, that was shared by all men, rich or poor. The
junta of colonels had not yet come to power and forbidden public
displays of opposition, but the politics of the time were turbulent

and the gathering had an air of protest because of the dead man's record of imprisonment. The applause as Spyros was carried to the grave was a moral victory over the stony-faced policemen and security operatives who were in attendance.

Mavros was five, missing his father but only dimly aware of what was going on around him as he gripped his brother Andonis's hand tightly. Andonis of the bright blue eyes. He was sixteen then, defiant and already trusted by his father's friends. But there was to be no funeral for him, no memorial, no mention alongside Spyros's name on the headstone. He had disappeared into the abyss in 1972 without a trace.

Mavros blinked hard and watched as the open coffin was carried out of the church by young men, the boy's relatives even more stricken than they had been as he came out into the sunlight for the last time. The one-armed old man was close behind, his heavily lined face expressionless. Damp-eyed women fussed around, their sighs and groans audible from where Mavros was standing. Then he saw the tall man who had gone hunting last night, the father of the drowned boy. His face was impassive, his muscle-bound limbs constricted in an ill-fitting suit. By his side was a thin woman, her face ravaged by suffering. Her prominence in the procession and the cowed glance she gave Lefteris showed that she was Yiangos's mother. As the procession set off for the cemetery, a collective moan rang out across the square above the sound of the villagers' shuffling feet. Over them all, the late September sun shone out in an indifferent blue sky.

Mavros had been intending to keep his distance, to soak up the atmosphere and try to make sense of the village, but he found himself drawn into the sombre parade. In Athens the funerals of people who weren't family or friends meant little to him. The cries of the mourners were drowned out by the unceasing din of traffic, the trees and flowers blighted by the lead-tainted air. But the ceremony on Trigono was different. It had struck him that by following this young man's coffin he would be sending a message to his brother across the years and the emptiness that lay between them, a message that might finally get through – even though he wasn't sure what he wanted to say to Andonis. Leave me in peace?

Across the square the Theocharis party had gathered around the Jeep. Mavros could hear the old man telling his son in a low, firm voice that he was tired and that Aris was to join the procession on his behalf. Aris's lips were twisted, his eyes screwed up, but he acquiesced.

'You too,' Panos Theocharis said to the archaeologist Eleni. 'Spend the rest of the day in the village.' He turned back to his son. 'Dhimitra will drive me home. She'll pick you up in the evening after the girl's funeral. Be sure to pass on the family's respects, do you hear, Ari?'

Mavros watched as the woman in the designer suit helped her husband into the vehicle then drove slowly out of the square. Aris Theocharis joined the column of villagers, his chest out and his face red.

'Hello,' Mavros said before Eleni was swallowed up in the crowd.

She looked at him, her eyes narrowing. 'So, Alex from the bar. Taking in the local colour?'

He nodded awkwardly. 'It's very moving,' he said, trying to maintain the guise of a tourist. 'Much more emotional than back home.'

Eleni turned away. 'Come, then,' she said brusquely. 'Maybe you'll see something – what's the word? – quaint to tell your friends about.' Despite the heavy accent, her command of English was good.

Mavros walked alongside her. They were about thirty metres from the front of the dense procession.

'Did you know the young man who died?' he asked, making his tone conversational rather than inquisitive.

The archaeologist nodded. 'It's a small place. Everybody knows everybody.'

'Are you from here?'

She glanced at him as they passed the last houses and followed a winding, unmetalled road to the west. 'No, I'm from Thessaloniki. But I've been excavating sites here for the last four years.'

Mavros could see cypress trees against the blue of the sea in the distance, their pointed green tips swaying gently in the breeze. 'So was the boy a friend?'

This time Eleni's eyes didn't move in his direction. 'I . . . I knew him quite well, yes.' She shook her head. 'Yiangos was a simple soul,' she said in a neutral voice. 'He always did what he was told.'

Mavros considered that brief obituary as the stone walls on either side of the track gave way to *pikrodhafnes*, the oleanders' dusty pink and white blossoms forming an undulating line to the white walls of the burial ground. From what he'd understood, the young man had taken the fishing boat when his father was away. Had he been told to do that or was it just a young lovers' illicit outing that had gone tragically wrong? The police, coastguard and Port Police had apparently seen nothing suspicious about the drownings – if any of them had, the funerals would have been delayed by autopsies and investigations. There were representatives from the three services in the procession, their dark blue uniforms standing out. The policeman Stamatis who had been in the bar was trying hard to look dignified.

Mavros shook his head to dispel the thoughts. The deaths of the young people were nothing to do with him. He had to start concentrating on Rosa Ozal. But the heart-rending beauty of the scene overwhelmed him. If custom required you to be laid to rest rather than cremated like his Scottish relatives, this burial ground with its view across the unquiet waves was as appealing a place as any he could imagine.

He heard familiar voices to his left. On a small outcrop of rock above a field that had been burned gold by the sun, the American couple he'd seen in the café and the Bar Astrapi were squatting beside a camera on a tripod.

'It's not close enough, Lance,' the woman was complaining. 'The images will be useless.'

'I'm not going any nearer, Gretchen,' the man countered, his usually calm voice registering annoyance. 'It's not some freak show you can just muscle into. You go if you have to.'

The woman glared at him and, picking up the camera, came over the field in a cloud of dust. She was wearing knee-length khaki shorts and a halter-neck top that displayed sun-reddened legs and shoulders.

'I think that's far enough,' Eleni said to her. 'You're not dressed properly.'

Gretchen stopped, looking at her arms and her unshaven legs as if she hadn't noticed them until then. 'What? Oh, for the love of God.' She turned back angrily towards her partner.

'Do you think I'm dressed properly?' Mavros said in a low voice.

Eleni looked at his T-shirt and jeans briefly. 'I suppose so. As long as you stay outside the wall.'

He nodded. Going inside the sanctuary wasn't something he had planned on doing. He wasn't a believer and the bereaved family was entitled to some privacy, at least as far as strangers were concerned. The procession had halted at the gate as people struggled to squeeze into the confined space. When they got closer, Mavros heard raised voices.

'You aren't going in, witch.' The old man with the missing arm was standing across the entrance like a statue, his expression fierce. There were gasps and then silence from the other villagers. 'You aren't family.'

All that could be heard above the running of the water up the shore beyond were the feeble sounds of an old woman's voice.

'But I am family, Manoli,' she said desperately. 'You can't say I'm not. I'm your sister. We are one family and Yiangos was part of it. You can't keep me out.'

Mavros looked over the mass of heads and saw a tiny creature in black, her head covered in a scarf. She was leaning against another woman, facing the old man like a songbird standing up to a predator. Another old man with similar features to Manolis had taken up a position next to him, his expression no less stern.

'You aren't going in, witch,' Manolis repeated.

The old woman looked around, her clouded eyes searching for support among the islanders, but none of them returned her gaze.

'Come, Kyra Maro,' said her companion. 'It's finished. You've accompanied Yiangos to his last home. Come away now.'

It was only as the woman turned, an arm round her charge's shrunken frame, that Mavros recognised his landlady Rena under the black scarf that was covering her head. She led the woman called Maro from the gate, the crowd parting to let them go. Only when they were several paces away did the islanders start pushing into the cemetery again.

'What was that all about?' Mavros asked Eleni.

'Poor woman,' she said, shaking her head. 'It's a family feud. They can go on for generations here.' She moved forward and then stopped. 'It's completely full in there.' There was a hint of relief in her voice. 'I think I'll stay outside with you.'

Mavros and the archaeologist moved towards a gnarled olive tree on the slope to the right of the cemetery. They stood under the shade of the silvery-green leaves and watched as the priest ran through the final ritual, his voice carrying through the clear air.

After the open coffin was placed in the shallow grave, he recited a prayer cast in the voice of the departed, asking people to mourn for him. 'Only yesterday I was talking with you, but suddenly the terrible hour of death overtook me . . .'

There was a loud, agony-stricken cry from one of the female relatives. Then the priest poured red wine in the shape of the cross over the body and tossed in a handful of earth. The villagers followed suit. When they'd finished, the shroud was raised over Yiangos's handsome but pallid face and the lid lowered over the coffin. People began to move away immediately, their duty fulfilled.

Mavros raised a hand to his eye and brushed away the dampness that had gathered. For a few seconds his brother Andonis's face had been before him rather than that of the young man in the grave. He gazed out over the blue water, pale and glistening in the strength of the sun that would soon reach its zenith. It was only as he turned back that he saw the direction of Eleni's gaze. She was staring at Aris Theocharis as he took the dead boy's father Lefteris by the arm and started speaking to him.

It was a look of pure hatred.

8

Mavros and Eleni walked back into the square behind the remnants of the procession.

'What are you doing now?' he asked as they stopped in the shade of the mulberry tree. From the conversation he'd overheard, he knew that she had been told to stay in Faros by Theocharis.

Eleni was watching Rena open a door in the lane under the *kastro* and usher in the old woman who had been barred from the cemetery. 'What?' she said distractedly. 'I have nothing planned. I must wait for poor Navsika's funeral in the afternoon. I'll find somewhere in the shade and write up my notes.' She patted the leather bag on her shoulder and gave a faint smile. 'I'm always weeks behind.'

Mavros remembered what the German woman Barbara had said about Eleni. She seemed more melancholic than loudmouthed. 'Would you like a coffee?' he asked, looking round at the *kafeneion*. It was still closed, a pair of tourists standing outside it with bemused expressions. 'I don't suppose anything's going to open until after the second funeral. You could come to my place.'

'Your place?' The archaeologist ran her eye over him as if he were a find she was appraising. 'And where is that, Alex?'

'Just down the street,' Mavros replied, extending his arm. Although Eleni had the worn look of someone who had spent too many years exposed to the elements, there was a vitality in her, but it seemed to be tarnished by some deep sadness. He was curious about her.

She considered the offer then nodded. 'All right.'

As they reached Rena's door, a pair of old women standing

in the middle of the street stopped talking and watched them with unfeigned interest. Eleni nodded to them but they didn't acknowledge the greeting.

'*Ilithies*,' she said under her breath as Mavros admitted her. She shook her head as he glanced at her. 'They are fools. They see me with a strange man and they immediately think I'm opening my legs for him.'

'Really?' Mavros replied, feigning surprise. He'd come across similar prejudice in Zakynthos.

'It's because I'm a *xeni*,' Eleni said. 'A stranger from outside the boundaries of their little world. For them it's impossible for men and women to have friendly relations, even to drink coffee together, without sex being involved.' She gave him a cool look as they walked into Rena's courtyard. 'You don't have attitudes like that in your country, do you?'

Mavros wasn't clear how serious Eleni's question was. 'In Scotland?' he said. 'No, men and women don't drink coffee together there. What they consume is much stronger.' As the words left his mouth, he remembered that she'd put a fair amount of alcohol away in the bar herself.

The archaeologist smiled, her face suddenly less tense. 'If that was an invitation, it's too early for me.'

Mavros laughed. 'And for me.' He pointed to the table under the pergola. 'Sit down. I'll have to raid my landlady's kitchen for coffee.'

'I prefer *chamomili*. Camomile?' Eleni pronounced the English version uncertainly. 'It's better for the stomach.'

Mavros nodded then checked his stride. He didn't think many bona fide Scotsmen would be able to identify the bundle of dried leaves that he'd seen hanging in the kitchen earlier. 'You'd better help me look for it,' he said over his shoulder.

She followed him in and pointed immediately to the camomile. 'Whose house is this?' she asked, glancing round at the spotless room.

'A woman called Rena,' he said. 'She was at the funeral with that old—'

'*O-pa*,' interrupted Eleni, her face showing concern. 'The widow. She is a . . . she is a difficult person.'

'What do you mean?'

She shook her head. 'Never mind. I'll wait for you outside.' She parted the muslin and stepped into the shaded yard.

Mavros heated water, looking out at Eleni through the partially curtained window. What could she have against Rena? He made the drinks, deciding regretfully that instant coffee would be more appropriate for him in his guise as a tourist, and loaded up a tray.

'There you are,' he said, setting it down. 'I don't know what yours will taste like.'

Eleni sipped and nodded in approval. 'You should be careful, Alex,' she said. 'Rena has a reputation.'

Mavros looked at her. The sunlight that was filtering through the leaves dappled her face. 'What for? She seemed like a decent enough person to me.'

Eleni opened her eyes wide at him. 'Decent?' she said with a sharp laugh. She didn't elaborate.

'Well, she's been kind to me.' When Mavros gathered she wasn't going to say any more, he asked, 'So where do you live on Trigono?'

'Theocharis has an estate out in the Kambos, the plain in the centre of the island where the best farmland is. He's given me one of the houses to use.'

He remembered the photo he'd found up the chimney. Could it be of the dig? 'The excavations are out there?'

'On the Paliopyrgos estate and the slopes of the mountain Vigla behind.'

Mavros swallowed coffee and grimaced. The powdered stuff was even worse than he'd expected. 'Have you found anything significant?'

Eleni held her gaze on him. He thought she had noticed the marking in his eye, but she didn't mention it. 'It depends what you call significant,' she said, looking away. 'A lot of skeletons, many broken pots, old foundation stones . . . are you interested in archaeology, Alex?'

He shrugged. 'A bit.'

'Of course,' she said with a mocking smile. 'You go to museums.'

'That's right. I'm very interested in the past. The past and how it affects the present.' He realised that he was talking obliquely about how he approached his business. When it came to finding out about his clients' backgrounds and relating them to the cases he'd taken on, past times influenced his daily life. But they were also part of the core of his being. The face of his brother Andonis flew up before him, the features less blurred than they often were. 'History and the present are inextricably linked, don't you think?' he said.

Eleni was studying him even more closely now, an expression of mild surprise on her round face. '*To varos tis istorias*,' she said. 'The weight of history, we call it. It can be very hard to bear, especially in this country. Tell me, what is your job, Alex?'

Mavros had been waiting for the question. 'I'm a writer,' he replied. He'd used the lie in the past. It was an easy one to carry off because he knew enough about the business from his mother, and he'd met enough writers to last him a lifetime.

'What do you write?'

'Stories, novels.'

'Anything translated into Greek? Anything I would have heard of?'

'No to both questions,' he said. 'I'm not one of those famous writers you read about in the newspapers, the ones who are on television and radio all the time. I'm a professional struggler.'

The archaeologist laughed. 'To struggle is good, comrade. I was a communist when I was young, so I learned that lesson well.'

Mavros's throat went dry. Although he'd never had much to do with the communist youth organisations, Eleni was old enough to know about his father. She might even have been to the old family house in Neapolis. He changed the subject. 'How do you get around on Trigono? Have you got a donkey?'

Eleni looked disappointed at the direction in which he'd steered the conversation. 'No, of course not. You don't have to become a peasant to live on the island. I have a motorbike.'

Mavros felt disappointed himself. He'd been hoping Trigono hadn't been taken over by the two-wheeled contraptions that had done so much to ruin Athens, and so far he hadn't seen many. The riders were probably keeping clear of the funerals.

The noise of the street door opening and closing came down the corridor. Eleni sat up and glanced around as if she was suddenly searching for an alternative exit.

Rena appeared, her head bowed. Mavros thought he heard a sob. She looked up and caught sight of him. A smile flickered across her lips but it died when she saw Eleni.

'I hope you don't mind,' Mavros said. 'I invited—'

'My house is your house, Alex,' Rena interrupted. She held her eyes on the archaeologist for a few moments and then nodded at her coldly. 'So,' she said in Greek. 'What do you want here?'

Eleni stood up, her cheeks reddening. 'Excuse me, Alex,' she said, avoiding the other woman's eyes. 'I don't think I'm welcome in this house. Thanks for the camomile.' She gave him a crooked smile. 'Maybe I'll see you at the Astrapi. I come in most nights.' She walked towards the passageway, stepping round Rena when the house owner didn't move. The door slammed after her.

'*Poutana*,' Rena said in a loud voice. Whore.

Mavros went over to her. 'Is there something wrong?' he asked disingenuously. 'I'm sorry, I shouldn't have—'

Rena raised a hand and took the black scarf from her head. 'You don't know . . . you didn't know,' she corrected herself, her brow furrowed. 'That woman, she is not good. She makes . . . she makes sex with people she should not.'

Mavros could see how disapproving Rena was. That probably explained the looks Eleni had got from the old women outside, as well as why she had hung back from entering the cemetery. He wondered if she'd been involved with the boy who had drowned.

'Makes sex,' Rena repeated, her face suddenly cracking into a smile. 'I mean makes love.' Then she gave a bitter laugh. 'But I do not think she understands anything about love.'

Mavros gathered up the cups and took the tray to the kitchen. So that was Eleni's reputation, he thought. What was the widow Rena's?

She followed him and nudged him out of the way. 'In my kitchen I do everything, Alex.' She glanced at the tray. 'You give her *chamomili*?'

He nodded, embarrassed at having been caught looting her stores.

'It's all right,' she assured him with a shy smile. 'It is good for bad women.'

'Rena?' he asked as she started to run water over the cups. 'What happened outside the cemetery? Why was the old woman you were with stopped from going in?'

She gave him a questioning look then shook her head. 'No, no, that is private business. You are *xenos*, stranger. You should not have come to the . . . what do you call it? Burial?' She made a hash of the vowels.

He nodded slowly at her. 'No, you're right, Rena. I shouldn't,' he said, turning and walking out of her kitchen.

Before he was halfway across the courtyard her voice rang out. 'But don't worry, Alex,' she said, smiling at him tentatively. 'I forgive you.' Her face turned stern again. 'If you stay away from her.'

Mavros shrugged and went into his room. So much for the simplicities of rural life. There seemed to be more happening on the small island than in most suburbs of Athens.

Kyra Maro was sitting at the table in her front room, thin arms crossed and fingers digging into the cracked skin of her elbows. Rena had just left, after bringing her bread and bean soup before going to beautiful, lost Navsika's funeral. Maro didn't feel able to follow the second procession, even though the dead girl's family had never shown open hostility to her. She knew that everyone in the village preferred her to keep out of the way. The entire island would weep for Navsika, given in marriage to the death spirit Charos rather than to a living bridegroom. She would hear the sighs and the bitter crying through the panels of her door. Soon Navsika would be in the ground, covered by the black earth and close to the boy she had died with.

My poor Yiango, she said to herself. You were a sweet child when you were little, but darkness came over you before the day of your death. Rena told me things about you that made me weep.

The old woman went back to the scene at the cemetery gate, her brother Manolis barring the way with his arm raised, the empty sleeve of his best shirt dangling at his side. She should have known that he would keep her out, stop her from fulfilling her family obligation to Yiangos. Manolis was hard, he'd always been like that, even before the catastrophe that came over them during the war. He would never forget or forgive. And he'd made his son Lefteris in his own image, a wave-lashed island standing out among weaker men, his character formed of stone. Neither of them spoke much, but other people understood what they wanted from the will in their eyes and the set of their limbs. They were harsh men who allowed no leeway. Yiangos hadn't been like that when he was a child; his mother Popi had managed to protect him. God knows at what cost to herself. The wretched woman often had bruises on her face and bald patches where hair had been ripped out of her scalp. But Lefteris had eventually brought Yiangos round. He worked on the boy's softness and made him do exactly what he wanted. And what was Lefteris doing now? She'd heard the women talking under their breath. He wasn't mourning his son. He was already preparing the *trata* that had brought death to Yiangos so that he wouldn't miss any fishing when the autumn season began.

'Ach, wretched family,' she said aloud. 'We have all been crushed by the bitter fate that has dogged us for decades, even the innocent young.'

The old woman leaned forward and buried her face in her gnarled hands. In years past she had felt foolish about talking to herself, but she had little choice. Until Rena started looking after her she had been alone; for many years she had spent the evenings reading and educating herself because she had no company. Her family had thought she was flighty, even before they shunned her. She had always lived in her own world, kept her thoughts to herself and tried to lose her pain in the collections of poetry and folk tales she had devoured when she could still make out the letters.

Maro looked down at the plate of *fasoladha* on the table. Rena was good to her. She didn't really understand why. Perhaps it was because they were both outcasts. Rena suffered the sharp stares of the married women who suspected all widows of lusting after their husbands and sons, but that was the least of her problems. She had no real family on Trigono, she was a *xeni*, so maybe that was another reason why she had taken Maro on as a duty. God knows there could be no idea of gain in Rena's mind. Maro had nothing except the contents of her tiny house and the few strips of stony ground on the slopes of Vigla that, for some reason, the widow had volunteered to work. Poor Rena, she thought. You should find yourself a man, you should go back to your own island. Trigono will grind you in the mill as it does all who live here, native or foreign. Trigono is death to all human hopes.

Maro stood up and walked unsteadily to the bedroom.

'So, Manoli,' she said quietly, remembering what her brother had called her outside the cemetery. 'You think I'm a *strigla*. Maybe I am. In the folk tales *strigles* are old women who turn themselves into owls and drink the blood of helpless children. Not only that. *Strigles* can bring about the deaths of the unfortunate children's parents. Do you really believe I could do that to your precious grandson Yiangos? Do you think I want to kill you and my own nephew Lefteris? Maybe it would be better for everyone if I could. Because you are the guilty one, you are the one responsible for the pain that has fallen on this family.'

She sank down on the bed, her eyes filled with tears. 'What am I saying?' she groaned. 'They hate me but I don't hate them. I should do after everything they've done to me as well as to the only two I ever really loved in my life. But hate doesn't bring them back. The only thing that calls them, that keeps them with me, is the love that I still have for them.'

Maro got down on her knees and pulled the box out from under the bed. She opened it and, moving her eyes constantly to the photograph in the icon niche, she lifted out the blackened skull. Inaudible words were streaming from her lips, tears running down her wrinkled cheeks. Then she reached over to the small bedside cabinet and picked up a small wooden box. She placed the small shrivelled objects she took from it carefully around the skull in a circle.

And waited patiently for the pomegranate seeds that in ancient times had been sacred to Persephone, Queen of the Underworld, to bring her beloved ones back across the river of lamentation.

Mavros didn't want to be in the village while the second funeral took place. Rena was looking so down that he kept his questions about Rosa Ozal to himself. Eleni's mention of the Kambos, the inland plain, and the grandeur of the southern massif had piqued his curiosity. He wanted to explore the island, as well as start earning Deniz Ozal's fee – he had rung his bank and confirmed the transfer of funds. According to the guidebook there was an asphalt road that ran down the east coast for six kilometres to the beach resort of Ayia Marina. He didn't like the look of the hotel blocks and tourist cafés in the photos, but it was possible that Rosa Ozal had worse taste than he had, so he decided to start the search for her there. If she'd come back to the island, maybe she had her reasons for staying outside the village this time. He was pretty sure that there would be some staff on duty despite the funerals. He exchanged jeans for shorts, noticing how white his legs were beneath the hairs, and went outside.

About twenty metres beyond Rena's house there was a small yard enclosed by a low wall, a new stone-built box of a building to the rear. Through the leaves of a well-watered fig tree, Mavros could see an engraved plaque stating that the Public Library of Trigono, built with a generous donation from Panos Theocharis, had been opened by the local prefect a couple of months earlier. He was about to walk on when it occurred to him that he might find books of local interest there. Going up the smooth marble steps, he remembered what the villagers were caught up in. The library was unlikely to be open when everyone was attending the funerals. Then he saw the key in the door.

The interior of the building was cool because of the thick walls and the closed shutters. Turning on the light, Mavros looked round the sparsely filled shelves. Either the local people were avid borrowers or funds had run out. There were more children's books visible than adults'. Someone had taken the setting up of the library seriously as there were handwritten labels on the ends of each shelf stating the subject matter. Although there was a section marked 'Local History and Culture', the only book in it was a lavishly printed study of Trigono's churches published by the diocese on Paros. He put it back after a few seconds, the air of devotion that rose from the volume stifling him.

There was a pair of rectangular wooden boxes on a table under the window, the word 'Catalogue' written in red on their upper surfaces. One series of cards classified the library's books by author name and the other by subject. There were four other books in the 'Local History and Culture' section, all in Greek, their titles, authors and publication details neatly inscribed. Three were religious studies concerning the island's experience of the Byzantine, Venetian and Ottoman empires, but it was the last one which caught his attention. It was entitled *Trigono 1941–1943: Endurance and Resistance*, written and apparently self-published by one Andhreas S. Vlastos of Paros in 1999. According to the card there were six copies of the book in the library. Either it was very popular or the catalogue was wrong, as it was conspicuous by its absence from the shelves. Mavros glanced around for a register of loans. There was no card or digital strip in the book he'd looked at so presumably the librarian kept a handwritten record. He caught sight of a leather-bound book on a shelf by the door and went over. Running his finger down the pages, he soon ascertained that no one had borrowed the book. He twitched his head in irritation. The war memorial with the name erased from it had piqued his curiosity. He noted down the details of the Parian author's book then put the register back and went outside, telling himself to stick to the job in hand.

The problem was that it was now past midday and the sun was blazing down. Walking six kilometres in this heat was the kind of thing that only demented foreigners did, especially as the light wind was blowing on to the far side of Trigono. He wondered if there would be a bus. A quick perusal of the roughly painted sign at the parking space on the outskirts of the village told him that he had a two-hour wait, and even then he wasn't convinced. His experience on Zakynthos had taught him to beware all signs concerning transport even under normal circumstances, when there wasn't potential disruption by general mourning. There was a car and bike hire place at the end of the track that led to the Bar Astrapi, but it was closed.

Mavros decided to try hitching. The road snaked away into the haze, its black strip separated from the sea by rocky uncultivated land and, about fifty metres to his left, by the dusty tamarisks that marked the edge of the beach. After a few minutes he came to a junction with a signpost pointing towards 'Psili Ammos Beach – Rooms, Bar and Souvlaki House'. He made a cross on the margin of his map to remind himself to show Rosa's photo there on the way back and kept going. So far not a single car or motorbike, not even a donkey, had passed in either direction.

The southern hills rose up sharply, the ridge between them standing against the blinding blue sky like a great fortified curtain. The wall that followed its contours reinforced that impression. Mavros was amazed that at some time in the island's history the locals had transported stone up to the windswept saddle, presumably to separate grazing land. It was a magnificent, almost surreal achievement – and all for a few goats. To the south-east the white patch of buildings that made up Ayia Marina danced in the heat like a mirage. It was then he realised that he hadn't brought any water with him.

He cursed under his breath. In Athens there were refrigerated cabinets attached to almost every kiosk, but in the Cyclades you obviously needed to plan ahead. He considered turning back but dismissed the idea. According to the book there was a beach called Makroyiali about halfway to Ayia Marina that had a café.

Shortly afterwards he heard the noise of an engine. He turned his head and saw a silver Suzuki four-by-four that glistened in the sunlight. It stopped when he stuck out a thumb.

'I thought I recognised you,' the man in the front passenger seat said. 'You were in the bar last night.' He gave Mavros a tentative smile.

'And in the *kastro* above Rinus's flat this morning,' the female driver added, her voice markedly less friendly than her companion's. 'Well, get in then. We'll melt if we stay here for long.'

The fair-haired man stepped out and collapsed his seat to give Mavros access to the back. 'It's Alex, isn't it?' he said with a smile.

'Thanks,' Mavros said. 'Yes, I'm Alex. I'm afraid I don't know your names.' He had picked them up in the Astrapi, but he didn't want to reveal that he'd been listening to their conversation with Aris Theocharis or to the one with the barman Rinus in the *kastro*.

'I'm Barbara,' said the woman as she pulled away. 'He's Mikkel. Where were you going? It's dangerous to walk in this heat if you're not used to it.' She glanced at his legs. 'And I can see you're not.'

'I was going to Ayia Marina,' Mavros said, glad that he didn't spend his weekends on the beaches of Attiki and the neighbouring islands like many Athenians. The smog kept even the exposed parts of his skin unburned and the lack of tan fitted in well with his cover story.

'Oh, you don't want to go there,' Barbara said firmly. 'It's a horrible tourist trap. If you want a beach, Makroyiali is much nicer and it's empty at this time of year. It's nearly a kilometre long. The name means Long Beach.'

'Does it?' Mavros said, letting the woman hold sway. The low profile the man was keeping suggested that she was used to running conversations. Close up, her appearance was marginally less severe than it had been under the lights of the bar. Her hair was pulled back from her face, emphasising the prominent cheekbones and an incongruous button nose, and her body, sheathed in an expensive-looking long-sleeved blouse and linen trousers, was amply proportioned. 'Do you live here?' he asked. 'You seem to know the place very well.'

His remark brought a satisfied smile to Barbara's face. 'I should do,' she said, driving over the carcass of a rabbit. 'I've lived here for over ten years. All year round, unlike the other foreign homeowners.' She announced this as if it were a notable achievement. 'Even the Athenians who've built houses here only come at Easter and for a few weeks in the summer.'

Probably because they had jobs to go to, Mavros thought. 'How interesting,' he said. 'So you decided to move to Greece, did you? What made you choose Trigono?'

'I first came here in 1972,' said Barbara. 'The place was so different then. I fell in love with it immediately. There was no electricity, no roads like this, no tourists.'

'Apart from you,' Mavros put in with a slack smile.

'I am not a tourist,' she said, looking at him in the mirror.

'Barbara was collecting ideas for furniture,' Mikkel said, turning round. 'Her designs are sold all over the world.'

'Hoeg,' she said. 'I'm Barbara Hoeg. Do you know the name?'

Mavros shrugged, feigning ignorance. He'd seen Hoeg designs in a shop patronised by his sister – tall, thin, tubular steel chairs with wicker bases, dressers that were a weird combination of folk carving and stainless steel – but he wasn't going to give the woman the satisfaction of admitting that. Her abrasive nature repelled him, but there was more to it than that – he had the impression that she was concealing something that disturbed her more than she could admit. 'I'm afraid I don't know much about furniture,' he said, wondering how she would react. 'I don't pay much attention to it.'

'Are you here for long, Alex?' Mikkel asked quickly. He was clearly concerned about the effect Mavros's words might have on Barbara. She narrowed her lips but didn't speak.

Mavros shook his head. 'A few days. I'm travelling from island to island.' He decided to take a chance. 'A friend gave me the idea. She went island-hopping in the early summer and she sent me a card recommending Trigono. I don't suppose you happened to meet her. Rosa Ozal?' He took the photo from his bag and showed it to Mikkel.

The German looked at it, his head bobbing as the car went over bumps in the asphalt. Barbara's arm banged into his. 'No,' he said, suddenly blinking his eyes as if to block out the sight of the image. 'I don't think I remember her.' He held the photo up in front of Barbara.

'I'm trying to drive, Mikkel,' she said in an irritated voice. 'No,' she said, 'no, I never saw her.'

Mavros was watching them carefully. 'It doesn't matter. I just wondered, since you know the island so well . . .'

Barbara pulled up outside a high stone wall surmounted by a bamboo fence. There was only a restricted view to the large house beyond. 'You'll have to get out here, I'm afraid. The beach is a few minutes' walk farther on.'

Mikkel let him out. 'Well,' he said apologetically, 'maybe we'll see you again.'

Mavros nodded, pretty sure that the man would have invited him in if left to his own devices. But Barbara's face was set hard, her fingers tapping the steering wheel and her eyes away from Mavros. 'Thanks for the lift,' he called to her.

She didn't respond, but that didn't bother him. He was convinced that she'd nudged Mikkel to shut him up. His nervous eye movements and the way she'd suddenly closed up had convinced him that they'd both seen Rosa Ozal in the flesh earlier in the year. Hitch-hiking had been a lot more productive than he'd imagined.

Walking on past the fence, he looked towards the sea and saw a fishing boat close to the shore, its winches turning but no net on them. He narrowed his eyes and read the name *Sotiria*, then recognised the hefty frame of Lefteris, the son of old, one-armed Manolis and father of the drowned boy. Not only was he staying away from the young woman Navsika's funeral, he was staring with frightening intensity at the house belonging to the German woman and the man she kept firmly under her thumb.

★　　★　　★

Barbara Hoeg strode into the large living room that featured many pieces she had designed. 'I don't like him,' she said, opening the French windows that led on to the terrace. The water in the swimming pool reflected the sky, while the sea lapped dark against the low cliff thirty metres beyond. 'There's something about the guy that gets my back up.' She took a step outside, her eyes fixed on the fishing boat, and raised a hand briefly.

'Alex?' Mikkel said, bringing her a glass of white wine. 'He's just a tourist, *agapi mou*.' He used the Greek term of endearment – 'my love' – that Barbara had liked ever since she'd heard it from the local boy she got involved with on her first visit to Trigono. Mikkel hadn't known her then. He was an accountant by profession and had met her when Hoeg Design took off in the early eighties. 'He'll be gone in a few days.' He sipped from his own glass. 'We probably won't even see him again.'

'I don't know why I stopped to pick him up,' Barbara said, gulping down her wine and lighting a cigarette. 'Why did you suggest it?' She stood by the windows looking out towards the bare flanks of Iraklia and the smaller islands to the east. The *trata* had begun to move away to the south, its helmsman with his back to the house now. She glanced round and saw the weak smile on Mikkel's face. She knew he would defer to her. He wouldn't ask why she'd warned him off talking about Rosa Ozal. She didn't care what she thought her interest in the woman had been. He always turned a blind eye to her involvement with other men. Perhaps he thought she'd been experimenting with her own sex for a change.

Barbara Hoeg pulled on her cigarette and thought about the long-haired Alex. It was undeniable that he was handsome, but there was something about him that didn't ring true. Was he really a friend of the Turkish-American woman? She'd better ask Rinus about him tonight in the bar. Rinus was good at finding out about people. God, Rosa Ozal. Who would have thought her name would have cropped up again? And today of all days, the day Lefteris's son was buried. Perhaps they should have attended the funeral, but she hadn't trusted herself to remain calm.

She stubbed out her cigarette in a swift movement, then unbuttoned her blouse and dropped her trousers. She wasn't wearing anything underneath. She ran forward and dived into the pool, her heavy breasts and thighs lit up for a moment by the sun.

As the sweat was dashed from her skin, she let out a silent scream as Rosa's face and lustrous hair loomed up before her like a water nymph hungry for prey.

9

Mavros woke before his alarm clock went off. The birds were shuttling across Rena's courtyard, their wings vibrating like miniature fans. He lay in the cool room and focused on the lines of light that were coming through the slats of the shutter. Lines that led nowhere. They cast themselves on to the white wall, beginning and ending in space, never connecting with each other.

He was thinking about Rosa Ozal. Her line started here, in this very room. All he knew was that she'd sent a postcard from Trigono and that she'd subsequently gone to Turkey, where the line ended. Was there another one leading back? Although Trigono wasn't one of the major holiday islands, it still received thousands of visitors during the season. By this time of year the locals were suffering from tourist blight and all visitors looked the same to them. That had been obvious when he'd shown the photograph in Ayia Marina and in the cafés on the beaches down the east coast. No one remembered her, no one showed a flicker of recognition. The only people so far who had done were the furniture designer Barbara Hoeg and her man Mikkel, and they hadn't meant to.

Mavros got up and pulled on shorts. For all the hair on them, his legs had started to burn yesterday. Fortunately a *periptero* in Ayia Marina still had high-factor lotion in stock. He was intending to ask Rena about Rosa and then head out into the Kambos. He reckoned that Faros would still be in deep mourning and information would be hard to come by in the village. He also wanted to talk to Eleni the archaeologist. The Bar Astrapi had been closed yesterday evening so he'd missed her. Deniz Ozal's business interest in antiquities had been nagging him. The police

commander Kriaras hadn't called him back, so presumably Ozal
had no recorded involvement in the black market. He wondered
if there could be a connection between the Turkish-American
and Panos Theocharis. It seemed unlikely, given the Greek's
reputation as a museum benefactor who had never been involved
in any illicit dealings, but Eleni might be persuaded to divulge
information – she didn't seem to be the old man's number-one
admirer. There was also the fact that Rosa Ozal worked in a
gallery in New York. Could she have been acting on behalf
of her brother? He reined in his imagination. Creative thinking
was a bad idea before the first coffee of the day.

He made it on the gas ring in his small kitchen, having
borrowed some Greek coffee from Rena when he returned the
previous evening. He'd said that he wanted to try it and she
gave him a quick lesson on how to use the *briki*, which he tried
to look engrossed in. Taking his cup out to the table under the
pergola, he heard Rena moving about in her kitchen. This was
his chance. He went back into his room to pick up Rosa's photo
and postcard, then walked over to the rear of the house.

His landlady was standing with her back towards him.

'Good morning,' he said cheerfully.

Rena seemed to freeze, her hands rising quickly to her face.
She didn't turn round.

'Are you all right?' Mavros asked uncertainly.

'Yes,' she replied in a low voice. 'Good morning, Alex.' The
words were muffled by her hands. She swallowed a sob.

He stepped forward, sticking the photo and card into the
waistband of his shorts under his T-shirt. 'Is something wrong?'
he asked. 'Can I help?'

Rena lowered her hands and looked over her shoulder at him,
displaying reddened eyes and damp cheeks. 'No . . . no,' she
said. 'I did not sleep so much. Thinking about the boy . . . the
boy and the girl who—' She broke off and sobbed again.

'I'm sorry,' Mavros said, raising a hand to touch her shoulder
but then holding back. She would be even more traumatised if
a tourist laid hands on her.

Rena took a deep breath, raised a handkerchief to her eyes and turned round. She gave him a brave smile. 'I'll be all right,' she said. 'Time is a good doctor, is he not? The only doctor.'

Mavros nodded dumbly.

'You are going to the beach today?' his landlady asked, nudging him gently out of the way. She started running water over crockery.

'Em, no,' he replied. 'I'm going to explore the Kambos.'

Rena glanced at him. 'Be careful out there, Alex,' she said, her voice concerned. 'Strange people live in the Kambos.'

Initially he took this as a reference to Eleni, but then he wondered if she meant the Theocharis family. He considered asking her about Rosa Ozal now that she seemed less upset, then decided to put it off. She obviously needed to get over the first shock of grief. She looked as devastated as anyone in the village, even though she'd said she wasn't a close relative of the dead.

As he walked into the shaded yard, he wondered about that again. She was a couple of decades older than the drowned kids, so she probably wouldn't have kept company with them. Then he remembered Rena's reference to Eleni making love with people she shouldn't. Was that what had upset her? Could Eleni, a city-born outsider with different standards of behaviour, have been involved with Yiangos? On the other hand, Eleni said that Rena had a reputation. He wondered what for. She seemed to be punctilious in observing the demands of widowhood and she didn't strike him as the sexually frustrated figure of popular myth, although there was something about the way she looked at him – he had caught her observing him surreptitiously from her bedroom window.

Mavros went back to his room and put the computer diskette he'd found in his bag, along with his Greek mobile phone – he didn't want his landlady to find that. His ID card was in the back pocket of his jeans where he always kept it. So far his cover as a foreigner was intact. He went out into the street and headed down to the public library, remembering the book about Trigono during the war that he'd been unable to locate.

Going up the steps and across the shaded space to the door, he noticed that the key wasn't in the lock. He tried the handle to no avail. Today the library wasn't open to the public.

Heading across the square towards the Internet café he'd noticed the day he arrived, Mavros felt a change in the atmosphere. There were more people around, islanders as well as tourists, and voices were not as restrained as they had been. It was almost as if the village had done its duty, had registered its grief for the passing of the young couple and was now starting the long haul back to normality. Shops on the long street leading down to the port were open and small children, who had been kept indoors until now, were playing in the sun. But the faces of the adults still showed the burden they were carrying, their eyes raw and ringed.

Outside Themis' Place – 'Drinks for Hackers,' according to the crudely painted sign – a couple of tables were occupied by bronzed tourists. Mavros went in, trying to keep his eyes off the ugly web patterns in silver paint that were on the black walls. There was a row of computers to the left. He inclined his head to the lugubrious, short-haired guy at the bar.

'You want Internet?' The English was rough but comprehensible.

Mavros shook his head, glad that his body language had made it clear he wasn't Greek. He held up the diskette.

'Okay,' the barman said. 'Fifteen hundred an hour. You want something to drink?'

Mavros didn't really want another coffee but it might be an idea to keep the guy sweet. He ordered a frappé and turned on the machine. It was a recent model, in good condition. Unfortunately it was no good to him. Whatever he tried, he couldn't get into the numbered files that were on the diskette marked 'GL 1'. A password was required and none of his attempts worked, nor did his efforts to get round it.

The barman arrived with his chilled coffee.

'Are you Themis?' Mavros asked.

'Yes.' The Greek nodded at the screen. 'Problem?'

'Stupid,' Mavros replied. 'I forgot the password.'

'I try.'

After ten minutes of swearing in Greek that Mavros tried not to show his amusement at, Themis gave up. 'Sorry. Sometimes is possible, but not with this disk.' He started to move away.

'Wait a minute,' Mavros said, determined to get his money's worth. 'The public library. Who's in charge?'

The Greek looked at him blankly.

'Who is number one? The boss?'

Themis raised his eyes. 'Why you want to know?'

'There's a book I'd like to see but the library is closed.'

The barman licked his lips as if there was suddenly something sour on them. 'One woman, name Rena,' he said, glancing away. '*Poutana*,' he said under his breath. 'Lives after square. Blue and . . . *kitrino* . . . how say? Yellow? Yes, blue-and-yellow door.'

Mavros nodded slowly. Everything seemed to lead to his landlady. He was going to have to talk to her, sooner rather than later. He had noticed that Rena had been characterised as a whore, the same term she had used for Eleni the archaeologist. He swallowed his coffee, paid and headed back to the house. On the way he passed the war memorial and stopped to look at the abraded patch with the faint marks on it. He was thinking of the photo he'd found, the one of the wartime officer. George Lawrence. Could that be the name that had been erased? It was hard to tell. Were the letters Greek or English? If they were Greek, 'PEN' could equate to the English letters 'REN' in the middle of the surname. And the first and last letters of the first name – 'T' and 'Z' – could come from Tzortz, the Greek transliteration of George. Who was this George Lawrence? It seemed clear that the files on the diskette also referred to him.

'Rena?' he called as he opened the door. 'Are you here, Rena?'

There was no reply. The kitchen door was closed, muslin blowing in front of the window.

Crossing to his room, Mavros had another thought. When he

was inside, he closed the door behind him and took out his mobile phone. The signal wasn't good, but he didn't want to go into the courtyard in case Rena was upstairs. He was going to be speaking Greek. After a couple of abortive attempts he managed to get through to directory enquiries. He was informed that there was only one Andhreas S. Vlastos, writer, on Paros, and was given the number. If he couldn't track the book down on Trigono, a conversation with the author was as good a solution as any. Perhaps he would know who George Lawrence was. Then all he would have to work out was why a photo of the soldier was up the chimney in the same folder as one with Rosa Ozal's writing on it.

He rang the number. A woman answered.

'Could I speak to Andhreas Vlastos?' he asked.

There was silence on the line. He repeated the question.

'Andhreas Vlastos does not exist,' the woman replied in a weak voice.

Mavros felt his stomach flip. 'I . . . I'm very sorry,' he stammered. 'When . . . when did he depart this life?'

'One month ago, God forgive him.' The woman suddenly became loquacious. 'It was that accursed writing that ruined him. His heart couldn't take it, working all day in the school and writing till the middle of the night. Then he would go to Athens at the weekends to the archives, the poor fool. He should never have—'

'There is a book he wrote about Trigono,' Mavros interrupted. 'I wanted to talk to him about it. Do you perhaps have a copy I could buy?'

'Ach, that was the book that did for Andhreas,' the woman said, her voice rising. 'That rich man over there, he tried to stop my husband publishing it. And when Andhreas refused his money and won the court case, he bought all the copies, he made sure no one could find it, the murderer, ach . . .' Her words trailed away in a bitter cry.

The murderer she was talking about – did she mean the weak old man with the sculpted beard Mavros had seen at the funeral?

He hazarded a question. 'You mean Theocharis?' he said. 'Panos Theocharis?'

'Of course I mean him, you fool,' the woman shouted. 'Now leave me in peace, all of you!' The connection was cut.

Mavros tossed the phone on to his bed. Eleni had told him that the museum benefactor lived in the Kambos. That was definitely the place to take a look at now. Maybe Theocharis was linked to Rosa Ozal. He seemed to have a tight grip on Trigono.

November 21st, 1942

I swore to myself a month ago that I would write no more in this book, that it was the height of folly to leave anything that could help the enemy if it fell into his hands. I kept my vow as the warmth of early autumn turned to heavy rainstorms and chill, starry nights. The worsening weather forced me to move down to a more sound hut near a now uninhabited hamlet in the Kambos, the central plain. Although the danger is minimal, Ajax having ensured that the locals steer clear, I've had to keep watch even more carefully and only go out after the work in the fields is over and the people have gone back to Faros.

And then it happened, the event that has changed everything, the event that has driven me back to this diary because of its monumental, glorious significance. I have fallen in love.

It was Ajax's fault. He'd been bringing me food and drink himself: rough island bread, bean stews, the occasional grilled fish, and sweet red wine that sent me to sleep more effectively than any pharmacist's pills. He would appear at the hut after dark and knock twice then twice again. Although I could never get more than a few words out of him, I gradually came to the conclusion that he approved of me. Our work was going well. The stock of supplies had been steadily rising and our plans for sabotage on other islands were advancing. All we were waiting for were the additional trained personnel we'd need to carry out operations. But the Greek unit is still being held up by the staff in Egypt. So, except when there were stores to be moved under cover of darkness, Ajax and I were stuck with going over our strategy every second night when he supplied me, sharing bottles of wine in the flickering candlelight.

Then, two weeks ago, the pattern of knocks was lighter, the sound hardly carrying into the sack-strewn hovel where I've holed up. I was instantly alert, hand on my service revolver, Ajax always came himself. He told me that he didn't want any of his comrades out after dark, but I was sure that he didn't want them to come into contact with the xenos; liaising with the foreigner was his prerogative. So who was at the door now? It was inconceivable that the hefty islander would have touched the wood so delicately. There was a window at the back of the hut with a loose-fitting shutter that I had prepared as an emergency exit but, when the weak tapping was repeated, I dismissed the idea of flight. If an Italian patrol had ended up at my front door, they wouldn't have been knocking so politely. I pulled the door open and admitted my visitor into the darkened hut. It was only when I lit a candle and held it up that I understood I was looking at a girl. The most beautiful girl I'd ever seen.

'To faï sas,' she said. Your food. Her voice was low and throaty. It made the hairs on my neck stand. She handed me a woven bag and smiled.

I was having difficulty speaking, my faculties stunned by the sublime contours of her face, the shining black hair that hung loose around it, and the lithe body that was standing only a few inches from my own. Stepping back to break the spell, I saw that her legs were bare under her knee-length skirt, the thin cotton jacket that she wore on the upper part of her body tight across her well-developed chest. She was short, no more than five foot two, but she radiated an irresistible, elemental power.

I finally rediscovered my tongue and asked her where Ajax was. She came closer to me, no sign of the shyness island women would normally be expected to display in the presence of a stranger. In her enchanting voice she advised me that her brother had damaged his leg and had sent her in his place.

I asked her name.

'Maro,' she replied, her dark eyes flashing and an innocent smile on lips that were redder than ripe cherries.

And so I was lost, willingly and completely. To be in love in this country, still so captivating despite the steely skies and the bite of the wind, is more than any man deserves.

Mavros went out into the street, shouldering his satchel that contained water, tanning lotion, guidebook and mobile phone. He'd also taken Rosa's photo and card, as well as the diskette and photos he'd found in the chimney. The morning was well progressed and the sun was shining down the east-facing street with plenty of vigour. He put his sunglasses on and walked down the uneven surface. There was a small spray of hibiscus, already withering, lying against a bottom step. He wondered if it had come from the funeral procession as it meandered round the village, someone's offering to the young people who had died. At the corner where the sign pointed to 'Kambos 2 km', he turned and walked up the gradually increasing slope.

He was passed by a succession of vehicles – battered pick-ups, white Japanese vans, ancient Rotavators towing mini-trailers and filling the air with their din. But Mavros wasn't hitching. This time he wanted to complete the journey on foot. It wasn't far and he felt it was time that he experienced the island's topography close up. He often did this when he was working on a case. It was one of the reasons that he walked around Athens so much. He reckoned that only by measuring out the place you were in could you begin to decode it – and Trigono was one of those multilayered locations that needed a lot of decoding. He looked southwards to the massif, the bare flanks glowing silvery brown in the morning light and the great ridge standing between the peaks like an impenetrable wall. Beyond it the young couple had drowned in a relatively calm sea. He wondered idly if anyone could have seen what happened from the hills. But a witness would surely have come forward by now.

As he walked on up the thin layer of asphalt to the low ridge that separated the north of the island from the central plain, Mavros looked to his right. The conical hill he'd seen from the cemetery road stood out against the southern extremity of Andiparos across the waves. According to the map that prominence was called Korakas, The Crow. A vision of black birds pecking at corpses rose up unbidden before him. He twitched his head. Trigono was doing disturbing things to his imagination.

Breathing hard as he reached the top of the incline, Mavros stopped and gazed down at the chequered pattern of fields and strips. The areas of bleached colours – pale gold, dusty green, freshly ploughed lustrous brown – were dotted with the matt white of houses and small churches. In the haze at the farthest extent of the Kambos he made out a large walled enclosure crossed by roads and tracks, a tall circular tower of dark stone rising up from a wide base against the lower flank of Mount Vigla. There was a jumble of white buildings around the old fortified structure, giving it the look of a shepherd protecting his flock. Mavros knew without consulting the map that this was Paliopyrgos, Old Tower, the estate owned by Panos Theocharis. Opening the guidebook, he read that the original tower had been built by a relative of Marco Sanudi, the first Duke of Naxos and the Archipelago way back in the thirteenth century.

The road snaked down the southern side of the ridge and soon led into farmland. In the wind-free plateau the heat was even greater, the air filled with the humming of insects and the rumble of agricultural machinery. Dry-stone walls had been built on either side of the road, hemming it in and forcing Mavros to stand on tiptoe to see around. As he passed a dilapidated, windowless building a donkey suddenly started braying close by. The sound continued, increasing in volume and becoming more high pitched. The panic and pain expressed in it were unmistakable.

Mavros ran through a rutted gateway and past a hut with a collapsed roof towards the source of the noise. He found it behind another wall, the sound of the stick that was being brought down repeatedly on the animal's thin sides audible before he got there.

'*Stamata!*' he shouted, ignoring his cover as a tourist. Stop! He dropped his bag and started to climb over the loose stones of the wall. 'For fuck's sake, stop!'

The wrinkled man with the stick was watching him through narrowed eyes, but he continued administering the beating until Mavros grabbed his arm. Despite the man's obvious age, his arm was strong. Finally Mavros wrestled the stick down and tugged it away with his other hand.

'What are you doing?' he continued in Greek, giving the donkey a quick examination. Its black eyes were shiny, its front legs hobbled and the tattered hide on its neck twitching. 'You'll kill the poor beast!' he yelled, turning his gaze back on the old man.

'What do I care?' the islander replied, his voice loud and steady. 'It's only a donkey.' He fixed Mavros with a stare. 'And it's mine.'

Mavros glared back at him. The concept of treating animals without cruelty wasn't widespread in rural Greece. He knew there was no point in lecturing the old man so he tried reasoning with him. 'I know it's your donkey,' he said. 'But what use is it to you dead or seriously injured?'

The farmer was still staring at him, chin high. Then he turned his head and spat a great lump of phlegm on to the dry earth.

Mavros stood with his hands on his hips then strode off down the road, his cheeks red and his breathing heavy. 'The old bastard,' he cursed. He could only hope that he hadn't made the poor creature's situation any worse. At least the agonised braying hadn't started up again as soon as he left. Then he remembered the farmer's solid features and unwavering eyes. He'd seen him the previous day beside the old man with one arm who'd blocked the entrance to the graveyard and shouted at the old woman. There was a definite resemblance; he guessed they were brothers. That would make this guy an uncle of the drowned boy's father Lefteris, the callous fisherman who'd gone hunting the night before the funerals. Presumably they were the village's family of violent headcases. Every isolated community had at least one.

Crossing a dusty junction in the middle of the baking plateau, he found himself in an open area that was uncultivated. A herd of goats were nibbling what remained of the pasture, the grass now tawny brown and only just protruding above the earth. A herdsman stood near the road, supporting himself on a long stick. He swivelled his eyes towards Mavros and ran them down his T-shirt and shorts. Then he raised an arm and came over, his legs taking giant strides. As he came close, Mavros realised he must be in his late teens. His eyes moved constantly and his lips were set in a slack smile. The wooden shaft of a roughly hewn wind instrument protruded from the pocket of his faded jeans.

'*Kali mera*,' Mavros greeted him, deciding that he might as well give up the guise of a foreigner for the time being. 'Hot, isn't it?'

The young man took in his words and then nodded solemnly, his eyes bright and questioning. 'Yes, very hot. My name is Dinos. Where are you going?'

Mavros asked him if he knew where Eleni the archaeologist was working. After some repetitions and clarifications, he was told that she was up on the slope above the old tower. Mavros raised an arm in salute and walked on, feeling curious eyes burning into his back. Then the swirling notes of the herdsman's pipe rose up into the air. It suddenly struck him that the sound would have been little different from when the island first supported livestock in ancient times.

Before Mavros had gone more than a hundred metres, he heard the roar of a powerful motorbike. It came over the rise in a cloud of dust and skidded to a halt in front of him. The engine was cut.

'Alex! What are you doing here?'

'Hello, Eleni,' he said. 'Looking for you, actually.' He wasn't going to mention the conversation he'd just had with the local. He was hoping that the weak-minded Dinos wasn't a friend of

Eleni who'd give her to understand that Mavros spoke Greek.
'I was looking around the Kambos and thought I'd come to see
you at work.'

The archaeologist gave him a sceptical look and drew a
dusty forearm across her face. 'See me at work?' she repeated.
'Wouldn't you prefer to be on the beach?'

Mavros grinned. 'Later, maybe. I don't want to get burned.'

Eleni looked up. 'There's sun in the Kambos too, you know.'

'Yes, but at least I'm vertical rather than horizontal out
here.'

She shrugged. 'All right. I'll show you around. I was going
for lunch but that can wait.' Her dark eyes held his for a
moment. 'Since you're so interested.' She kick-started the
bike and turned it back up the hill. 'Come on then,' she
said, looking over her shoulder and indicating the seat behind
her.

Mavros swore under his breath at the prospect of mounting
the bike. The way it had come down the hill suggested that Eleni
was as reckless as any Athenian kamikaze rider. 'How far is it?'
he asked, raising his voice over the noise.

'Get on,' Eleni said impatiently. 'I'm not wasting any more
time than I have to.'

Mavros bit his lip than swung a leg over the ripped plastic
seat. He managed to shove the footrests down but couldn't find
any handholds.

'Put your arms round me!' Eleni shouted. 'Don't worry, I
won't bite.'

Mavros slung his bag over his back and slid his arms round
the archaeologist's midriff. Her shirt was damp with sweat and
he felt her loose breasts on his forearms. Then the engine was
revved and he was forced to close his eyes by the cloud of dust
that rose immediately. The wheels started to slam up and down
on the rutted track and more than once he thought they were
going to cant over. The thought of his unprotected legs hitting
the bone-hard ground at speed made him close his eyes even
tighter. After what seemed like a long time, Eleni slewed the

bike round and killed the engine. He loosened his grip on her and dismounted, his legs weak.

'What's the matter?' she asked. 'You look like a ghost. Was my driving that bad?'

'No, no,' Mavros said, blinking to clear his eyes. 'I just don't like two-wheeled vehicles.'

'Really?' she said dubiously. 'Don't you have them in Scotland?'

He finished beating the dust from his T-shirt. 'What? Oh, yes. But I don't ride one. Too wet, too cold.' He looked around, taking in the panorama of scorched slopes then, beyond them, the islands and fishing boats dancing on the shimmering blue. 'Unlike here.'

The archaeologist moved away towards an outcrop of rock surrounded by a small plateau. The ground all around was steep, the flanks of Vigla scored by fissures and small watercourses that had been dry for months. The area surrounded by a barbed wire fence was the only flat one in the vicinity. Mavros followed Eleni and, as he got closer, he saw a low roof of corrugated plastic beneath a perforated cliff-face. He didn't need to take out the photo he'd found in the chimney to be sure that it was the same place.

Eleni undid a pair of heavy padlocks on the barred gate in the fence and led him in. 'Mitso! Where are you?' she called in Greek. 'Wake up, you lazy slob!' She turned to Mavros, shaking her head. 'I've told Theocharis a hundred times that we need electronic security, but he insists on using his own people. They're ex-sailors and they spend most of their time drinking.'

A heavily built man in his late thirties appeared from under the shelter, scratching his groin and regarding Eleni with a grin. 'I thought you'd gone to lie down,' he said, his eyes moving to Mavros. 'Or is that what you're going to do with your friend?'

'Screw you!' the archaeologist yelled. 'Go back to your dirty magazines.' She pointed towards an orange tent beneath the rocks.

Feigning incomprehension, Mavros watched as the muscle-bound guard loped away with a grin on his face. He turned to Eleni. 'So what was this place? There don't seem to be any buildings or fortifications.'

Without a word she went to the excavated area and ducked down under the cover. Mavros followed, moving his feet down a flight of uneven steps till he found himself on the floor of a wide trench. The heat under the plastic was intense.

'Christ,' he gasped. 'How do you work down here?'

'At this time of day I don't,' Eleni replied drily. 'I get up early in the morning.'

For a second he wondered how she managed that after nights drinking in the Bar Astrapi, then he was distracted by the head-high stone wall in front of him. Although it was irregular, the large blocks had been fitted with obvious skill. In the centre of them was a narrow space, the heavy lintel showing that it was a doorway.

'You asked what this place was,' the archaeologist said, her eyes off him and concentrating on the wall. 'This is the entrance to a series of Bronze Age grave chambers.'

Mavros leaned forward, breathing in the musty, mineral air. Nothing was visible in the gloom beyond the doorway. 'My God,' he said in a low voice. 'It's incredible. Have you been digging inside?'

'Yes,' Eleni replied. 'It is indeed incredible. The hill of Vigla is full of natural caves and man-made tunnels, most cut by miners in the early 1900s but some by Trigono's prehistoric inhabitants. In recent weeks I have made some major finds. It is potentially the most important site in the whole of the Cyclades – in the whole of Greece, as far as I'm concerned.' She looked at him seriously. 'And you are one of the few outsiders to be allowed into the site. You must promise me to tell no one about what you see.'

Mavros gave her the pledge she demanded without hesitation, his heart beating fast. He'd have liked to have known why she'd chosen him to be the first witness of her work, but the look in her eye put him off. Not for the first time, the island had taken him completely by surprise.

10

The darkness that enveloped them was intense, an impenetrable shroud. Then there was an explosion of bright yellow light.

'Don't worry,' Eleni said. 'You'll soon get used to it.'

Mavros peered into the illuminated passage, vaguely aware of the sound of a generator on the surface. 'How far does this tunnel go?'

The archaeologist handed him a hard hat and jammed one over her thick curls. 'We've penetrated about twenty-five metres. Come on, I'll show you.' She gave him a sharp look. 'Don't touch anything, all right?'

Mavros raised his hands. 'Don't worry. I'm terrified I'll bring the whole place down around me.'

Eleni laughed ironically. 'I don't know, Alex,' she said over her shoulder. 'Motorbikes, enclosed spaces – what aren't you frightened of?'

He swallowed a riposte and moved off after her. She stopped a few metres into the passage and pointed to the left.

'This is the first chamber,' she said, standing back to let him approach the red-and-white tape that barred the entrance.

Mavros bent down and looked into the shoulder-high opening in the rock. When he saw what was laid out on the level floor he took a deep breath.

'You're not scared of bones as well, are you?' the archaeologist asked.

Kneeling down, Mavros took in the well-preserved remains. The torso was a jumble of ribs and arm bones, the arms having apparently been folded across the chest, but the legs were straight and separate. The head lay on its right side, the lower jaw hanging loose. 'No,' he said, 'I'm not scared of bones.'

'They are of primary importance, the human remains in these chambers,' Eleni said. 'In other Cycladic sites, the dead are on their sides, their knees drawn up to their chins. Here the people took advantage of the natural rock formations and laid the bodies out straight, their knees only slightly bent. Like the Cycladic figurines.'

Mavros looked up and saw a series of empty niches, some of them as large as half a metre, in the wall above the skull. 'Did you find things in those holes?' he asked.

'Yes,' the archaeologist replied. 'Oh, yes.' She was kneeling beside him now and he could smell the sweat on her. 'There were many grave goods.'

'So where are they? In the National Museum in Athens?'

She glanced at him and stood up quickly. 'Don't you want to see the rest of the site?' she asked.

He followed her down the passage, the air getting cooler and mustier as they went. There were three more chambers in the rock, each containing a single body. The last one was only partially excavated, the top of the cranium protruding from a layer of gritty earth. There was a box of tools by the entrance.

'This is where I'm working now,' Eleni said. She turned to her right and pointed to the last light. Beyond it there was a wall of rock. 'We haven't got any farther but the geologist told us there's a network of natural passages that has been blocked by rockfalls over the centuries. When we've finished here we'll clear a way through. I'm sure there are more grave chambers.' She moved towards the exit.

'You didn't answer my question,' Mavros said. 'There's nothing but bones in the chambers. What happened to the grave goods you found?'

Eleni ducked under the lintel and into the outer trench. It was too hot to stay there for long. Back on the surface, blinking in the sun, she wiped her hands on her shirt and looked at Mavros doubtfully. 'I don't know why I showed you the dig. I know nothing about you. Are you really a writer? Oh God, don't tell me you're an antiquities dealer.'

Mavros returned her gaze. 'An antiquities dealer?' he repeated, the sallow features of Deniz Ozal flashing before him. 'Why do you say that?'

'You wouldn't be the first we've had snooping around the site,' she replied, heading for the gate. 'You seem to be very interested in the artefacts we've found.'

'I'm not a dealer,' he said, catching her up. 'Or a smuggler, or anything else like that. I told you. I tell stories and I have an interest in all kinds of human culture, that's all.'

The archaeologist didn't look convinced. 'All right,' she said after a long pause. 'I'll take your word for it.' She unlocked the gate. 'What you have to understand is that this land belongs to Panos Theocharis.' She raised an arm towards the north. 'The Paliopyrgos estate is down there and all of the hills are his too. The family had mines on Vigla from the beginning of the twentieth century.'

Mavros took the water bottle from his bag and offered it to her. 'And Theocharis runs a museum dedicated to funerary art,' he said as she was drinking. 'What are you saying, Eleni? That the artefacts are his?'

She looked past him. 'Mitso?' she shouted. 'I'm finished for now.'

There was a muffled grunt of acknowledgement from the tent.

'Sorry,' she said. 'I don't let him in the site when I'm here. He's an animal.' She glanced at Mavros. 'Of course the artefacts aren't Theocharis's. They belong to the state. This is an official excavation, you know. Although Theocharis is funding it, I work for the Ministry of Culture.'

'I see,' Mavros said, looking around the enclosure. There were none of the signs normally seen at sites indicating the name of the ephor in charge or the responsible ministry directorate, only a series of warnings to keep out in several languages. He had the feeling that Eleni wasn't being straight with him. But if the dig was illicit, why had she taken him to see it?

'Would you like something more interesting to drink?' the archaeologist asked. 'And something to eat?'

Mavros wiped the sweat from his brow. 'That sounds like a good idea. Shall we go to the village?'

'Not necessary,' she said, moving towards the motorbike. 'I have everything we need in my house.'

The ride down the track to the Paliopyrgos estate didn't take more than five minutes, but Mavros had his heart in his mouth all the way. He felt like he'd had his arms wrapped around Eleni for hours by the time she stopped outside a high metal gate. It would have been better suited to a government minister's residence in Athens than a quiet Aegean island. Eleni pulled out a remote control and activated the mechanism. Then she drove into the estate and the extent of Theocharis's wealth became apparent. Despite the chronic water shortage in the Cyclades, Paliopyrgos was an oasis of luxuriant growth. The high wall was lined on the inside by privet and pine, while the open ground had been cleared and tilled to give the orchards of vines, citrus and fig trees the opportunity for maximum growth. As she swung the motorbike off the main asphalt road towards a single-storey white house, Mavros saw the great stone curve of the tower and the complex of buildings that surrounded it. He couldn't help being impressed. His father and the Fat Man would have hated it.

'This is where I live,' Eleni said, swinging her leg over the seat after he'd dismounted.

'Not bad,' Mavros said, eyeing the simple but expansive house. There were blue wooden railings and shutters opening on to a series of small terraces. The ubiquitous bougainvillaea was weighing down pergolas, its purple-pink flowers and green leaves contrasting with the limestone wash on the walls.

'Come on in,' Eleni said, looking into his eyes and taking his hand. 'I've got something for you.'

At first Mavros thought he was going to see some grave goods from the dig, but when he was led into a cool bedroom, a mosquito net parted over a double bed, he realised she had something else in mind.

'Em, Eleni,' he said. 'I . . .'

She raised a finger to her lips. 'Shhh. You got a tour of the site. Now you have to pay.' She finished undoing the buttons of her shirt and opened it to display large breasts with firm brown nipples. Her hand was on the buckle of his belt before he could move. 'Don't worry,' she said with a soft smile. 'I'm sure a beautiful man like you is already involved. This means nothing more than what it means now.'

Mavros spent a few seconds trying to make sense of the words. It was only after Eleni's hand squeezed the swelling in his groin that he thought of Niki.

'For God's sake, hurry up, Mikkel,' Barbara Hoeg said, her restless eyes turning on him. 'If I'd known you were going to go so slowly I'd have driven myself.'

'What's the rush?' her husband asked, trying to sound cheerful. 'It's a beautiful day, most of the tourists have left and we're going to have a good lunch in the port.'

Barbara looked away, her lower lip between her teeth. 'I would like to get to Faros before the post office closes, if you don't mind.' She was running her hand up and down her forearm.

Mikkel glanced at her as he overtook a tractor. 'Are you all right, my love? You seem uptight.'

'Yes, I am uptight, if it's any concern of yours,' she said, her voice hoarse. 'Now just park the bloody car and let me out.' She didn't wait till he had stopped outside the Bar Astrapi to open her door. 'I'll see you at the restaurant in half an hour.' She didn't bother to close the door, moving away at a rapid pace.

Mikkel got out and followed her down the track after picking up the shopping bag. Now that the season had ended the shops closed in the afternoon, so he would have to buy the few things they needed before lunch. By the time he was halfway down the street leading to the square, Barbara was under the shade of the mulberry tree. But instead of turning right towards the

post office, she kept on going and disappeared up the lane that
ran past the old castle walls.

A sourness rising in his throat, Mikkel walked past the supermarket and followed her into the *kastro*. It was as he suspected –
she had gone to Rinus's flat. Oh God. He'd thought it was over
between Barbara and the Dutchman. She'd been going with him
for a few months last year when she couldn't find anyone with a
more rugged body, but lately she'd seemed to use the bar to drink
in rather than as a trysting-place. He should have known better.
Then he remembered the conversation that Rinus had initiated
from his balcony with Alex, the guy they'd picked up in the car
yesterday. He'd been up on the walls above the barman's flat.

Mikkel went round the back, past the raised stone-covered
mound containing the village's water cistern. He climbed the
steps and moved cautiously towards the edge where Alex had
been, making sure that his shadow didn't fall on the balcony.
Then he leaned forward and listened.

'. . . got time for a quick one?' Rinus's voice was playful. 'Like
we used to have in the old days when the fool was doing the
shopping?'

'No.' Barbara's voice was firm, making Mikkel sigh with relief.
'What are we going to do about the tourist?'

'Alex is all right,' the Dutchman said blandly. 'So what if he's
a friend of Rosa?'

There was a pause. 'Rosa was a friend of yours too, wasn't
she, Rinus?' Barbara sounded breathless. 'And you saw her leave
Trigono, didn't you?' Her voice hardened even more. 'You saw
her leave.'

'Yeah, yeah, I saw her leave. Satisfied?'

There was the sound of a slap. Mikkel gave up trying to work
out what Barbara meant about Rosa Ozal and smiled.

'No, I'm not fucking satisfied,' Barbara shouted. 'You know
I'm not.' Her voice dropped and became almost inaudible.

There was a sudden noise behind Mikkel. He turned to see
an old woman in black heaving herself up the steps, a basket
of washing in her hands. A line had been strung between the

branches of the large fig tree that had put roots down into the main village cistern.

'*Kali mera*,' she said with a toothless grin as she recognised Mikkel.

He nodded to her, not wanting to speak, then went quickly down to ground level. If Barbara caught him eavesdropping, his life wouldn't be worth a bean. Then he remembered the way she and the skinny Dutchman had talked about him. His life was already worthless.

Mavros woke up and tried to get his bearings. In his dream a scaly creature with folded bat wings and needle-sharp teeth had been working its way up his legs. Just before it reached his crotch, it looked up and snarled at him. Under the matted locks Niki's features were instantly recognisable.

Mavros lay flat and took in the mosquito net that was moving in the breeze from the slatted shutters. He was on his own in the guest room. He'd just managed to fend Eleni off before his cock betrayed him. She had taken the rejection of her advances with a bitter laugh and pointed him to the room next to hers before retiring to her bed. He'd thought about setting off back to the village on foot, but the stifling heat had put him off. It seemed that Rena was right. Eleni did have a penchant for making advances to people she shouldn't, although as an unattached foreigner he was fair game. Not for the first time in his life he cursed the brown mark in his left eye. He reckoned the archaeologist had noticed it and been attracted by its weirdness. Or maybe she was just open about her desires. He wondered who else might have passed through her bedroom.

Mavros sat up slowly and slipped out between the flaps of the net. Through the partially open door he could see Eleni fast asleep on her front. Not bothering to dress, he walked towards the bathroom then changed direction. He was feeling guilty, embarrassed that he had almost let Niki down despite the shaky nature of his relationship with her, and he was looking for a way to distract himself. This was the perfect time to take a look at Eleni's house. The photo of the dig that he'd found up the chimney in his room – Rosa Ozal's former room – was nagging him.

He went into the living room. The far end of it was obviously the archaeologist's work area, with a wide rustic table covered in papers and books. There were also cardboard boxes full of plastic bags containing finds. A cursory glance at them revealed nothing spectacular. There were pieces of rock and shards of pottery, but nothing of obvious value – certainly no marble statuettes or gold jewellery. Then he saw a black photograph album on the first shelf above the table.

Glancing over his shoulder and registering the regular sound of Eleni's breathing, Mavros opened the pages. There were some shots of Eleni at work – he recognised the site on Vigla at different stages of the dig – but most were social shots. The ones on the last pages showed Eleni with a fair-haired, strikingly attractive but stern woman he didn't recognise. There were shots in restaurants, shots on beaches, shots in the sea. There were also a couple taken in the Bar Astrapi. Two things struck Mavros about the photographs. The first was that Eleni and the unknown woman were definitely attached; in several cases they were holding hands and there were three shots of them kissing. Maybe that explained why she hadn't reacted much when her seduction of him had failed. And the second thought he had was that someone else had been on hand in the various locations to point the camera, someone who, judging by the intimate poses, knew the two women well.

Then he went back through the album and felt a rush in his veins. This time the female couple was different. Eleni was still in shot, but now she was embracing a dark-haired woman who Mavros recognised immediately. It was Rosa Ozal. So the missing woman knew the archaeologist. That went some way to explaining the photo of the dig. But why had it been hidden in the chimney at Rena's house?

Before he could think farther about the discovery, he heard the sound of a car drawing up outside. Mavros put the album back where he'd found it and moved quickly to the bathroom. Heavy footsteps pounded across the terrace and he didn't make it. He grabbed a magazine.

'Eleni?' Aris Theocharis bellowed from the open door. '*Edho eisai?*' Are you here? Then he noticed Mavros, who was shielding his naked groin.

'She's sleeping,' Mavros said in English.

The visitor pursed his fleshy lips and nodded slowly. 'I saw you in the bar, didn't I?' He didn't look particularly surprised to find an undressed man in the archaeologist's house.

'Did you?' Mavros replied. 'My name's Alex. Eleni invited me for lunch.'

'The naked lunch?' The big man laughed coarsely.

'*Ti gyreveis?*' What do you want? Eleni was standing at the bedroom door, wrapping a robe around her body. There was a look of extreme distaste on her face.

'We're speaking English, Eleni,' Aris said, giving her a mocking look. 'Your boyfriend and me.'

'In that case I'll say what I'm thinking in English,' the archaeologist said, stepping up to him. 'Fuck off.'

Aris Theocharis laughed again. 'Charming. And all I'm doing is delivering a message from my father.'

'Why didn't he phone me?' Eleni demanded.

'He was going to,' Aris replied, glancing at Mavros. 'But I volunteered to come down.' He winked at her. 'Keeping an eye on you, lover girl. And the company you keep.'

Eleni pursed her lips. 'What's the message?'

Aris nodded slowly. 'I almost forgot. You're to come to dinner tonight.' He grinned at Mavros. 'Your presence is required too.' He looked back at Eleni. 'Mitsos reported that you took a visitor into the site. Naughty, naughty.' He laughed then stared at her, his expression suddenly serious, and walked away.

Eleni sent a string of insults in Greek after him.

'What's the matter?' Mavros asked when she'd finished.

She gave him an infuriated glare. 'Oh, nothing. That bastard's only here for a few weeks every year but he . . . he makes me so angry.' She went towards the bathroom in a flurry of towelling. 'The useless pig.'

Mavros watched her go thoughtfully. He had picked up an uncharacteristic hint of fear in her voice. Eleni gave the impression of being a strong woman, but Aris Theocharis had some kind of hold over her.

He spent the rest of the afternoon debating whether to ask Eleni about Rosa Ozal, but decided against it. He suspected that in the mood she was in she'd just brush him off. It would be better to talk to her when she was less irritable. At one point he told her that he'd pass up Theocharis's invitation and go back to the village, but she wouldn't let him.

'No, no, it will be so exciting for you, Alex,' she said, looking up from the notes she was writing at her table. 'Meeting a person like Panos Theocharis will be a very useful experience for a writer. I can tell you that there's no one else like him anywhere.'

Mavros could tell from Eleni's tone that she wasn't paying the museum benefactor a compliment.

Dinos led the goats through the gap in the wall on the ridge and let them spread out over the slope above the ruins of Vathy, the pair of mongrel dogs circling his feet. He went over to the heaps of stone near by, all that remained of the herdsman's hut built by his great-grandfather, and sent a rising string of notes from his pipe into the air. The sea beyond the inlet was blinding blue, the pair of islands at the far end floating like turtles on the water. Farther out, Eschati was the curve of a seal's back, almost swallowed by the waves. This afternoon there were no boats.

Dinos was thinking about the *trata* he'd been watching the other day. His cousin Yiangos, he'd been at the helm. And Navsika, her chest bare. They had swum to the little beach; Dinos hadn't been able to see what they'd done, but he knew all the same. He had gone hard when he thought about it, had emptied himself on to the thin soil. And then . . . and then the other boats had come. He blinked and forced the images away, wouldn't think about them.

The goats had headed west. He got up and went after them,

suddenly worried that they were homing in on the cultivated terraces over there. The widow Rena worked the old madwoman's strips now and she sometimes spoke sharply to him. But not as sharply as Lefteris. Even though Yiangos's father was a fisherman he often came out here; Dinos didn't know why. He hadn't planted anything on his terraces, the ones beyond Rena's. But Dinos had seen the gleaming new pick-up over by the rocks where they used to dig the minerals, usually in the evening, its headlights never on. He was probably looking for ancient things in the caves, like the woman with curly hair who spent her days digging. Lefteris was a fierce man. One time he had spotted Dinos as he looked down from the ridge. The goatherd shivered as he recalled the burning eyes and the clenched fists. But Lefteris hadn't done anything more. Like everyone else on the island, he thought Dinos was a moron, the son of a drink-addled farmer and a shrewish mother, not even worthy of a clout on the back of the head the next time he saw him in the village. Dinos was pleased that he had fooled them.

The clanging of the goat bells was interrupted by a shout. Dinos looked round and saw the only person he knew who didn't treat him like a fool. Smiling as he stuffed the pipe back in his pocket, he ran with loping strides towards the shattered walls of the old hut. To the devil with the goats.

A little before eight o'clock they set off on foot towards the tower. Eleni had given Mavros a pair of cream trousers and a loose-fitting shirt that a previous occupant of her house had left behind. She'd pulled her hair back and put on a pale yellow dress that flattered her figure, but she'd made no other concession to evening wear. Make-up apparently wasn't her thing either. At least her tanned face gave her a healthy glow that was just the right side of rugged.

'How many people work on the estate?' Mavros asked as they passed out of the orchards and entered a rock garden filled with a plethora of plants and blooms, insects buzzing somnolently around them in the gathering gloom.

'Dozens,' Eleni replied. 'I think most of the families on the island work for Theocharis one way or another. He gives the locals work even though it would be much cheaper for him to use Albanians.'

That made an impression on Mavros. Most Greeks with money used workers from the former communist stronghold to do the shitty jobs for shitty wages. It seemed that Theocharis believed in looking after the islanders. He took in the complex of buildings. Close up he could see that there was accommodation for numerous guests, though most of the houses were unlit. The old tower was even more imposing from beneath, the medieval stonework picked out by floodlights and the terrace beneath it covered in light-coloured tenting. He followed Eleni up a wide staircase. Reaching the top, he saw that a large part of the platform in front of the tower was filled by a swimming pool, the water gleaming pale blue in the lights. Beyond it Panos Theocharis was standing at the rail of the belvedere, looking out over his glittering nocturnal domain. Above him the dome of the sky curved into the darkness, the Milky Way and the stars much more intense than Mavros was used to in the big city.

'Ah, there you are,' the old man said in English. 'I hope you don't mind yet another dinner, Eleni?' He nodded at her once, the set of his face beneath the sculpted white beard discouraging a reply. 'Please introduce your friend.'

'Alex Cochrane,' Mavros put in, using his mother's maiden name. He suspected the multimillionaire would have met Dorothy at cultural receptions in Athens, but he was hoping that he wouldn't remember that half of her surname or connect it with him.

'I prefer to use first names, Alex,' Theocharis said. 'I hope you don't mind.'

'Of course not,' Mavros replied. Eleni's stiffness gave him the feeling that following suit and addressing Theocharis by his first name was probably not a good idea, despite the offer of informality. The old man was wearing a perfectly pressed pair of white trousers and an open-necked silk shirt that didn't need a tie to emphasise its quality.

'And what do you do, Alex?' Theocharis asked.

'I'm a writer,' Mavros replied glibly.

'Really?' The museum benefactor suddenly sounded less friendly. 'You're not a journalist, I hope.'

Mavros shook his head. 'Fiction,' he said.

'Anything I might have read?' The Greek's English had only the slightest hint of a non-native speaker's accent.

'I doubt it. I write trashy thrillers.' Mavros went for an extra layer of security. 'Under several noms de plume.'

Theocharis looked slightly more at ease. 'How interesting,' he said. He glanced at Eleni as a white-coated waiter came up with glasses of champagne. 'And are you planning a scene in an archaeological site?' There was an edge to his voice again.

'Em, no,' Mavros said, realising that he had to take the pressure off Eleni. 'No, I'm in the middle of a book set in the United States. When I heard that Eleni was working on a dig here, I asked her if I could have a look. I've no special interest in Cycladic culture, though I found the excavations fascinating.' He sipped the wine. It was as good as anything he'd ever tasted.

Panos Theocharis was nodding slowly, his eyes still on the archaeologist. 'Eleni is an expert, Alex,' he said, enunciating the words clearly. 'But sometimes she acts beyond her authority.' He gave a tight smile, and it was suddenly apparent where his son Aris's malicious side originated. 'That site is on my land.' Now he turned his gaze on Mavros. 'Visitors are only allowed with my personal permission, as Eleni knows very well.'

Mavros felt his heart begin to beat faster. The museum benefactor may have been old but his voice was underpinned by a young man's strength of will. He wondered what had happened to the gorilla Mitsos. Presumably he should have denied Mavros entry rather than let Eleni do as she pleased. Or was the tycoon just playing at being a tyrant? 'I'm sorry . . .' he began.

Theocharis raised a hand and smiled with a little more warmth. 'It's all right. You're not the first one. Eleni takes her friends up

there quite often, even though I've asked her not to.' The tension
went out of his upper body and he leaned heavily on a stick that
had been standing against the wall. 'We'll say no more about it.'
He looked past Mavros. 'Ah, there you are, my dear.'

Eleni and Mavros turned and watched as the statuesque figure
of a middle-aged woman approached them. She was tall, her
unnaturally blonde hair set in a cascade that reached her bare
shoulders. The black evening gown she was wearing would have
been excessive at an embassy reception in the capital and the
silver high-heeled shoes made loud clicks on the tiles of the
terrace. Behind her three Alsatians padded across the tiles, their
eyes fixed on the stranger.

Theocharis bowed to her with old-fashioned courtesy. 'May I
present my wife Dhimitra?' he said to Mavros. 'My dear, this is
Alex . . . ah, Alex Cochrane. He is a writer from—' He broke
off. 'I'm sorry, I haven't yet discovered where he's from.'

It wasn't clear to Mavros if his host was mocking him. There was
a touch of irony in his voice but that may just have been his nature.
The only way he could have discovered Mavros's true identity was
by examining the Greek ID card, and that was buttoned securely
in his back pocket.

'I'm from Scotland,' Mavros said, taking the hand that Dhimitra
Theochari extended.

'Really,' she said. 'How fascinating.' Her English was much
more heavily accented than her husband's and the sardonic
edge was more pronounced as well. She gave Eleni a brief and
disapproving glance. 'Back again?' she asked in Greek, her tone
coarser.

Theocharis took a glass of champagne from the waiter and
handed it to his wife. 'I asked Eleni to bring Alex to dinner
because he visited the site this afternoon.'

Dhimitra was looking at Mavros over the rim of her glass, her
kohl-lined eyes wide open and penetrating. There was a visible
tension about her.

'As he showed such curiosity,' the host continued, emphasising
the final word, 'I thought he might like to see the collection.'

His wife turned her gaze on him. 'Are you sure, Pano?' she asked. 'Things from graves are not interesting to everyone.' She took a long sip of champagne. 'Where is Aris?'

Theocharis raised his chin. 'Who knows? Chasing tourist women in the bars, no doubt.' He gave Dhimitra a brief smile. 'Don't worry, your step-son can look after himself.'

Mavros was watching the woman. There was something false about her, something out of place. He couldn't work out what that element might be. She was decades younger than her husband, but that was hardly unusual in the families of the super-rich. And her hair colour obviously came from a bottle, though again, that was par for the course among women of her status. There was an ill-concealed scowl on her face now, as if the absence of the blustering Aris had ruined her evening.

'Well, Alex?' Theocharis said, turning to him. 'You decide. Would you like a brief tour of my private collection before dinner?'

Mavros felt Eleni's elbow jab into his side. She was looking at him expectantly. Showing interest was obviously de rigueur in the old tower.

'Why, yes,' he said. 'That would be very kind of you.' He looked at Dhimitra. 'I don't have much experience of grave goods, but I'm very keen to see some. Are they from the site Eleni's been excavating?'

He felt her elbow again, this time harder.

Theocharis put his still-full glass on the waiter's tray. 'Certainly not,' he replied firmly. 'All new finds are handed over to the relevant experts for analysis and classification.' He moved slowly away from the edge of the terrace. 'As I'm sure Eleni told you. What I'm going to show you are the fruits of my passion for collecting over the last forty years.'

'I'll wait for you out here, Pano,' Dhimitra called after him, her voice suggesting that she'd seen this particular passion fruit often enough.

Theocharis stopped briefly and then limped on towards the house, his weight on the stick. When Mavros caught up with him he said in a low voice, 'Museum pieces aren't Dhimitra's major preoccupation.' He smiled in a curious way, his lips twisting. 'She didn't always live like this.' He glanced around the opulent terrace. 'I rescued her from a hard life, but at times I think she resents me for it.'

Mavros gave his host a polite nod and tried to place Dhimitra Theochari. He was sure he'd seen her somewhere before, not dressed in the products of haute couture.

Theocharis led them into the cool house. Mavros took in the huge open reception rooms with their gleaming marble floors and ornate furniture that had been built around the medieval tower. The base of the original curved wall was now inside, and the great arch of the gate was protected from the elements. He suspected that the development had contravened numerous building regulations, but Theocharis clearly had enough clout – and wealth – to cut though any bureaucratic tangle.

'The tower was in danger of collapse,' the old man said as he led them down a broad stone staircase. 'So we dug out the foundations and strengthened them.' They came out into a large, dimly lit area. 'That gave me the perfect space for the pieces I haven't donated to the museum.' He took a remote control from his pocket and pressed a button. 'Behold the glory of death.'

Mavros didn't have time to quibble at the melodramatic introduction. As soon as the lights brightened he temporarily lost the power of speech. He stepped forward and moved his eyes slowly around the display cases and the walls behind them, aware that both Theocharis and Eleni were studying his reaction. The strains of doom-laden orchestral music came from speakers in the corners.

'It's . . . it's amazing,' he said feebly. 'This must be worth a fortune.'

Theocharis nodded. 'Indeed. That's why I have the security that you may notice.' He inclined his head towards the closed-circuit TV cameras that were suspended from the ceiling. 'Let me show you around. Do you recognise the musical accompaniment, by the way? No? Rachmaninov's symphonic poem *The Isle of the*

Dead. It was inspired by the famous painting by Böcklin of an oarsman steering a white-clad figure to its final resting place.'

Mavros followed his host around the display cases. There were exquisite pots and flasks from the classical period, including several lekythi like the one he'd seen on the poster for the museum in Athens; there were grave markers of all kinds, from head-high, unadorned columns to miniature statues of humans and animals; and there was a line of sarcophagi labelled as coming from the Hellenistic period, their sides carved in magnificent detail. But, as he went farther into the underground room, Mavros realised that the most important part of the collection was on the far wall. A few metres in front of the wide panel, Theocharis pressed another button to activate additional lights.

'Do you know where you find yourself now, Alex?' the museum benefactor said, the breath scratching in his throat.

Mavros looked at him and saw that the skin of his face was taut under the pointed, pure white beard. He looked up at the great mural, some parts with brighter colours that had clearly been restored, and made out a sylvan landscape with a river snaking through it. All around were marsh flowers and drooping trees. The music's intense rhythm suggested the regular movements of an oarsman.

'Is that Charon in his bark?' Mavros asked, pointing to the figure at the stern of a small craft in the middle of the stream.

'The ferryman of dead souls,' Theocharis said. 'Excellent. You appear to have more than a passing interest in Greek mythology, Alex.'

Mavros glanced at the old man and shrugged. 'The benefits of a classical education,' he lied. Although he went to school in Athens and the Greek system drummed ancient culture into pupils relentlessly, he'd met people at university in the UK who were much better informed than he was about the subject. 'Where did this come from?' he asked. 'I presume you weren't lucky enough to find it here.'

Eleni shook her head at him as if he were a particularly dense student.

Theocharis put a wrinkled hand on Mavros's arm. 'This mural dates from the fifth century BC. It is from a palace in Sicily.' He gave a brief smile. 'I have contacts over there who enabled me to obtain it. Master restorers worked for years to complete it and to install it here. It has been assigned to the great master Polygnotos, whose painting of the underworld in Delphi is one of the lost masterpieces of the ancient world.'

Mavros was looking at the depiction of the old ferryman, his beard unkempt and his thin arms bent against the flow of the infernal river. This section of the work seemed to be original. The piece would be worth millions, its value to scholars priceless. So what was it doing in Theocharis's cellar? And why was it being shown to him?

'Charon was a shadowy figure in classical literature and art,' his host said as he dimmed the lights, 'but in later Greece, as Charos, he was equated with the ineluctability of death. In effect, he personified death.' He clasped Mavros's forearm again. 'When you die, it is believed that you fight with Charos.' He gave a hollow laugh. 'And inevitably you lose.' He turned away.

Mavros looked at Eleni and raised his shoulders, trying to understand why he'd been brought here. She gazed back at him blankly then followed the old man out. As Mavros moved off, the music rose to a strident climax. He suddenly thought he could feel the eyes of the death god burning into his back from the underground wall.

If Theocharis was making some kind of oblique threat, it was having the desired effect.

11

The screen flickered in the darkened room, then the image consolidated.

The woman was cowering in the corner of the cave, her bound hands clenched between her legs. She was trying to cover her breasts with her tanned upper arms. The screams she was emitting could not be heard as the sound had been deactivated. Then the light, which up till then had come only from a single torch, was increased. An oil lamp was placed by hands with varnished nails on either side of the captive, out of reach of her flailing legs. These were quickly stilled when the rope around her ankles was stretched.

The image was suddenly unsteady, the camera held now in hands that were shaking. The woman kept her eyes off the lens, as if by looking at it she would become complicit in what was about to happen to her. Now that her bonds were taut, she stopped struggling and let her head droop to one side, her chest heaving for breath.

A male figure appeared on the screen, the heavily muscled upper part of the body naked, jeans and heavy boots on the lower part. He turned to face the camera without reservation. His face was split by a vicious grin, his eyes staring and wild. After holding his gaze on the lens for a few more seconds, he loosened the rope attached to the woman's ankles. Grabbing her by the hair, he forced her into a kneeling position. The ropes had drawn blood on her wrists and she was mouthing inaudible words, her lips cracked. Then she was hit by a series of heavy slaps on both cheeks and she slumped as far as her bonds would allow. The assailant manoeuvred her towards the wall and then calculatedly drove her head three times against the stone. She collapsed forward, her backside raised above her crumpled legs.

The position of her body seemed to enrage her attacker even more. He glared at the lens then pulled down his jeans and massaged his half-erect penis. Pushing the woman farther forward with his knees, he raised her buttocks into a higher position. Then he inserted his now stiff member between them and started riding his victim like a cowboy on a steer, one arm pulling the rope around her wrists. The camera stayed on him until he arched backwards and rammed his groin into her with quicker thrusts, mouth hanging open as he reached his climax. As soon as he withdrew, the screen went blank, dots and flashes of colour running past.

The scene gradually composed itself again, the torch beam back on the woman's naked, motionless form. Resting against her darkly bruised knee was a square of cardboard on which the words 'One week' had been written in large red letters. The image faded then re-formed, this time with a sign saying 'Two weeks' to the fore. And so it continued until the final image with the board marked 'Seven weeks'.

The captive woman's skin was now black and distended. The camera moved in closer and substantial insect life became apparent, green blowflies clustering around the facial orifices.

Then the image disappeared.

'All right, Alex,' Eleni said as the two of them walked down the road to her house. 'It's time you told the truth.'

Mavros felt his stomach somersault. 'What do you mean?' He glanced over his shoulder at the terrace beneath the tower. The lights were still bright but there was no sign of Panos Theocharis. He had retired soon after dinner, leaving his wife to pass around liqueurs. Dhimitra had made a substantial hole in a decanter of cognac, her hands trembling as if the evening air were chill. She had made little effort at conversation and obviously wanted Mavros and the archaeologist to leave.

'What do I mean?' Eleni laughed and shook her head. 'You aren't who you say you are, I'm sure of that.'

Mavros was running through the events of the evening, trying to remember when he might have given himself away. After the viewing of his host's collection, they'd been served dinner on the terrace. Dhimitra had been difficult, directing a series of complaints in Greek at her husband and the waiters as well as complaining about Aris's continued absence, but Mavros was pretty sure he hadn't shown any understanding of what had been said. He also made sure that he didn't eat the head of the grilled bream he'd been served. Few Greeks would pass up the opportunity of gnawing and sucking that part of the fish, but a bona fide Scotsman would be much more reticent.

Eleni stopped outside her house and turned to face him. 'You're in the antiquities trade, aren't you?' she said, her tone unequivocal. 'The criminal side of it.'

'What?' Mavros responded, relief rushing through him. 'You're joking, aren't you?'

She stood there with her hands on her hips. 'No, I'm not. Theocharis knows your sort better than anyone and he was convinced. Why do you think he showed you the contents of his cellar? He was laughing at you, my friend. He was saying, "See what I've got – and you can't have it."' She frowned at him. 'Didn't you understand the threat, Alex? He's daring you to take him on, to try to steal from him. He's like that. But not all his people are as careless as Mitsos up at the site. Theocharis has this island in his pocket. Don't even think of trying to get your hands on any of his pieces. Even if you manage to get past the alarm system, the locals will tear you apart before you can get off the island.'

As Mavros stood listening, Deniz Ozal came into his thoughts. Unlike him, his client really was an antiquities dealer, one who was possibly involved with Tryfon Roufos, the most notorious smuggler and fence in the country. He wondered why he hadn't heard from the Turkish-American.

'Look,' he said, opening his arms wide. 'I'm not a dealer.

How can I prove it? Try out my knowledge of ancient pots or statues, if you want. I don't know a red-figure vase painter from a black-figure one.'

The archaeologist turned towards the house. 'I think you're an expert at concealing things, Alex,' she said over her shoulder.

Mavros followed her in and caught sight of the photograph album above the desk. It struck him that asking Eleni about Rosa would be a good way to distract her, but he would have to find the right moment – and calm her down first. 'I'm not concealing anything,' he said, going into the main room after her. 'But I admit I am interested in your work.' In his experience, nobody could resist talking about their ruling passion for long. Maybe that would make Eleni more amenable to questioning.

The archaeologist laughed. 'I'm sure you are.' Then she turned towards him, her expression suddenly avid. 'You don't know how important these excavations might be. If I can establish a pattern, a systematic mode of burial that matches the style of the Cycladic sculptures, it will be a major breakthrough.'

Mavros was trying to keep up. 'A breakthrough in what way?' he asked.

Eleni led him over to her worktop and took a handful of photographs from a file. 'See these?' she asked, spreading out on the table shots of blank-faced marble figures with their arms crossed. 'Nobody has ever been sure if they represent the dead or the culture's deities, nor if they are lying down or standing up. I hope my work will prove that they are people who have passed away rather than gods.' She looked up at him, her face bright with enthusiasm. 'That would have a major effect on the way the Early Aegean Bronze Age is viewed. A concentration on real men and women rather than supernatural beings might even be said to prefigure classical Greek civilisation's human values.'

Mavros was following her line of argument, but he had allowed his eyes to stray from her. It had just struck him that there had been no Cycladic objects in Theocharis's collection. Surely he must have some. But where were they? Had he consigned them all to the museum?

Eleni's expression lost its ardour. She presumably thought that she was boring him. She moved towards the bedroom.

'That's . . . that's fascinating,' Mavros stammered as he went after her.

'Of course it is.' Eleni's tone was ironic. She turned as he reached the door, her dress slipping from her shoulders. She gave him a taunting smile and let it fall farther, exposing her breasts. 'Are you sure you don't see anything you like? You with your strange left eye?'

Mavros gave a sigh and bit his lip.

December 12th, 1942

An extraordinary day. We are still waiting for the Greek contingent to land – all I've been told on the radio is that 'operational delays' have occurred. Ajax has been laid up with his leg for weeks now, though he's apparently started to hobble around, shouting at the women in his family if they try to get him to lie down again. This I know from my beautiful messenger, my lover, my Maro. She has come every evening. She has managed to stay late by telling her mother that I am ill and need nursing, though how much longer that excuse can continue I don't know. I don't care. I love her so much that I have had to resist the temptation to run out of the hut in daylight and profess my infatuation to anyone I might meet in the Kambos. Fortunately the more restrained, British side of my nature prevailed. Ah, but I love her! When she is gone I feel that part of me has been ripped away. But when she is here I am whole again, lost in her soft arms and the scents of her perfect body.

It was after midnight when Maro left and I sank into a sweet dream in which I was following her through a field of tall corn, the wind tossing the ears from side to side and the sea running away towards the neighbouring islands. It was well into the morning when I was woken, the loud cries of women jerking me out of my enchanted world. I stumbled to the slats over the window, grabbing my service revolver as I went. The noise was terrifying, the screams of agony making me think that a massacre was taking place outside

*the hut. I put my eye to the wood and peered out towards the source
of the disturbance. About twenty yards away is a small cemetery.
The church of Ayios Dhimitrios that used to serve the abandoned
village of Myli is a little farther off, and in all the weeks I've been
here, I've never seen anyone worship at it. But this was different.
There must have been dozens of islanders inside the uneven wall of
the graveyard. The majority of them were women in black clothes,
their heads shrouded in scarves.*

*I moved my ear to the slats and tried to understand what was going
on. My Greek has improved enormously in recent weeks owing to my
lengthy conversations with Maro. But there was such a confusion of
cries and what sounded like discordant singing that I struggled to
follow what was happening. Then the tight grouping of people moved
apart and the noise grew weaker, only a few cracked voices carrying
on a kind of chant. Looking between the black-clad figures, I caught
sight of a bent old woman. I felt my heart pound in my chest. She
was holding up a human skull.*

*What were they doing? Digging up a body? I watched in horror
as the skull was wiped with a cloth, what looked like remnants of
hair coming away in the old woman's hand. Now there was a wild
shouting, the watchers bewailing the fate of the grave's occupant. I
heard the word* eirene, *which means 'peace', being repeated over and
over again, then some other words I couldn't understand. And then
a cloth was placed on the bare cranium and the old woman kissed
it reverently.*

*'My daughter, why did you leave us?' screamed a middle-aged
woman, her eyes red. 'Why were you walking on the mountain when
you should have been at home?'*

*The lament was taken up by other women, some of whom were
putting coins into the rectangular metal box that was being filled with
the earth-stained bones. Then a larger gap appeared in the crowd
and a priest walked forward. The smell of incense drifted across to
my hut through the still air. I heard the divine pronounce words in
ecclesiastical Greek. These I could mostly make sense of as that form
of the language is closer to the ancient Greek that I studied.*

'May your memory be everlasting, sister,' he recited. 'May the

holy, the mighty, the immortal God have mercy.' Then he upturned
a bottle of wine over the box containing the bones, making the shape
of the cross three times. *'You shall wash me and I shall be whiter
than white,'* he said, taking on the dead woman's voice. *'Dust are
you, and to dust you will return,'* he concluded, reverting to the role
of priest.

I watched as the crowd began to break up, the old woman carrying
the box off to a small building at the corner of the cemetery. People
moved towards the church and I could see wine and food being
handed out. To my relief no one came towards the hut, and soon
I was on my own again. I was surprised to find myself quivering,
my eyes damp. Who was the dead woman and what had happened
to her? The emotions displayed by the islanders, the heart-rending
screams they'd let out, had shaken me badly.

This evening Maro came again and I asked her about the
ceremony. She apologised that she hadn't warned me about it
and told me that it is the Orthodox ritual to dig up the bones of
the dead after some five years and to transfer them to the ossuary.
As I witnessed in part, people run through a mixture of sentiments.
Initially they are almost joyful to be in close proximity to the departed
one, and then they are torn apart by the ravages of a grief even worse
than that they experienced after the burial as they realise that bones
are now all that remain.

'Who was the deceased?' I asked.

Maro looked at me with wide eyes, her expression one of great
tenderness. 'She wasn't a close relative of mine,' she replied, 'but I
remember her very well. She was twenty when she died. She was
beautiful, her hair jet black and curled, her eyes bright. Everyone
loved her, she was the village's favourite daughter.' She stifled a
sob. 'And then one evening she followed a stray goat up the slopes
of Vigla. They found her the next day at the bottom of a cliff, her
neck broken. Poor Eirene.'

I held her tighter, wiping the tears from her cheeks. I realised my
mistake. Eirene *is also a name.* There is so much I have to learn
about the modern country I am fighting for. 'I'm sorry,' I said. The
irony of exhuming the bones of a woman whose name meant 'peace'

during times of war also struck me, but I kept that to myself. 'That must have been terrible for the island.'

Maro looked at me and then nodded solemnly. 'It was. Not just because a young woman had died before her time, but because her father was maddened by grief. He wouldn't let her be buried in the village cemetery, saying that she'd invited her fate.' Maro raised her shoulders and shook her head. 'He got it into his head that Eirene had gone to meet a boy. But no one else thought that, at least not at the beginning. Eirene hadn't been interested in any of the young men's approaches. She . . . she was her own mistress.' She bit her lip. 'That's why my father and my brother wouldn't let me come to the rite today. Like a lot of the men they think Eirene is a bad example. The fools.'

The sudden strength of her voice and her unaccustomed criticism of the males in her family took me aback. I kissed her tear-stained cheek and she huddled closer to me. But this evening, for the first time, we didn't make love. It was as if the loss of the young woman and the brief exposure of her remains to the sun for the last time had diminished our happiness.

Maro went back to the village earlier than usual and I climbed up to the ridge to make the scheduled call on the radio to base. Things are moving at last. I was told to expect the detachment of men tomorrow night.

So the war is about to intrude into my Cycladic idyll. I am still enthusiastic about the action that lies ahead, desperate to strike a blow for my adopted fatherland, but I am also nervous because now I have Maro to think about. There is so much more to lose. I will have to steel myself, put the struggle before my beautiful lover.

Have I the strength to do that?

Mavros felt his cheeks redden. 'I'm . . . I'm sorry, Eleni,' he said. 'Like I told you, I've got a partner back home.'

The archaeologist took the second rejection less indulgently than the first. 'How lucky she is,' she said acidly, dropping the dress to the floor and stepping out of it. Her thighs and the skimpy knickers she was wearing provoked a stir in Mavros's groin before he could look away. She started pulling on her jeans. 'I'll take you as far as the Bar Astrapi.' She shot him a penetrating glance. 'If you can bear to put your arms around me.'

Mavros shrugged weakly. 'Can't we just be friends?' he asked, angry with himself for messing up. So much for getting her in the mood to answer his questions.

'Acquaintances, I think,' Eleni said. 'Isn't that the word?' She smoothed a white T-shirt over her torso and pushed past him. 'Come on.'

He reached out a hand to stop her. 'Eleni, there's something I want to ask you.' He took the folded photo of Rosa Ozal out of his pocket. 'A friend of mine was here in the early summer. I was wondering if you'd met her.' He opened up the photo and held it up, watching her carefully.

There were a few seconds of silence that were broken only by the high-pitched buzzing of a mosquito, then the archaeologist shook her head and moved away.

'No,' she said, 'I never saw her.'

Mavros had seen the flicker of her eyes and the way her face had momentarily changed. What was it she'd expressed without wanting to? Wistful sorrow? Pain? Whatever the emotion was, it didn't sit well with the firm tone of her denial. 'Are you sure?' he asked. 'She had a very good time here. You didn't see her in the Astrapi or any of the restaurants?'

'I told you,' she said, keeping her back to him as she closed the shutters, 'I never saw her.'

Mavros was caught in a dilemma. Either he disproved Eleni's answer by opening up her album and confronting her with the photo of her and Rosa that he'd viewed illicitly, or he tried to discover why she was lying. He decided on the latter course. After all, the photo and his own experience suggested that Eleni was bisexual. Perhaps she was just grieving for a brief romance she'd had with Rosa. On the other hand, she was the third person on the island to mislead him about the missing woman and, like the furniture designer Barbara Hoeg and the compliant Mikkel, she was nervous about it. He didn't have much to report to Deniz

Ozal when his client took it into his head to call, but at least the case was starting to move.

A few minutes later he was clutching on to Eleni as she drove the motorbike down the empty, unlit roads of the Kambos, past the old church and its unkempt cemetery, and then on to the farm where he'd seen the old man beating his donkey. He wondered if Theocharis used him on the estate. From what Eleni had said, it sounded like the museum benefactor had no shortage of work for hard men.

Rena slipped into the narrow lane by the *kastro*, head covered by her usual black scarf. The music from one of the few bars still open in the centre of the village was reverberating off the heavy stone walls, but there weren't many people around. The locals were already sinking into winter habits, spending the evenings in their own or their relatives' homes rather than parading around the streets in their best clothes with their families in tow.

She glanced up at the wooden balcony outside Rinus's flat and saw that there were no lights on. No doubt the bastard was at the Astrapi, selling his filth to the tourists. Yiangos had something to do with that, Rena knew it. But surely that couldn't have led to his death and that of poor Navsika. Merciful God, what happened to them?

There was no answer when she knocked on Kyra Maro's door. She swivelled the handle and found that the door was locked. Worried that something had happened to the old woman, she put down the bowl of soup that she'd covered with a cloth. She checked that the street was empty and took out the key she'd had cut on Paros for an occasion like this. Fortunately the key wasn't in the lock on the other side. There was a single feeble light burning in the corner but she could make out no sign of the tiny flat's occupant. She couldn't be out at this time of night. The whole village shunned her and she kept away from the church except on major festivals. She must have gone to bed – the partition door was closed – but that was strange as well;

Kyra Maro hardly slept, and when she did it was in her chair in the main room.

Feeling a stir of disquiet, Rena retrieved the soup from outside and laid it on the table. Then she went over to the bedroom door and tapped on it, gently at first and then more urgently. There was no response. She turned the handle and pushed the flimsy panel open. And swallowed a scream.

The small chamber, its internal wall hewn out of the rocky base of the *kastro*, was lit by a multitude of candles, the heavy scent of wax hanging in the air. Kyra Maro was kneeling on the floor, her tiny head on the embroidered bedspread. Rena could see no movement in her chest, but that wasn't what frightened her. There was an open tin box on the floor and the bed was laid out with darkly stained objects that she knew immediately were human bones. And between the old woman's outstretched arms was a skull, the eye sockets gaping and the cranium disfigured by an uneven bulge on the top.

Rena's knees were weak and her breath was coming in rapid gasps. She forced herself to go closer and bend over Kyra Maro. Touching her fleshless wrist, she found a pulse that was stronger than she'd expected. She stepped back, unsure what to do. The way the room had been arranged gave the impression of ritual. Perhaps the old woman did this every night, there was no way of knowing, and she might be upset to be discovered with the bones.

Kneeling down beside the box, Rena looked at its lid. A white cross had been painted roughly on it, along with the capital letters alpha and gamma, and the numbers 1943–1964. She rocked back on her heels and tried to make sense of this. The gamma may have referred to a member of Kyra Maro's family – her surname was Grypari. But whose bones could they be? As far as Rena knew, the old woman had never married or had children. She assumed the numbers were dates; 1943 – Maro would have been about twenty then. But whose were the initials? And why had his or her bones been taken from the ossuary?

Rena shivered and got slowly to her feet, having decided to

go without waking the old woman. Though faint, her breathing was regular and she didn't seem to be ill. It was as she ran her eyes around the cell-like room one last time that Rena saw the faded photograph in the icon niche. She recognised it immediately. She had come across it in the room across her courtyard that she rented out. Her surprise at seeing it again in Kyra Maro's bedroom diluted the shock she'd got from the bones. Then the old woman twitched, her eyes suddenly flickering.

Not wanting to be caught in her sanctuary, Rena moved quickly out of the room towards the front door. She remembered to take the bowl of soup to cover her tracks – she'd come back with it later. Outside, she turned the key in the door and started quickly down the street, almost colliding with Manolis Gryparis. The old man with the single arm stared hard at her as he brushed past. She was halfway home when it occurred to her that now Kyra Maro's brother was aware that she had a key to the old woman's house. As far as she knew, no one else in Maro's family had one. It was the kind of knowledge that the old bastard was quite capable of using to his advantage – or to that of his terrible son Lefteris.

Eleni pulled up in front of the Bar Astrapi, dust rising in the bright lights. Mavros let go of her and got off the bike, his thighs aching. He'd been trying to grip the seat in order to reduce his hold on her, but she'd driven so fast that he'd been forced to encircle her midriff with his arms as he'd done earlier in the day.

'You can buy me a drink for the ride,' Eleni said, her voice humourless. 'I won't charge you for anything else.'

'Yes, I'll get you a drink,' Mavros replied. 'In a few minutes. First I want to go back to my place to change so that you can take these clothes back.' He also wanted to call Niki, but he wasn't going to tell Eleni that.

The archaeologist gave a shrug. 'You do what you like, Alex,' she said indifferently. 'You know where to find me.' She turned away and went into the bar, the sound of heavy rock music increasing as the door was opened.

Mavros walked down the unlit track towards the village. He could have done without another late night, but there were people he needed to talk to and he reckoned that their guard would be down and their tongues looser in the Astrapi. That was, unless Eleni warned them about his interest in Rosa. Even if she did, their reactions might be revealing.

He entered the village street and in the sparse lights made out his landlady approaching her front door from the opposite direction, a plate in her hands. He gave her a wave, but her head was down and she didn't respond.

'Hello,' he said as he got closer.

Rena's head shot up and she gazed at him with wide eyes. 'Oh, Alex.' She gave him a nod as she put her key in the lock, holding the plate firmly in one hand.

'Is something wrong?' he asked as he followed her in.

'Wrong?' she repeated, eyes to the front. 'No.' She turned when she came out of the passage to the yard. 'You know, the dead young persons . . .'

Mavros nodded. 'It must be very hard for everyone.'

'No,' she said bitterly. 'Not for everyone. There are people who do not care so much.'

He looked at her and saw that her eyes were damp. 'Excuse me, I have to . . .' He moved towards his rooms.

'You stay in now?' Rena asked, her expression lightening slightly. 'You would like coffee?'

Mavros shook his head. 'No, I'm meeting—' He broke off. Maybe this was the time to question Rena. But she still looked very upset. It would be better to talk to her in the morning. 'I'm meeting some people.' He smiled awkwardly as he remembered Rena's aversion to Eleni. 'Goodnight.'

The widow kept her eyes on him for a second then nodded. 'Goodnight,' she said in a low voice.

Mavros went into his bedroom and changed out of the clothes Eleni had given him. He was wondering about Rena. Underneath the black clothes and scarf she was attractive, young enough to find another husband and smarter than most island women. But there was something worrying about her, something that at times made him feel like a naughty child. It was as if she lived in a different dimension to everyone else on the island, as if she had access to mysteries denied to other people. He grunted as he pulled on a clean T-shirt. Maybe she was just more subtle than her rivals about taking the tourists' money without making them feel they'd been milked.

He took his mobile out and called Niki's flat. His encounters with Eleni had brought her closer and he wanted to hear her voice. Niki may have been volatile and trying, but he knew her feelings for him were genuine. As it turned out, he heard her voice only on the recorded message. He told her he'd call again the next day and cut the connection. The same happened with her mobile number. She'd probably passed out with a case file on her face – when she wasn't with him, she took her work to bed and turned off the phones.

He checked his own voicemail. Nothing from her and nothing from Deniz Ozal. His suspicions that the Turkish-American wasn't particularly concerned about his sister were deepening. He hoped his client hadn't been slapping any more hookers. If he hadn't been so set on taking a break from Athens and Niki, that might have put him off the case. As far as he was concerned, men who hit women were scum.

Mavros went out again, seeing Rena through the open window of the upper room. She was holding something out in front of her and examining it, her expression intense. He went out into the street and back towards the bar. Walking up the dark track beyond the village, about fifty metres from the Astrapi he heard what he initially thought were animal sounds over the wall to his left – breath being drawn in hard, limbs rubbing against the dry-stone wall. Then he heard a human voice, a loud whisper.

'Keep still, will you?' A male speaking Greek.

A female laugh. 'Keep still? I didn't come here to do that.'

There was a pause and then a dull slap.

'Fuck you, Ari,' said the woman. 'Is that the best you can do?' Mavros recognised the throaty voice now. It was Dhimitra Theochari's. It seemed she'd managed to meet up with her step-son. Now Mavros could see why she'd been so restless at the dinner table. Her husband, so much older than she was, obviously didn't satisfy her. But did she want to be hit? He thought about intervening to help her out.

'I told you,' Aris said. 'Stop jerking around.'

There was a sultry laugh. 'All right, do it as fast as you like. I don't care.'

Mavros walked on. It sounded like the mining tycoon's wife could look after herself.

'Liar,' Aris grunted, his breath coming fast.

Mavros entered the glow of light around the bar and glanced over his shoulder. Two linked bodies were just visible in the field, Aris behind his stepmother, trousers round his knees. Dhimitra was up against the wall, her head bowed and her hands on the top. Her expensive clothes would be getting dirty.

He opened the door and entered the bar. The first table he passed was taken by the English tourists he'd seen before.

'Where's Aris got to?' he heard the shaven-headed Roy say. 'We need more drink.'

'Don't worry, he'll be back in a minute,' replied the bulky Trace. 'He told me he likes peeing under the stars. I'm not surprised. The toilet in here's disgusting.'

Mavros took in the rest of the tables as he went to the bar. The Americans, Gretchen and Lance, were starting on a bottle of red wine, their faces suggesting that they weren't fans of Aerosmith – the band's first album was blasting from the speakers. In the far corner, Mikkel raised a glass to Mavros and gave him a weak smile. Barbara was at the bar, cigarette in one hand and bottle of beer in the other, her eyes down. She looked exhausted. Near her was Eleni, deep in conversation with the barman. She kept her eyes off Mavros when he handed over the clothes he'd borrowed.

'Good evening, Alex!' Rinus shouted through the buzz of

guitars. 'What'll you have? This one's on me.' He gave a tight smile and cocked his ear to hear the reply to his offer.

Mavros shrugged. 'Very good of you,' he said. 'I'll have a beer.' He pointed to Barbara's. 'One of those.'

The German woman slowly raised her eyes and surveyed him with a blank expression. He nodded to her but received no acknowledgement. Either she was nearly out for the count or he wasn't her favourite person.

'So,' Rinus said, lowering the volume of the music marginally and handing him a bottle of Amstel. 'Eleni tells me you were asking about a woman.' He gave Mavros a guileless look.

'That's right,' Mavros replied, surprised by the directness of the approach and feeling the archaeologist's eyes on him. He delved in his pocket and took out the photograph. 'This is my friend. Did you ever meet her?'

Rinus flattened the photo out on the bar top and gave it a brief look. 'Sure,' he replied. 'It's Rosa.' He nodded at Mavros. 'She used to come in here. She was a lot of fun.' He scratched behind his ear. 'June, it must have been. Yeah, June.' He slid the photo to Eleni. 'Don't you remember Rosa?'

Eleni shook her head insistently then pushed the photo on to Barbara, who stared at it and then flicked it back, her expression blank but her eyes less glazed.

The barman laughed. 'You must both have been pissed. I'm sure she was in here at the same time you were some nights.' He turned back to Mavros. 'Anyway, how is Rosa? She said she might come back.'

'And she hasn't?' Mavros said.

'No, man.' Rinus stared at him. 'She hasn't come back. New York is where she lives, isn't it? Long way.' He raised an eyebrow. 'I thought you were from Scotland. Have you seen her recently?'

Mavros was studying him. So far the barman hadn't let drop any hint that he might be lying. 'No, I haven't seen her for a couple of years. She used to study in Edinburgh,' he said, fabricating a background. 'She sent me a card telling me how wonderful Trigono was. I don't suppose you remember her leaving the island, do you?'

Rinus folded the photo and handed it back to Mavros. 'Yes, as it happens I do. I was down at the port waiting for a delivery of booze. I saw her get on the ferry that the truck came off.' He smiled loosely, glancing towards Barbara. 'I even remember her waving to me.' He nodded at Mavros again, this time giving him a wink. 'Beautiful woman, wouldn't you say?'

Mavros held his eyes for a moment and then put the photo back in his pocket. As he raised the beer bottle to his lips, he thought about that wink. He was pretty sure the implication was that Rinus had been involved with Rosa. 'Have you heard from her since then?' he asked.

'From Rosa?' Rinus shook his head. 'Nah. They come, so to speak . . .' He laughed. '. . . and they go. I don't expect letters.' He glanced at Eleni. 'Hey, have you told our Scottish friend what Trigono was called in ancient times?' There was an expectant smile on his lips.

'Oh for God's sake, Rinus,' the archaeologist said, shaking her head at him.

'Pesinthos,' the barman said. 'Get it? Pe-*sin*-thos,' he repeated, stressing the middle syllable. 'That's what we like around here. Plenty of sin.'

Mavros raised an eyebrow. 'Is that right?' he said. 'I'm afraid I'm an atheist. I've got a pretty limited conception of sin.'

The Dutchman stared at him, his mouth half open.

Then the door banged open and everyone swung round. Aris Theocharis blundered in, a grin on his heavy face. Behind him walked Dhimitra, holding her head high. She was wearing a tight red dress that emphasised her breasts and tanned legs. There were dust marks on her front. The couple sat down next to Mikkel at the rear of the bar. As he turned to face forwards again, Mavros caught sight of Eleni and Barbara. Both of the women had their eyes on the barman, their faces set in taut expressions. Rinus didn't seem to be concerned. He leaned across to the sound system and changed the record. The sound of Status Quo made Mavros's mind up for him. He'd find another opportunity to ask Aris and Dhimitra if they'd ever met Rosa.

Outside, the air was warmer than it had been the previous night. The constellations were wheeling across the velvet black dome of the sky and the breeze was light. If Trigono, aka Pesinthos, hadn't been full of crazy people, Mavros could almost have seen the attraction of the place.

12

Mavros slept badly. Although the night was cool, he woke up sweating several times, the top sheet tangled round his limbs. He kept dreaming that he was in the sea, his arms flailing as his legs were impeded by the dark red nets he'd seen on the fishing boats in the harbour. Images flashed before him of a young couple flailing, their naked flesh puckered by the chill water and their mouths open in desperate screams.

The muffled ring of his mobile phone brought him back to reality. He'd left it on overnight in case Niki called before she went to work, placing it under his clothes so that Rena wouldn't hear it. He mumbled an answer.

'That you, dick?' Deniz Ozal's voice was loud, the sound of an announcement in the background. 'Jesus, my ancestors like to shout.'

'It's me,' Mavros replied, fumbling for his watch. It was six in the morning, which explained the absence of light from the slatted shutters. 'You're in Turkey.'

Ozal laughed. 'Pretty sharp, my man. Did I wake you?'

'Don't worry about it. You're paying for a twenty-four-hour service.'

'You got that right, the rates you charge. So, what have you found out?'

'Not much,' Mavros said. 'There's been a tragedy on the island and people aren't in the mood for talking.'

'Couple of kids drowned? I saw that on the news.'

'In Turkey?'

'No, I just got here. I've been in Athens. You don't reckon Rosa could have gone back to Trigono, then?'

'I certainly haven't seen any sign of her. But I'm working on a couple of angles. There's a guy in a bar who remembers her.'

Ozal grunted. 'Yeah, Rosa was a party girl when the mood took her.' He broke off. 'Hey, I've gotta go. I'm being paged. I'll be in touch in a couple of days.'

The connection was cut.

Mavros lay back in the darkness, phone by his side. Yet again Deniz Ozal hadn't seemed very concerned about his missing sister. Still, he was paying the fee and at least he'd finally called in. But Mavros had the feeling his client would choke off the funds after the minimum five days if he didn't come up with something concrete about Rosa. He was going to have to put the squeeze on Rena as soon as he saw her. In the meantime he thought about the other angles he'd mentioned. It seemed that, one way or another, everyone and everything on Trigono were linked to Panos Theocharis. He needed information on the museum benefactor and he knew where to get it. He picked up his phone again and highlighted a number in the address book.

'Anna, good morning.'

'Alex?' His sister's voice was immediately tense. 'What's happened?'

'Calm down. Nothing's happened.' Mavros heard his brother-in-law asking what was going on. 'Tell Nondas to keep his mind on making money.'

'Oh, be quiet. Are you still on Trigono?'

'Yes. Listen, what do you know about the Theocharis family? I had dinner at the old man's place last night.'

'Did you indeed?' Anna sounded interested. 'I hope this is going to be an exchange of information, Alex. Can you give me the low-down on the place? He never allows media people in. It's some kind of medieval tower, isn't it?'

Mavros sighed. Anna's journalistic instincts were irrepressible. 'Yes, it is. All right, I'll tell you all about Paliopyrgos when I get back. What can you give me about Panos Theocharis?'

'Nothing right now.' She paused for him to register annoyance, but he resisted the temptation – she liked to exercise power over him whenever she got the opportunity. 'But you're in luck. I did a story on him for one of the magazines last year. After I've got the children to school, I'll fax you it.'

'E-mail it to me and I'll access my server from here,' Mavros said, remembering the Internet café. 'Thanks, Anna.'

'I'll be expecting lots of gossip in return,' she said with a brittle laugh. 'Don't enjoy the sun too much.'

Mavros put the phone down and looked at the faint grey light that was creeping across the floor. In the distance he could hear the first crows of Trigono's cockerels from the villagers' runs. Getting up, he padded to the shutters and looked through the narrow gap between the slats and into the courtyard. His eyelids sprang wide apart as he saw his landlady standing by the wellhead. Her face was contorted, she held a long-bladed knife in her right hand and she was staring straight at his room.

Mavros bided his time before going out. Rena stood motionless in the yard for over ten minutes, and he had no idea how long she'd been there. As the sky lightened further, she seemed to come back to herself, going into her kitchen and busying herself with what the rich smell suggested was a *baklavas*. It was when she emerged wiping her hands on a cloth, her expression less bleak, that Mavros decided to approach her.

Rena gave a shy smile as he came across the courtyard. 'Good morning, Alex,' she said, stuffing the cloth under her apron.

'Good morning, Rena,' he said, returning her smile.'

Spots of red had appeared on her cheeks. 'You like coffee?' she asked, glancing towards her kitchen. 'I make a honey pastry but it is not ready yet.'

Mavros nodded. 'I would like a Greek coffee, no sugar, thank you. I can wait for whatever it is that you're baking. It smells fantastic.'

Rena stepped away briskly, her demeanour now very different to what it had been earlier. Mavros felt bad about deceiving her, pretending that he didn't know what the sweet filo pastry was. But, as her appearance with the knife had emphasised, she was a complex character. If he was to prise information from her, he'd need all his skills. That Rena was obviously grieving but was still eager to please made him feel even worse. The way that she looked at him suggested that she might have more than just a landlady's interest in him. He wondered if his blue-brown eye had caught her attention as well as Eleni's, and swallowed a groan.

When she came back out with his coffee on a tray, he took the plunge. 'Rena, there's something I want to ask you about. Is this a good time?'

She looked alarmed at his serious tone. 'Of course.' She sat down opposite him at the table under the bougainvillaea. 'What is it, Alex?' she said, her eyes on his.

Mavros smiled to put her at ease. 'I wondered if you'd ever seen this woman on the island.' He held out the folded photograph of Rosa Ozal.

Rena took it and opened it. She tried to dissemble but her lips parted and she blinked several times, one hand rising quickly to the corner of an eye.

'Are you all right?' Mavros asked, leaning forward and watching her carefully.

Rena raised a hand. 'Do not worry,' she said, breathing deeply. 'I . . . I sometimes feel . . . how do you say? Dizzy?'

'I'm sorry,' he said, 'I shouldn't have bothered you with this.' He tried to take the photo from her hand.

She tightened her grip on it. 'No, no,' she said in a low voice. 'Please forgive me, Alex. I have been working in the fields too much these days and the sun is a devil, even at this time of the year.' She looked down at the photograph again. 'Yes, I know this woman,' she said slowly. She raised her head and met his eyes again. 'She stayed in my house.'

'Did she?' Mavros was relieved that Rena had told the truth. But why had she seemed so shocked by the photo? He didn't buy what she said about the effect of the sun. She would have been used to it.

'I remember her name,' Rena continued, her voice still soft. 'Rosa. She was American, I think.'

'That's right,' he said. 'Do you remember when was she here?'

Rena thought about it. 'In June, I think. She stayed for about ten days. If you like, I can check in my book.' She stood up and went to the kitchen. 'The *eforia*, the tax office, makes us keep records,' she said as she came out. 'Most people do not bother, but I like to be careful.' She turned the pages of a large cardboard-covered book. 'Yes, here she is.' She held the book out to him.

'Rosa Ozal,' he read, then stopped. He wasn't supposed to be able to understand Greek. 'What's all this?' he asked, pointing to the handwritten columns.

'Nationality American,' Rena said, leaning forward. 'There is her passport number. Arrived June fifth, left June sixteenth. Paid fifty thousand drachmas in advance.'

Mavros had taken a pen and a small notebook from his pocket and was writing down the dates. He looked back up at her. 'She's a friend of mine,' he explained with a brief smile. 'She recommended that I come to Trigono.'

Rena was studying him and he could almost hear the question she was asking herself. Why was he taking down details about the woman? That was hardly the action of a friend. He put his notebook on the table quickly.

'Can you give me your passport, please?' Rena asked, her voice suddenly more formal. 'I need to write down your name and the number.'

'I . . . I had to leave it at the bank,' he said, the words coming out in a rush. 'I'll give you it tomorrow, all right?' He had only his ID card with him and he didn't want her to see that.

Rena nodded slowly, her eyes questioning. 'Alex,' she said, 'is there something wrong?' She looked at him and it struck him that maybe she was in the same position as he was; maybe she was trying to decide how much to disclose. 'Has something happened to Rosa?'

'She sent a card in June,' he said. 'From Trigono. And then it seems she went to Turkey. But no one who knows her has seen her since she left the US for Greece.'

Rena's eyes were wide, her mouth open. Then she twitched her head and glanced at Mavros nervously. 'Rosa has disappeared?'

Mavros raised his shoulders. 'So it seems.'

'And you are a friend? You are looking for her?' Rena's face was glowing red, her expression almost as pained as it had been at dawn.

He nodded.

'But you said Rosa went to Turkey?' Rena asked. 'Shouldn't you be looking for her there?'

'I thought that maybe she enjoyed herself so much here that she came back. You haven't seen her since June?'

Rena shook her head, her eyes down. There was something about the way she was reacting that Mavros had noticed from the start, something that made him think Rosa meant more to the widow than the average tourist who stayed with her.

'Alex,' she said, raising her eyes to his again. 'There is a man called Rinus. He has a bar called—'

'The Astrapi,' he interrupted. 'Yes, I've been there. And met him.'

'Yes. This Rinus, he and Rosa spent time together.' The words seemed to burn her mouth as she spoke them. 'And Alex? Rosa left Trigono very quickly, before she was going to. I think . . . I think there was some trouble between them.'

He leaned closer. 'Trouble?' he said, his eyes on hers again. 'What kind of trouble?'

Rena raised her shoulders. 'I don't know. Someone told me they were shouting at each other outside the bar. I heard . . . I heard he hit her.'

Mavros thought about the Dutchman and the way he'd spoken openly about Rosa. The barman was very sure of himself despite his small stature. Mavros would have to find a way of using Rena's accusation to shake his confidence.

He took out the photos he'd found in the chimney and pushed

them across the table to the widow. 'Do these mean anything to you?'

Rena examined the photo of the dig, turning it round to see the writing in Rosa's hand on the rear. A look of suspicion that turned into barely suppressed anger came over her face. 'It's where that woman works, the archaeologist,' she said slowly. 'But why was Rosa at . . .' The words trailed away.

'Rosa and Eleni were friends,' Mavros said, remembering the photo he'd seen in the archaeologist's album. He wondered why Rena despised her so much, but he didn't think he'd get an answer to that question. 'Did you know that?'

For a few moments it looked like Rena was going to speak, her mouth opening and closing like a fish's, but she kept silent and glanced at the photo of the war memorial. It was only when she picked up the faded shot of the wartime officer that she found her tongue again.

'George Lawrence,' she said, reading the inscription on the back. 'I know this photograph.' She stared at Mavros. 'Where did you get this?'

'They were all together, in a plastic bag up the chimney in my room. I think Rosa may have put them there.' He was returning her look. 'What do you mean, you know this photograph? You've seen it before?'

'I . . . I don't remember,' the widow said, shaking her head in a way that suggested confusion – or the attempt to imply it. She glared at him. 'Why were you looking up my chimney? It is not for you to do that.'

Mavros gave an embarrassed shrug. 'I saw the edge of the plastic bag hanging down,' he lied. 'Rena, was Rosa interested in this man?' He held up the portrait. 'Did she ask you about him?'

She shook her head emphatically. 'No, but—' She broke off.

'You said Rosa went in a hurry. Did she leave anything behind?'

Rena felt the force of his eyes and looked down. 'No, nothing,' she mumbled.

He reckoned she might be lying. That was something else he'd have to follow up. 'All right,' he said, standing up and moving away from the table. 'Oh, one more thing. I heard that you are the village librarian. You look after the books.'

His landlady looked up and nodded. 'Yes, I look after the books. Nobody else wanted to do it and I like to read when I have time.' She shook her head. 'But it is not for you. There is nothing in English.'

Mavros realised the flaw in his plan. As long as he maintained the guise of foreigner, he couldn't ask her about the dead historian Vlastos's book. This was getting complicated.

'Oh,' he said, giving a disappointed shrug. 'I wanted to find out more about the island.'

Rena raised her chin in a negative movement. 'I am sorry. There is nothing for you in the library.'

The small birds were drilling and darting between the branches. Mavros felt the widow's eyes follow him across the yard to his room. His questions had yielded some useful answers, but he was convinced that Rena knew more about Rosa Ozal than she'd admitted. He'd also seen new and disturbing sides of his landlady's nature. In the later part of the morning she'd been evasive; while earlier she'd stood in the cold grey of dawn, clutching a large knife and staring across the courtyard at his room – the room that Rosa Ozal had once occupied.

Later Mavros sat at a table in the shade of the main square's mulberry tree, riffling through the sheaf of pages he'd printed out in the Internet café. The barman had tried to look over his shoulder at the article Anna had sent, which drove him away. The last thing Mavros needed was Theocharis being informed that the foreigner he thought might be an antiquities thief was reading a profile of him.

Although his sister wrote for magazines that he rarely read because their glossy fashion pages and envy-fuelled gossip columns depressed him, Anna was a talented journalist with a knack for unearthing things her subjects would have preferred to remain out of the public domain. Mavros had eventually realised that he had more in common with her than he thought. Reading the in-depth article, he found himself admiring her piercing wit almost as much as the details yielded by her research. Panos Theocharis, 'a businessman who combines the acumen of Onassis with the moray eel's ability to make snap decisions', was generously praised for his charity work and the establishment of the museum – although Anna made it clear that his core business activities had hardly suffered from the free advertising and profile-raising engendered by these activities. There was a fair amount about how Theocharis had expanded the family mining business across the world after the war, but this was less interesting to Mavros than the information his sister had dug out about the family. It seemed that many of the lurid stories peddled by the gutter press were true.

For instance, Aris, the only child that Theocharis had fathered on his three wives, had written off more cars and needed more hush money than a dozen other tycoons' spoiled sons. The old man had been forced to send his son to New York when he was in his twenties to keep him away from the Athenian police as well as the media. He was overseen by a company of very discreet and very expensive lawyers, but stories had slipped out about sessions in drinking clubs with well-known hoodlums. No one took any of that seriously – Aris was perceived to be too much of a buffoon to become a serious criminal himself. But that hadn't stopped him picking on people smaller than himself. One indiscretion that the lawyers failed to suppress was made public by a nightclub hostess who sold her story detailing a night of sexual and physical abuse to a New York tabloid. Aris had shown no remorse. He remained defiant and was apparently proud of the fact that his low-life friends referred to him as 'Kojak', alopecia having caused his hair to fall out in his early thirties.

There was no mud like that on Panos Theocharis. He had apparently been a devoted enough husband to his first two wives, although neither of them had lasted the course. The first, Aris's mother, died of cirrhosis in 1970. The second had been killed in a road accident, her Mercedes shunted off a hairpin bend near the family's house in Gstaad by a car that was never traced. The post-mortem found a large quantity of diazepam in her stomach. Both of the women had been Athenian heiresses and it seemed that Theocharis, in his seventies when he became a widower for the second time, had decided to marry beyond the confines of his class.

Mavros slapped his thigh when he realised who the old man had chosen. He knew there had been something familiar about Aris's stepmother and, as he'd seen outside the Astrapi, lover Dhimitra. Fifteen years ago she'd been the popular singer Mimi, whose heavily made-up face adorned hoardings all over Athens. Mavros couldn't remember the name of any of her hits – she had been a purveyor of eardrum-bursting love songs to the tone deaf – but he remembered her blowsy, come-hither poses. Unsurprisingly she hadn't been accepted into Athenian high society with open arms. That was why Theocharis and she spent most of the year on Trigono.

Mavros ran his fingers through the pages when he finished the article. The material about Aris and Dhimitra was revealing, but there were some things about the old man that he found more intriguing. The first concerned the museum and the acquisition of the numerous pieces he'd bought. Anna quoted an expert at one of the great international auction houses, who stated that there had never been even a hint of malpractice or illicit dealing by Theocharis, something that was apparently very unusual with private museums. Mavros reckoned that had to be horse shit, especially in Greece. The fact that Theocharis had apparently suspected him of being a thief or a bent dealer only made him more suspicious – it took one to know one. Anna also pointed out that the family had recently been hit by several business failures around the world, though she didn't specify them or say how serious they'd been to the overall Theocharis fortune.

The other thing that struck him was what Anna had written about Theocharis's activities during the Second World War. He had served with a specially trained unit that had been in action in the Cyclades and the Peloponnese. Although few records were available, there were rumours at the time that his activities had led to unacceptably high losses – of Allied as well as enemy personnel. Coupled with the fact that the book about Trigono during the Italian occupation by the Paros historian had disappeared from the library, this hint of savagery beneath the millionaire's urbane surface made Mavros even more curious.

Now he was more keen than ever to learn whether Theocharis or his unruly son had met Rosa Ozal.

The woman woke up and knew immediately that something had been done to her. She sniffed the air and picked up a chemical smell, the residue of an oil-based fuel. The only light in the hole or cave or wherever she was being held was the grey line in front of her, the faint, tantalising hint of a world outside. She moved her hands, feeling the rope bite but also aware of the numbness throughout her body. Scrabbling on the gritty floor, she tried to locate the water bottle. Nothing. Her throat was parched and she could hear the rumble of her empty stomach. It was difficult to calculate the passage of time. She thought it was at least a day since she'd drunk or eaten. But she hadn't been abandoned. The cloying smell and the pain between her legs proved that. She moved her fingers towards her groin then stopped them, frightened of what they might find. Dragging herself as far away as she could from where she'd been lying, she emptied her bladder and felt a stinging sensation.

She stilled her breath and listened hard, tried to pick up any clue to where she was. There was a gentle soughing of wind coming from the line of light and, farther off, a current of what must have been water, a great body of water in restless motion. The sea, yes, it was the sea, but it wasn't so close, she wasn't in a sea cave. It made her think of a beach and a coastline again, but she couldn't place them, couldn't conjure up a name.

'What's happening to me?' she said aloud, her voice hoarse and cracked. She smelled the rankness of her breath. 'Who brought me here?'

She struggled with her memory, dredging up a flight on an

aeroplane, vile food and the stewardesses with their noses in the air. But she could bring back nothing of where she'd come from or where she'd been going, no names or faces of people she'd met, no landscapes other than the beach that had appeared to her. Was she on an island?

Then the idea hit her like a kick in the stomach, the sudden, unreasoning fear that whoever was keeping her captive had decided not to give her anything else to eat or drink. She tried to scream, but she was already falling into an even blacker hole.

Just before it closed around her she was sure that she heard the notes of a pipe and, farther away, the muffled barking of what sounded like more than one dog.

Out of the corner of his eye Mavros noticed a person approaching him. He quickly folded up the printed pages.

'Hello, Alex.'

The German stood smiling, a faded Ferrari cap on his head. He gave the impression of a lost child, unsure whether to approach a stranger.

'Ah, Mikkel,' he said. 'Good morning. On your own?'

The older man set down the blue plastic bags of shopping he was carrying and nodded distractedly. 'Barbara's at the house.' He said the words as if they were a standard response rather than one he had much faith in.

'Is she working?' Mavros asked, taking in the German's nervous expression. He remembered Barbara's nudge in Mikkel's ribs when he had asked them about Rosa Ozal. Maybe this was the time to exert some pressure on the couple's weaker link.

'Yes.' Mikkel took off his cap and smoothed down his thinning fair hair. 'She works on her designs in the morning. I leave her on her own.'

Mavros gave him an encouraging smile. 'It must be difficult, submitting designs and so on from Trigono.'

Mikkel shrugged. 'It's all right now. We have a computer, e-mail and so on. It wasn't so easy in the past.' He looked away, lower lip between his teeth. 'But she has her reasons for living on the island.'

Mavros was pretty sure that, whatever those reasons were, they weren't all shared by her husband. 'It must be tricky for foreign women in a small community like this.'

Mikkel's eyes jerked back on to him. 'What do you mean?'

'Well,' Mavros said, nodding towards a pair of muscle-bound young islanders in cement-stained clothes, 'the local men view foreign women as easy targets, don't they?'

The German's face flushed. 'I . . . I don't know where you get that idea from,' he said, turning his head away again. 'Anyway, Barbara is quite capable of looking after herself when I'm not here.'

'Oh, you aren't here all the time?'

Mikkel shook his head. 'I am required to attend board meetings and finalise the accounts every month. I'm going to Hamburg next week.'

'So were you actually on the island in the first half of June?' Mavros asked, keeping up the attack. 'When my friend Rosa was here.' He was watching the German carefully and noticed that his eyes widened when the name was spoken.

'Em, yes, yes, I think so.' Mikkel glanced at him anxiously, as if he might have given something away. 'We told you, we didn't meet her.'

Mavros took out the photo and held it up in front of him. 'Are you quite sure? Only, Rinus told me she was in the Bar Astrapi several times. You go there often, don't you?'

Mikkel gathered up his shopping bags. 'I have to get home now. Barbara will be wondering what's happened to me.' He looked at Mavros, the lines on his face taut. 'You shouldn't believe everything Rinus tells you,' he said in a low voice. Then he moved quickly away across the square.

Mavros watched him go. Was Mikkel just a jealous husband or was there something more disturbing beneath the timorous exterior? No, Barbara Hoeg was obviously the strong one in that couple. He had the feeling the world-famous designer was capable of anything if she put her mind to it. But she was a troubled person beneath the hard shell, and he had the feeling that she drank to escape.

At the corner the German almost collided with Aris Theocharis. They spoke for a few seconds, the big man shooting a glance at Mavros and then heading towards him. He was wearing loose cream chinos and boating shoes, the green eyeshade he favoured splitting his egg-like head in two horizontally.

'You again,' Aris said as he approached the table. He sat down opposite Mavros without waiting for an invitation. 'How did you get on with my father last night? I'll bet the old man dazzled you with his precious possessions, didn't he?' He gazed across the table with a belligerent grin that faded slightly when Mavros didn't answer. Leaning forward, he lowered his voice. 'Someone told me you're a friend of a woman called Rosa.'

'That's right,' Mavros replied, wondering who that 'someone' was. Rinus the barman? 'Her full name's Rosa Ozal. Do you know her?'

Aris shook his head. 'Not personally.' The grin widened. 'Not carnally.' He paused to see Mavros's reaction, but there was none. 'I wasn't here when she was. But I heard a lot about her.'

'Really? You've got a bit of an American accent. Have you spent time in the USA?'

Aris looked at him thoughtfully. 'Yeah, I have. Office in Manhattan. Why?'

'Well, Rosa's from New York City too. You never ran into—'

Aris was shaking his head. 'I told you, I never met her.' The grin reappeared. 'But she got very friendly with a lot of people here, I can tell you.'

'Is that right?' Mavros said. 'Who, for example? I can't find many people who remember her, apart from Rinus in the Astrapi.' He kept quiet about Rena.

Aris suddenly looked less assured. 'I don't know about that,' he mumbled, looking away.

Mavros decided against showing any more of his hand by winkling out second-hand information from the tycoon's son.

'Hey, wanna see my boat?' the big man asked, grabbing Mavros's arm. 'Come on, you'll like it. Where are you from? The fucked-up old UK? You haven't got anything like her there, I can tell you.'

Mavros shook off Aris's grip and picked up his bag. 'All right,' he said. 'Why not?'

The large four-by-four was parked in the street off the square. As Aris climbed in, he waved at the shopkeeper opposite. The wizened old man acknowledged the greeting, but scowled as soon as Theocharis's back was turned. The son didn't get anything like the degree of respect from the islanders that his father did.

Aris drove down the narrow tiled street, ignoring the 'No Entry' signs and forcing pedestrians – women with buggies, a tourist with a rucksack – to press against the walls. 'Out of the way, *gria*,' he said, gesticulating at a bent old woman in black.

Mavros said nothing. There was no shortage of loudmouthed rich men's heirs in Athens, but they were less incongruous there. Aris Theocharis stuck out on Trigono like a slug in a salad.

'There she is,' the driver said, pointing as they swung into the port. 'Forty feet of glory.'

Mavros followed his arm to the *kaïki* that was bobbing on the light swell at the quayside. Its hull and large cabin were blue and white respectively, the mast and rigging in perfect condition. It looked like an old boat that had been expertly renovated, the general layout being that of the craft that used to carry freight between the islands before the large ferries started operating.

'*Artemis*,' Mavros read from the bow.

'My daughter,' Aris said, jumping down.

'How old is she?'

The big man glanced at him. 'Thirteen, fourteen. I don't see her much. Her mother's a bitch who made the mistake of thinking I'd stay with her for life.' He laughed as he hauled on the mooring rope. 'Jump on. I'll give you the tour.'

Mavros made the small leap and held the rope to enable Aris to join him. He wasn't much of an enthusiast of boats – like children and cars, they required you to lift the toilet lid and pour in your bank account – but he could see that the *Artemis* had unusual charm. The wood on the deck was stained a deep brown, and through the windows he made out a well-appointed cabin below.

'Superb, isn't she?' Aris said, running his hand along the gunwale. 'I wish I could spend more time on her.'

Mavros was looking at the mast. 'You don't sail her, though?'

'Uh-uh. Engine only. Beautiful new Volvo. Gives her plenty of power and range.'

Mavros nodded. 'I imagine. Were you on a trip a couple of days ago? She wasn't here the day I arrived.'

'Ah, no,' the younger Theocharis said, glancing beyond him towards another boat. 'No, I had her in the yard over on Paros. They brought her back yesterday.'

Mavros didn't ask what the *Artemis* had been in for. Before he embarked, he'd noticed a section on the waterline amidships with fresh blue paint, the wood smoother than the other planking. He remembered what the men on the ferry had said about the scrape along the side of the boat the young drowned couple had been on – according to them, there had been traces of blue in the wood.

Then he saw where Aris was looking.

The old, one-armed man Manolis was staring across the water at them from the deck of the *trata Sotiria*, his heavily built son Lefteris also fixing them with his eyes as he coiled a rope. The faces of the two islanders expressed a barely concealed hostility that made Mavros shiver in the bright sunlight.

13

It didn't take long for Aris to lose interest in showing off the *Artemis* to Mavros. His mood changed from effusive to irritable, though Mavros couldn't be sure how much this had been brought about by the sullen stares of Manolis and his son Lefteris. Leaving the port, he headed up the main street to the OTE to run a check on Aris's boat.

The telephone office was located in a cubby-hole in the northern wall of the *kastro*, a guy with a grizzled moustache behind the counter. Mavros spotted the local Golden Guide behind him and pointed to it. There were several boatyards listed on Paros, most of them under the names of their owners. There was only one with a company name, Blue Wave Dock SA in Naoussa. He wrote down all the numbers and went outside to call the first one on his mobile, looking around to check there was no one in the vicinity.

'Blue Wave Dock,' came a languid female voice.

'Yes, good day,' Mavros said in Greek. 'This is Worldwide Marine Insurance in Piraeus. I understand that you recently undertook repair work on behalf of Mr Aris Theocharis.' He was taking a chance that the big man would have taken his precious *kaïki* to what looked like the most professional operation on Paros.

'That is correct,' the woman answered after a pause, responding to Mavros's formal language with a marked increase in courtesy. 'How may I help?'

'No doubt we'll shortly be receiving the documents from the insured, but I would be grateful if you could give me a run-down of the work you carried out.' Mavros moved into the centre of

the square to distance himself from a pair of voluble Italian
tourists.

'Certainly,' came the reply. 'Kindly give me your fax number.'

'I require an outline on the telephone,' Mavros said in the firm
tone used by business people to prevail over minor functionaries.
'Now, if you please.'

There was a pause and then the sound of fingers tapping on
a keyboard. 'Yes, here we are, Mr . . . what did you say your
name was?'

'Mitsotakis,' Mavros said without hesitation. Using the family
name of the country's last right-wing prime minister would keep
the woman on her toes.

'Mr Mitsotakis,' the woman repeated slowly, clearly impressed.
The tactic had worked – it usually did with employees in private
companies. Civil servants needed a different approach after
years of socialist government. 'The work carried out on Mr
Theocharis's boat was put in hand immediately. Remove and
replace section of hull measuring one point five by nought
point four metres, bond joints, seal and paint new section. The
total cost—'

'That does not concern me at this stage,' Mavros interrupted.
'I need to know how the damage to the hull occurred in case of
litigation.'

'Surely your client will furnish you with the relevant details,'
the woman said.

'Yes, but I need your company's appraisal,' Mavros said
coldly.

There was another pause as the woman shouted for someone
called Mikis. A conversation ensued that Mavros couldn't make
out. Finally the woman came back to the phone. 'Apparently there had been heavy contact with another vessel. There
were traces of white paint in the damaged section. If Mr
Theocharis hadn't brought the boat in promptly, the gradual
influx of water would have given rise to serious danger of
sinking.'

'Thank you,' Mavros said. 'I'll make sure that your cooperation in this matter is noted.'

'Thank you, Mr Mitsotakis. Good day, and please remember us whenever—'

Mavros cut the connection and sat down under the mulberry tree. When he'd been on the *Artemis* he had managed to cast an eye over the *trata* the young couple had been on. Its hull had not been as seriously damaged as Aris's, but there was enough of an abrasion to suggest there had indeed been heavy contact. The likelihood of Aris having run into a different white boat didn't seem overwhelming. But did that mean he had some involvement in the drownings? If so, why had the men of the dead boy's family stared at him rather than confronting him? Maybe they'd been paid off.

Head bowed in thought, Mavros started walking. He had come to Trigono to find a missing woman, but it seemed that this was only one of several curious issues: the drownings, Aris's damaged boat, the war memorial with the erased name, the photos linking Eleni the archaeologist to Rosa Ozal, the photos and the diskette that seemed to link Rosa to the wartime officer George Lawrence and to the dig – the dig which was on old man Theocharis's land. Things seemed to lead back to Panos Theocharis. He even found himself wondering if his client Deniz Ozal could be tied up with everything – after all, he was an antiquities dealer and he'd visited the notorious operator Tryfon Roufos in Athens. Not only that, his sister Rosa worked in a gallery back in Manhattan. Did either of the Ozals know one or other of the Theocharis men?

It was time Mavros found out more about the museum benefactor's activities on the island, and he knew where he was going to start. But there was someone else he wanted to question first.

December 19th, 1942

Suddenly how different it all is. Hiding from the Italians has been easy enough. They've only been as far as the village since I landed, and then just for a few hours each week to buy provisions at rates that

*are highly unfavourable to the Trigoniotes. But now I'm also having
to conceal part of my activities from Ajax and from the leader of the
Greek Sacred Band unit that has arrived. I'm sure that Ajax, who is
limping but mobile again, suspects that I have been up to something
that his family wouldn't approve of with Maro. I'm also sure that
Captain Th. would insist on my immediate replacement if he found
me involved with a local woman. He is a stickler for discipline who
doesn't cut his four men any slack at all. I can tell by the way he
looks at me, his eyes hooded and reserved, and by the formal way
he addresses me that he resents my presence on the island.*

*For it seems that Captain Th. – Agamemnon is the code-name
he has been allocated – is a local of sorts himself, although he only
spent the summers here when he was a boy. Apparently his father
owns the large estate beneath Vigla. Its eastern extent is on the other
side of the track from my hut in the Kambos. The old man is close
to death in a clinic in Athens, which means that the captain, an
only child, stands to inherit the wide stretch of cultivated land as
well as the land above it, not that the worked-out mine shafts and
the cave systems around them are worth much now. To say that
Agamemnon regards the island with a seigneurial eye would be to
indulge in the grossest of understatements. On the other hand, the
islanders seem to respect him: even Ajax, who has never concealed
his communist leanings from me.*

*My life has become much more complicated with the arrival of
the Greeks. The main problem is that my mission and Agamemnon's
have not been properly coordinated. Every time I call base, I am
instructed to proceed with sabotage operations on Paros and the
neighbouring islands. A good stock of explosives and other equipment
has now been landed at Vathy, and I have lugged a fair amount of
the former up to the caves on Vigla myself. The question is, what do
we do with it? Ever since Agamemnon and his men set up camp in
the sheltered watercourses above Vathy, Ajax seems to have lost his
appetite for action. Maybe the good captain is set against hostilities
or maybe the injury to Ajax's leg has made him think long and hard
about the potential effects of operations against the enemy – which
are reprisals against the local population. My God, I'm aware of*

that consequence too. How could I not be? The idea of anything happening to Maro keeps me awake through the darkness after she has gone. But I was sent to Trigono to do a job and I can't ignore my orders.

Ah, Maro, we have been unlucky to find ourselves in love at this time of blood and fury! But then, we would never have found each other in peacetime. Even if I'd stopped off on this wave-lapped, gull-haunted island, I would never have been able to get close to you. Although it is now fraught with danger because of the influx of men trained in watch-keeping and observation techniques, we have still managed to meet. Now you take your donkey to the Kambos every morning to work the isolated strips of land that are part of your dowry, and you slip away for an hour to the secret place we have taken over. They never last for long, but I live for those times when we take refuge from the hostile outside world and lose ourselves in each other. Ah, Maro, how I worship your perfect body that bursts with such a frenzy of youth when I cling to it! How I rejoice in your breasts, small but ripe, and your white thighs that press so tightly to mine when I die in you, the tears dripping from my eyes and mingling with those you are already shedding for the beauty of our love.

But these interludes of bliss cannot continue. I saw a movement on the ridge leading to Profitis Ilias when we parted today. Whether it was one of Ajax's men or a lookout posted by Agamemnon doesn't matter. Sooner or later we will be seen. But I don't care. My intentions towards Maro are honourable. I would marry her tomorrow if the custom allowed it. My love for her has made me more alive than I've ever been before. Passion may blind men, but I am in complete control of myself. I will push ahead with the mission I have been planning with or without the help of the Greeks.

Outside, the night is still. The wind that has been blowing hard from the north these last few days is finally exhausted. In the distance I can hear the run of the sea and the faint clang of goat bells up on the heights.

The blood is coursing through my veins like liquid fire. Ah, Greece! It is time for me to strike a blow against the oppressor. Everything has come together. I feel that all my life has been leading up to this glorious act. I cannot die. I shall become one of the immortals. I shall live for ever. With Maro.

Mavros followed the narrow street into the *kastro* and went up the steps to Rinus's flat. Although he could hear music playing at low volume, there was no answer to his knocking. He couldn't be sure, but he thought he picked up the sound of careful footsteps behind the door. There was a crack in the panelling and he saw a shadowy movement through it. An image was flickering on the screen of a large television, and to the side of it he could see a pile of video cassettes. It seemed that the barman wasn't receiving visitors – or perhaps he just wasn't receiving Mavros. Short of breaking the door down, there wasn't much he could do.

He headed back past Rena's house, skirting a heap of fresh donkey droppings, towards a car and bike hire place he'd noticed earlier. Although the sun was high in the sky, its rays making the back of his neck tingle, he'd made his mind up – no motorised transport. The island was already too redolent of diesel and tractor oil. He pointed to the solitary mountain bike outside the ramshackle office and made a deal that didn't strain his wallet. The broad-girthed girl watched him with ill-disguised contempt as he checked the tyre pressures and adjusted the seat height. Push-bikes were for kids or demented tourists – sensible people drove.

Mavros cycled out past the Bar Astrapi, feeling his thigh muscles stretch. The bike was in surprisingly good condition; there probably hadn't been much call for it over the summer. He was going out to the dig to surprise Eleni. He reckoned she was as good a lead to Theocharis as any, despite her antagonism towards Mavros after he'd spurned her advances. But more important, the photo in the album proved that she knew Rosa Ozal. He wasn't planning on confronting her over that until he'd regained her confidence, but he was curious. Why had she been lying to him?

He freewheeled down the slope to the Kambos, glancing to

the right as he passed the farm where he'd seen the donkey being beaten. This time there was no sign either of the old bastard with the stick or of the sad-eyed creature. He remembered reading in a Greek novel at school about an island farmer who drove his decrepit mule over a cliff with a big stone lashed around it when it could no longer work. The thought that the animal he'd tried to save may have suffered that fate made him shiver.

At a dusty junction in the middle of the Kambos, Mavros saw an old church, the whitewash fresh on its walls but the stonework beneath heavily pockmarked. He stopped and dismounted, rubbing the backs of his legs. He took the guidebook from his bag. The Theocharis estate, the old tower hovering in the haze, was farther to the west. This had to be Ayios Dhimitrios, the church that once served the deserted village of Myli where the windmills to grind the corn produced in the fertile plateau had been built. Now the two round structures were only a single storey high, the upper walls collapsed around their bases. Going closer to the church, Mavros examined the holes around the door. There were a lot of them, some narrow and deep, the other indentations more spread out. They looked very like they'd been made by bullets of varying sizes. Glancing back at the ruined mills, he wondered if there had been action here during the war.

Behind Ayios Dhimitrios a narrow path wound between two high walls to a graveyard. Mavros clambered over the remains of the gate and walked around between uneven metal crosses and dirt-encrusted marble slabs. The place was almost completely overgrown, the crops of mallow and thistles that had leaped up in spring now brown and withered. No one had been buried here for a long time. Over in the corner was the ossuary. He moved towards it, stepping over the desiccated vegetation, and forced the door open. Like the graveyard, it was no longer in use. Only one tin box rested in the corner. He kneeled down in front of it and wiped the dust away. A cross had been painted on the top, along with the name Eirene Kasdhagli and the dates 1917–1937. Just a girl, he thought. Only twenty when she died, her bones abandoned to moulder here alone.

He pulled the door shut behind him and left the young woman's remains in peace. Maybe Rena would know something about her. Walking back between the stunted crosses, he caught sight of a low hut about twenty metres away, the wall facing him completely shattered and the end walls leaning inwards like the converging sides of a triangle. It looked like the building had been blown out by some explosive device. He shook his head, wondering what had happened in Myli.

Back on the bicycle, Mavros followed an asphalt road southwards, the great curtain of the hills looming. Up on Profitis Ilias – the Prophet Elijah – he could see the customary chapel on the highest point whence, according to the scriptures, the holy man ascended to heaven. The breeze carried the undulating sound of a pipe to him. Stopping for a moment, he made out a figure surrounded by grey, black and white shapes on the flank of the hill. Maybe it was the simple lad he had met the other day. There was nothing simple about his music. The notes soared and danced like birdsong.

The road became a heavily potholed track. Mavros went along it to the west, where it eventually joined up with the ascent to the dig. He stopped to catch his breath and lifted his eyes to the wall of scarred rock that rose up from the lower, bush-dotted slopes. He saw a couple of other figures ahead and rubbed the dust from his eyes with his forearm to look more closely. They were behind an outcrop about two hundred metres from the level area of the dig, their heads craning to the west. He followed the direction of their gaze and two more people came into view. This pair were moving around each other like fighters eyeing up an opponent. With a shock, Mavros realised that the one dressed in a black blouse and skirt was his landlady Rena. Suddenly she went into a clinch with the other figure.

Mavros left the bike by the side of the track and started to run up the incline, his breath catching in his throat. After what seemed like a lot more than the minute that he calculated from his watch, he came within shouting range of the antagonists. He ignored the two observers behind the rocks and focused on

Rena. She was still grappling with her opponent, who was now kneeling.

'Rena!' he bellowed. 'What are you doing?' He moved forward again.

The black-clad woman let go of the other person and watched as he approached.

'What's going on?' he demanded. 'Rinus?' he said in surprise as the barman straightened up, his jeans torn at the knee. If he was out here, who'd been watching a video in his flat? 'What the hell is going on?' He glanced over his shoulder and saw a single head above the rocky bluff to the left – the other watcher had ducked out of sight. To the rear of Rena a donkey stood with a wooden saddle on its back, its head lowered over a patch of thistles. A high-powered motorbike was on its side behind Rinus.

Rena's face was red, her arms still extended towards her opponent. 'This man is a pig, Alex,' she said. 'He nearly . . . he nearly hit my donkey.'

Rinus laughed breathlessly. 'Pity you weren't on it, bitch,' he said in a low voice.

Mavros looked at the animal again and realised that it was the one he'd seen being beaten. The marks of the old man's stick were still visible on its thin flanks. At least it was still alive, although it didn't seem to be endowed with much luck.

'Are you all right, Rena?' he asked, stepping between them.

She nodded, her eyes defiant. 'Oh yes, I'm all right, Alex. But if you hadn't come, I would have crushed this *skouliki*, this worm, into the dirt.'

Mavros glanced at the Dutchman. Although his eyes were also belligerent, he was hanging back and it was pretty clear that Rena would have got the better of him. 'Maybe you should climb back on your bike and hit the road, my friend,' he said.

Rinus took up the suggestion quickly, struggling to right the BMW 750 and then mounting it. Once he was on it and had kicked the engine into life, he leaned towards them. '*Tha se kapso, poutana,*' he said to Rena, mangling the Greek words.

I'll burn you, whore. Then he revved hard and shot off down the steep track.

Mavros watched the dust cloud as it drifted away over the fields of the Kambos, then turned his eyes to the outcrop of rock. Two figures were now on their way down from it, both of them in white shirt and shorts. He recognised the American couple, Gretchen and Lance. Neither of them was looking in his direction. He would catch up with them later.

'That wasn't just about the donkey, was it, Rena?' he said, watching as she ran her hand down the creature's neck.

She held her eyes on him for a few seconds. 'Well . . . the donkey was part of it. I'm very . . . how do you say? . . . sensible?'

Mavros smiled. 'Yes, you're very sensible, but right now I think you mean sensitive.'

Rena's cheeks reddened again. 'Yes, sensitive. I am very sensitive about poor Melpo. Some *bastardhos* has been hitting her.'

Mavros decided to keep what he knew about this to himself.

'You see, I keep her in a field in the Kambos when I'm not using her. I think old Thodhoris likes to think she is me. That family doesn't like me.'

Mavros nodded slowly. 'I saw a man there.' He remembered the scene outside the cemetery. 'Is he another brother of Kyra Maro? He looks like Manolis.'

Rena looked at him thoughtfully and inclined her head. 'Yes, they are brothers. You are very clever, Alex. Already you have learned much about the island.'

He raised his shoulders, trying to conceal his interest. Why did the family of the old woman Maro dislike her? Because she helped the relative they shunned?

She led the donkey gently on to the track, head tilted up. 'I must do my work now,' she said.

'What work have you got up here?' Mavros asked.

'There are some small fields farther on.' Her chin jutted forward. 'They belong to Kyra Maro. I work them to grow food for

Melpo.' She stroked the donkey's sparse mane. 'What are you doing on the hills, Alex?' she asked, her eyes on his.

'I'm a tourist, remember?' He smiled. 'I'm touring the island.'

She nodded, her face blank. 'Of course.' She turned away up the track, the donkey's hooves kicking up grit and small stones. 'Goodbye.'

Mavros watched her go then raised his eyes towards the rocks that concealed the excavated area. The bulky figure of the watchman Mitsos was there, staring down at him. After meeting his gaze for a while, Mavros started walking towards the dig. Several things puzzled him about the stand-off between his landlady and the barman. Rena hadn't answered his question and he was sure there was more between them than Melpo's hide. She had spoken about Rinus to him in unflattering terms before. What was the Dutchman doing up here? Had he been to see Eleni? Or Mitsos? And was he in the flat when Mavros knocked? Rinus might just have been able to make it out here before him on the BMW, though he hadn't seen or heard the bike on the other roads in the Kambos. Finally, what had the Americans been doing hiding behind the rocks? They had watched Rena and Rinus square up, but they hadn't intervened.

As he went to find Eleni, the element of surprise lost now that the watchman had spotted him, Mavros failed to come up with any answers. Life on Trigono was getting more complicated by the hour.

Panos Theocharis was sitting in the shade by the pool, his eyes on the naked and oiled torso of his wife. Dhimitra, supine on a lounger, was well aware of his gaze. She gave him a lazy look then slid her hand down her belly and under the fabric of the sarong she was wearing on the lower half of her body.

'Where is Aris?' she asked in a low voice.

Theocharis knew she was taunting him. The same thing happened every September. His son came to Trigono and blundered around antagonising people, sticking his nose where it wasn't wanted – and screwing Dhimitra. Panos didn't blame his wife for taking advantage of a functioning male organ. He couldn't get hard these days. Even the most extreme videos that his supplier dredged up from the backstreets around Omonia had little effect. And when Aris wasn't around, Dhimitra comforted herself with the servants and estate workers, and with young male tourists whose initial delight at their good fortune was soon replaced by admissions of their inadequacy – for Dhimitra only liked men who gave it to her without any kind of reserve. Maybe, Theocharis reflected, he should be proud that his son was one of the few men who could satisfy her. But he wasn't. Aris was a braggart and a waster who was bleeding the family dry.

'Where is Aris?' he repeated, getting up and shuffling over to the belvedere with his stick. 'How would I know, woman? The idiot is probably entertaining a bevy of tourist bitches on the *Artemis*.' He regretted the outburst immediately. There was no point in trying to make Dhimitra jealous. She was ruled by her appetites and, underneath the patina of wealth that he'd given her, she was coarser than a three-client-an-hour Piraeus tart. But that was what had led him to her. He'd got so sick of the society women at the gallery openings and the weekend villa parties with their refined accents and their alley-cat morals. At least Dhimitra was open about her needs. Unlike his first wife Tatiana. Latterly Aris's mother had fallen for a communist and was soon opening her legs in the name of fraternal goodwill for any comrade who raised an eyebrow at her.

'Pano,' his third wife called. 'Come and sit by me.'

'In a minute,' Theocharis said, wondering what she wanted from him now. He looked out over the estate, the silver-green leaves of the olive trees below the tower trembling in the breeze. In the distance he could see the white blur of the village against the southern cliffs of Paros. He blinked, feeling the strain on his eyes, and focused on objects at closer range. The roof of Eleni's house was visible through the foliage of the orange trees.

That made him think about the archaeologist. She'd been behaving strangely in recent months, even more so in the last few days. What had she been doing showing that foreigner around the dig? Alex – what was his other name? – Alex Cochrane, that was it. There was something very wrong about him. First Theocharis had taken him for a common thief or a dealer, but he didn't display any sign of cold-blooded calculation when confronted by the collection. So what was he? An undercover ministry official? You could usually see through them in a matter of minutes. No, the man was smooth, his smoothness was too well practised. He definitely wasn't the innocent writer on holiday that he purported to be. Not that writers were ever innocent in Theocharis's experience. They were even more single-minded in their search for profitable material than antiquities dealers, and much more two-faced. What was it about his surname? Cochrane. It had set off an alarm bell deep in his mind the moment he heard it.

'Pano,' Dhimitra said, her voice more strident. 'Come here.'

Theocharis moved back, dragging his sandals on the shining tiles. He knew this was going to hurt in some way.

'Pano,' she said as he sat down in the chair next to her lounger. Her hand slid over his knee. 'I want to go into the village tonight.'

'But you've only just come back from the village,' he complained. 'There's no life in the place now. The season's over and the restaurants and bars are all closing.'

A smile crept across her glossed lips. 'Most of the places are shut, it's true. But I know one or two that are still lively.'

'Well, don't be too late,' Theocharis said, giving up the fight. There was no question of him going, he knew that well enough. When Dhimitra expressed a wish to taste Trigono's night life, she never included him in her plans. All he could hope was that she'd be discreet, and that she wasn't falling back into old, destructive habits. No doubt she would be going with Aris, and he certainly wasn't capable of upholding the family's dignity.

A servant appeared, keeping his eyes off Dhimitra's bare flesh.

'A vodka and tonic,' she said, eyeing the young man up.

'Iced water,' Theocharis said. He dismissed the boy with a movement of his head.

His wife was watching him. 'You're so sharp with them,' she said. 'If you're going to turn the islanders into slaves, you might at least be polite to them.'

The museum benefactor turned away. Whenever his wife started lecturing him about how to behave, he conjured up a vision he'd had of her in the dressing room at the nightclub not long after he'd started taking her out. The door had swung open and he'd walked in on her with the bouzouki player from her band, her red taffeta skirt halfway up her back and her upper body bent forward over a chair. He couldn't identify the orifice the musician had penetrated, but whichever one it was, Dhimitra was grunting in delirious abandon.

Anyway, he had more important things than social graces on his mind. It was time to decide what to do about this supposed writer, Alex Cochrane. Apparently he'd been asking questions about Rosa Ozal, and that made Theocharis even more suspicious. Mitsos had just called to say the snoop was on the track leading to the dig, along with several other people. He needed to talk to the watchman about how to handle this. Whatever was going on, Eleni had some explaining to do. Christ and the Holy Mother, he appealed silently. What was it about women? They were all the same – Dhimitra, Eleni, Rosa Ozal, that other one with the tight face and the superb body. Why could they never keep their painted, faithless mouths shut?

But at least they gave him something to think about, something to take his mind off the feelings he had begun to experience from reading the idiot British soldier's diary. Guilt? Fear? Those emotions had finally taken hold of him after so many years of self-control. Could it really be that he was fated to live with the same doubts and agonies that had racked George Lawrence?

Panos Theocharis looked out over the dusty earth towards the glinting blue of the Aegean. The colours were vivid now, but when the sun sank in the west Trigono would again become what it always had been – a well-worn threshold to the eternal dark.

*   *   *

Mavros carried on up to the excavation plateau, the sun doing more now than just tingling on his neck. He'd left his bag where he'd dumped the bike, and it was a long way down just to get the suntan lotion. He had his ID and wallet in his pocket, so the only potentially compromising thing that any inquisitive passer-by would find was his Greek mobile phone. He decided to take a chance and leave it where it was. There wasn't much of a signal out in the hills.

According to the lumpen Mitsos, Eleni wasn't at the dig. It was impossible to tell if she was beneath the sheeting at the tunnel entrance, but there was no sign of her motorbike. Mavros walked away and continued climbing. This was an opportunity to have a look at the southern massif which, according to the map that he'd left in his bag, was criss-crossed only by goat tracks.

After an ascent that left him blowing hard, he reached the saddle joining two peaks, the ridge between them with its stone wall twisting away precipitously on either side. Apart from the chapel on Profitis Ilias and a ramshackle herdsman's hut, the hills were desolate, their upper slopes devoid of vegetation and scored by rockfalls and seasonal watercourses. There was no sign of Rena. The land she was working must be beyond the cliffs. The stone flanks of Vigla were pierced by holes, some of them surrounded by mounds of reddish earth that marked abandoned mine shafts. There were also natural caves, the entrances overhung by stalactites of varying lengths. A feeling of melancholy settled over Mavros, a crushing hopelessness brought about by the unforgiving landscape that thousands of years of human civilisation had done little to temper.

Then he looked farther away and felt a burst of exhilaration as the sea filled his eyes. It was pale blue in the coastal reaches, but swiftly deepening in colour as it stretched away to the neighbouring islands. The capes at the corners of Trigono pointed to the south-east and the south-west, the long snout to his left like an extended finger. Through the strait between Ios and Sikinos, Santorini was visible, its cliffs circling the burning heart of the underwater volcano. Closer at hand, he could see a narrow track leading down to a huddle of houses at the end of a long inlet, the grey, unwhitewashed walls showing that no one had lived there for years. This was Vathy, Mavros remembered from the guidebook, and the islets at the end of the inlet were Mavronisi and Aspronisi. Floating serenely on the calm water farther out was the smudge of the last island, Eschati. It was down there that the fishing boat with the drowned young lovers in its nets had been found.

Having taken in the panorama, Mavros turned back towards the caves and man-made holes. He wanted to go and investigate them – they were drawing him to them like a boy caught by a spell in an enchanted landscape. Then he felt the back of his neck with the palm of his hand and realised that he had to do something about the sun quickly. Stepping over the hard ground, he skirted the eastern flank of Vigla and headed back down the path. A seagull hovered above him as he went, its cry a blend of aggression and a weird, mewing sadness. He scanned the dig from above but still could see no sign of Eleni. Back at the mountain bike, he opened his bag and slapped lotion over his neck. As far as he could tell, nothing had been tampered with. The satchel was where he'd left it, buckle in place, and all his possessions were there.

The road back to the village was deserted, people with any sense keeping out of the still-vicious sun of early autumn. Looking back at the hills, he still couldn't see the donkey Melpo or Rena. He wondered why she was sweating in the sun to provide for the beast. Surely she could buy fodder. If she were to spend more time at the port, she might be able to rent her other rooms out to the few tourists that arrived on the ferry each day.

As he was freewheeling down the slope towards the village, he saw a figure go into the Bar Astrapi, and applied his brakes. This was a good opportunity to talk to Rinus – he'd recognised the barman's black T-shirt and jeans through the haze. Keeping out of sight of the windows, he propped the bike up against the wall. He stood by the door and placed his ear against the join in the woodwork. It was immediately apparent that the Dutchman was not alone.

'Where the hell have you been?' The voice was that of the furniture designer, Barbara Hoeg. 'I've been waiting in your flat for hours. I came in on the bus. Mikkel will have been looking everywhere for me.'

'Nice to see you too, Barb,' Rinus replied. 'I thought I told you only to use the key I gave you in emergencies.'

'This is a fucking emergency.' There was a pause. 'Yes, all right, you can take that smile off your face. I've run out of stuff.'

'Barb, Barb, this isn't what I want to hear.' The barman's tone was almost playful. 'Have a drink instead.'

There was the sound of a heavy slap.

'Don't fuck with me, little man. I need more now.'

'Screw you, Barb.' Rinus sounded like a child who had been unjustly scolded. 'Where do you get off on hitting me? Not even my ex-wife did that.' A bottle rattled against a glass. 'Anyway,' he said in a loud whisper, 'do you really think I've got any gear now? After what happened to Yiangos?'

There was another silence, this one longer. It was broken by a long intake of breath.

'Oh my God,' Barbara moaned, her domineering tone gone. 'Haven't you got anything left?'

'You've had every last grain,' Rinus said. Mavros was sure he was grinning. 'Don't worry, I'm working on it. The next delivery's due in a week.'

'In a week – oh Christ, Rinus, you've got to help me. What else have you got?'

The Dutchman laughed briefly. 'A bit of grass, a few Es—'

'Shit!' the woman screamed. 'That's all shit!'

Mavros slipped away round the corner of the wall when he heard rapid footsteps approaching the door. Barbara ran out unsteadily and down the cleared space towards the track. If she saw the mountain bike, it didn't seem to make any impression on her. Mavros moved back to the entrance.

'Hello, Rinus,' he said, striding towards the bar. 'I've been wanting to have a talk.'

The diminutive figure on the other side of the counter swallowed the rest of his large measure of whisky and tried to disguise his alarm. 'Alex,' he mumbled. 'I suppose I owe you a drink for getting that mad cow off me in the Kambos.'

'Never mind Rena,' Mavros said, leaning forward and grabbing the Dutchman's arm. He didn't often resort to physical coercion, but there were times when it was a necessary part of the job. 'It's time you opened up to me. Or would you prefer me to call in that policeman friend of yours? What was his name? Stamatis, wasn't it? I don't think that gleaming motorbike of yours will be enough to keep him off your back if I tell him you're peddling dope.' He smiled maliciously. 'Better still, I could tell his superiors in Paros.'

'What the fuck are you talking about?' Rinus gabbled. 'I'm not a—' His eyes screwed up in pain. 'Ow! Let go, for Christ's sake. Let go!'

Mavros reduced the pressure on his wrist, but kept hold of it. Ever since a school-friend had overdosed on heroin, he'd had an aversion to pushers like the Dutchman. He didn't care about adults like Barbara Hoeg using, but mention of the dead boy Yiangos suggested that Rinus had involved the local kids. Mavros had no hesitation in giving him a hard time. Now he had the means to squeeze information out of the barman.

'Let's hear it then, Rinus,' he said, moving the whisky bottle out of range. It wouldn't have been the first time that a panic-stricken dealer had tried to crown him in a bar. 'First, everything you know about Rosa Ozal. Then everything about your no doubt highly profitable sideline.' He gave his captive a slack grin. 'And, last but not least, what was behind your pathetic attempt to fight my landlady?'

The barman raised his eyes to Mavros's and gave him a weary look. 'Who are you, man? Eleni was right. You're no fucking tourist.'

The grin disappeared from Mavros's face. 'That reminds me.

I want to know all about Eleni and Aris as well. And everyone else who comes to this dump.' He leaned closer and breathed over the Dutchman. 'Who am I? I'm your worst nightmare, you little shit.'

14

Mavros was sitting on the small hill near the village, looking down over the cemetery. The line of pink and white oleanders snaking through the barren ground and the square enclosure of whitewashed walls were set against the blue backdrop of the sea, the cypresses pointing to the cloud-flecked sky like the sappy fingers of a giant trapped underground. The wind was stronger now and the neighbouring coastlines, Andiparos with its gentle slopes and the marble mountains of Paros, were rimmed with foam.

Rinus had insisted on leaving the bar, as if talking about his activities there would bring bad luck on the place. He answered Mavros's questions willingly enough, but that only made him sure that the Dutchman was a skilled liar. While he admitted shifting small amounts of grass and hash, he denied any involvement with hard drugs. Mavros reminded him of Barbara Hoeg's desperate demands, but Rinus just laughed and said that she always spun out of control when she missed an appointment with her analyst in Hamburg – apparently she should have gone in the middle of September. The fact that the German woman was having therapy didn't surprise Mavros. She'd struck him as unstable even before he'd overheard her last conversation with the barman.

'Where do you get the stuff?' Mavros asked, placing himself in the barman's line of vision.

Rinus shrugged. 'I've got contacts here and there.' He opened his eyes wide. 'Who the fuck are you, man? Why are you so interested? If you were some kind of cop, you'd have nailed me or sent the narco squad in by now.'

'Never mind who I am.' Mavros grabbed his scrawny wrist

again. 'Do the local people know what you're peddling in the Astrapi, you bastard? Would you like me to tell them?'

The barman's bravado vanished and his thin frame drooped. 'Christ, it's only a sideline,' he whined. 'Do you know how difficult it is to make any money here? The islanders screw you for rent and never spend any money in the bar themselves. They—'

'Spare me the hard-luck story,' Mavros interrupted. 'You could always sell your motorbike. That would keep you in beer and cigarettes for a few years.' He caught the Dutchman's eye. 'Was the dead boy Yiangos moving the gear on his father's boat?'

Rinus's eyes narrowed. 'Shit, Alex, the guy's in the ground down there,' he said, inclining his head towards the graveyard. 'What fucking difference does it make now?'

Mavros stepped up close to him again. 'Are you sure it was an accident?' He was thinking about the damage to Aris Theocharis's boat. The big man was a regular in the Bar Astrapi. Maybe he was involved with the Dutchman's dealing. Anna's article had said that he had criminal friends in the States. Then again he only came to the island for a month every year.

Rinus licked his cracked lips. 'What do you mean? Yiangos and Navsika got dragged over by the net. The idiot was probably showing off to her.'

Mavros raised his shoulders. 'That isn't what I heard.' He studied the barman's face. 'I heard that another boat collided with the *Sotiria*. Is that why you missed your delivery?' He put his mouth close to the other man's ear. 'Maybe you've got yourself tied up in a murder case.'

For a few moments it looked like the pressure was going to tell. Rinus's eyes twitched and his breathing quickened. Then he clenched his arms to his fleshless sides and reasserted control.

'Go to hell, Alex,' he said. 'I'm not buying that. Lefteris would have caught his son's killer and torn his head off by now.' He looked at the dusty ground. 'It must have been an accident.'

Mavros saw he was losing momentum, so he tried another angle. He wanted to hold off asking about Rosa Ozal and what Rena had said about Rinus hitting her until he'd reduced the

Dutchman's defences. 'You've got a lot of friends on the island, haven't you?' he said. 'Aris Theocharis must be a useful guy to know. And his stepmother, Dhimitra.' He raised an eyebrow. 'Quite a woman, isn't she? Not to mention the archaeologist Eleni. She's another link to the Theocharis family.'

The Dutchman was looking at him nervously, trying to work out what he was building up to. 'Yeah, we're all friends here. Not that old man Theocharis ever comes into the Astrapi.'

'No, I don't suppose he does. Panos Theocharis more or less runs Trigono, doesn't he? Not on the surface, of course, but he's got his fingers on most of the strings.'

'Yeah, he has,' Rinus agreed.

'So does *he* know that you sell dope, soft or otherwise?' Mavros asked.

The barman's eyes flew open in alarm. He quickly tried to disguise it. 'No, I don't think so. Aris—'

'Never mind Aris for now,' Mavros said. 'Tell me about Rosa Ozal and I'll consider letting old Theocharis remain in a state of ignorance.'

'Rosa?' The barman looked alarmed, though only for a few seconds. 'What's Rosa got to do with anything?' he demanded, seemingly surprised by the change of tack.

'That's what I want you to tell me,' Mavros said, glancing over his shoulder as he heard voices. He watched as the American couple he'd seen out on Vigla earlier came up the slope towards them. 'Shit,' he said under his breath.

'Hello, Gretchen,' Rinus called. 'Hello, Lance.' He gave Mavros a mocking glance. 'Just in time. Alex here was about to start strangling me.'

'What?' Gretchen's face was red beneath her sunhat, her eyes wide open and displaying bloodshot whites. 'What are you saying, Rinus?' She suddenly seemed interested in what was going on.

'It's a joke, dear,' Lance said drily. 'At least I hope it is. What are you guys doing up here? Taking in the view?'

'Something like that,' Mavros said, shaking his head dis- piritedly.

'And unfortunately I've got to go,' the Dutchman said. 'Catch you later, Alex,' he added with a relieved smile. 'Don't jump to any hasty conclusions.' He waved to the Americans and set off down the hill in a miniature dust storm.

'What was that all about?' Gretchen asked. 'You two looked as if you were about to start brawling.' She squatted down and rummaged in her small rucksack, coming up with a half-full bottle of water.

Mavros took in legs covered in black hairs and watched as she emptied the bottle without offering it to anyone else. 'Speaking of fighting,' he said, 'what were you two doing earlier on? I saw you watching Rinus and my landlady Rena almost come to blows. Why did you do nothing to separate them?'

Lance looked down. 'Well, you see,' he said in an embarrassed voice, 'Gretchen . . . Gretchen here's an anthropologist and she—'

'Oh for goodness sake, Lance,' the woman interrupted. 'There's no need to stutter like a teenager.' She stood up and faced Mavros. 'We were taking a walk in the hills down there. It so happens that one of my research interests in anger management. I was interested to see how two people of different gender and background handled themselves.'

'Really?' Mavros looked at her sceptically. 'I don't suppose you know why they were fighting?'

Gretchen returned his gaze then shook her head. 'No. That doesn't concern me.' She turned away and started drawing the lines of the cemetery walls in a small sketchbook.

Mavros glanced at Lance, who raised his shoulders.

'Sorry,' he mumbled, going over to stand beside his partner.

'Are graveyards one of your research interests as well?' Mavros asked.

Gretchen looked over at him. 'As a matter of fact they are. Anger and death studies are my two fields of expertise. I am the author of the definitive study of certain Native American funerary practices.' She shook her head at Lance. 'If this oversensitive soul hadn't forced me to keep my distance, the recent funerals here would have provided me with excellent material for comparison.'

Mavros walked past them, his hands in his pockets. He wasn't aware that death studies were an academic subject. 'Maybe you should ask one more of the locals to die so there's another funeral for you to study.'

He heard a scandalised snort from the woman as he went down towards the track. Ahead of him, seagulls were hovering on the thermals above a white-hulled *trata*, their mournful yelps carrying on the breeze towards the southern massif of Trigono.

In the darkness Kyra Maro found herself high on the hillside above Paliopyrgos, her back straight, the skin on her face unwrinkled and her legs strong again. The southerly wind was being funnelled up the watercourse that had eaten into the ridge between Vigla and Profitis Ilias, its damp breath carrying a hint of the distant African desert. Her eighteen-year-old heart was fluttering like a caged bird in her chest, her breath coming quickly despite the fact that her lungs were accustomed to the steep ascent. All because of him: her lover, the man who had appeared on the island like one of the ancient gods she'd learned about from the island's schoolmaster before he went off to die fighting the Italians in the snows of the Albanian front. Yes, that was what Tzortz was to her, an Olympian god, fleet of foot and sharp of eye. But tender, oh so tender, more gentle with her than any man from the island could ever be. And he was waiting for her in their secret cave.

She stopped by the rocky outcrop and listened, her ear to the night sky. There was no sound apart from the sighing of the waves as they ran into the sea caves far below. The stars were bright tonight, burning their shapes into the sky's dark ceiling while the moon's curved sliver sank away in the west. Maro knew that a watcher from the Sacred Band had been posted on the saddle between the hills, but she was sure she had flitted past without him noticing. Her aunt had died of the consumption a week ago so she was wearing black, her face obscured by the loose folds of a scarf. Outside the cave entrance she stopped and ran her hand over the rock to find the loose stone in its position. Tzortz had told her always to check that. If there was danger he would knock it away. Her fingers touched the smooth surface of the large jet pebble and felt it move soundlessly against the rougher sandstone. Her heart soared free like a lark in the spring.

'My love,' came the soft voice with the educated foreign accent as she ducked her head and entered the low outer cave. 'Come to me.'

He was there, beyond the solid wall that even in daylight looked impenetrable but which concealed a narrow passage leading into a chamber larger than the room Maro shared with her three sisters. She slid round the jagged corner and moved into the circle of light cast by the oil lamp. In heavy peasant clothes, her man was kneeling on a blanket facing her with his arms open wide. His face had been darkened by the sun, but he still didn't look like an islander. His skin wasn't rough enough, his eyes unburdened by the demands of work on the boats or in the stony fields. That made him seem even more of a god to her.

They nestled together, his arms tight around her, not muscular like her brother Manolis's, the hands not calloused by a lifetime hauling nets like her father's, but safer and more caring. The protection this wiry foreigner could offer was worth more to her than that of her family. The men stood as a bulwark between her and the world because that was what the custom required, not because they loved her.

'Ah, Maro,' Tzortz said, his mouth close to her ear. The way he spoke her name always made the hairs on her neck and arms rise, the sound full of a longing that was all the more powerful because they'd been able to satisfy it every night since her brother's accident.

They made love on the blanket, the light turned lower so that their naked limbs and secret places kept some of their mystery. Their movements were slow and deliberate; they bit each other's lips gently as they concentrated on reaching the point where they fell together into the deep river of passion. Then they swam for what seemed like hours in a world beyond time, only coming back to the surface when the delirium began to wear off.

'Ach, Tzortz,' she said, her hand on him damp and softening. 'How is it that you love me? I am nobody, a girl who knows nothing. I will live on Trigono and die on Trigono, but you? You will sail far away when the war is finished. You will go back to your own people and forget me.' Her eyes filled with tears but, even before he spoke, she knew there was no need for them.

'I will never leave you, Maro,' he whispered, the words dripping from his lips like honey. 'You know that. I will stay on Trigono after the war and we will raise a flock of little Maros and Tzortzes.' He stroked her chin as she laughed. 'I promise you,' he said, looking at her with blue eyes that burned as bright as any star in the pastures of heaven. 'I will never leave Trigono.'

They stayed close together and the drug of their love gradually wore off.

'But Tzortz,' she said. 'We must be careful. My brother suspects us, I'm sure of that. And that Theocharis, you must not trust him. His father owned the mines here, you know that.' She bowed her head. 'He worked the men terribly. Many died in the shafts and caves around here. The families of the local ones were paid only enough to keep them quiet and the ones who came from distant places were left to rot where they fell unless their friends scraped a hole for them.' She looked back into her lover's eyes. 'Beware of Panos Theocharis. And of Manolis Gryparis. They are not your friends.'

He nodded slowly at her then smiled. 'Don't worry, Maro. I know what I'm doing. Nothing can come between us.' He drew her tightly to him. 'Our love has made us immortal.'

It was then that Kyra Maro came back to herself and blinked, the narrow confines of her bedroom gathering around her like a cell. She sat up with difficulty and wiped the rheum and the tears from her eyes. Immortal, she thought. Tzortz was wrong about that. He'd been wrong about many things. She looked under the bed at the box containing Tasos's remains. No one was immortal. The creaking in her own bones would soon cease for ever. And her lover? He had come back as he promised, but she had gained no relief – only a terrible agony that had never left her. There was no immortality, whatever the idiot priests said.

She got off the bed and walked unsteadily into the front room. There was a loaf of bread and a piece of hard goat's cheese on the table. Rena must have been in when she was asleep. At least she hadn't come when Maro was speaking to Tasos.

'Ach, Rena,' she said under her breath. 'You're a good woman at heart, you look after me even though we aren't related. But people fear you, they think they know the truth about you. Eventually they will crush you like they crushed me. The village is harsh to its women if they stray from the path laid down by custom. But the men, why is it that they can do as they please? My brother Manolis and his vicious, animal son Lefteris, they have both escaped punishment for their sins. And what about Theocharis in his tower, as cruel as any king in the old stories? There has been no retribution for him either.'

Kyra Maro sat down and scrabbled to break off the end of the loaf. Before she put a morsel of bread into her mouth, she cleared her throat and spat into her handkerchief.

'My curse on them all,' she said, raising her head defiantly. But her eyes were still wet with tears.

Mavros rode the mountain bike to the hire office and then walked back to Rena's. He crossed the courtyard to his room and sniffed the air inside. There was something different about the place. He looked in the bathroom and saw that the toilet paper bin had been emptied. Rena had obviously been in to clean before she left the village. Then it struck him that she could have been nosing around. Since he'd seen her in such an animated state on Vigla, her eyes burning and her face set firm against the Dutchman, he had wondered about his landlady. She was usually quiet and reserved, but she seemed to be harbouring some painful secret. He wouldn't like to be around when it got too much for her – there was something frighteningly intense about her. And yet she was kind to the old woman and to the wretched donkey, and she'd been hospitable to him. Perhaps he

wasn't making enough of an allowance for the extremes of the
Cycladic character.

He checked his possessions. They were all as he had left them,
though the drawers in the small chest were uneven, as if they had
been opened and closed again. Rena was an obsessive cleaner.
There was no dust in the rooms and the windows shone in the
afternoon sun, so maybe she was nothing more than fastidious
about her housework. Anyway, he had everything important with
him in his pockets and his bag.

Mavros walked out into the courtyard. There was no sign of
Rena; the kitchen door was pulled to and the shutters closed
upstairs. He called her name but there was no response. She
was presumably still out on the slopes above the Kambos or
putting her donkey back in the field that belonged to old Manolis's
brother. This was his chance to check her house. He thought about
the ethics of his profession for a second or two and then went into
the unlit passageway. He opened the door farther down and ran
his eyes over the standard, spotless *saloni* that was reserved for
formal occasions, the walls lined with dark-stained furniture and
the armchairs and sofa covered with transparent plastic sheeting. It
was unlikely that there would be anything pertaining to Rosa Ozal
in it, and a quick examination of the cabinet confirmed that.

Mavros went upstairs and opened the doors quietly. There was
a well-appointed bathroom with unusually tasteful pale cream tiles
– many islanders went for the most garish colours and patterns
that they could find. The two guest rooms were pretty spartan
– wood-frame beds, posters of Greek tourist attractions on the
walls and cheap panelled wardrobes. He checked them and found
nothing apart from spare blankets and electric anti-mosquito
devices, the flex neatly wrapped round each one.

He went into Rena's bedroom, having carefully closed the other
doors. It was more ornately decorated, the double bed under a
bright embroidered cover and the walls painted in a pale shade
of pink. Mavros wondered if they would have been that colour
when Rena's husband was alive and decided that they would not.
Then it struck him that he'd seen no photographs of her departed

family in any of the rooms, not even in the *saloni* – in fact, he'd seen no photographs of any people. That was unusual. Most Greeks, especially in rural areas, cherished the faded sepia shots of their ancestors. Wedding photos of grandparents and parents, memorial portraits of lost family members, were treasured almost as much as the smoke-blackened icons that were handed down from generation to generation. Rena had no such photos on display, nor did she have any icons. He wasn't sure what to make of that.

Taking a deep breath, Mavros opened the wardrobe. He wasn't comfortable poking his nose into his landlady's possessions, but he couldn't think of any other way to make progress with the case. Rosa Ozal had stayed in this house and he wasn't convinced when Rena said that nothing had been left behind when the woman left suddenly. There were the standard island woman's clothes, the formal suits for feast days in plastic covers, the black blouses and skirts neatly pressed. It seemed that Rena had disposed of all her brightly coloured clothing after her husband's death. But if she was so adamant about mourning him in the traditional way, why was his photograph absent? There were a few pairs of high-heeled black shoes but other than that, her footwear was simple and unfashionable. He didn't think it likely that his landlady attended many of the *glendia*, the eating, drinking and dancing sessions with which the locals kept themselves amused in the winter months.

After running his fingers quickly through drawers full of sensible underwear and cotton nightdresses, Mavros looked around the room. There was a bedside table by the single pillow but, apart from a pristine copy of the Bible, the drawer was empty. There were no other books in the room, or anywhere else in the house. He dropped to his knees and glanced under the chest and wardrobe. Nothing, not even a layer of dust. He swore in frustration, as much because he didn't know what he was looking for as because he couldn't find anything. Then he inclined his head and saw something protruding from beneath the pillow. It was the corner of what looked like a blue plastic folder.

Feeling a rush of excitement, Mavros slid his hand under the counterpane and pulled out the object. Here were the photographs that should have been in frames in the main room. He opened the flap and took out a blurred image of an elderly couple, the man's thick moustache failing to disguise a weak and unassuming face, the woman's hard gaze giving the impression of an unbreakable will. Their clothes and the condition of the photo suggested it had been taken in the late fifties or early sixties. He assumed they were Rena's parents, not that there was much family resemblance. The photo had been crumpled up at some stage then smoothed out, which struck him as odd.

The next image was that of a youngish man with a mocking smile, his hair thin and his cheekbones unusually fleshless. If he hadn't been gazing at the lens so arrogantly, he'd have given the impression of an invalid who was soon to succumb. Mavros wondered if he was Rena's husband. This photo too had been crushed and then flattened out again, the surface creased by numerous broken lines. Why had she done that? If she'd disliked her parents and her husband, she would surely just have thrown the photos away. Perhaps family loyalty had made her relent.

All that was left in the folder now was a Kodak envelope containing a batch of photos. He took them out and immediately felt his head jerk back. Here she was, the woman he was looking for. There were several shots of Rosa Ozal sitting in Rena's kitchen, her fine features adorned with broad smiles. In one photo she had her arms wide open, as if she were about to wrap them round the photographer. And then there was an image of the missing woman on the bed that Mavros was standing beside – the cover was identical. In this one Rosa was naked, her arms folded beneath well-formed, tanned breasts, the nipples hard and extended. She was looking straight at the lens, her lips parted and her expression rapt.

Mavros stood with one hand cupping his chin. Now at least he could see why Rena had been reticent when he'd questioned her about Rosa. A local widow engaging in a physical relationship with a foreign woman wouldn't impress the residents of Trigono.

Then he came to the last photograph and got another surprise. This time there was a different woman on Rena's bed. He recognised her immediately. She was the one he'd seen in Eleni the archaeologist's album, the blonde with the finely sculpted, severe features. Her hair was wet and close to her scalp as if she'd just come out of the shower. She too was naked, her legs apart at the knees and her right hand over her pubis. Her left arm was under her firm breasts and her eyes were locked on the camera.

Mavros wondered if Rena was the photographer in both cases. It seemed likely, given the location. That would explain her guarded manner and the removal of her husband's photo. Had she discovered her sexuality and fallen in with lesbian tourists? There were plenty of those in the archipelago every summer. But how did that fit in with what Rena had told him about Rosa and Rinus? Did the Dutchman hit the missing Turkish-American woman because she'd rejected his advances? Or could there be more to it, given his sideline in pushing drugs?

Moving his foot, Mavros felt something under the bed. He put the photos back in the folder and replaced it under the pillow, then dropped to his knees and felt around with one hand, his fingers closing around the handle of a suitcase. He pulled it out, registering that it was fairly heavy. The two clasps had been locked. He thought about what he was about to do for a few seconds then decided to go ahead. He had already stuck his nose into his landlady's life so far that breaking into her case wasn't any worse – not that he felt proud of himself. He fumbled around in his bag for the paper clip he always carried, straightened it out and inserted it into the first lock. It was stiff but eventually the hinge flipped open. The second one was easier. He took a deep breath, hoping both that it was worth it and that Rena wouldn't notice the locks were disengaged. Then he raised the lid.

There were two objects inside the suitcase. The more striking one was a marble Cycladic figurine about thirty centimetres long. It was a female form, lying with the knees together and slightly raised, the arms crossed beneath small breasts. The surface of the cream-coloured stone was smooth, the blank oval head angled back so that, had there been eyes, they would have been staring straight up. Mavros lifted the piece and felt its weight, then held it to his chest as if it were a child. As far as he could tell, it was an original rather than a copy – and the fact that Rena had hidden it away gave support to this conclusion. But where did it come from? Could Eleni have something to do with it? And what about the photos with her and Rosa Ozal? The archaeologist had hinted at finds that she'd made at the dig, but she and Rena seemed to hate each other. Then Mavros remembered the pose that Rosa had struck in the photo, arms folded beneath her breasts. Could the figurine be linked to Rosa in some way?

Mavros rocked back on his heels after he'd replaced the piece, feeling pins and needles but remaining in a squat. He had just read the words in Greek that were on the front cover of the small blue volume in the case. *Trigono 1941–1943: Endurance and Resistance* by Andhreas S. Vlastos. Here it was at last, the book that had disappeared from the public library and which, according to the author's widow, Panos Theocharis had taken steps to suppress. Why had Rena secreted a copy under her bed? He flicked through the pages, aware that the longer he spent in the room, the greater the chance of being caught by his landlady on her return. But taking the book away to study it in depth was an even bigger risk. He would be the obvious suspect given his earlier questions about the library, and the idea of being caught out by Rena was repellent. So he tried to speed-read through the densely packed text, noticing the name Panos Theocharis several times. But the references mentioned only anodyne details of his family background and his war service in Egypt. Then he stopped, his eye caught by another familiar name. It was written in Latin characters and prefaced by the word *Ipolochagos*, Greek for the rank of lieutenant. George Lawrence. The officer in the photo he'd found in the chimney and whose name he suspected had been erased from the village's memorial.

Mavros pulled out his notebook and scribbled down the sparse details given by Vlastos. Lieutenant George Lawrence had been sent to Trigono in October 1942 to plan and execute sabotage operations. He had a minor reputation as a poet in Egypt and had published some work in the magazines of the time. But his service on Trigono was marked by disagreements with the local resistance leaders and with Panos Theocharis, who had been sent to the island with a unit of Greek commandos. And that was it. Nothing more about the mysterious Lawrence, as far as a rapid trawl through the rest of the book showed. He shook his head in frustration. Could there be some kind of connection, via George Lawrence, between Panos Theocharis and Rosa Ozal? Why had the photos and the diskette been put in the chimney? He was still assuming that Rosa had been responsible for that.

There was a sound from the street below. Mavros went over quickly to the shuttered window and saw Rena in her dusty scarf, blouse and skirt at the door. He considered what to do for a moment, then put the book back in the suitcase, closed it and replaced it under the bed. He went downstairs three steps at a time, making it to the passageway as the door was opening and darting round the corner into the yard. Keeping close to the wall, he slid round to the table and sat down, assuming a relaxed pose.

As Rena came into the light, he looked up and saw an old woman staring down at him from the neighbouring house. She must have seen him sidling round the wall. If she told Rena about his behaviour, he'd have some explaining to do. Then it struck him that he had omitted to close her bedroom door after him. He was probably in trouble even if she didn't spot the unlocked suitcase.

Rena gave him a tentative smile and walked to her kitchen. Mavros got his breathing under control. It seemed he was losing his touch in more ways than one. What he'd discovered in Rena's bedroom – the photos of Rosa and the other woman, the Cycladic figurine, the book with its references to Theocharis and George Lawrence – had left him as confused as he'd ever been during an investigation. The only angle to check that he could come up with was the detail about Lawrence being a published poet. A call to his mother, publisher of many minor writers, might cast light on the officer who'd been on Trigono during the war – the officer who had been in dispute with Panos Theocharis.

It wasn't much but, since no one wanted to discuss Rosa Ozal, he couldn't see how else to call up her shadowy presence.

15

Mikkel parked the Suzuki on the concrete area outside the house and went back to close the gate. Before the heavy panels swung to, the sky to the west filled his eyes. The sun had dropped beyond the southern ridge of Andiparos into a bath of crimson. He looked at his watch. Nearly eight. He'd been in the village and on the road for over three hours trying to find Barbara, without success. He had woken after his siesta to find her side of the bed empty. Walking through the cool rooms of the house, he'd realised by the absence of cigarette smoke that she wasn't inside. There had been no sign of her by the pool either. He was immediately concerned because she'd been even more on edge than usual for the last couple of days, but when he called her mobile it rang in the study. Not for the first time she'd omitted to take it with her, despite his repeated requests. She didn't like to be tied down, which was exactly why he'd given her the thing.

Now he was at the end of his tether. Where the hell had she got to? No one in the village had seen her and she never went anywhere without the car. He had wondered if she was with the shitbag Dutchman she'd been spending so much time with recently, but he'd seen him on the hill above the village with the tourist Alex. Why was it that Barbara had taken against him so much? Then the American couple, the sharp-tongued woman and her quiet man, had joined them and Rinus had left. He claimed he hadn't seen Barbara all day when Mikkel asked him outside the bar.

Opening the antique door that Barbara had bought at great expense from a dealer in Athens – he'd assured her it came from an *archontiko*, a traditional gentleman's house, on Pelion, but Mikkel had his doubts – he felt a wave of relief dash over him. The unmistakable smell of her beloved Camels hung in the air. Mikkel walked in quickly, the bottle of seven-star Metaxas brandy that he'd bought her in one hand. She must have wandered off to an out-of-the-way beach and fallen asleep. He shook his head as he skirted the pine-and-steel chairs in the main room and cursed himself for a fool. There he'd been imagining the worst – Barbara having one of her unstable episodes and running in front of a car, Barbara drinking herself into a stupor and falling off a cliff – and here she was back home. She'd be fine again soon, he was sure of that. After her next session with the analyst in Hamburg.

The French windows leading to the terrace were open, the bamboo blinds behind them rattling gently in the breeze that had started to get up in the late afternoon. Mikkel called his wife's name but got no reply. He was about to check her study when he saw her on her front in the swimming pool. As usual she was naked with her arms extended, her all-over tan visible through the limpid water and her long legs leading to the shapely backside that still made him hard. He went outside, his eye automatically following the line from pool to retaining wall to darkening blue sea and the tawny flanks of the islands beyond. Then his eyes jerked back to the swimming pool as he realised that his wife was well beneath the surface, her hair spread out around her head like an inflated halo.

'Barbara!' Mikkel cried, the name sounding hollow in his ears as if there were already an insurmountable barrier between him and the person who bore it. 'Jesus, Barbara!'

Without thinking, he dropped the bottle of brandy into the flower-bed beside the pool and launched himself into the water. He flailed through it until his hands touched her upper torso. Manoeuvring the waterlogged body was difficult and he was panting, treading water frantically, by the time he got it to the side. He needed several attempts to haul his wife up the ladder and lay her on the wet tiles. He rolled her on to her side and tried to empty her lungs, but it wasn't long before he gave up.

There was no pulse and her eyes, though they were as cloudy blue as ever and shining from their immersion in the water, had no more life in them than the pebbles on the beach.

'Jesus Christ!' Mikkel said under his breath. 'Jesus Christ, you crazy woman, what have you done?' He stood up and went over to the table at the head of the pool. There were three Camel butts in the ashtray, an empty wineglass on its side. He sniffed it and picked up the smell of the sharp Thessalian white wine Barbara favoured. He was sure there wouldn't be much left in the bottle in the fridge 'Shit!' he said, glancing back at the body. 'You stupid, stupid bitch.' The words turned into a wail of misery. 'You got yourself drunk and then passed out in the pool. I told you a thousand times to be careful about that.'

He ran into the living room and snatched up the multicoloured cover Barbara had outsourced to a factory in Rwanda; the designs went well with hers and it made her feel good to support a developing country. Mikkel swallowed a bitter laugh. As she'd pointed out to him, the covers were also dirt cheap. He spread it out over a dry part of the terrace and gently dragged Barbara across. Then, before he wrapped her in the cover, he bent his head over her arms. His heart missed a beat. No, it couldn't be. There were track marks on the skin of her upper arm. Christ, how had he failed to spot them? The cunning bitch – she'd taken to wearing long-sleeved blouses and he'd thought it was because the worst of the heat had passed. She'd sworn to him that she was off the stuff. That was why they'd moved out here, why they spent so much time on Trigono. She could score in ten seconds back home, but here there was no easy supply. Jesus. How could he have been so blind? That was what the bastard Rinus was up to, that was why Barbara hung around him like a blowfly over a carcass. And that must have been where she was all day.

Mikkel remained squatting by his wife until his legs were attacked by cramp. He rolled on to his side, then moved closer to Barbara. God, how had he missed what she'd been doing? Never mind the long sleeves – her moods and her distance should have alerted him. And the way she warned him off with her eyes if he looked in her direction when she was in the pool. Stupid bastard. He'd spent the last few weeks pretending that things weren't happening – that Barbara's addiction hadn't reclaimed her, that Rinus Smit wasn't a poisonous dwarf who treated women like so much meat, that Aris Theocharis wasn't a lunatic who was capable of anything. Oh God. He could have saved Barbara, he could have taken her away from this terrible island. Trigono consumed the people who lived there like a beast turning on its offspring.

But now . . . now he could look after her as much as he liked. He drew close to her and pulled her slack arm over his shoulders. Looking into her vacant eyes, he began to speak to her in a low, loving voice.

'Don't worry, my darling, I'm here. From now on it's just the two of us. The others don't matter any more. The muck you depended on has no more power over you, it can't hurt you now. We're going to stay here together, you and me. I won't let anyone else lay a finger on you. No, never again . . . never . . .'

Mikkel continued talking as the shroud of darkness fell over Trigono, his voice lilting like a priest's and his hand clenched around his wife's lifeless fingers.

Mavros stood on the end of the pier as the darkness took over. There was a line of lights leading back to the harbour front, but he stood outside the glow cast by the one nearest to him. Though he didn't think there was anyone close, he wanted to be sure no one saw him making the call or overheard what he was going to say.

'Hello, Mother.'

'Alex! How lovely to hear your voice. Where are you?'

'Still on the island. How are you?'

He let her describe the ups and downs she'd experienced in the last few days, her main concern being the incompetence of the man who'd come to repair her washing-machine.

'But you don't want to hear about that, Alex,' Dorothy said. 'Is everything all right down there? Those poor young people.'

'Yes, the atmosphere's pretty angst-ridden,' Mavros confirmed. 'Listen, this is a bit of a long shot, but have you ever heard of a man called George Lawrence? He was a—'

'Soldier-poet in Egypt during the war,' his mother said. 'Yes, he was a friend of Durrell, moved in the same circle.'

'Amazing,' Mavros said under his breath. Dorothy had the most encyclopaedic memory he'd ever encountered. His own wasn't bad, but he hadn't inherited the full, twenty-four-volume Cochrane edition.

'I'm just checking something,' she said, papers rustling in the background. 'Ah, yes, here it is. I made some notes about him a few years ago for an essay I contributed to the *TLS*.' There was a pause. 'Why are you interested in an obscure bard, young man? Not that I'm complaining. Your life could do with more poetry in it. All those fearful cases you—'

'It seems he was on Trigono during the war,' Mavros said, cutting off her standard diatribe about his profession. 'Have you got anything about that?' He watched as a fishing boat chugged past the end of the pier, a cigarette blossoming red as the man at the helm inhaled.

'Really? He was a Cambridge classicist, but I haven't got anything about him being on Trigono. In fact, I have nothing about what happened to him in wartime after Cairo.'

Mavros let out a groan.

'Hold on, dear,' Dorothy said with a laugh. 'I do know the names of the two collections he published in the UK in the late forties. Let me see. There was *Cycladic Twilight* in 1948 and then *Nights in the Archipelago* in 1949. After that he disappeared.'

Mavros pricked up his ears. 'Pardon?'

'He disappeared. You know well enough what that means. I remember that it was a bit of a mystery at the time. He just upped and left his flat in Bloomsbury – no note, no nothing. He was never seen again. Rather romantic, don't you think?'

'Maybe.' Mavros was chewing his lip. 'It's certainly interesting. Are the poems any good?'

'Some of them are quite moving,' Dorothy said, again shuffling pages. 'A lot about love and the Greek landscape. But they're very dark. He seemed to have become disillusioned, no doubt during the war. Many of that generation did.'

'Any references to Trigono?'

Dorothy laughed again. 'I don't remember, dear. I don't have the books, only some poems I copied myself in the British Council library. They were published by an independent poetry press with small print runs. They're probably worth quite a lot now, so if you come across any on your island . . .'

'I'll keep my eyes open, Mother,' Mavros said. 'Let me know if you find any direct references to Trigono in the poems you have.' He signed off, telling her that he'd be back in a few days.

Walking towards a restaurant he'd noticed on the main street, Mavros told himself to forget George Lawrence. Even if Rosa Ozal did have some interest in the guy as the material from the chimney suggested, and even if he had disappeared – could he have returned to Trigono after the war? – time was running out. He'd have to find a more direct route to the heart of the case, and soon.

The restaurant down a lane near the school was one of the few that were still open at this late stage in the season. Mavros was glad to discover that the food, though basic, was fresh and well prepared – grilled squid, *patates* and a salad – and the local white wine was surprisingly subtle.

One of the other tables had been taken by a group of local men, among them one-armed Manolis and his son Lefteris. Their conversation was loud and boisterous, mainly concerning the inadequacies of the government and its fishing policy. Mavros eavesdropped casually, fixing his gaze on the grease-stained wall above the grill. At one point he felt eyes on him and looked down to find father and son watching him intensely. He returned their stare briefly, their hostility burning him like acid. Wondering what he'd done to antagonise them – being seen with Aris Theocharis on his boat? – he turned towards the table in the corner by the window. The two English couples he'd seen before were working their way through heaps of *souvlaki* and chips, beer bottles crowding out the plates.

'Don't worry, Trace,' said one of the shaven-headed men. 'I'll sort the tosser out.'

The woman with the large chest shook her head. 'Oh, forget it, Roy. He's not the first barman who's tried it on.'

'Is that right?' said her man, brow furrowed. 'Dutch bastard.'

'Be quiet, Roy,' said the other woman, her face red from the sun. 'Don't be such a racist.' She put her hand on Trace's arm. 'Doesn't matter where blokes come from, they're all after the same thing.' She cocked an eye at their partners.

Mavros glanced away after Trace raised her eyes and met his for a few seconds. That was long enough for her sombre look to make him feel guilty. The way he was treating Niki wasn't exactly a master-class in caring masculinity.

'Yeah, well,' Trace said, drinking from her bottle. 'That little tosser thinks he's something really special.'

Roy leaned forward. 'What did he say, then? It must have been bad. You don't normally get this bothered. Tell me and I'll have his balls.'

'Yeah, bloody right,' Norm put in avidly.

Trace shook her head. 'Oh, leave off,' she said, glaring at her companions. 'He . . . he just scared me a bit. He's weird. Let's go somewhere else tonight.'

'No chance,' said Roy, a wicked grin spreading across his face. 'I want a word with that Rinus.'

Mavros laid some banknotes down and stood up. It was clear that Rinus had tried it on once too often. It would be interesting to see what happened to him tonight. But more interesting was what the episode said about the barman's way with women. Trace was safe enough, given the muscular back-up she had, but what happened to unaccompanied women who spurned the Dutchman? What had happened between him and Rosa Ozal?

On his way out Mavros nodded at the English table and received cheerful waves from the two men. The women gave him sceptical looks. Whatever Rinus had said to Trace seemed to have made them suspicious of men. He had a feeling that Roy and Norm wouldn't be enjoying the rest of their holiday much.

Mavros passed the last of the village's dim streetlights and moved up the narrow track, the usual rustles and shuffles coming from behind the high stone walls. The sounds were from animals this time. It was too early for illicit human couplings. The stars were spread out across the dome of the night in all their glory, the constellation of Orion the Hunter hanging low in the eastern quadrant. Mavros had always felt an affinity with the mythological figure, with his dogs around him and the great sword hanging from his angled belt. But this time he hadn't succeeded in tracking down Rosa Ozal, the object of his hunt. Suddenly the image of his brother Andonis flashed before him, the piercing blue eyes and the smiling face seemingly sympathetic despite the long-standing failure to find him. All these years and still Mavros felt the loss, all these years and he hadn't been able to uncover the slightest trace of Andonis. Instead of slackening, the pain of that failure was becoming harder to live with as he got older. It seemed that time didn't heal all wounds.

He entered the pool of light outside the bar and glanced around. The large green Jeep was parked by the wall, as was Eleni's motorbike. The regulars were here, though there was no sign of Barbara and Mikkel's Suzuki.

Inside the bar was smoke-filled, the organ-heavy sound of The Doors cascading from the speakers.

'Alex,' Eleni said, turning to him as he reached the counter. 'I wondered if I might see you.' Her thick hair was pulled back in a knot and her face was made up more than usual. The buttons of her denim shirt were open halfway down her chest.

Mavros nodded to her. Looking beyond, he made out Aris Theocharis in the corner, his stepmother Dhimitra beside him. The bald man ignored Mavros, but the museum benefactor's wife give him a nod and a loose smile as she raised a martini glass to her glistening scarlet lips. There was no sign of the old man.

'I came to see you at the dig this afternoon,' he said, leaning on the bar beside Eleni. He watched as her eyebrows shot up. 'But you weren't around.'

'No,' she said, looking down at her beer. 'No, I was working with Theocharis in the tower. Some . . . some cataloguing.' She lifted her gaze back to him. 'Why? Did you want something?'

Mavros watched as Rinus went round the end of the bar and started talking to Aris and Dhimitra. 'Well, yes, I did actually.' He smiled at her, trying to dispel the suspicion in her voice. He edged closer. 'You remember that woman Rosa Ozal I asked you about?' Her expression was blank. 'I was just wondering if you were sure you didn't know her. After all, Rinus remembers her coming in here quite often, and you do too . . .' He smiled again, letting the words trail away.

The archaeologist's eyes narrowed and for a moment he thought she was going to lose her temper. Then she let out a long breath and pursed her lips. 'God, you don't give up, do you, Alex?' she said, shaking her head then relaxing slightly. 'All right. Yes, I knew her. If you must know, we had a brief affair.' She held her eyes on his. 'Although I tried to get you interested – God knows why – I prefer women. Satisfied?'

Mavros watched as the barman turned in their direction, still talking to the Greeks. 'What about Rinus? Did he have something going with her too?'

Eleni gave a dismissive snort, the sound catching in her throat. 'Rinus thinks he's a ladies' man. Rosa put him in his place.'

'Was that near the time she left?' Mavros asked quickly. Rinus was moving back towards the bar.

Eleni thought and nodded. 'A day or two before. Why?'

Mavros shrugged as the Dutchman arrived. He also wanted to find out how likely it was that the Cycladic figurine he'd found in Rena's bedroom was genuine, but he hadn't worked out how to do so without mentioning the widow. He'd have to find another opportunity.

'Alex,' Rinus said, 'I didn't see you there.' His voice dripped false bonhomie. 'What would you like?'

'What I'd really like,' Mavros replied, 'is a private conversation with you, but I don't suppose I'm going to get one right now.'

The barman gave him a half-nervous, half-mocking look and raised his shoulders. 'I'm busy with my customers. How about later?'

'I'll be waiting,' Mavros said.

Rinus smiled weakly. 'Whatever. Dhimitra would like you both to join her. What are you drinking?'

Eleni's face was set hard. 'You go, Alex,' she said. 'I see enough of that woman.'

Mavros didn't want to miss the opportunity of talking to Dhimitra without her husband. 'I'll see *you* later too,' he said. 'Brandy,' he added, turning to Rinus. 'Seven stars, since the rich lady's buying.'

The barman grunted, eyes on the glasses he was filling.

As Mavros approached the table, he heard Aris's voice thunder out.

'Where's Barbara? Where's her wimp of a husband? They're always here by now.'

Rinus shrugged as he arrived with the tray of drinks. 'Don't know. I haven't seen either of them all—' He broke off as he picked up Mavros's questioning glance. 'I haven't seen either of them this evening.' This time he didn't hang around to make conversation.

'So, Alex,' Dhimitra said in her throaty voice. 'What have you been up to today?' The question sounded innocent, but Mavros got the immediate impression that he was being probed.

He raised the cognac glass to her, aware that Aris was staring at him bullishly. 'Me? I've been doing what tourists do. Exploring the locale, sampling the food and drink—'

'And asking questions,' the bald man interrupted.

Mavros held his gaze and then nodded. 'Yes, I've been asking questions. I'm going to ask Mrs Theocharis one now. A friend of mine was here earlier in the year. She hasn't been seen since.' He took the photo of Rosa from his pocket and held it up in front of the woman opposite him. 'I don't suppose you met her in June?'

Dhimitra waved away the pungent smoke from her untipped Assos and stared at the image. 'No,' she said. 'No, I never saw her. I . . .' She looked at Mavros and smiled apologetically. 'I don't get out of the estate as much as I'd like. My husband is very—'

'Demanding,' Aris Theocharis interrupted again, laughing coarsely. 'I don't think so.'

'I don't suppose your husband could have met her?' Mavros asked Dhimitra.

The former nightclub singer laughed, the smoke pluming from her nostrils. In the low lights of the Astrapi her blonde hair looked almost natural and the heavy foundation covering the wrinkles on her face and neck was less visible. 'Panos? No, he keeps himself very much to himself these days.'

'Beating his ancient meat in front of *tsondes*,' Aris said with a guffaw.

'What?' Mavros asked, feigning incomprehension.

'*Tsondes*?' Aris looked at him as if he were a moron. 'Blue movies, porn, shagfests. You get my meaning?'

Mavros caught his eye and held it. Aris Theocharis had a big mouth, but he wasn't sure what lay beneath the bravado. The big man dropped his gaze after a few seconds. Nothing much, maybe.

'My husband . . .' Dhimitra began, her heavy hand with its immaculate purple nails suddenly on Mavros's forearm. 'My husband lives for the past, as you understand from the collection he showed you. His sexual interests are – how shall I put it? – restricted.'

Aris grunted. 'At least the guys in the movies stay hard.'

'Stop it, Ari,' Dhimitra said, flashing him a stern look. 'Alex doesn't want to know about your father's private life.'

'Doesn't he?' Aris demanded, glancing at Mavros. 'Excuse me. I have to talk to Rinus.'

They watched him shamble over to the bar, his bulky frame looming over the Dutchman.

'I must apologise for my step-son,' Dhimitra said, lips parting over gleaming capped teeth. 'He can be very crude.' She smiled expansively and Mavros suddenly felt the weight of her hand on his thigh under the table. 'You, on the other hand, are sensitive, are you not?' The tips of her fingers approached his groin.

Mavros pushed his chair back and nodded. 'Yes, I'm very sensitive,' he said. 'And I know how to avoid trouble.' He looked across at the heavily made-up woman, wondering if she was after him for sex or if she had another agenda. Maybe Theocharis had told her to find out if he was in the antiquities trade. If he played along, he might pick up information about Rosa – but he couldn't face getting closer to the vulpine Dhimitra.

'Your husband is one of this country's most influential and powerful men,' he added. 'Find someone else to drop in the shit.' He turned away and headed for the door, aware that Eleni's eyes were on him but not intending to stop. He'd made the rebuff of Dhimitra as unsubtle as he could. It was time he showed his teeth to people other than Rinus.

Outside, he stood in the light for a time, trying to get his thoughts in order. Aris talked tougher than he was, Dhimitra was a scheming nymphomaniac, Eleni was a lesbian who tried it on with men, and Rinus was a dope dealer with wandering eyes and hands. There was no shortage of suspicious characters who either knew or could have known Rosa Ozal, but none of them was about to tell him what caused her to leave before she'd planned to. He stepped into the darkness, the constellations higher now and the cotton-wool traces of distant galaxies more faint. He knew it was time to make things happen. Rather than waiting for Rinus to close up, he decided to see if he could get into his flat. That was the most likely place to find something linking the Dutchman to Rosa.

Before he was more than ten metres down the track he heard

the long-drawn-out screech of an owl. Seconds later there was a heavy blow on the back of his head.

'Ah!' Mavros heard himself exclaim, the sound of his voice somehow insulated. He dropped to the ground and felt sharp stones pierce the skin on his kneecaps.

More blows followed, a narrow torch beam playing over his head and shoulders to direct the hits. Some were random, rebounding off his shoulders and upper arms, but others were well aimed, fists making contact with his chin and temples. He began to sink into unconsciousness, his eyes filling with sticky blood and his breath rushing in his throat. Then, as if from far away, he heard voices. Loud voices.

Male. 'Oi, what are you doing?'

Female. 'Get off him. Go on, get away.'

Male. 'Grab him, Norm. Quick, he's getting over the wall. No, Trace, don't.'

Mavros heard a sharp blow and a gasp.

Female. 'That'll teach you, two of you ganging up on a defenceless guy. Oh, shit, I've broken my heel on the bastard.'

Stones rattled around, thudding on to the ground near Mavros. He heard rapid footsteps moving away.

Male. 'They've cleared off. How many were there?'

Female. 'Two on the track, I think, Roy. There might have been someone else behind the wall. This travel torch of mine's not too bright.'

The other female. 'Here, it's the bloke from the restaurant. He was in the bar last night and all.'

Male. 'Oh yeah, so it is. We'd better get him up to the Astrapi.'

Another male. 'No, no.' Mavros realised it was his own voice. 'Get me to my place. House on the street leading to the square. Blue door with yellow panels.' He felt himself fall away again. 'Please.'

He was vaguely aware of being lifted up as his head was smothered in darkness, his breathing loud, far too loud. Then everything went completely silent.

January 5th, 1943

We have struck our first blow and the blood is running quick in our veins!

I won't pretend things have been easy. In fact, I've been so busy organising the operation and wrangling with the Greeks that I have been unable to keep this diary for weeks. And unwilling in case Agamemnon or his men should discover it, which would be catastrophic for Maro and me. But now we have holed up on Vigla again and I have more time. I have even seen Maro, though only briefly and in the presence of her brother. My love for her still burns strong, so strong. How I wish we could slip away to our secret place and lose ourselves in each other, but the mission is what counts now. We have blooded the Italians and it will not be long before we must do so again.

I have to say that Agamemnon and his squad have been less than helpful. As soon as I outlined my plan to blow up the enemy garrison's stores depot and an electricity substation in Parikia, the main town of Paros, the Sacred Band turned its collective face against me. Agamemnon had obviously been working on Ajax as well. The local men refused to take any part in the sabotage operation, following the position established by the captain – that any subversive action would bring the wrath of the enemy down upon innocent islanders' heads. I tried in vain to convince them that we would leave no traces, that the Italians would be unable to establish any connection with Trigono, but it was no good. Many of the Trigoniotes have relatives on Paros and the threat of reprisals against the population of the neighbouring island disturbed them just as much. It was pointless to remind them that the Italians are in no way as vindictive as the Germans on the mainland, and that we would make sure our activities injured no enemy personnel. They were adamant. Agamemnon has heard reports of Cretan peasants being forced to dig their own graves, of women and children being herded into churches and burned to death, and those accounts seemed to scare even the redoubtable Ajax. So much for the spirit of resistance. I understood their fears – my God,

I have Maro to think about – but the struggle has to take precedence. Being in love is wonderful, but standing up to tyranny is the greater glory. Byron knew both and he chose to die in the Greeks' own war of independence rather than in the arms of a woman.

But I had an ace up my sleeve. I informed base of the stalemate we had reached and they supported my line. In the brass hats' view, civilian casualties, though regrettable, are sometimes unavoidable. So they ordered Agamemnon to keep his distance and sent me a pair of experienced sabotage hands to back me up. From now on this would be an all-British operation. I had enough local knowledge to get us to the target area and the fact that we would be wearing army-issue boots and using British weapons would get the locals off the hook.

Corporals Rees and Griffin of the Royal Marines duly arrived on the supply kaïki *on Boxing Day, the former a wiry, red-faced Welshman and the latter a monosyllabic Yorkshireman with a vicious glint in his eye. They are both explosives experts and apparently Griffin is well versed in the black arts of silent killing. I told him that he was unlikely to have to use those on the somnolent Italian detachment on Paros and that he was only to strike on my direct order. He raised a sceptical eyebrow and went on checking his kit. My God, I'm glad he's on our side!*

And so the day of the operation dawned, the sun bright over the eastern islands and the north wind no more than Force 3 as I looked out of the herdsman's hut below the ridge. I had left the hut in the Kambos when the other two arrived, thinking it best to be out of the way of the islanders who worked the land. The move meant that I saw less of Maro, but she seemed to understand. She even came to the cave the night after Rees and Griffin landed. I don't think they saw her – she is always very careful – or heard the cries we couldn't silence. Ah, Maro!

I made my final preparations independently of Agamemnon, using Ajax only to find us a small fishing boat. Rees was a fisherman before the war and he was quite capable of getting us to a deserted cove on the south coast of Paros. Ajax had the boat brought to the inlet of Vathy and the three of us filed down the track in the afternoon, feeling the eyes of the Sacred Band men on us from the scrub. Their officer was waiting for us in the deserted village at the head of the inlet, his expression grim and disapproving.

'I ask you to reconsider your operation, Lieutenant,' *he said, taking my arm and drawing me aside. His English is excellent, the fruit, no doubt, of expensive tutors.* 'The dangers to the local population must be obvious to you. In a week our people will have completed their reconnaissance of Naxos and Amorgos. I will gladly assist you in operations there.'

'And what about the danger of reprisals to the populations of those islands?' *I demanded.* 'Why are they any less important? Because your family happens to own an estate on Trigono?'

That took the wind from his sails. He glared at me and then marched away, his face set hard. I don't think I'll be having any more trouble from that quarter.

Rees and Griffin stored the equipment below deck and we cast off. The Ersi *was a battered old hulk, her timbers heavily scraped and her hull in need of several coats of paint, but her engine sounded healthy enough and Ajax had managed to obtain a supply of diesel from the black market on Paros. The light was fading over the western islands as we steered between Mavronisi and Aspronisi at the opening of the inlet. Eschati, the last island, floated like a piece of eggshell on the darkening waters and we turned to the west, Rees handling the boat with the light hand of a born seaman. I felt my heart pound in my chest. What more could a man ask from life than to sail through the most beautiful archipelago in the world and wage war on an unjust enemy? The last of the sun's rays were turning the sheer cliffs of Trigono a lambent red and I blinked the tears from my eyes before the gruff Yorkshireman beside me noticed. I was in my element at last. I felt then that not even the joy Maro brought me could compare with this.*

I will not write about the operation in too much detail. I have already taken a chance by consigning my thoughts to print. Suffice to say that it was a resounding success. After mooring the boat in a cut that was almost invisible from land or sea, we marched through the night to the hillside above the town and holed up in an overgrown watercourse during the day. At nightfall we slipped silently down to the outskirts and flitted like ghosts between the shuttered houses. There seemed to be no one about and the only danger came from dogs that growled when they heard unfamiliar footsteps and from chickens squawking on their roosts. We located the Italian depot without difficulty and the only tricky moment came when a sentry walked within a foot of Rees's crouching body. But he disappeared round a corner soon enough and we didn't see him again. Griffin went after him to make sure he kept walking away from us. The charges were laid, the timer set for 4 a.m. By then we would be long gone.

Soon afterwards we moved on to the electricity substation, which lay to the north of the silent town. There were no sentries on it and we had no alarms as the corporals repeated their actions with the explosives. Then we were away into the darkness, our legs straining as we scaled the flank of the marble mountain, the gorse tugging at our trousers. We heard the explosions when we were a mile or so from the boat. Time passed in a flash and we were soon back on the gentle swell, carving an arc round the long tail of Oura at the south-eastern point of Trig. The sun came up as we swung into Vathy inlet and I shook hands with my men. We were home and dry.

Tomorrow, January 6th, is Twelfth Night. In the Orthodox Church it is the Fota, *the blessing of the waters. Ajax has already taken the trusty* Ersi *back to the village so she isn't missed during the festival. The young men dive into the sea to fetch the cross thrown in by the priest and there is great rejoicing. We are already celebrating, Griffin having cracked open a bottle of whisky that he brought, against orders, from base. Maro will not come tonight as the women will be preparing for the feast day. I miss her already, but I have enough to console myself with.*

Agamemnon gave us the same stony glare when we returned, the fool. We have achieved something, we have struck a blow. What have he and his precious Sacred Band done to rid Greece of the invader?

Mavros struggled to get himself into a sitting position, gasping as the pain in his ribs knifed in. He was still woozy, and the owl's shrill call that he'd heard before he was attacked was running through his mind like a record that had stuck. The owl. In Greek popular belief, its cry was an evil omen, a harbinger of death. He blinked to dispel the thought. The bedside light in his room at Rena's was on and he could make out his face in the mirror. It could have been worse. There was a large black swelling above his left eye and a bloody scrape along the line of his jaw on the other side. His head was pounding and he badly needed something to drink. Reaching out for the glass on the cabinet, he misjudged the distance and watched helplessly as it toppled on to the tiled floor.

The crash brought his landlady running.

'Alex, what are you doing?' she said, an expression of alarm on her face as she came in the door. 'You must lie down. The doctor said that—'

'I'm all right,' Mavros said, raising an arm and wincing.

'The doctor said that you might have a—' The widow broke off and searched for the word. 'A concussion?'

'Very good,' Mavros said with a weak smile. 'Where did you learn that difficult piece of English vocabulary?'

'From the dictionary,' she said, not returning the smile. 'I looked it up a few minutes ago.' She frowned and pushed him gently back on to the bed. 'You should be careful, Alex,' she warned. 'You must tell me if you are dizzy so I can call the doctor back.' She shook her head. 'He's drunk, of course. He always is. But he knows his work.'

'Where are the people who brought me here?' he asked, swallowing hard as he felt the throb of pain in his head worsen. He wasn't going to mention it to Rena. She'd probably tie him to the bed till the doctor returned. It was then that he realised he'd been undressed. Had she done that? He glanced over to the chair where his clothes had been draped and saw his satchel. Although it was buckled, he wondered if anyone had looked inside it.

'The English?' Rena twitched her nose. 'I thought they were horrible people when I first saw them. They smelled of beer.

But they helped you and they were very friendly. They went away when the doctor came.'

Mavros nodded slowly, the ache still there. 'I wanted to thank them.'

'They said some people attacked you, Alex.' Rena's eyes were wide. 'Who could have done that? You must talk to the policeman tomorrow.'

He shook his head and immediately regretted the movement. 'No, it was only some drunken idiots. I'll find them myself.'

Rena drew the chair nearer and sat down. 'Will you? Like you will find Rosa Ozal?'

Mavros caught the sharper tone in her voice. 'Yes, I hope I'll find Rosa,' he said cautiously.

'*Vre psefti*,' she said, leaning over him. Liar. 'Why are you pretending that you're a foreigner?' she continued in Greek. 'Why have you been deceiving me and everyone else? What are you? An undercover cop?' She used the derogatory term *batsos*.

Shit, Mavros thought, letting his limbs go slack. It looked like he would have to come clean with his landlady. Otherwise she might square up to him as she had to the Dutchman, and he was definitely in no condition to take another beating.

16

Kyra Maro was sitting at the table in her front room, the first light of dawn filtering through the half-closed shutters. The birds were chattering in the morning sun, flitting between the chimneys of the *kastro* and the branches of the fig tree that spread over the water cistern. She could hear the yowls of the skinny cats as they looked up longingly at prey they rarely caught. Some of the old women in the neighbourhood put poison down for them, but Maro never did. She felt sympathy for the outcast creatures, even took them into her home on occasion.

But not this morning. She was taking a chance opening the shutters at all. If any of the villagers peeked in and saw what she had on the table, she'd be shunned even more. But she couldn't help it. The oil lamp had been burning all night and she couldn't stand the fumes any longer. And today was his day, today was Tasos's day. For the rest of the year the poor boy was confined in the box and in the artificial light of her bedroom. He needed to feel the sun's warmth once a year, he needed to be brought back to the living world.

Maro looked down at the pile of bones she'd carefully arranged on the table, the misshapen skull on top. Her eyes filled with tears and she extended a twisted hand, put the tips of her fingers on the discoloured surface of her son's head. Tradition said that if the bones came up black or unclean at exhumation, the deceased was a sinner or a vampire. But no one else knew the condition of Tasos's remains. She'd been forced to have him buried in the disused cemetery at Myli in the Kambos. Five years later the priest and all the village women had refused to attend the exhumation, her brother Manolis made sure of that. So Maro had dug her son up unattended, had sung the laments for him on her own. Afterwards, instead of consigning his box to the ossuary, she had taken it back to her house under a blanket on the donkey's back. Tasos was always with her and he was even closer to her on this day, October 2nd, the day of his birth.

'Ach, Taso,' she said in a low voice. 'You were blameless, you didn't deserve your fate. It was my fault, it was the war that eats men and families then spits them out on the ground.' She moved her fingers across the table and felt the small heap of dried pomegranate seeds.

'Anastasios, I called you,' she continued, her voice cracking, 'even though the name wasn't handed down in our family. Anastasios after the resurrection, because I knew you would not be with me for long. But I never celebrate your feast day at Easter – no, there is too much joy and hope at that time.' She bent her head and let out a great sob. 'And I know you will never come back, even in the twisted form that was your unfair fate. Today is your day, your birthday. The foreigners celebrate that more than we do, so Tzortz told me. He had his birthday during that terrible January.' She was caught up in the throes of weeping, only swallowing her cries when she heard footsteps in the street. She hobbled over to the window and drew the shutters to as the black figure of one of her neighbours passed the house. There was no call, no offer of help. They were all waiting for her to die.

'Ach, Taso,' she said, touching the bones again. 'You were twenty when you left me, your body that of a man but your mind a smiling child's. The doctor said you would die before you were a year old, but you stayed much longer and I loved you even more for that.' She picked up the skull and held it close to her withered breasts. 'My son,' she whispered, 'come back to me.' She looked over the pile of bones at the framed photograph, her eyes narrowing in the gloom. 'And you, Tzortz, you must come back too. You said we were immortal and in one way you were right.' She sobbed again. 'But only for as long as I am here to remember you.'

And suddenly Maro was back on the flanks of Vigla, the evening wind tugging her jet-black hair and her young legs traversing the stony ground with ease. The sun had been swallowed by the western sea an hour earlier and her lover would be waiting for her in their secret cave. She had taken a great risk by slipping out of the house during the celebrations. At the festival of Epiphany one of her cousins had found the cross in the waters of the harbour and the family was rejoicing. Manolis and the other men had been drinking *tsikoudhia* all day, giving her the opportunity to leave unnoticed.

'Stop,' said a low male voice to her left. 'Where are you going?' The unmistakable sound of a revolver being cocked followed the words.

She waited as the man came out of the bushes with a faint rustle. In the dim light of the rising moon she made out the features of the landowner's son.

'Where are you going, girl?' he repeated when she kept silent, his voice harsher.

'I have a message for the English officer,' she said, staring into his dark-ringed eyes.

'Give it to me,' Panos Theocharis said. 'I will take it.'

She shook her head, her heart pounding. 'No,' she said. 'I don't trust you.' She knew such words, directed by a peasant girl to a rich family's heir, would sting him. Before he could react she darted away behind an outcrop of rock, leading him in the opposite direction from her destination.

She soon lost the captain's footfall, her knowledge of the terrain much better than his. After waiting for a long time, she moved on towards the cave, taking a roundabout route through the steep watercourses on the western slopes. But still she failed to approach the cave unnoticed.

The Englishman with the frightening eyes swung down in front of her from the top of a boulder, a knife between his teeth. He took it out and held it against her throat and she felt her knees give way, so intense was the way he was looking at her as he bore down.

Then she heard Tzortz's voice, low but angry. Her attacker

stepped back and disappeared into the night after they exchanged some words.

'I'm sorry, my love,' he said, drawing her close. 'I told him to stay near the hut, but he does what he wants. Don't worry, he won't tell anyone you were here.'

Maro told him about her meeting with Theocharis as they moved towards the cave.

'Never fear,' he said. 'We'll think of a story. We'll say you heard some news from Paros.' He turned up the lamp and looked at her anxiously. 'Have you heard anything?'

She stared at him, seeing how ravaged his expression was. She shook her head. 'No, Tzortz. It's the *Fota*. Everyone is celebrating.'

He shook his head. 'Not the Italians. I've had a message on the wireless. The operators at base intercepted an enemy transmission.' He lowered his eyes. 'It seems that some of the enemy were killed during our operation.'

'My God,' she said. 'What will they do?'

He raised his shoulders. 'Arrest people on Paros? Search the neighbouring islands for us? Take hostages here? I don't know, Maro.'

She went to him and put her arms around his thin frame, feeling him shake. He was a boy again, all his soldier's zeal gone. 'Maybe they won't follow you to Trigono,' she heard herself say, the words ringing hollow in her ears. 'Maybe they'll think the attackers came from far away and sailed back there afterwards.'

He nodded slowly, tightening his arms around her. 'Do you know what day it is?' he said shyly. 'It's my birthday. I'm twenty-five years old.' He inclined his head towards the tins of food and the flask laid out on the blanket. 'I was going to celebrate on my own, but now you're here . . .'

Maro kissed him, pressed him down to the ground. They made love with more passion than she had ever experienced; she thought she was going to die when he came into her and the world broke into tiny pieces, smaller than the grains of sand that were washed by the restless waters around the island.

It was as if they both knew that their dream would soon be over. The years of stone had already started to harden around them.

It was awkward, it took some time, but Mavros managed to convince Rena that he wasn't the great deceiver she had taken him for. The fact that it was after three in the morning and they were both yawning probably helped. He had some business cards secreted inside the cover of his mobile phone and one of them seemed to reassure her more than his protestations.

'I am disappointed in you, Alex,' she complained. 'You pretended you were a tourist and you spoke only English to me.'

'I *am* a tourist,' he replied. 'I've never been to Trigono before.'

Her expression was disapproving. 'But you are not truly foreign.'

'Okay, I'm half Scottish and I'm half Greek. So I told you half a lie.'

She dismissed his smile with a stern stare. It was only after she'd examined his card and asked about his interest in Rosa Ozal that the atmosphere lightened. Although his head was aching, he tried to keep the conversation going. He had the feeling that Rena was about to open up to him. But she noticed he was struggling and forced him to take a pill that the doctor had left. 'We'll talk about this again in the morning,' she'd said, pulling the sheet over his upper torso. 'Go to sleep now, liar.' Her brief smile diluted the annoyance in her voice.

Mavros woke feeling slightly less pulverised. His body still gave howls of pain when he moved in certain ways, but his head was clear. He decided to leave the five-day stubble, the livid red patch on his jaw putting him off shaving. After a cold shower he pulled on his jeans, feeling the plastic cover of his ID card bend against his buttock. Rena had obviously noticed it when she was undressing him. In future he'd have to be more careful when he played the undercover game.

'Good morning,' Rena called in Greek as he walked into the courtyard. A concerned look appeared on her face. 'Are you all right? Sit down. I will make you coffee.'

Mavros allowed her to pander to him, watching the birds fuss in the bougainvillaea, the purple flowers with their yellow inner parts soaking up the sun.

It was after she'd brought him a Greek coffee and a plate of home-made *koulouria*, ring-shaped biscuits, that he asked her how she'd felt about Rosa. The photographs he'd seen in the folder under her pillow showed they'd been close. It was time to be more direct with his landlady. The attack on him last night meant that he had to make rapid progress with the Ozal case as well as identify who had laid into him before another attack was made.

Rena looked at him thoughtfully, one hand at her throat above the top button of her black blouse. 'How I felt about her?' Her eyes bored into him. 'I know you have been in my bedroom,' she said slowly. 'You left the door open.'

Mavros felt his cheeks redden. 'I had to—'

The widow raised a hand. 'Don't give me excuses. I want you to tell me one thing and then I will help you. Who are you working for?'

Mavros should have kept his client's name confidential but he knew he had to prove that he was being straight with her. So he told her about Deniz Ozal, not mentioning the Turkish-American's apparent lack of concern about Rosa's disappearance. He hadn't heard from his client since the call from Istanbul airport.

Rena shook her head. 'Rosa mentioned her mother, but she never said anything about a brother.'

'She went to Turkey after she was here,' Mavros said. 'She sent a postcard from there saying she had met a man.'

Rena's eyes widened. 'A man?' She gave a hollow laugh. 'I wonder.' She looked away, her gaze fixed on the wellhead. 'Do you know how difficult it is for a widow on a small island like this, Mr Private Detective?' she said in a low voice. 'This isn't Athens where you can do anything you like behind closed shutters and doors.' She glanced back at him. 'Here, they know what you're doing – or they think they know what you're doing, which can be worse – even if you put a hundred locks on your house.'

He nodded, concealing his surprise. He hadn't expected her to open up so easily. Then again, maybe it was easier to do so to a stranger. He decided to press harder. 'You're still a young woman. You . . . how shall I put this? You have desires.'

Rena lowered her head. 'Yes, Alex, I have desires. I have many desires. You see . . . you see, I discovered that I am attracted to men and to women. I never knew about liking women until I started renting rooms, after the worm died.' This description of her husband made Mavros blink. Now he could see why there were no photos of him displayed in the house. But why did she keep the crumpled one under her pillow along with that of her parents?

'Rosa,' she continued, the words beginning to flow, 'she showed me things I had never imagined. She made me laugh again, she made me cry from the beauty of it. No man ever made me do that.'

'And then she left without saying goodbye?'

The widow nodded, eyes still down. 'I don't know why she did that. I went out to the fields one day and when I came back her things were gone. There was no note on the table, no message with the neighbour.' She turned to the house on her right. 'Not that the old gossip would have given me it. She thinks I'm a witch.' She gave a contemptuous snort.

'Did . . .' Mavros hesitated, remembering the fury she'd displayed with Rinus. 'Did Rosa like men as well?'

Rena's tongue played across her lips. 'She liked to go out in the evenings. I told you she went to the pervert Dutchman's bar.' She bowed her head again. 'Yes, I think she may have liked men too.'

Mavros leaned across the table, swallowing a gasp as his ribs creaked painfully. 'Does that explain why you were fighting with Rinus?'

'Over Rosa?' she said, her eyes wide. 'Is that what you think?' She gave a laugh and then choked on it. 'No, I have other problems with the Dutchman.'

Mavros waited, but Rena didn't elaborate. Did she know

about the drugs dealing? He didn't want to mention what he'd discovered about that until he spoke to the barman again.

'I miss her,' she said. 'We were only together for a few days but I miss her still.' She shook her head. 'And then it happened again a week ago.'

He turned an ear towards her, unsure that he'd heard correctly. 'What did you say?' he asked.

She looked straight at him. 'It happened again. A woman who was staying here, a woman I . . . I became friendly with left without a word.'

Mavros was thinking of the other woman in the photo upstairs, the one he'd seen in Eleni's album as well. 'Who was she?' But the words were scarcely out of his mouth when the doorbell rang.

Rena got up, shrugging helplessly, and admitted the English couples who had rescued him.

Panos Theocharis was sitting in front of the widescreen television in his study on the first floor of the tower, fingering the handset. The images on the screen were scanning forward at speed, the bare flesh a blur of colours and movements. He pressed 'Play' and watched as the blur took solid shape. The woman was on her hands and knees, breasts hanging and quivering as she was penetrated from behind. Her hands and feet were bound so the man had his legs on either side of her narrow hips. As he climaxed, he turned to the camera and looked straight at it, his eyes fixed and his mouth half open. It was formed in a rictus that contained no hint of pleasure. Theocharis knew how he felt. He couldn't even get hard any more, could do no more than watch other people having sex, but at least it was a distraction – a distraction from the diary that was locked in his desk. Although the book was out of sight, he couldn't get the English lieutenant's words out of his mind. Cloying and sentimental they may have been, even arrogant at times, but they were making him feel the shame he'd always managed to block out until now. First there had been guilt and fear, now there was shame.

The door opened and Dhimitra came in, her heels clicking on the varnished floor.

'Mother of God, Pano,' she exclaimed. 'Are you watching that filth again?'

Theocharis swivelled his head slowly towards his wife. 'Filth? You used to work in the industry, didn't you?' He gave a bitter smile.

'Only when the singing didn't pay enough,' she replied, sitting at the far end of the leather sofa from him and picking up a fashion magazine.

'And when your narcotics bill mounted up,' Theocharis said, turning the video off.

Dhimitra held her eyes on the glossy photograph of a model in a short skirt. 'Well, you saved me from that life, Pano.'

He turned to her. 'Did I? I hope you haven't managed to find someone on the island to supply you, Dhimitra. I'd be extremely disappointed.'

The edge to his voice made her sit up straight. She put down the magazine and faced him. 'I'm not using, Pano.' She stretched out her arms, forearms upwards, the sleeves of her red silk blouse riding up.

'That proves nothing,' her husband said, running his eyes up her torso.

'You want me to strip?' Dhimitra asked hoarsely.

He nodded slowly. 'Why not? You have your own room and you never come to my bed nowadays. And not even I would carry out an inspection for track marks in front of the servants.'

She stood up, her lips set in a tight line. She stepped out of her Versace skirt and shrugged off her blouse, then unhooked her lacy black bra. She pulled down the matching knickers in a quick movement. 'Satisfied?'

Theocharis had come closer, his thin shanks rubbing along the sofa, to examine her ankles, the backs of her knees and her thighs. 'No,' he said, his bony fingers resting on the lips of her sex. He leaned forward and took some time to finish with that area, then he moved on to her armpits and lifted her breasts to look at the skin beneath them.

Dhimitra's breathing was shallow, her face taut.

'That surgery I paid so much for in Switzerland enhanced your bosom very successfully, didn't it?' her husband said, sitting back. 'Yes, it seems you're clean.'

'Fuck you, Pano,' she said. 'Even sticking your fingers inside me didn't make your old cock stiff, did it?' She started pulling on her clothes, jerking her head round as the door opened without warning.

'Oh, excuse me,' said Aris, a grin spreading across his heavy face. 'It never occurred to me that sex still played a part in your relationship.'

'Be quiet and come over here,' the old man said. 'You, stay,' he said as his wife started to move away, her blouse still open. 'The three of us need to talk.'

Aris pulled a chair in front of the sofa, the flesh of his thighs wobbling beneath his shorts. He was wearing the green shade on his head even though the sun was kept from the room by blinds. 'Talk?' he asked, suddenly less sure of himself. 'What about?'

Theocharis waited until Dhimitra had sat down, his eyes directed out of the high French windows towards the white mass of the village in the distance. The surface of the sea in the straits beyond was cutting up, the waves whipped by a strengthening northerly wind. 'What about?' he repeated, glaring at his son and then his wife. 'This man Alex, the one who calls himself Cochrane. I have made an interesting discovery about him.' He pointed to his desk. 'Fetch me that black file, Ari.'

His son clumped across the room and returned, handing over a document wallet. 'He's just a tourist, for Christ's sake,' Aris said under his breath.

'I'm afraid he isn't,' Theocharis said, taking a photograph out and holding it up to them. 'Do you recognise the couple he's with? I know it's an old photo, but the youth is plainly Alex.'

'Christ and the Holy Mother,' said Dhimitra. 'That's Mavros the communist, isn't it?'

'Very good,' her husband replied. 'And the woman is his wife, Dorothy Cochrane-Mavrou. The name Cochrane meant something to me the moment he said it, but I couldn't place it until yesterday.'

'So what?' Aris demanded, his brow furrowed. 'So the guy's father was a communist. Are we supposed to torture him like your friends the Colonels did with his kind during the dictatorship?'

Theocharis turned on him. 'Shut up, you fool. This has nothing to do with politics.' Then he ran a hand through his pointed white beard. 'Though maybe that is a way of tackling it.' He thought for a few moments then focused on his son again. 'The point is that he is not just a tourist as he pretends. He speaks Greek and he holds dual Greek and British nationality.'

Dhimitra was staring at him. 'Why the pretence?' She moved closer to her husband. 'How do you know about his background, Pano?'

'I was suspicious of him from the beginning. Remember, he talked Eleni Trypani into showing him the dig. That made me sure he was a thief or a dealer. I invited him to the tower to gauge his reaction to the collection, but that was inconclusive.' Theocharis gave his wife a scathing look. 'Mainly because, despite the fact that I asked you to be welcoming, you were interested only in making a spectacle of yourself.'

Dhimitra stuck her chin forward. 'You should have told me why you wanted my help.'

'It doesn't matter now,' the old man said, holding up a photocopied sheet. The printed script was blurred but legible.

'Jesus,' Aris said, straining forward. 'He's a private dick.' His expression had darkened. 'That's all we need.'

'How did you get this?' Dhimitra asked. 'It's a Justice Ministry authorisation.'

'One of my people here obtained this and his ID card last night. Mavros doesn't know they disappeared for a time.'

'I don't get it,' Aris said. 'What's he doing here?'

Theocharis stood up and took his stick from the end of the sofa. 'Ostensibly, as you both know, he's trying to locate Rosa

Ozal.' He looked at them in turn. 'More disturbing as far as I'm concerned, his interest in the dig suggests that he may in reality be investigating illicit antiquities trading, either freelance or on behalf of one of the ministries. I've got my people in Athens checking in the relevant offices.'

Aris's expression was less sombre now. 'It sounds to me like it's time this Alex Mavros received a dose of pain to keep him in his place.' He got to his feet and stood by his father. 'Want me to organise something?'

'I have already organised a dose of pain, as you put it,' Theocharis said, keeping his eyes off his son. 'It didn't run as smoothly as I hoped, but I don't think Mavros will be asking any more questions for a day or two. Now it's time we discovered what Eleni has told him. My tame archaeologist has been behaving rather erratically in recent weeks.'

'Shall I bring her to the cellar tonight?' Aris said, his tone avid.

His father shook his head. 'No, we'll handle it differently. We still need her, at least in the short term.' He glanced at Dhimitra. 'I presume you'll want to be involved. I know how much you dislike Eleni.'

The former singer nodded, her fingers with their painted nails wrapped tightly around the old man's fleshless arm.

Mavros finally managed to get rid of the English tourists by feigning a worse headache than he had. He was grateful to them, but their noisy bonhomie was not what he wanted right now, and the darkness meant they had seen nothing that would identify his attackers. They didn't look particularly bothered that he wasn't going to involve the police. His main concern was to talk to Rena again before she left for the fields. She had already put bread and olives and a flask of water into a wicker basket.

As his rescuers headed for the door, the woman Jane giving him a questioning look, he remembered what they had been saying about Rinus in the restaurant. Had Roy made good his threat to avenge his woman's honour?

'Did you ever get to the Astrapi last night?' he called after them.

'Nah, mate,' Roy replied, running his hand over his shaved and scarred scalp. 'But we'll be there tonight. You make sure you join us. There's going to be some fun.' He laughed in a worrying way and then disappeared into the passage.

It looked like Rinus's escape would only be temporary.

'I must go,' Rena said. 'Melpo is waiting for me.'

'Melpo?' Mavros said, trying to place the name.

'My donkey,' the widow said with a smile. 'Well, the donkey I use. You are losing your memory, Mr Investigator.'

Mavros got up from his chair. 'Now I remember. You keep her out at the old man's farm.' He extended a hand towards her. 'Wait, Rena, we must talk more.'

She stared at him doggedly and then put down her basket. 'All right. But not for long.' She came back to the table under the pergola and sat down.

'This woman,' Mavros said. 'The other one you said left suddenly. Who was she?'

A cloud seemed to pass over Rena's face. 'Ach, Alex. I don't want to talk about her. She . . . she was here and now she's gone.' She bowed her head.

Mavros remembered his mother saying something similar about his father and his brother Andonis, but he suppressed the thought. 'What was her name?' he asked gently.

Rena kept silent and then raised her eyes to his. 'Liz,' she said. 'Elizabeth.' She pronounced the English version of the name carefully, then got up and went into the kitchen, returning with her accounts book. 'Here you are,' she said, opening it and pointing to an entry only a few lines above his own incomplete details. 'This time you don't have to pretend you can't follow the Greek.'

Mavros gave a rueful smile then looked at the neat script. 'Clifton, Elizabeth,' he read. 'Nationality British, date of birth 4/9/67, arrived September thirteenth, departed September twenty-third.' He glanced up. 'That's under a week before I came to Trigono.'

Rena was nodding. 'Yes. She had your room. She was . . . she was a very good woman. Very friendly.'

Mavros was thinking about the photos and the computer diskette he'd found. He'd assumed they were put up the chimney by Rosa Ozal because of the handwriting on the back of the photo showing the dig, but maybe this woman Liz was responsible for hiding the package. He looked back at the entry.

'Paid a hundred thousand drachmas in advance.' He looked at Rena. 'When was she supposed to leave?'

'Tomorrow,' Rena said, blinking several times.

'What happened?'

Rena raised a hand to her forehead then met his eyes. 'I don't know, Alex. I came back from the fields in the afternoon and . . . and she was gone. The door to her room, your room, was open and I went to greet her. As soon as I looked in I realised she had left. There was nothing belonging to her anywhere. Even the wastepaper bin in the bedroom was empty and it was often full of papers.' The widow gave a sad smile. 'She was always writing on a notepad or on her computer.' She shook her head. 'We had got quite close,' she said softly. 'I'd have expected a message.'

'Did anyone else see her leave?' Mavros asked. The similarity of this second unexpected departure to Rosa's bothered him. The barman Rinus had supposedly witnessed the Turkish-American woman get on the ferry.

Rena raised her shoulders. 'I don't know. I didn't ask anyone.' She looked down. 'I didn't want people to think . . .' Her words trailed away.

'That you had become over-friendly with her?' he said gently.

She nodded. 'I'd already been cursed when Liz and I were seen touching each other.' She chewed her lip for a few moments. 'That animal Lefteris.' She stood up. 'I must go to Melpo.'

Mavros got up too. 'Are you walking out to the farm?'

'Yes. I have no choice. Old Thodhoris won't let me keep Melpo anywhere closer to the village.'

'I'll come with you to the junction.' Mavros needed to check the place where he was attacked, but he also didn't want to leave his conversation with Rena unfinished. Her mention of Lefteris and the way the blood rushed to her neck and face had caught his attention. He went into his room and picked up his bag.

On the street Rena drew her black scarf over her hair. 'I think she was a journalist,' she said, unprompted. 'I mean Liz. She asked me a lot of questions about the island. She was very interested in what happened during the war.' As they passed a pair of old women, she wished them a good day. They muttered a grudging response. 'She had some old books about it, one of them filled with tiny handwriting.'

Mavros was thinking of the photo of George Lawrence and the war memorial, as well as the diskette with his initials on it. He'd also remembered the Paros historian's book, the one that Panos Theocharis had apparently suppressed. Was the copy in Rena's suitcase connected in some way to Liz Clifton?

'Old crows,' Rena was saying under her breath, looking back at the women. 'They are relatives of Lefteris . . .'

They had reached the end of the village and the track that led to the Bar Astrapi was on their left. Mavros stopped and tossed a coin in his mind. He reckoned Rena would only leave the donkey waiting for one more question. Should he ask about Liz or Lefteris? He went for the latter, the fisherman's muscular bulk looming up before him. The way he and his father had stared at him in the restaurant made them good candidates to be his assailants – old Manolis looked capable enough of violence despite having only one arm.

'What has Lefteris done to make you hate him?' he asked, raising his sunglasses to look into the widow's eyes.

Rena's cheeks blanched. 'What has he done?' she said in a tight voice. 'What has he done?' She dropped her gaze. 'I was drawn to him for a while. He sensed my weakness after Argyris died, he came to me and overwhelmed me. For a while he made me feel like a woman again.' Her voice dwindled to a whisper. 'And then I realised that he only wanted to dominate me, to mount me like a bull.' She gave a bitter laugh. 'Until something happened to him in the summer and he couldn't . . . he couldn't do it any more.'

She looked up. 'But that only made him more violent than he used to be.' She opened the top button of her blouse and pointed to a scarred patch of skin. 'Cigarettes. He told me not to scream and I . . . I obeyed him.' Her eyes were clouded with tears. 'And . . . and I saw what he was doing to his son. He and that bastard Dutchman, they're in it together. Lefteris rents the bar to him and they do their filthy business there. But why did they have to involve poor Yiangos? He used to be such a sweet boy but Lefteris was making him hard, in his own image. Oh, God . . .' Rena drew her sleeve over her eyes. 'I have to go, Alex. I've said too much.' She twitched her head as if to deny everything she'd told him and hurried away, the wicker basket banging against her leg.

Mavros stood watching her as she moved up the asphalt road towards the Kambos. It sounded like she knew about the drug dealing. He hadn't expected such an outpouring of information, let alone emotion. He wasn't sure where it all left him. He would have to talk to Rena again, though much of what she'd said was only tangentially linked to Rosa Ozal. But he was getting a bad feeling about the case. Someone else was too. The attack on him wasn't a random one. He went up the narrow path to confirm this impression. So Lefteris and Rinus were in business together. The barman was still serving customers when Mavros had left so he couldn't have attacked him, but he might have put his partner up to it.

There were plenty of footprints on the dusty earth both inside and over the walls, far too many to be much help. It was easy enough to find the location where he had been assaulted. There was a patch of his blood on a large stone by the side where he had fallen, and the footprints in this area were even more chaotic – mainly trainers, the ones worn by both the Englishmen. He climbed over the wall to his left, the bones in his side complaining, and found more prints among the mule and goat tracks. These were from heavy boots, as worn by the village men, some of them no doubt left by the farmer who worked the field. But others must have been from his assailants. His rescuers were unsure how many there had been – they admitted they'd all been half pissed – but there had been at least two. He followed a faint line of double tracks then lost them in a patch of earth where the animals must have congregated. And then he found a length of thick metal piping.

Biting his lip, he kneeled down and picked it up in a handkerchief before putting it in his satchel. It was about forty centimetres long, the metal grey and dented in several places at one end. Through the dust Mavros thought he could see traces of blood. If he decided to get the police involved this would be useful evidence, especially if the person holding it hadn't been wearing gloves. But he didn't intend talking to the local policeman, not even now. He'd seen the guy in the bar on his first night and it was obvious he was in Rinus's pocket. But this was serious. Whoever laid into him hadn't just been using fists. The piping was potentially a lethal weapon. If the British couples hadn't arrived when they did, he might have been in a much worse state than he was. Someone on Trigono had upped the stakes in a big way.

Trying unsuccessfully to protect his aching ribs as he clambered back over the wall, Mavros walked back to the outskirts of the village and hired the same mountain bike from the girl with the pitying expression. He mounted up and headed out towards the Kambos. He was hoping Eleni would be at the dig as he wanted to ask her about Liz. The photo he'd seen in her album showed that she had known the Englishwoman too. Now this was more significant since perhaps she had disappeared too. Was there a connection between Liz Clifton and Rosa Ozal, or had they both suddenly left the island by coincidence? Maybe Liz Clifton had just found the photo with Rosa's writing in the room at Rena's. But why would she, or someone else, have put it up the chimney along with the other photos and the diskette?

When he reached the top of the slope between the village and the plateau, Mavros stopped to catch his breath. Looking around at the patchwork of cultivated land, he felt the wind on his back. The sea to his right was choppy, the vibrant blue cut with white. He hadn't heard a weather forecast since he'd been on the island. At last he was experiencing the rapid increase in wind that was

notorious in the Cyclades. Storms often messed up ferry schedules
and forced urgent medical cases to be transported to the mainland
by helicopter.

This gave him even more motivation to wrap up the case.
The idea of being marooned on Trigono was filling him with
trepidation.

17

Mavros followed the road through the cultivated plain. When it turned to the rough track beyond the Paliopyrgos estate and began to steepen, he ditched the bike behind a boulder overgrown with bone-dry thistles and continued on foot. The wind whistled past his head as he climbed towards the dig plateau and he felt his breath catching in his throat. The clink of goat bells made him look to his left. The coats of the animals were visible on the western slopes of Profitis Ilias, the young herdsman he'd met waving at him. At first Mavros thought something was wrong, so vigorously was the arm moving, then he realised that it was just an overstated greeting and returned it less effusively. That didn't put the islander off. He came loping down the hillside, his dog barking at his heels.

'I remember you,' the young man said with a wide smile. His teeth were surprisingly white, the skin on his face smooth and tanned.

'I remember you too,' Mavros said, nodding and making to move on.

'Dinos,' the herdsman said. 'I am Dinos.'

'Yes,' Mavros replied, staying where he was and resigning himself to a conversation with the lonely local. 'I am Alex.'

'Cigarette?' There was another smile.

Mavros shook his head, looking past Dinos up the slope. Some of the goats were right up on the ridge. An idea came to him. 'You go up there?'

'I go up there every day,' Dinos said. 'The goats can get over the old wall. I must stop them going to the edge of the cliff.'

'You can see very far from the top, I suppose.' Mavros kept

his voice level, displaying no more than passing interest. He didn't want to scare the herdsman off.

'Yes, to all the islands.' Dinos swept his arm round in a great sweep.

'There are islands near Trigono, are there not?'

'Aspronisi, Mavronisi, Eschati,' the herdsman recited.

Mavros nodded, a smile on his lips, then he put his hand on Dinos's arm and caught his eye. 'I imagine you see boats too. Fishing boats.'

The islander stiffened and tried to pull away, but Mavros didn't let him.

'You saw Yiangos and Navsika, didn't you?' Mavros had moved close, his mouth up to Dinos's ear. 'Don't worry, I won't tell anyone your secret.'

The herdsman was breathing hard and suddenly he let out a long groan, his chest heaving.

'It was Aris Theocharis's boat that hit theirs, wasn't it?' Mavros said quietly. He felt sympathy for the simple boy who had obviously bottled up what he'd seen and was burning with guilt. 'I won't tell anyone you told me, I promise.'

Dinos fought to get his breathing under control. He blinked tears from his eyes then leaned his head against Mavros's shoulder. 'He hit the *trata* but he didn't help Yiangos and Navsika until it was . . . until it was too late,' he said, sliding his tongue over chapped lips. Then he jerked away and started running up the slope towards his goats.

Mavros squatted down and thought about what he'd heard. His call to the boatyard on Paros had made him pretty sure that Aris had been involved in the accident, but this unexpected confirmation had thrown him. He didn't think it would be worth much in a court. The Theocharis family lawyers wouldn't need long to discredit Dinos's testimony on the grounds of mental deficiency, even if the old man failed to bribe the goatherd or his family into silence. But it gave him something to hold against the multimillionaire.

He had the feeling that he'd soon need everything he could

find to defend himself against Trigono's self-appointed lord and master.

January 8th, 1943

Disaster has come to Trigono; disaster that I am, at least in part, responsible for. But I must be firm. I must not allow myself to be diverted from the objectives of my mission.

We were unlucky on several counts. Or perhaps we brought the wrath of the enemy on our own heads. I cannot be sure. The Italians have continued to claim that during 'a cowardly act of sabotage' two of their garrison, a sentry and, worse, an officer doing his rounds at the supply depot, were killed in 'the most barbaric fashion, their throats slit like animals in a slaughterhouse'. So say the proclamations that have been posted in Paros, Andiparos and Trigono. I knew nothing about this during the operation, although I remember Griffin disappearing on his own into the dark on more than one occasion. When I questioned him this morning he said in his terse way that he was not to blame and I had to take his word for that, but he has a wicked look in his eye, a cold, inhuman stare. Rees is in awe of him and since the raid he has kept his distance.

Perhaps Trigono would have escaped retribution if the trail of footprints from British army boots hadn't been followed to the cove on the south of Paros: and if a goatherd on the hillside above hadn't sighted the Ersi on her voyage back to Trig. The Italians beat that information out of the poor boy. Apparently his jaw was broken and one eye badly damaged. There are fears that he will lose the sight in it. But even those terrible injuries pale into insignificance in comparison with the Italians' actions here today.

From the summit of Vigla we watched as the enemy approached the harbour of Faros in three commandeered kaïkia, Agamemnon having learned from a runner sent by Ajax that they were on their way. The word had been spread around the village that everyone should be as compliant as possible. At any rate, the majority of the locals knew nothing about us. According to Maro, Ajax and his men were tight lipped even with their families. I was worried about Maro and wished that she could be with me in the hills. Obviously that was impossible as it would only have drawn attention to her, as well as raising her brother's suspicions about the two of us even more. When I saw him yesterday, he gave me a searching look and then turned away to talk to the Sacred Band group. He deals only with Agamemnon now.

The Italians came round Cape Fonias and moored in the port, men immediately moving through the village in pairs. We could only sit and wait helplessly, hoping that they didn't harm any Trigoniotes and that they wouldn't pick up any hint of our presence. Until midday there was no sign of trouble. Then we saw a larger group of enemy soldiers on mules come over the brow of the hill above the Kambos and head towards the buildings of Myli, where the hut I used before I came up to the caves is located. We watched them as they moved down the track and waited. There were men and women working in the fields around the windmills and we saw them suddenly rush towards the old church. They were soon shut up inside, an Italian on the door, his rifle at the ready. I wondered what was about to happen, a sense of foreboding settling over me like a cloud of poison gas.

Agamemnon crawled up the hill behind us and raised his binoculars. 'They have learned from the Germans in Crete,' he said, his voice taut. 'The enemy herded villagers into churches there. You can be sure they will be interrogating them.' I could feel his eyes on me. 'Did any of the islanders see you when you were living down there?'

'I don't think so,' I replied.

'What about the girl Maro?' he asked, moving closer so that I could smell his sour breath. 'She was taking supplies to you, was she not?'

I kept my eyes on the buildings in the distance. A man had just been dragged out of the church. 'When Ajax was injured, yes,' I replied, my heart beating fast. I sensed his disapproval. 'She won't tell the Italians anything. I am sure of that.'

'I hope so, for our sakes and for the sake of the island,' he said. 'If they find even the slightest trace of enemy presence, they will feel

*justified to act as harshly as the Germans.' He jabbed his elbow into
my side. 'Have you any idea how little value our oppressors put on
human lives?'*

*I saw a puff of smoke between the windmills then heard the crump
of an explosion in the clear air.*

'Grenade,' Griffin said, his ear cocked. 'And another.'

*There was a long rattle of gunfire, a combination of rifle shots and
the repetitive drill of sub-machine guns. We listened as the sounds
continued, then saw the men on the door move away. They were
joined by others and they all directed their fire at the church.*

*'Bloody hell,' Rees said under his breath. 'How many people are
in there?'*

*'Sixteen,' Griffin replied. 'I counted them in.' He turned and gave
a tight smile. 'I wonder how many will be walking out.'*

*Agamemnon stared at him, an expression of disgust twisting his
face. 'My God, Lieutenant,' he said, 'what kind of men are you?'
He withdrew to the ridge and rejoined his unit.*

*At last the Italians ceased fire and opened the doors to the church.
Soldiers entered and soon reappeared, dragging six men and one
woman out. At first I thought they were dead, then I saw them
stand up, their legs unsteady. Relief dashed over me. And then I
made out that they were being attached to the mules by long ropes.
The Italians set off at a brisk pace, their captives forced to run after
them or be dragged along the stony road. My heart was pounding
as I tried to make out the faces of the islanders, in particular the
woman. But all I could see were black clothes and bare legs. Could
it be Maro? Would she have been in the fields? I didn't know
and everything suddenly shifted. My life went into an uncontrolled
descent, like a paratrooper's whose chute fails to open.*

*We waited until they had disappeared over the hill, a cloud of
dust marking their passing towards the village. Ordering Griffin
to stay on watch, which he didn't like, I took Rees with me down
the slope. Over to our right the Greeks were also making their way
towards the mills, Agamemnon running with great strides over the
bushes. I wondered if Myli and its buildings were part of his family
estate, but dismissed that unworthy thought.*

As we approached the scene of the shooting. I heard shrill screams above my desperate gasps, loud wails similar to the ones I'd heard from the hut during the exhumation. Scarcely able to breathe, I followed Agamemnon round the last bend between the high walls.

The body of an elderly man lay in the clear space in front of the church, women on their knees around him. There were explosion craters near by, smoke rising from the devastated mills. I assumed the man had been killed during the firing, but Agamemnon turned to me from the body and said that he must have died of heart failure. There was no mark on him. Going towards the church, which was pocked by dozens of bullet holes, I counted the islanders and came to nine including the dead man. Nine plus the seven captives came to sixteen. If Griffin's numbers were correct, there were no casualties apart from the old man. That was a miracle. The Italians must have been trying to frighten the locals with the gunfire and grenades. Taking hostages meant that they had effectively neutralised us. Their assumption was that the islanders would no longer help or harbour us. That way they could avoid casualties by leaving the southern massif uncombed.

'Who was the woman they took?' I demanded of a tear-stained peasant woman. 'Was it Maro Grypari?' She stared at me blankly and I felt the fear rise up in me. I grabbed her arms and shook her. 'Was it Maro Grypari?' I heard myself shout.

'No, it wasn't,' Agamemnon said, detaching the woman from my grasp and giving her into the care of another female islander. 'Do you care about anyone apart from the girl you are corrupting?' he said bitterly. 'Do you know why they did this, Lieutenant? Do you know why they terrified these people and destroyed the mills and defaced the church?'

The cloud of foreboding I had felt now enveloped me completely. 'Why?' I asked, my voice weak.

Agamemnon stepped up to me and spoke in a low, hard voice, his spittle soaking my face. 'Because they found a book in English in the hut over there.' He was pointing at the hovel where I'd lived after my arrival on Trigono. No, it couldn't be. I knew I had lost my copy of Byron, but I'd assumed it was in one of the caves or on the slopes I'd been crawling over for weeks. Then it came back to me. The last time I read from it had been the night before Maro came, the night before we first made love. I hadn't needed it after that, I had been so caught up in my own dream of love and war. Oh, God, what have I done?

Agamemnon was staring at me, his eyes bulging. I thought he was going to hit me, but he managed to restrain himself and stepped away to talk to the islanders. Before I lowered my head I saw their empty expressions, their damp eyes looking at me without accusation, only with profound sadness. They seemed to understand that I had involved myself in things that were far beyond my powers.

Back in the cave I tried to come to terms with what had happened. By my carelessness I had brought destruction on Myli; I had indirectly caused the death of the old man; I had probably consigned seven innocent people to the horror of the occupiers' prisons. And what had I achieved? Our sabotage had interrupted the power supply for a few hours and destroyed part of the Italians' stores, which they had no doubt already replenished. They clearly still had plenty of ammunition and any deficit of food they would have taken from the local population.

But soon I thought again, regrouped, as we were taught to do in basic training. This is still a just struggle, a struggle that must continue. We will have to lie low for some time. That will give us the opportunity to plan more operations. I can't expect to see Maro much in the near future, but our love can wait. It is strong enough to survive this setback. The war is the priority. I must be as clear about that as were the ancient warriors – Leonidas and the Spartans who died at Thermopylae, the original Sacred Band of Thebans who perished en masse at the hands of the Macedonians of Philip and Alexander in the great defeat at Chaironeia. In fact, I must be cold and deadly like Griffin. Yes, I must become ruthless if the enemy is to be prevented from hurting more innocent people.

A devastating thought has just struck me. Perhaps my love for Maro is weakening me, corrupting my ability to fight. Perhaps Maro is actually my fatal flaw, my own Achilles' heel. If I really *was the soldier I was trained to be, I would reject her. Send her back to the harsh discipline of her family.*

But am I man enough to do that?

As Mavros reached the beginning of the flat area and turned to take in the panorama of Trigono's northern sector, he thought he saw a sudden movement on the heights of Vigla to his left. Raising his hand to his eyes and blinking in the wind, he saw two heads above the line of the hill. One was indistinguishable, but he recognised the white sunhat habitually worn by the crabby American anthropologist Gretchen. Presumably she had dragged the unusually laid-back Lance out here again. He wondered what more she could expect to learn about anger management out on the hills – unless discovering how long her partner could last without laying into her was the subject of her studies. Then he remembered that she was also a specialist on funerary practices. Did she have an interest in the graves Eleni was excavating?

He was glad to see that the archaeologist's motorbike was standing by the fence, but less happy to spot the muscle-bound form of Mitsos emerge from his tent.

'What you want?' the ex-seaman said in heavily accented English, his eyes narrowing as he took in the damage to Mavros's face.

Resisting the temptation to give him an earful of abuse in Piraeus argot, Mavros pointed to the plastic roof of the excavation. 'Eleni?' he asked.

'Working,' Mitsos replied. 'You not be here.' He pulled a mobile phone from the back pocket of his jeans and pressed a button. 'Calling boss.'

Mavros raised his eyes to the sky. 'Eleni!' he shouted. 'It's Alex. Come and save me from King Kong.'

There was a pause during which Mitsos told someone – Panos Theocharis? Aris? – that the foreigner was at the dig again. Eleni appeared from the shelter and sauntered across, wiping her hands on her grimy T-shirt. Her face was drenched in sweat and she didn't give him more than a cursory glance.

'You wait,' Mitsos said, putting the phone away. 'Boss coming.'

'What's going on?' Eleni asked in Greek, listening to the watchman's sullen explanation. 'Wanker,' she cursed. 'You don't have to tell them about people I invite.'

'Yes I do,' he replied, keeping his eyes off her.

'You'd better come in,' Eleni said to Alex, pointing to the lock which Mitsos opened reluctantly. 'Animal,' she said under her breath. 'What are you doing out here?' she asked, wiping the sweat from her brow with the back of her arm. 'Still looking for Rosa?' She stared at him. 'My God, what happened to you?'

'I fell over on the way back from the bar last night,' he replied, following the archaeologist under the roof and into the inferno. He didn't want to tell her about the attack in case that put her off answering his questions. 'I want to talk to you.'

'Come into the passage,' she said. 'It's much cooler.' She looked over her shoulder. 'You sound very serious.'

'I am serious,' he said, lowering his head as he went under the heavy lintel. 'I'm serious about finding Rosa Ozal.' He glanced to each side as they moved down the passage. The burial chambers were as he remembered them, the skeletons in the positions where they'd been preserved for over four millennia. He breathed in the smell of the dusty space. 'I'm still trying to find out what she did on Trigono before her sudden departure.'

Eleni stopped. She turned and looked at him in the artificial light, the generator's hum penetrating to the subterranean corridor. 'And?'

Mavros returned her gaze. 'And . . . it seems that another woman left the island in similar circumstances.' He was watching her carefully. 'Just a few days ago.'

The archaeologist's eyes widened and her lips parted. 'Another woman?'

Mavros was curious to see if Eleni would admit that she knew Liz Clifton, as proved by the photo in her album.

'Yes. A very attractive woman with an austere look to her. Blonde, in her thirties.' He focused on Eleni's face in the confines of the hewn passageway. She kept quiet and he decided to tell an untruth. 'You were seen in a clinch with her.'

'What?' The archaeologist's expression cracked, the aura of calm assurance gone. 'Where? Who by?' The questions came rapidly.

Mavros decided to increase the pressure by bending the truth. 'Rena saw you together.'

Eleni gave a bitter laugh. 'You shouldn't believe anything that woman says, Alex.' She drew closer to him. 'Do you know what they say in the village?'

He raised his shoulders. 'How would I?'

Eleni's voice was low. 'They say she murdered her husband.' Her eyes locked on his. 'And that she seduces the boys. Including Yiangos, the one who drowned.'

Mavros inhaled deeply, the inert metallic air making his nose twitch. The idea of Rena killing anyone seemed ridiculous. Then he remembered her fight with the Dutchman. He forced himself to concentrate on Eleni. 'Why are you being so evasive?' He stared into the dark brown eyes that suddenly were no longer raised to his. 'I saw the photographs of you and Elizabeth Clifton in your album.'

Suddenly the archaeologist's mouth was half open, the tongue protruding. She took a deep breath and looked at him, then nodded. It seemed she was finally going to come clean about Liz and Rosa.

And then a voice boomed down the passage from the covered trench outside.

'Eleni? Are you there?' It was Aris Theocharis, speaking Greek. 'Come out.' There was a pause. 'Alex? Alex Mavros? I know you're in there. Come out before I turn the lights off.' There was a burst of coarse laughter. 'We're coming to get you.'

Eleni was staring at him. 'Mavros?' she said in a sharp voice. 'What's he saying?'

Mavros struggled to speak. 'I—'

'You're not a foreigner, are you?' the archaeologist interrupted in Greek. 'You understand, don't you? Christ. I knew there was something about you.' She pushed him away angrily. 'I don't want to meet that bastard in here. He frightens me enough in the daylight.' She darted into the last chamber and came back out with a torch. 'Follow me.' She glanced at him. 'And keep your head down, you lying shit.'

Mavros accepted the insult. He had some explaining to do, but maybe he'd be able to turn the revelation to his advantage. Rena had opened up to him when she discovered who he was. As he went after Eleni, he caught a glimpse of a pair of partially uncovered skeletons, and then the lights flickered and went out. In the second before Eleni's torch came on, he collided with the wall at the end of the passage.

'Here,' she said. 'To the right.'

Biting his lip from the pain in his knee, Mavros realised that there was a narrow gap beyond a heap of recently fallen stone. Eleni had already scrambled over it, bending double to squeeze through a low aperture. He wasn't sure if he would fit, but he pushed himself forward, feeling his hair pick up grit as it scraped the surface above. Then he found himself in an open space, the torchlight revealing what seemed to be a natural cave that was about ten metres long, the floor covered in a layer of small stony fragments. Mavros noticed that the surface was disturbed in the area nearest the entrance they'd used.

Eleni was squatting by the wall, the hand that wasn't holding the torch resting on something on the cave floor. 'Keep quiet,' she whispered. 'If we're lucky he won't find the gap.' The light was extinguished.

Mavros sat down next to her in the darkness. After a while the distant sound of the generator could be heard again, but only the faintest glow came through into their hiding place. He was wondering why Eleni had run at the sound of Aris Theocharis's voice, and he was trying to figure out how the big man had discovered his surname. Someone must have been through his pockets. Had Rena told Aris, or had someone else found his ID? Eleni's words about his landlady came back to him. Rena a killer? He couldn't believe it. But perhaps she had a link to the Theocharis family; most people in the village did.

'Eleni?' boomed a voice in the passage behind the rock wall. 'Where the fuck are you? Alex? Alex Mavros? I want to talk to you.' Aris was close now, the sound of his heavy feet loud. 'Come here, Mitso,' he shouted, then demanded if the watchman was sure that Eleni and her visitor had come down into the dig.

The watchman's reply wasn't clear. The shouting continued for a while, then began to fade away.

Eleni waited, keeping the torch off. 'I wouldn't like to be Mitsos right now,' she said in a cautious whisper. 'I discovered this area yesterday, but I kept it to myself.'

'Is there another way out of the dig?' Mavros asked.

'Yes, there's a gate at the far end where the rubble from the grave chambers is tipped. As far as anyone knows, I don't have a key. They may suspect I do now.'

'We haven't left any footprints there, though,' Mavros said. 'Won't they notice?'

'That pair of apes?' Eleni said in Greek. 'They're only interested in nipples and arses.' Her tone was scathing, but there was still an undercurrent of fear in her voice. She switched on the torch and shone the light in his face. 'So, Mr Mavros, now will you tell me what game you've been playing?'

Mavros put a hand up to shield his eyes. 'No game,' he said, deciding that the only way to gain the archaeologist's confidence was to be honest. 'I'm an investigator.'

'A what?' she said in a hoarse whisper. 'Christ and the Holy Mother. Theocharis will throw me off the cliffs if he thinks I've told you anything. Who are you working for? The Culture Ministry?'

'Don't panic,' he said, stretching across and pushing the torch beam on to the stony floor. 'I'm a private investigator. Rosa Ozal's brother hired me to find out if she was on Trigono or if anything happened to her here. The family hasn't seen her since she came to Greece in June.'

Eleni was silent for a while. 'So why are you asking about . . . about Liz?' she asked, her head down. Then she looked up. 'And why have you been pretending to be a Scottish tourist?'

'My mother's Scottish,' he replied. 'You've probably heard of my father – Spyros Mavros.'

'Not the communist? My God, you're Mavros's son? He had died by the time I was in the KNE, but people still talked about him.' She paused. 'Didn't you have a brother who was . . . who was lost during the dictatorship?'

'Yes. Andonis.' He blinked. 'So you were in the youth party?'

'Along with all of my friends,' Eleni replied, her voice growing sombre. 'Then we grew up and realised that things weren't so simple.'

'The innocence of youth.' Mavros touched her knee. 'I'm sorry about the deception. It seemed easier to play up my non-Greek side.'

'I don't know how you can do it,' she replied angrily. 'Don't you feel dirty?'

He shrugged, feeling the rock scratch him through his shirt. 'It's the curse of growing up with more than one language and culture. You're always deceiving someone about who you are.' He gave a bitter laugh. 'The problem is, you're never really sure who you are yourself. There's a danger that you become the perpetual outsider.'

Eleni snorted and then was quiet for a few moments. 'I suppose that's true. I've never really thought about it.'

'So?' he said. 'Who was the other woman? And what about Rosa? Are you sure you've told me all you know about her?'

Eleni stood up. He could see an object that he couldn't fully make out under her arm. 'Not now. Those bastards will be waiting for us outside. I want to see if this cave leads anywhere. Aris will look even more of a fool if we turn up outside the wire.'

'What's that?' Mavros asked, trying to see what she was carrying.

'I'll show you when we get out,' she said.

'You're making a lot of commitments, Eleni.'

'So?' she said, turning to him and flashing the light in his eyes. 'Are you worried that I won't stick to them?'

He waved the beam away and watched as she shone it over the other end of the cave. The roof there was hung with stalactites, some of them broken off and lying on the floor.

'I think there must have been a minor earthquake,' Eleni said. 'I didn't feel anything until rocks came down at the end of the passage when I was working in the last chamber yesterday. I think there was some damage here too.' The light played over a heap of stones by the wall. Behind them a large crack was visible, and another hole.

'We're in luck,' Mavros said, leaning forward and breathing in what seemed like fresher air. 'Let me go first.' He pushed past her, his elbow hitting the obscure shape under her arm. It was hard and uneven, and he felt the nerves in his arm go dead. 'Shit,' he said in English.

He had to get on his hands and knees to crawl through the gap. When he was halfway, he was struck by the thought that if the rocks had moved once recently they could easily do so again. Heart pounding, he pulled himself through. 'Give me the torch,' he said. 'I'll light the way.' When she passed it through, he shone it on the hole. 'You'd better give me whatever it is that you're carrying too.'

There was a brief silence. 'All right. But be very careful with it, Alex. I'm serious. It's priceless. Are you ready? I'm wrapping it in my shirt.'

Mavros waited and then took the denim-covered object, the torch clenched in his armpit. It wasn't as heavy as he'd expected and he could feel carved lines and recesses. He was thinking about the Cycladic figure he'd seen in Rena's suitcase. Was this another one? Was it why Eleni was trying to elude Aris? He took a step back and waited for her to crawl through.

'Give it to me,' Eleni said, standing up and brushing dust from her bare chest.

'You mean your shirt?' Before she could protest, Mavros unwound the garment and handed it to her. He was left holding a marble figurine, the torchlight making it glow pale, translucent blue, and he felt the breath stop in his throat. His fingers played involuntarily over the smooth stone, touching the sublime curves and lines. 'My God,' he said, his voice no more than a whisper. 'This is amazing.' The carving was more skilful than the piece under Rena's bed. He'd never seen marble of that colour before.

'I told you,' the archaeologist said, taking it gently out of his hands. 'It's very precious. Only the fourth artefact from the Cycladic civilisation ever found on Trigono. And the last three are the only ones in this blue stone ever found anywhere in the Aegean.'

'Amazing,' Mavros repeated. He was wondering if Eleni knew anything about Rena's figurine, which wasn't blue. Now probably wasn't the time to ask. He examined the female figure with its stylised breasts, the arms crossed beneath them. The elliptical face with only a triangular nose in the centre, no eyes or mouth, had an otherworldly air, managing to be both alien and quintessentially human in its geometry. The knees were pressed together and slightly bent. 'Presumably you regard this as a depiction of a dead loved one. You said the skeletons in the same pose lend weight to that theory.'

'Are you sure you aren't from the ministry?' Eleni demanded. Her expression lightened. 'Sorry, I'm getting as paranoid as Theocharis.' She ran her fingers down the front of the figurine. 'Perhaps the sculptor was mourning a woman he loved,' she said in a low voice. 'The piece is imbued with emotion, isn't it?'

Mavros looked at the archaeologist. Her shirt was still unbuttoned. 'Theocharis doesn't have any Cycladic figures in the museum or his private collection,' he mused.

'Correct.' Eleni moved forward to the end of this smaller cave. There was a hollowed alcove which led into another, from which daylight could be seen. She turned to him after they had made their way to the light and nodded as if she'd made a decision. 'But he does have two in his possession.'

Mavros glanced out of the gaps through which the sun was pouring, seeing that they were far too small for a human body to get through. He turned back to the archaeologist. 'You mean he's kept the first pieces you found?'

She nodded, her eyes lowered. 'Yes. He's planning to sell them illicitly, which is why he was so worried by the possibility that you were a thief or a dealer.' She kept her head down. 'And I've been too much of a coward to say anything about it.' She looked up at him. 'I lied to you when I said the important finds had gone to the relevant authorities.'

Mavros shrugged his shoulders to put her at ease. 'That makes us even, then.'

'But he's not getting this one,' Eleni said fiercely. 'And neither is his sick fool of a son.'

'I can understand that,' Mavros said. He turned to examine the rest of the cave. 'How are we going to get out of here?' he asked. 'This looks like a dead end.'

It was then that he noticed the edge of a tarpaulin sticking out from a heap of dusty rubble. He went over quickly and pulled it up, his jaw dropping as he made out several discoloured haversacks and a pile of green wooden boxes.

Mikkel was sitting on the floor in the utility room, his back against the large chest freezer. He could hear the wind blowing hard across the terrace, making the bamboo on the pergolas rattle and dashing the water of the pool over the tiled edge. That brought him to his senses. The swimming pool. The lethal blue element. The place of death. It was time that he moved Barbara.

Staggering as he stood up, having had no sleep overnight or during the day, he opened the lid and looked at the neatly

ordered contents. He was the one who'd done that. Barbara
had no interest in food or cooking. On the left he'd arranged
the fish and seafood that he had bought from the fishermen
on the quay when they returned from their expeditions. He
knew they overcharged him despite the facts that he was a
local resident and spoke some Greek, but he didn't care.
It was enough to take possession of the lustrous creatures,
their scales glinting in the sun and their eyes still wet. He
started pulling out the bags with the dates written in his hand,
throwing them carelessly across the room. There were bream
and mullet, octopus with the suckers frozen into the shape
of inverted nipples, *kalamaria*, even a couple of lobsters that
he'd had to withdraw extra money from the cash machine
to pay for. Soon that side was empty and he started on
the meat. Barbara preferred it – she couldn't stand fish
bones in her mouth. There were huge beef chops hacked
by the untrained butcher from animals that had grazed in
the fields near the house, crystallised sacks full of lamb ribs,
local corn-fed chicken with their bright yellow skins. He sent
the wire baskets crashing across the floor. The sarcophagus
was ready.

Going into the bedroom, Mikkel knelt by Barbara. He'd
laid her on her side of the bed. He touched her arm and felt
that it was even harder than it had been during the night.
Rigor mortis was well advanced. He ran his eyes up and
down the naked body, calculating if it would fit. It would be
close. The only thing to do was try. He wanted his Barbara
to be as perfect as possible, and if he left her much longer
the smell of putrefaction would be unbearable. He wrapped
a sheet around her, tying it at top and bottom, and heaved
her on to the floor. Her head hit the stone floor with a crack
and he felt his heart jump, then he shrugged. His poor darling
was past having any more of the headaches that had dogged
her for so long.

Mikkel got her to the utility room easily enough, the shrouded
corpse sliding smoothly over the floor, but the transfer to the

freezer was difficult. He tried until his arms ached, but she was too heavy, the rigid limbs catching against the edges and foiling his efforts. And then he thought of the Dutchman. Rinus's smirking features hovered in front of him like a mocking demon and he found new strength, tugged the body up and rolled it in with a loud crash. He had to force one leg down and, as he did, he noticed bruises that had somehow escaped him the evening before. There was a thick livid line round each ankle. He stood looking at the marks for a long time, painful thoughts running through his mind, then swallowed hard and went back to the bedroom to find the African bedcover. He laid it carefully over Barbara, obscuring all but her head. It was propped up against the inside of the freezer at an angle, the eyes already misty and the lower lip extended unevenly. My Barbara, he thought. What did he do to you?

He closed the lid reverentially and went out to the main room, returning with an oak cutlery box that she had designed and placing it on top of the freezer. The symmetry pleased him, Barbara's body weighed down, given a memorial, by something she herself had created. Then Mikkel went to the window, suddenly aware of the regular phutting sound of a fishing-boat engine. Parting the venetian blind he looked out through binoculars – Barbara kept a pair in every sea-facing room so she could study the views – and recognised Lefteris's *trata*, the *Sotiria*. He couldn't make out the fisherman's broad form, but he assumed he was on board. How did he do it? His son had died on that boat only a few days ago and here he was fishing from it.

Mikkel stepped back, suddenly feeling stronger than he had for years. He knew what he was going to do. Like the fisherman, he would stand up to death. And make Rinus pay for what he had done to Barbara.

Gretchen the anthropologist peered through her top-of-the-range Zeiss binoculars from the ridge between Vigla and Profitis Ilias, her eyes on the fence surrounding the excavations. She couldn't understand what the two men were

doing with the motorbike. They had each bent down by a
wheel, before the bald one – Aris Theocharis, she reckoned
– moved quickly to the Jeep and headed down the track in
a cloud of dust that was quickly whipped away by the wind.
She glanced over her shoulder, trying to see where Lance
had got to. The fool, he hadn't done what she asked. All
she wanted was some moral support. It was bad enough
trying to find a way into the dig without him wandering off.
If she could only get a look at the graves she was positive
were being excavated, her curiosity would be satisfied. Maybe
she'd even be able to work a grant application up along the
lines of 'Similarities and Differences between Native American
and Prehistoric Aegean Burial Customs'.

To the north she heard a clattering noise and strained to see
round the flank of the hill. A helicopter was hovering over the
Theocharis estate, slowly lowering itself towards a clear patch
between the lines of trees. In the corner of her eye she saw
the goatherd who was short of wits watching from high on the
other slope.

She swung the glasses around Vigla, along the irregular
pattern of caves and holes left by the mine workings. Lance
hadn't said he was going over there, but you never knew with
him. Sometimes he deliberately ignored her instructions. As
she moved her eyes, she caught a glint at the edge of her
vision and homed in on it. Another motorbike, this one larger
and more powerful. She hadn't seen it go up the track, but
they'd been over on the Vathy side until recently. She'd had
no luck there. This side was the one with the graves inside
the wire fence.

A braying noise was carried to her on a gust of wind, a
strange sound that she realised came from a donkey that had
been tethered on the slope round the side of Vigla where a few
strips of land were still cultivated. That island woman who was
fighting the barman yesterday worked up there. She remembered
now. The motorbike belonged to Rinus.

Then two things happened in quick succession. First Gretchen saw a pair of heads appear at some window-like apertures in the rock face, one male and one female. She recognised the archaeologist Eleni but couldn't make out the man. A split second later, from the western side of Vigla, she heard a high-pitched scream. The cry was brief, almost immediately blown away on the gusting wind's blast, but she had no trouble recognising the voice.

18

Inside the cave Eleni knelt down by the tarpaulin and shone the torch on the boxes and bags. 'What is this stuff?' she asked.

'Army supplies,' Mavros said. 'They look old.' The face of the British lieutenant in the photograph he'd found in the chimney flashed up before him. Could this be another link to Rosa and Liz, the women who'd stayed in the room in Rena's house before him? 'There was some undercover activity on Trigono during the war.'

The archaeologist shrugged. 'I don't know. You'd have to ask Theocharis. He was here. I heard him talking about it once to Aris.' She put her hand on one of the boxes.

'I wouldn't touch that,' Mavros said, carefully lowering the lid he'd raised. 'From what I can tell, there are explosives in there.'

'What?' Eleni gasped, pulling her hand away. 'Let's get out of this place.'

Mavros was on his knees at the rock face beyond the tarpaulin. 'There's been some movement of the wall here, but I don't think we can get through.' He glanced round at her, the sunlight from the narrow gaps in the far wall momentarily blinding him. 'If you want to leave, we'll need to go back.'

Eleni squatted down under the natural windows. 'Do we have to?' she said reluctantly. 'I really don't want to see Aris. All he'll do is shout at me for letting you on the site.' She shook her head. 'Not that it's any of the bastard's business. He comes here for a month every year and throws his weight around, then flies off back to his whores in New York.'

'All right, all right,' Mavros said, giving her a tentative smile.

'We'll wait. Those explosives have probably been here for half a century. If we leave them alone, why should they blow up now?'

Eleni didn't look convinced but she nodded, clutching the Cycladic figurine closer to her chest.

Mavros moved over and sat down beside her. 'So what are you going to do with it?' he asked, inclining his head towards the sculpted blue marble.

'I'm not sure,' she said, running a hand through her hair. 'I made the mistake of handing the first two to Theocharis. He told me he would pass them to the ephor of antiquities, but he didn't.'

'You could give it to me for safe-keeping,' Mavros said, patting his satchel. 'It would be out of sight in here.'

'I don't think so,' Eleni replied, drawing back from him. 'I'm not sure you are who you say you are, you liar.'

Mavros realised he still had some convincing to do.

As soon as she had put her son's bones away, Kyra Maro felt a wave of exhaustion dash over her that was more than physical weakness; it was a terrible emptiness of spirit. She toppled on to her bed and managed to pull a blanket across her legs. Suddenly they were freezing. The shrivelled muscles and wrinkled skin seemed to be starting to detach themselves. She lay there, heart racing, and wondered what was happening. Was this the end at last? She opened her eyes and saw the photograph of her lover looking out from the recess in the wall with the hesitant smile she remembered so well.

'Ach, Tzortz!' she said in a faint voice. 'Are you waiting for me in the dark country beneath the surface of the earth?'

And in a flash she was young again, the wind on her shoulders as she scaled the steep northern slope of Vigla, keeping away from the tracks to avoid prying eyes. Her family had been openly hostile since the Italians went to Myli and captured seven of their fellow islanders. She wasn't sure, but she suspected the landowner Theocharis of saying something about her and Tzortz. She had been kept out of everything to do with the supply of provisions to the British and Greek groups and told to stay in the village. But it had been a week since she'd seen her lover and she wasn't going to wait any longer. She had climbed out of the window of the room she shared with her sisters when they were asleep and slipped through the empty streets like a ghost. It must have been after two when she approached the cave. She had stopped frequently to check that she wasn't drawing attention to herself, and her legs were aching from the walk. Her absence, and that of the goat leg she'd taken from the kitchen, would be discovered at first light. This time she would not escape Manolis's wrath.

The moon was bright as she came round the western flank of the hill, casting her shadow long over the scrub and rocks. This forced her to slow her pace. She could see the great sweep of the ridge leading to Profitis Ilias and she knew that a Sacred Band sentry would be on it. And where was the Englishman with the murderer's eyes? He would be watching somewhere near. Breathing deeply to calm herself, she looked out over the silver-grey water, ripples cutting across it under the moonlight like the lines on the back of a giant lizard. Even though she'd grown up on the island and seen its beauties a thousand times, they could still make her stare in amazement, a failing that her family regarded as evidence of her flightiness. For them Trigono's stony earth and the man-consuming sea around it were proof of life's bitterness, not of its bounty. Maro steeled herself and made the last zigzag approach to the cave. She arrived there without being stopped.

The interior of their secret place – the second cave beyond the almost invisible gap at the edge of the rock face – was pitch black, the moon's brightness reaching only as far as the outer area. For a moment she thought he wasn't there, even though the marker stone was in place. Then she heard a swift movement and a hand slipped over her mouth.

'Maro?' he asked in a whisper. 'Is it you? What are you doing here?' Then he kissed her and everything became sweet again.

After they had lain together for a long and beautiful time in the heavy air of the underground chamber, Tzortz lit the lamp and looked into her eyes.

'Ah, Maro,' he said, his voice full of pain. 'I didn't think I would see you again in our own place. I . . . I have been thinking of other things.'

'You forgot me?' she said, pushing an elbow into his bare abdomen and laughing. She wasn't concerned by his serious expression; she was sure their love was more important to him than anything. 'How could you?'

He smiled at her, sadness in his eyes. 'What news from the village?' he asked. 'Ajax . . . I mean your brother never speaks to me now and Theocharis thinks that my men and I should be sent away. Has anything been heard about the hostages?'

'Only that they are in the prison outside Athens,' she said. 'Chaïdhari is a very bad place.'

Tzortz nodded, his expression distracted. 'It . . . it was my fault, Maro,' he said. 'They found a book of mine in the—'

'I know they did,' she said, drawing him close and feeling his shoulders shake. 'But you mustn't blame yourself, my love. This is war and the people know that. Most of them still want to help in any way they can.'

'But the seven that were taken may be tortured, they may be shot,' he said, his eyes flickering. 'I could have their blood on my conscience for the rest of my life.'

Maro shook her head, soothed him, told him the Trigoniotes would willingly sacrifice themselves for their country's salvation. Eventually she persuaded him. He grew less agitated and kissed her again with the passion she had grown used to. Poor Tzortz. He must have been tormented for years by those wasted lives. What did it do to him, the knowledge that three of the men were executed after refusing to name resistance members; that two of the others died from typhus and malnutrition; and that one more was sent to Dachau and never heard of again? And Styliani, the sole woman to be taken? What might he have felt about brave Styliani? She had returned to Trigono after the war a shadow of herself, never speaking of what had happened to her before her untimely death in the late forties.

'You know we're going to carry out more sabotage, Maro,' her lover said after they'd joined their bodies again, unable to resist the urging of desire. 'There may be more reprisals, worse reprisals.' His voice was strong again. 'But the struggle must go on.'

And she had nodded eagerly in her innocence, saying, 'I will stay with you and help you, my love. I cannot go back to my family now.'

Tzortz had looked at her sternly, as if her words had been unwelcome, then he gave her a sweet, sad smile.

But life is not as simple as war. Maro had learned that lesson in the long years that followed. Life is a valley of woe. It begins in pain and ends in eternal darkness. She wanted to believe that there was companionship in the underworld, that she would see her loved ones again – the one she'd given herself to so joyfully and the one she'd carried inside her body.

Maro closed her eyes, shutting out the images of Tzortz and Tasos. If only she had faith that there would be a meeting beyond the grave. If only . . .

Eleni was glaring at him, the torchlight in the cave turning her face sallow. 'How do I know who you're really working for? This brother of Rosa could just be a front. You could be collecting information for one of the big dealers.'

Mavros shrugged. 'It's up to you,' he said, looking into her eyes. 'Eleni, did anyone leave the bar after me last night? You stayed, didn't you?'

She extended a hand to his chin and turned his injured jaw to the light. 'That's very nasty, Alex. Are you sure the doctor said you could be on your feet?'

'Answer the question,' he said, watching as her eyes widened at the roughness of his tone.

She pursed her lips and then nodded. 'Yes, I stayed for another hour or so. And no. No one left for quite a long time after you.'

She ran a hand through her curls. 'I think Aris and Dhimitra were the first to go, but that must have been at least half an hour afterwards.'

'Did anyone make a phone call?'

Eleni's brow creased as she thought about that. 'No, not that I saw. There was music playing, people shouting above it. I can't be sure.'

'How about Rinus?' Mavros persisted.

Her eyes flashed in irritation then her face slackened. 'Yes,' she said, raising her hand. 'I remember now. He made a call on his mobile phone, but it was at least ten minutes after you went. And I heard who he was talking to—'

'Who was it?' Mavros demanded.

'Or rather, who he left a message for,' Eleni continued. 'It was Barbara – you know, German Barbara? Obviously her mobile had been off for some time. Rinus was annoyed. He told her to call him as soon as possible.' She shrugged. 'He seemed worried.'

Mavros slumped against the wall, things no clearer to him than they had been. He suddenly felt exhausted, mention of Rinus bringing back what had happened to him on the narrow track from the bar. He was about to ask Eleni if she knew anything about the Dutchman's drug dealing when he heard sounds from behind the tarpaulin-shrouded boxes.

'What was that?' he asked, stepping across the cave.

'What was what?' Eleni asked, one eyebrow raised.

He listened, his ear to the rough surface of the rock. 'I don't know. I thought I heard scratching and then what sounded like a moan.' He leaned closer. 'Yes, there it is again.' He looked over his shoulder to find Eleni close behind him. 'Can you hear it?' he asked, moving back to let her get to the wall.

After a few moments she shook her head. 'No, I can't hear anything.'

Mavros listened again, this time picking up only a faint scratching. Then there was nothing.

Eleni was studying him thoughtfully. 'Are you sure you're all

right? You took some heavy blows to the head, didn't you?
Maybe you're—'

'Hearing things?' He gave her a testy look. 'No, I'm not. I
think there's someone behind there.'

Eleni stood with the figurine in her arms then looked at her
watch. 'Let's head back to the dig. Aris will have gone by now.
He's more impatient than a teenage boy in a brothel.'

Mavros turned away slowly. 'All right, you lead the way.'

She gave a twitch of her head. 'No. I want to concentrate on
the piece. You take the torch and go first.'

He nodded and headed back to the low hole. Bending down,
he held the light on the stones piled up in the breach. It was
then that he heard Eleni's voice rise in alarm.

'Alex, watch your—'

But Mavros had already slipped into freefall, the wind screaming past his outstretched arms and into his eyes, blurring his vision
and making him blink in the abyss of darkness. He thought he
heard the word 'head' the moment before he hit rock bottom.

'What is your name?'

A long silence.

'My name . . . my name is . . . oh God, what is my name?
Say it! I need to hear my name. I need to know who I am.'

The woman panted for breath, the dank air passing over
her broken lips. Now she could hardly speak out loud any
more, hardly had the strength to moan. She thought she had
heard a man's voice, muffled and distant, and she'd been
trying to scrape at the rock around the ring-bolt that had
been driven into it. But soon her nails were split again, the
grit and splinters jammed into the cuticles, and she'd had
to stop.

'Please,' she begged, 'let me drop into a sleep that I never
wake up from . . . before they come again . . . the pair of psychos
who stand behind the camera . . . recording my rotting body . . .
making a film for sick bastards to drool over . . .' The rasp of
her breath in the gravel pit of her throat seemed louder than the

words. 'Oh God, let me fall into oblivion . . . let the waters of Lethe wash me away.'

To her amazement she felt a painful gurgle of laughter well up. She wondered what she was saying. This made her laugh again, though there was very little noise. Just an unlikely lightening of her spirits. Why? What was so funny about Lethe, river of forgetfulness, river of the ancient underworld? Perhaps it was the incongruity of what she'd learned in classical studies coming back to her in this underground pit when she couldn't even remember her name. Or, more likely, it was her subconscious self showing her that water was the only important thing now – a bottle, a bucket, a river in spate, it didn't matter. Laugh out loud at this thought, she told herself. There isn't a drop for you to drink. What consolation is that, to think about water when you have nothing to drink? She swallowed a stabbing laugh. Not funny, not funny at all. But still her spirits were flying. Maybe the drugs she was sure she'd been slipped were still having some effect, even though she'd had nothing to eat or drink for what seemed like days. What was so funny about dying of thirst?

Wait. Something was coming back to her. Lethe. The river of forgetting. She'd seen the name in the recent past, not just when she was a fifteen-year-old schoolgirl. Lethe. Yes, that was it. In a bar. There was a bottle of ouzo called Lethe. She'd made a joke about it to the barman – what was he called? She'd said that was a good name for an industrial-strength spirit, something like that. Ouzo. Add water and watch it go cloudy. Water. The sea was all around. And now she remembered. She had been on an island. It didn't have much water, the shower ran dry every evening, the stuff from the tap was brackish, you had to buy bottles or queue up at the well in the square. Water. The island didn't have enough, you could see it in the people's faces, lined and wrinkled, sun darkened, long suffering; their characters hard, kindness and generosity rationed not from spite towards outsiders but out of necessity.

Come on, woman, she said to herself, get a grip. Lethe. What was the barman's name? Rinus, yes, that was it. A Dutchman who spoke perfect English, a skinny guy, earrings like a gypsy. And the other one, the big, bald man with the green sunshade on even at night? Aris. Yes, Aris. He showed me Lethe, he showed me the underworld. Didn't he?

'What is all this?' the woman said aloud, her voice muted. 'What am I thinking?' She tried to move her arms, but found that she had no power over them. She wanted to flex her muscles, wanted at least to feel that she could fight the rope even if she couldn't beat it. But there was nothing. She was stretched out in the darkness like a stunned heifer waiting for the spike to be pounded into her head. That's how they do it on Trigono, the big man told her when they were driving through the fields. Trigono. Yes, that was the name of the island.

And suddenly she found herself back in the Jeep with the man called Aris, the suspension moving easily over the surface of a road that led to a large stone tower surrounded by white buildings and lines of trees, the earth smelling of water. Oh God, water, she thought. Was that a swimming pool there? Then she was in front of a great painting, a mural, parts of it ancient and other parts restored. Yes, there was the river, there was Lethe, a small boat and a figure steering it with an oar across the stream – Charon the ferryman. Other faces flashed up before her – a heavily built middle-aged man with penetrating eyes, another man of the same stock, older, with only one arm. And a woman, golden hair and golden skin, overstated nose and lips, inflated bosom and a voice that was harsh, came from deep in her throat. She had three big dogs in tow. There was another woman, this one smiling beneath dark curls, her expression kind. And someone else behind her, an old man with a stick. Yes, an old man with a white beard and an imperious air. Who was he? And who am I?

The captive woman felt herself drift away from the people who were gathering around her like mourners around a body that had been laid out. She was floating away on Lethe's stream, unable now to remember what those people meant to her, or why she was remembering them one moment, forgetting them the next, remembering, forgetting, remembering . . .

And then she came back to herself, her mind clear again but her throat drier than ever.

'Water,' she gasped. 'Give me water. I'm dying for the need of it. Why have I been brought here to rot? Help me.'

The words boomed in her ears as she mouthed them, but the woman knew that they had made little sound. She no longer had the energy even to scratch the rock wall.

At that moment hope was extinguished. Now all she could do was wait for the racking pains to end.

No, she told herself. There was a man's voice near by, a different voice. Don't give up, don't . . .

The faint light faded and darkness closed in on her again.

The noise in Mavros's head was repetitive and regular, like the clanging of a bell rung by an over-enthusiastic priest on a Sunday morning. He blinked and focused on the narrow line of light to his right, then made the mistake of moving. The pain shot through his body, causing him to keep completely still for a period of time that he couldn't quantify. The pounding gradually reduced in volume and he realised that it was the beat of his heart. He moved his hand to the top of his cranium, feeling a familiar twinge in his side. There was a new matted patch in his hair, the blood still damp.

As Mavros sat up slowly he recognised the cave with the natural windows, the dusty tarpaulin still in place over the explosives and the other military equipment. Then he remembered who he'd been with. Where was she, where was Eleni? He turned his head, swallowing bitter-tasting liquid as the pain knifed in again. No sign of her, nor of the exquisite Cycladic piece. He fingered his head gingerly. Eleni had been behind him, she'd shouted out a warning. The blows he'd taken outside the Astrapi must have affected his judgement. He must have driven himself into the rock. He looked round and examined the jagged surface above the hole he'd been bending into. He couldn't see any mark on the stone, though the outer area was fractured by numerous small cracks and the cave floor dotted with fragments. He touched his scalp again, but felt only drying blood – no fragments of stone came away on his hand. Was it possible that Eleni had hit him? Surely not. And what would she have used? The priceless work of ancient art? He rejected the thought. The torch was gone – she must have headed back through the caves to get help. He stumbled over to the holes in the cave wall that were letting in the light.

What he saw made him draw his arm across his eyes and blink even harder than he'd done when he came round.

There was a motionless body on the hillside about ten metres away from him.

'I think you will have to stay the night,' Panos Theocharis said to his visitor. 'The helicopter is grounded. The wind is very strong now and I don't think it will drop for some time.'

Tryfon Roufos shrugged. 'I took a chance, given the weather forecast.' He nodded at his host, a grim expression on his sallow face. 'I hope it's going to be worth it. You are serious about selling the two Cycladic pieces?'

'Yes, Roufos, I'm serious all right.' Theocharis leaned on his stick and looked out over the northern point of Trigono. 'Unfortunately. That idiot son of mine has lost the family a fortune over the last two years in New York. Even the overpaid lawyers I employ have been unable to keep him under control. If the museum is to remain open, I must dispose of pieces that would otherwise have raised its profile immeasurably.' He lowered his eyes. 'I suppose there is an irony in that, but it's not one that gives me any pleasure.'

The antiquities dealer smiled, his mouth twisting and giving him the look of a hungry carnivore. 'Ah, what it is to have children,' he said, his tone light. 'I have made sure that I avoid the creatures.'

'That's not what I've heard,' Theocharis said with a knowing glance.

'I meant children of my own,' Roufos said, meeting the old

man's eyes. 'Other people's I am happy to use in whatever ways please me.'

Theocharis sat down, despair swamping him. That it should come to this. Aris out of control, the business floundering because of him, the museum's funding threatened. Was this what he was reduced to? Hiding the first Cycladic figurines to be found on Trigono for decades from the authorities and selling them illegally? He had played hard in business, operated beyond the law whenever necessary, driven more scrupulous operators to bankruptcy, even to suicide, more times than he could remember. But the Theocharis Foundation had always been above board, he had never done anything to blacken its name. What would happen if the deals that Roufos was setting up ever became public knowledge? Arrests. Law suits. Ridicule. He wouldn't last many more years, but he didn't want to spend that time fighting a losing battle against imprisonment.

He watched as the antiquities dealer moved to the window and took in the windswept central plain. Apparently the jackal already had a couple of clients lined up for the unique pieces. He felt his breath creak in his lungs as he leaned back in the sofa. Oh God, how was it going to end? There was too much to think about. Why did he have to be the one to fix everything? If only Aris had been more reliable, if only Dhimitra could restrain herself. What had they been doing? What happened to the seductive Rosa Ozal, the woman that the undercover investigator Mavros had been asking about? And the other one, the one who came asking about George Lawrence – what had happened to her? In the space of a few months Trigono had become a foreign land to him. Was this what it was like to go senile, to lose your wits? He would soon be crossing Lethe. He'd been preparing himself for that passage since he was a boy. The river of forgetfulness would claim him and wipe his memory clean. But when? And would the corrosive emotions that had been eating into him since he'd started reading Lawrence's diary be washed away at the same time?

'Pano? Pano?' Roufos's voice had risen in volume. 'The

phone,' he said, pointing at the instrument on the table in front
of the old man.

Theocharis came back to himself and picked it up. 'Yes?'

'It's me.' Aris sounded very uneasy.

'What's happened?' the old man demanded, instantly alert.

'We can't . . . we can't find the archaeologist. We lost her and
Mavros in the caves. There must be another way out.'

Eyes on his guest, Theocharis covered his mouth with his hand.
'Fool,' he hissed. 'Where are Mitsos and the other guards?'

'On the hills. Don't worry, *baba*, we'll find them soon.'

'You'd better. Get back to the site. I'm giving you another
hour. After that Lefteris will take charge.'

'No, *ba*—'

Theocharis put the phone down and wiped the sweat from his
upper lip. 'A drink, Roufos,' he said, indicating the well-stocked
bar. 'Please help yourself. I don't want the servants listening to
our conversation.'

Roufos took the lid off a crystal decanter and sniffed. 'When
do I see the pieces?' he asked.

'Shortly,' the old man replied. 'The final preparations are being
made as we speak.'

It looked like he might have to do the presentation without
Eleni. Maybe that would be just as well.

'Fuck this phone!' Aris threw the handset against the wall of
Dhimitra's bedroom and watched it shatter. 'I can't get hold of
Mitsos. We have to find the bitch Eleni and Mavros. Lefteris is
taking over in an hour.'

'It's the hills,' his stepmother said, applying the final touch
to her extended lips. 'You can never get a good signal south
of the estate. You'll just have to hope that the watchmen track
them down.' She smoothed her skirt over her hips and glanced
at him. 'You have to go and take charge.' She caught the lustful
look in his eye. 'Not again, you fool. You've got other things to
worry about.'

Aris nodded slowly. 'You're right. If Lefteris comes looking for me because of what happened with the *Sotiria*, I'm dead meat.' He stared at her again, this time his eyes cold. 'And if the lunatic tells my father, the dirt will land all over you too, be sure of that.'

Dhimitra walked up to him, a smile on her crimson lips. 'Ari,' she said, her voice even more throaty than usual. She grabbed his crotch and met his agonised look. 'Don't ever threaten me. We're in this together. Act like a grown-up and we'll inherit a fortune.' She squeezed harder. 'Act like a spoiled child and your stepmother will be very unhappy.'

She wiped her hand slowly down his chest and walked past him to the door.

Aris shook his head and wondered how he was going to get out of this shit storm. He was a betting man and he'd always liked long odds, but he wasn't attracted by this game at all. It was time to cut those odds. The best way to do that was to lower the number of people who could talk. He knew where to start. The information his father's people in Athens had gathered on Mavros would get him off their backs for good, even though the old man had so far held off using it. He must be going soft.

But he didn't know where the dick and the dyke had got to. He had to find them fast.

Straining forward, his heart pounding, Mavros took in the scene. The body was on its left side, facing away from him. The legs were drawn up and all he could see of the lower half was khaki shorts and a pair of thick-soled trainers. The torso was covered in a short-sleeved white shirt, but it was the head that drew his attention and set off stabs of pain in his own cranium. He was pretty sure it was a man from the dense brown hair on the outstretched arm, but the length and colour of the hair on the head were hard to make out. The skull had shattered into a mass of blood and other matter. He looked down, breathing hard, and tried to get a grip on his thoughts. He'd seen those shoes before, he knew he had, but he couldn't place them. Christ. He sank to his knees and retched up a great gush of sour vomit, then spat out as much as he could of what remained in his mouth. He pulled away from the mess on the cave floor and felt his mind clear. Move, he heard himself say, move, Alex. There's a chance the guy outside is still alive.

Feeling his way blindly through the caves, Mavros touched rough walls before he located the obscured corner that led into the excavation tunnel. He slid through and headed towards the yellowish light from the corrugated roof outside, glancing into each grave chamber as he went. There was no sign of the archaeologist. He raised his head cautiously from the trench and looked around. Mitsos the guard was also nowhere to be seen. Mavros ran unsteadily across the bare ground. The wind was blowing hard, making the damaged parts of his head ache even more. The gusts were stronger than they had been earlier.

'Mitso!' he shouted, eager to get to the body and no longer concerned about concealing himself. 'Come and let me out.'

There was no reply, no heavy form appearing from the watchman's tent. He yelled again, then took a deep breath and started to clamber over the fence. It was difficult as there was nothing to get a grip on and the points of his shoes kept slipping out of the spaces between the strands of wire, but eventually he managed to swing himself over the top. The barbed wire caught his T-shirt in several places without cutting into his skin. Turning to gauge where the cave system extended inside the hill, he estimated the position of the body he'd seen and headed up the slope. As he came into the open round a steep rock face, the wind blasted into him from the north and nearly knocked him over. Looking out to the sea between Trigono and Paros, he saw a maelstrom of white wave tops and a complete absence of boats. There wasn't any doubt about it. The island and everyone on it were cut off from the outside world.

Lungs bursting and throat gummed up, Mavros rounded another outcrop and stopped to orientate himself. He was close now. The angle of the ridge that he'd seen through the natural windows in the cave was almost identical, the great wall between Vigla and Profitis Ilias rising up to his left. Craning his head forward, he ran his eyes over the grey slabs of rock and the barren slopes. Although the other hillsides were dotted with clumps of gorse and hardy green bushes, the area near by was bare scree cut with mounds of dark red earth from the mine shafts. It was near one of those ore casts that the body lay, the white shirt catching his eye.

Mavros ran down towards it. Slowing as he approached the body, he looked around for prints or other traces but saw nothing. He kneeled down by the damaged head and immediately realised that there was no chance the man had survived what he calculated was a fall of at least fifty metres from the saddle above. And then he remembered who he'd seen wearing the trainers with the knobbly tread. He stepped over the body and looked at the face, the upper teeth driven into the lower lip and the eyes rolled to display bloodshot white.

It was Lance, the partner of the bad-tempered American anthropologist. Mavros felt for a pulse but couldn't detect one. The wide patch of blood and soft matter on the stones and earth suggested that the unfortunate man had sustained his massive head injuries at this location.

Mavros swung his satchel round and took out his mobile phone. The signal indicator was blank and he couldn't pick anything up by lifting it higher or by moving around. He was completely blocked in by the hills. He ran through his options. Go for help or look for the woman. Where was Gretchen? From what he'd seen, she and Lance went everywhere together. Maybe she'd already left to find help, but he couldn't let himself assume that. The first thing to do was to leave Lance where he was and find a spot in line with a phone mast so he could call the police. At least that way he wouldn't be too far away if Gretchen appeared. He looked back at the dead man, unwilling to abandon him without some cover, but all he had were the clothes he was wearing.

Then Mavros heard a rattle of stones, a miniature cascade down the slope, and gave a smile of relief. Back-up had arrived and it had transport. He shouted and waved, stopping only when he saw the look on the rider's face.

A demon from the pit couldn't have glared at him with more malevolence.

19

Mikkel had parked the Suzuki inside the gateway to a barren field on the outskirts of the village in mid-morning. He could see the Bar Astrapi from the position he took up at the uneven wall. Although he was aware that Rinus often didn't appear until the early afternoon to clean up, he wasn't taking any chances. Because of potential witnesses he didn't want to risk taking on the Dutchman in his flat in the *kastro*, and he knew that Rinus kept the motorbike he was so proud of in the storeroom at the back of the bar. Sooner or later he'd go out for a ride on it – he did most days – and Mikkel would be on his tail.

He had a long wait. By the time the wind started to blow hard, Mikkel had chewed his nails down to the quick. The back of his neck, which he usually took care to protect, was blistering in the sun and Rinus still hadn't shown up. A few locals on their way back from the Kambos waved at Mikkel with curious expressions, but he knew that they didn't really care what he was doing; he was foreign and there was no point in trying to account for the ways of his kind.

The German spent the hours at the wall replaying his life with Barbara, trying to concentrate on the good times: the openings of new design ranges when she'd moved around the crowded display rooms back home with her head held higher than a queen's; the days on Trigono long ago when she'd smiled at him and even let him touch her; her laughter in the bars before the combination of drugs and alcohol ruined her. She'd always been self-obsessed and overbearing – she said all creative people were – but when she was high she could turn into a wild beast. That was how it always went when Mikkel thought too much about his relationship with her: the bad times prevailed – the times when she swore at him and humiliated him in front of embarrassed guests, mocking him for being an accountant rather than an artist. For years he had managed to block out Barbara's bad side, but he was struggling now.

'Jesus, Barbara,' he heard himself say over and over again, the wind scattering the words across the stony earth. 'Jesus. Why did you let the little pimp destroy you? Why did you ever let him lay a finger on you?'

Mikkel retched as he was overwhelmed by shame. Barbara had been screwing the Dutchman, and no doubt plenty of others who came on to her after he walked home from the bar nursing alcohol-induced headaches. He'd been suppressing the suspicions for years but now they had conquered him. Before he left the house he'd opened the freezer lid again and looked at the bruises on his wife's ankles. Though the skin was now sparkling with ice crystals, the blue-black marks beneath were still clear. Was Rinus strong enough to hold Barbara's larger frame under the water? Of course he was. She had probably passed out from the muck he supplied. The bastard. He deserved to die in a crumpled heap on the roadside and that was what would happen – as soon as he woke up from his drunken, doped-up coma.

And finally the Dutchman did appear, walking at an unusually quick pace, his head turning from side to side. He looked nervous as hell. That made Mikkel even more sure of his guilt. Rinus went into the Astrapi and came out again almost immediately, putting his back into wheeling the powerful BMW across the concrete terrace. Then, with another worried glance around, he put on his black helmet, dipped the visor and started the engine. He was off down the road to the Kambos before Mikkel could get back to the Suzuki, but that wasn't a problem. The island was small and there weren't many roads. Besides, he didn't want the Dutchman to spot him until they were in a more deserted spot.

Mikkel kept his speed down until Rinus crested the brow of the hill between the village and the central plain, then accelerated hard before gliding to a halt just below the summit. The cloud of dust that the BMW was raising made the Dutchman easy to track, the northerly wind blowing it to the dun-coloured massif beyond. Mikkel watched as his prey passed the ruined windmills and the church at Myli, cutting along the eastern wall of the Theocharis estate. Where was he going? There were nothing more than rough tracks in that area. The thought that Rinus might not just be going for a recreational ride struck him. Could he be meeting someone? He drove down the slope quickly in case the barman glanced back. As he passed the abandoned graveyard, Mikkel saw the dust cloud move up the flank of the hill towards the archaeological dig. He thought he could see someone up on the ridge. Perhaps Rinus was going to see Eleni – after all, they seemed to be close, they were always talking at the bar like conspirators. Shit. He didn't want her to see what he was going to do to the Dutchman. Shit. He sped up even more, feeling the wheels of the four-by-four judder as the asphalt ran into the potholed track.

And then Mikkel caught sight of a figure standing in the narrow space between the walls straight ahead of him. He gave a long blast of his horn, but there was no movement in response.

'For God's sake,' he shouted, jamming his foot on the brake and screeching to a halt a few metres in front of the heavily built man. Pressing the electric window button, Mikkel stuck his head out. 'Please,' he said in Greek. 'I want to get past.' He looked up in surprise at the islander, recognising the impassive features. 'Please, I—'

The last thing he saw was the fisherman Lefteris's thick-fingered fist as it was swung at lightning speed into his face.

Mavros looked up the steep fall of scree, shielding his eyes against the sun. 'Rena?' he shouted. 'What is it? What's the matter?' He felt her eyes burning into him, her face set in what seemed to be a rictus of hatred. Only after a long time did her eyes move to the crumpled form on the ground beside him.

'Wait,' she said. 'I'm coming.' She got off the donkey and led it down the slope with encouraging noises.

Mavros watched as the woman and the beast of burden nego-
tiated the difficult surface of the hillside, stones tumbling down
around him. He stepped forward to shield the body of the
American, aware that it was an unnecessary action but doing so all
the same. He tried to make out Rena's face as she descended. Why
had she been looking at him as if she had caught him molesting a
child? Could she have had anything to do with Lance's fall? He
gauged the angles and wondered about it. No. She would have
been on her way back from the fields she worked on the terraced
slope farther along the ridge. She was probably just shocked by
the scene, maybe thinking that he had something to do with it.

'So,' the widow said as she reached the bottom, turning to check
that the donkey Melpo had cleared the last of the stones safely.
'What happened here? Is this part of your investigation?'

Mavros examined Rena's face at close range, puzzled by the
change in her. Although her expression was no longer full of
loathing, there wasn't any friendliness in the way she was regarding
him. 'No, of course not,' he replied. 'I saw the body from there.'
He pointed to the small holes in the rock through which he'd been
looking from the cave.

Rena's eyes opened wide. 'You were inside there?' she asked,
her tone expressing surprise. 'You were in the caves?'

'Yes,' Mavros replied. 'Do you know them?'

The widow nodded slowly, her head inclining to the left. 'I've
seen the entrances to some over there, yes.' She shivered. 'But I
don't go inside. I can't stand the dark and the dirty air, never mind
the bats.' She shook her head. 'The old people say that miners
used to live in there before the war. The Theocharis family treated
them like slaves, let them rot.' She glanced down at the American.
'What do you think happened to him?'

Mavros raised his shoulders. 'I don't know. It looks like he fell
from the ridge.' He stripped off his T-shirt and made to lay it
over the dead man's head.

'Don't,' Rena said, touching his arm. 'He doesn't care any more
and I've seen worse. The wind's chill now. You'll need your shirt.'

Mavros pulled the T-shirt back on. She was right. Even though the small valley they were in was sheltered, his skin was already covered in goose pimples. 'Did you see him or anyone else when you were working?'

She shook her head, manoeuvring Melpo round so her head was facing the opposite direction. The donkey had been tugging away from the body. 'The fields are out of sight from here and from where he'd have fallen.' Her chin jutted forward as she turned her hands up and looked at the soil-encrusted skin. 'Anyway, I've been busy.'

Mavros stepped back and ran his eye around the higher ground on each side. 'I can't understand where his woman has got to. They're always together and I saw them from the bottom of the track earlier on.' He held up his phone and checked the signal again. 'Nothing.'

Rena was looking at the dead man dispassionately. 'You must help me lift him on to Melpo,' she said in a calm voice.

Mavros shook his head. 'The police will want him to be left where he is. The area must be—'

'You're not in the big city now,' Rena interrupted. 'If we leave him here, the crows will have his eyes before we reach the Kambos.' She stared at him. 'Do you want his woman to see that?'

Mavros shrugged then nodded his acquiescence. The local policeman was unlikely to be an expert on crime scene procedures, and Lance had probably just slipped. If anyone asked, he could always say that the unfortunate American had still been alive when they moved him and that Rena was taking him to the village doctor.

'We'll approach Melpo from her hindquarters so she doesn't panic,' the widow said. 'Wait. There's an old blanket under the saddle. I'll wrap it round the man's head.'

Between them they got Lance on to the donkey.

Mavros stood back, wiping his hands on his jeans. 'If you meet anyone with a phone, ask them to call the police.'

'Aren't you coming?' Rena asked, her brow furrowed and her expression dark again.

He shook his head. 'I want to see if the American woman is anywhere near by.'

She looked at him uncertainly then made a clicking sound and led the donkey towards the track. Lance's arms and feet were hanging close to the rough ground, his swaddled head jerking up and down against the bottom of the wooden saddle. Then Melpo and her burden were round the wall of rock and Mavros was alone again. But Rena remained in his thoughts. What had she meant when she said she'd seen worse? Worse sights than a man with his head broken apart? And why had she been staring down at him with such belligerence?

Not for the first time Mavros found himself wondering what secrets were concealed beneath the normally placid face that the widow displayed to the world.

January 23rd, 1943

Our secret place. Despite the disaster at Myli and the horrors that the hostages must be undergoing in the prison on the mainland, the last week has been wonderful. The island has been bathed in bright sunshine. This time is the 'Alkyonidhes Meres', *the unexpectedly warm halcyon days when, in ancient myth, the kingfishers laid their eggs on nests floating on the sea's placid surface. The air has been so limpid that you almost believe you could stretch out a hand to touch Santorini or Anydhros despite the great expanse of light blue, shining water.*

And Maro has been here to share these days with me. Agamemnon has been asking where she is and her brother has been looking at me with eyes burning with malice, but at her request I have denied all knowledge of her whereabouts. No one else knows the location of our cave, not even Rees or the madman Griffin, so she is safe with me. She is very skilful at melting into the landscape when we go out at night to take in the glories of the moon and the constellations. I have been able to push away the bitter memories of the events at Myli and get them into perspective through her love. Such unquestioning devotion has helped me to plan our next operation, an attack on the main Italian supply depot on Naxos. This will be much more difficult, the distances greater and the Italians now very much on the alert. The attitude of the Greeks, both islanders and Sacred Band, has not helped. It has taken days of pleading for them to agree to supply a boat, but they will not come with us. I don't know what Agamemnon's idea of warfare is. In my view sending his men to keep watch on the ridge is hardly going to weaken the enemy's resolve. It seems that it is up to us to show them how to make life difficult for the Italians.

So tomorrow night we will set off from Vathy in the fishing boat to be provided by Ajax, trusting in Rees's seamanship and the navigation skills that I learned in the desert. The explosives will be carried down by locals and Sacred Band men. I plan to use half of our stock, leaving the rest in the store cave for future use. Base has advised that further supplies will arrive by kaïki *in a week's time, so I will be able to plan several more operations. Assuming, of course, that the Naxos show works out.*

Oh God, I have to stop myself turning into an unfeeling machine of destruction. The piercing beauty of the Greek landscape helps, as it has done throughout my sojourn on Trig, but the most valuable support has come from the lover I never expected to meet here or in any other place on earth. Maro is with me in the fight, but her presence also reminds me that there is more than war in this blood-drenched time. She understands the war and the need for sacrifice. If I allowed it, she would willingly come with us, but I have told her that she must stay in the cave. I cannot contemplate harm coming to her. She understands the war and yet she also humanises me. She makes me realise that there are more important things than the struggle, things that will last beyond the fighting. She laughs when I tell her that I will marry her when it's all over – that I will work in the British School in Athens and spend the summers on Trigono, that she will be with me all the time, that we will never be parted. If we can survive on Trigono in wartime, survive the Italians and the hostility of her family, we can survive anywhere. Ah, Maro.

'Tzortz?' *she said to me last night after we had made love, her arm on my chest.* 'You will be careful on this voyage to Naxos, will you not? You will come back for me.' *Her voice has the timbre of a girl's but the way she speaks, honest and proud, is that of a woman who has experienced much. 'I am not afraid for myself, but I worry for you. The man with the empty eyes, he is dangerous.'*

'I know Griffin is dangerous,' I replied with a smile. 'That is why he is here.' I have resisted great pressure from Agamemnon to have my man recalled to base because of the killings he carried out on Paros. If only his Sacred Band had proved so effective against the enemy.

She looked at me seriously, her eyes glinting in the oil lamp's flickering light. 'And my brother is dangerous too. The enemy wears a uniform you can recognise, but the people on your own side are sometimes more to be feared.'

I squeezed her hand. 'I will be careful.' Then I laughed, confident as perhaps only a young man in love can be. 'What are you saying, Maro? That the islanders will turn against me because of Griffin's fearsome eyes, or because they suspect that you and I are lovers? The Italians are the ones who sent their relatives to rot in Chaïdhari, not the British.'

She nodded but still her eyes were troubled.

'Come to me, little Maro,' I said, drawing her close. 'No matter what happens, we will always be together. I promise you that.'

'I know,' she said, her eyes wide and suddenly damp 'Athanati agapi,' she whispered. Love that doesn't die.

I repeated the words, my lips meeting hers.

Ah, Maro. Ah, Greece. What sacrifice would I not make for you?

Mavros looked around the hillsides. He considered shouting out Gretchen's name, but the blast of the wind above the enclosed space he was occupying showed how pointless that would be. The only thing to do was to climb up to the ridge and use the higher ground to locate her or anyone else who was in the vicinity. Eleni was also troubling him. She might be on her way back to the caves beyond the dig with help for him by now, but he had the feeling that something strange was going on. Where had the watchman Mitsos got to? It didn't seem likely that Theocharis would have given him the afternoon off without sending a replacement.

The least sheer of the slopes rising up from the sunken valley was to his right. The fact that Rena had brought Melpo down a steeper descent showed how experienced both woman and donkey were on the terrain. As Mavros traversed the scree near the cliff wall, he came to a narrow space almost completely concealed by a rock face, the formation similar to the blind door inside the excavated passage by the burial chambers. Peering into it, he saw a narrow zigzag channel leading into the hill. The stony floor was uneven, but when he bent down he could make out the ridged marks of shoes and boots on the sandy deposits on some areas of the rock. They looked recent. He moved into the passageway, feeling the rough walls tug at his shirt. As he approached the dark cave the half-sweet, half-sharp smell of decay flooded his nostrils. He wondered if one of the simple goatherd's animals had strayed into the subterranean labyrinth and permanently lost the light.

Then he heard the faint scraping noise, something abrading the rock, that he had heard in the other cave before he'd been knocked out. The hairs rose on his neck as he went into the darkness, breath catching in his throat as the stench worsened. He wished he still had the torch that Eleni had taken. The murk was so impenetrable that when he closed his eyes his vision was no worse.

The scream, long and shrill, from the slopes outside made him jump, the top of his head making contact with the uneven ceiling.

'Shit,' he said, raising his hand to the crack he'd received earlier. 'What next?' Turning on his heel, arms extended and hands on the stone walls, he made his way towards the faint line of light that was visible at the twisting entrance corridor.

Back in the open air, he ran his eye around the ridge, seeing no sign of the person – a woman, he reckoned – who had shrieked in what sounded like pain or panic. He started the ascent of the scree chute, immediately losing his footing and falling on his hands. It took him several minutes to get to the top, his thighs tight and his lungs bursting. The instant he made it to the saddle, the wind buffeted him like a straw in a hurricane, forcing him to crouch down low as he surveyed the island's southern cliffs. The sea was raging all around Trigono, the white foam that was bursting over the north-facing headlands giving them the appearance of the bows of ships slicing through the water at high speed. The great snake of the ridge between Vigla and Profitis Ilias was to his left, the dark green bushes and low trees that dotted its flanks straining in the blast like hounds pulling on the leash. But he could see no living creature apart from the gulls that were riding the wind currents. Even the nimble goats must have taken shelter on the lower ground or in one of the overgrown watercourses.

Mavros moved a few metres southwards into the lee of the howling northerly and squatted down. Had he imagined the scream? Could it have been the wind caught in a distorted rock, or a large seabird screeching its disapproval of the change in the weather? He didn't think so. It had to be Gretchen. But where was she?

Standing up against the pounding gusts, he headed east. It wasn't long before he was above the wired compound of the dig. He could see Eleni's motorbike by the gate, but there were no other vehicles and no people visible. He decided to go down and use the machine to get to the village. He could spend days searching for the American woman on the slopes and in the ravines, let alone in the caves and the disused mine shafts. Rena should be at least halfway to the village by now. He could probably catch her up, though the prospect of riding the powerful bike hardly filled him with joy.

He scrambled down the slope, the muscles in his calves complaining. The first thing that struck him was that Eleni would surely have taken her motorbike if she'd gone to get help for him. And the second, as he finally reached level ground and hobbled towards the machine, was that the rims of both wheels were pressing into the ground. The tyres were completely flat. He didn't bother calculating the odds of that happening accidentally. Something was very wrong.

Setting off down the track towards the place where he'd left his bicycle, Mavros thought he heard the wind's blast increase in volume. Then he saw the roof of a large vehicle come over the brow ahead. Before he could move, it skidded to a halt in front of him, the doors opening and two bulky figures running towards him.

Mitsos got to him first, the watchman's heavy hands gripping his upper arms hard.

Aris arrived, the flesh on his bare arms wobbling. 'So, Alex,' he said in Greek. 'It's time we had a talk.' He jerked his head towards the Jeep. 'Get him in the back, Mitso.'

'What's going on?' Mavros asked over his shoulder as he was marched away.

'Don't worry, Mister Brilliant Detective,' the big man said scornfully. 'You'll hear soon enough.' He gave a harsh laugh. 'And I think you'll be interested, very interested indeed.'

'Not if you're doing the talking,' Mavros muttered as Mitsos thrust him into the Jeep and sat beside him, hand still clutching his arm. 'Where's Eleni?' he demanded. 'Have you kidnapped her as well? What about Gretchen, the American woman? Have you seen her?'

Aris started the engine and turned to him. 'We've got everyone you want, my friend.' He laughed again, his eyes narrowing. 'And we've got news of your brother Andonis.'

Mavros felt his stomach somersault as the Jeep swung round, but the nausea that coursed through him wasn't caused by Aris's driving. Andonis? His brother's face rose up before him, the eyes as bright blue as ever. What did Aris mean? Jesus Christ. Andonis. What did the museum benefactor's son know about him? Was this finally the breakthrough he'd spent most of his life waiting for?

He passed the rest of the short journey in another world, the innocent one he'd grown up in before his brother went into the dark. Could it really be that Andonis had got a message through from the underworld after all this time? Could it really be?

Rinus was lying inside the roofless herdsman's hut on the southern side of the ridge watching the seagulls soar on the violent updraughts and trying to make sense of what he'd seen. He asked himself what the fuck was going on. That stuff he'd kept back from the last shipment Lefteris brought in – shit, what had it done to him? He had felt jittery from the minute he took it, had felt the stone walls drawing around him as he walked to the Astrapi. It was only when he was on the BMW, racing down the road to the Kambos with the wind whistling past his helmet, that he began to get a grip. But after he'd stashed the bike in the usual place behind the bushes, things had gone even more crazy.

First, as he followed the winding watercourse up to the ridge, sure that no one could see him in the heavy growth of evergreens and gorse, he'd caught sight of the two Americans who came to the bar. The woman Gretchen was a surly cow but Lance was okay, pretty straight but okay. They were up on the ridge to the west, staring down at something. He guessed it was Eleni's dig but he couldn't be sure from where he was. He lost them after a while as he ascended the dry line of stones created by the winter torrents. It changed direction all the time according to the contours of the hillside.

Then, when he was making the final approach to the ridge, he'd caught a glimpse of the mad widow Rena up on the heights to his right. She was crouching over, also peering at something below her. She may have been taking protection from the bastard wind, but it looked more like she was taking care no one saw her, like she was up to nothing that was good. The witch. Thank Christ his ex-wife Kate hadn't been as demented as her. Otherwise he might have ended up in a wooden box like the one the villagers said Rena put her husband in.

Just before he took cover behind the walls of the ruined hut, he saw Eleni on the track below. God, the stupid woman was running, heavy legs pounding and loose tits all over the place. She didn't make it, though. Aris caught up with her easily and dragged her into the Jeep. Shit, what had she been doing to upset the Theocharis family?

Crazy people, they were all crazy. Why couldn't they leave him alone? He stretched out on the flat rock and tried to get his head together. This was his routine; it had been for a long time now. Ever since his tart of a wife had taken the girls and left him. Bit of gear, hammer down the road on the bike, chill out in the hut and then . . . and then the other. It was a weird way to live, but it was his own. He'd made it, without help from anyone else. Later on he'd go back and sort the bar out, get ready for the drinkers. Not that there would be many of those from now until April. Winter was on its way, the season for planning next year's operations. Yeah. Next year. Hey, hold on, guy. This year's operations were still going on. This year's operations had to be sorted out after what had happened to Yiangos. Things were getting a bit hot for comfort. That fucker Alex, he had to be fixed soon. Before he left the island and shot his mouth off.

Then he felt himself begin to sink. It sometimes happened this way. The rush from the gear and the climb up the watercourse made him close his eyes and sink into the other world, leaving the muck to fly away and hit someone else. He let himself be surrounded by the bodies from the videos he watched – hard faces, dirty and cursing, but soft bodies, wet and willing. Yes, climb all over them, open their cracks and stick it to them wherever he wanted. Bitches, he'd show them, he'd show them all. Sinking into the dark . . .

But everything was different when he came round. It had never been like this before. The seagulls hovering and banking, yes, the sun westering into its crimson fall, but on his own – he was usually alone in the old hut. Alone or with the only one who trusted him. What were these other people doing here?

Rinus sat up with a jerk. Fuck. Who were they, the types on each side of him? They were naked, their faces battered and bloody, their arms tied behind their backs and their ankles roped. Eyes closed, lips smashed, were they breathing? He leaned over and touched the man's neck. Yes, a faint pulse. And in the woman's. Fucking shit, who were they? Did he have anything to do with what had happened to them? Jesus, had he blacked out and gone psycho?

He ran an eye over the woman's body. Flaccid breasts, dark hair in her groin and on her legs. He was having difficulty identifying the face because of the bruises and blood. Christ, yes, he thought. It was the American he'd seen up here earlier. Gretchen. So was the guy her partner? Yes, partner, not husband – she'd been very sharp about that the first night in the bar. Was this Lance? He looked more closely, taking in the small, limp dick and the puny chest and arms. No, Lance was tall and fit, and besides, his hair wasn't blond. Fuck, it was Mikkel, Barbara's Mikkel. How did he and Gretchen get here? Who tied them up? Could he have done it himself, stoned and out of control?

Rinus got to his feet, his mind reeling. He had to get organised, had to sort this mess out. But how? And then, as the wind made his eyes flood with salt tears and the heaving surface of the surrounding sea darkened, he understood what he had to do. There was no viable option.

He had to tell someone.

Rena reached the outskirts of the village without seeing anyone on the road, the other workers from the fields and the building sites having already returned. It was as she passed the Bar Astrapi that she was spotted by a group of little boys playing football. She heard their alarmed cries as they realised what was over the donkey's back, so she quickened her pace. Her legs were aching from the long walk and she could hear Melpo's rapid breathing. The poor beast had been expecting to turn into her field in the Kambos, but she had kept going without complaint. Fortunately old Thodhoris hadn't been there.

By the time Rena came out of the narrow track and into the paved street that led to her house and the square beyond, there was a crowd of screaming children behind her. Mothers dashed from their houses at the sound and joined the procession, voices raised as they asked about the body on the donkey. Who is it? Is it one of ours? A sharp-tongued old she-devil who had a particular dislike of Rena wondered out loud if she'd killed another man.

The hubbub roused the men of Trigono from their seats in the *kafeneion*. They formed a wall, blocking the road ahead and craning their heads towards her. Rena hurried on, hoping they would let her pass so that she could take the dead American to the police station near the school. But nobody showed any sign of moving and she was forced to stop. The voices all around her were gradually silenced, until the only sounds were those made by the wind as it rustled the leaves of the mulberry tree and whipped the electricity wires that hung between the houses.

Then the line of men parted and Manolis stepped out, the empty sleeve of his shirt pinned up beneath the black armband he was wearing for his grandson Yiangos.

'What is this?' he demanded, nodding at the body. 'Why are you bringing such a thing into the village to frighten the women and children?' The old fisherman's eyes, hard as a millstone, were fixed on Rena.

She glanced around the crowd. 'I don't see too many frightened people here,' she replied. 'Besides, as soon as you let me through, the object will be removed.'

'Who is it?' Manolis asked. 'One of ours?'

'No, it's not one of ours,' Rena said sharply. 'Not one of *yours*,' she emphasised. 'Not anyone from this island.' Her eyes flashed as she surveyed the villagers again. 'Though if you were good Christians you would care about every human being, not just Trigoniotes.' She stepped close to the line of men, tugging Melpo's rope. 'It is a foreigner, a tourist. I think he fell from the ridge near Vigla.' She looked up to the grey-blue sky. 'In the name of God, let us pass.'

There was a murmur from the crowd and Manolis stepped back. A gap appeared ahead of her and she ushered Melpo through, the people moving away to avoid the swaying arms and legs of the dead man and the bloodstained blanket round his head as the donkey shied.

Rena felt hundreds of eyes on her. They lanced into her body, making her skin tingle as if the threads of a huge jellyfish had wrapped themselves around her. Heading for the police station, she knew that the islanders would make her pay for this outrage. As well as for all the others they were convinced she had perpetrated.

20

It seemed to Kyra Maro that there was a lot of noise outside – women and children, the clamour of their voices, the village dogs yelping. She raised herself out of her chair with difficulty and went to the window. The shutters were hooked a few centimetres open to allow the air in. People were going past quickly, avid expressions on their faces.

Maro wondered what was happening. Had they found someone else to torment? Where was Rena? She hadn't been in yet today.

'Ach, Rena,' she mouthed. 'Is it you they're picking on? Ever since your worthless husband died – the animal who clawed at you and struck you every time he was drunk – Trigono has been suspicious of you. You're not a native, you came from another island. They will never accept you as one of their own.'

The old woman staggered back to her chair, her mind already filling with images from the past. She knew what it was like to be the target of the islanders' anger, of their poisonous disapproval. But for her it had been different. Her trouble started with her own family, with her brother Manolis in particular. He had always treated her like a slave, even when she was a child. It was the way of things in those days. The girls were used as servants until they were old enough to marry. Then, if their husbands and mothers-in-law had a mind, they were treated no better after they became wives. And the elder brothers of girls often resented them, because they had to wait until their sisters were provided with a dowry – which usually meant they had to build each female a house – before they themselves could marry.

So she had actually done Manolis a favour by running to Tzortz. Her lover would not have required a dowry, he would have taken her away so the family need not have felt shame every time Maro went outdoors. She gave a bitter laugh, feeling a stab of pain in her throat. As if her brother would ever have seen it that way. Her virtue was her family's virtue. By giving it away unmarried, and to a foreigner, she became unclean for Manolis, a common prostitute who had dishonoured the name of Gryparis. She'd known he would react that way, that was why she had slipped out of the family house and gone to Tzortz. But at that time she had no idea how things would end. Ach, Tzortz, you were too trusting. You should have listened to me.

And suddenly Maro was back in the cave on Vigla, in what her lover called their secret place. It was the night he and his men were going to Naxos to destroy the Italians' weapons and supplies. She had begged him to let her come with them. She could move through the undergrowth as quietly as any of them, she could carry heavy loads. But he had refused to allow it, told her that it was too dangerous, that he needed her to watch over the radio and the equipment. She accepted his words – what else could she do? – and she embraced him before he set out to join the other two British soldiers on the ridge. From there they would make their way down to the boat that was waiting in the inlet at Vathy. He was excited, his eyes restless and his hands trembling. She had never been able to understand it, this great love he had for her country and the way it inspired him to fight and take risks.

'I will return to you, Maro,' he said, kissing her on the lips then pushing her gently back. 'Be sure you are waiting.'

She had nodded, willing the tears not to flood her eyes so that his enthusiasm for the attack would not be affected. Then she bent her head and kissed his hand, the hand that had been on her breast only an hour before. 'Safe return, my love,' she whispered.

Tzortz left the cave, his shoulders bent under the weight of his pack. Maro gave him a few minutes then, contrary to his instructions, padded lightly though the twisting passage and into the light of the clouded half-moon. Glancing all around, she made sure she was on her own, then moved noiselessly through the patches of scrub and up the steep slope to the saddle.

There was nobody on the northern side of the wall separating the goat pastures. She kept to it, head down, and went towards the point where the British would start their descent on the southern side. And then the half-moon sailed out of the clouds that had been obscuring it, casting a silvery light on the hills and the ridge. Raising her eyes above the uneven wall, Maro saw a sight that froze the blood in her veins.

Tzortz and his men found their way barred by a group of Sacred Band men and islanders. Among them she saw her brothers Manolis and Thodhoris, their faces set in unnatural smiles. Close by she could see Captain Theocharis, his hand in his pocket. Then, before she could do anything, before she could shout a warning, Manolis stepped forward, his arms wide as if to embrace Tzortz. It appeared that he was wishing her lover luck on the mission, but she knew that look on her brother's face, she knew that it concealed violent intentions. Tzortz had already opened his own arms and accepted the embrace, as had the other two British, the friendlier one letting a Sacred Band member approach him and the dangerous one receiving her brother Thodhoris more reluctantly. The Greeks' knives glinted in the moonlight as they slid out of their coat sleeves and were plunged into the saboteurs' backs.

'Get off to the lower world, whore's son,' Manolis shouted triumphantly.

Maro was paralysed, could move no part of herself for seconds, watched helplessly as the men toppled backwards. Thodhoris and the Sacred Band member were bending over the two English soldiers, drawing their knives across the stricken men's throats. Panos Theocharis stood close at hand, following their actions with a look of grim satisfaction. Then scudding clouds passed in front of the moon and she blinked to get her night vision back. She could hear groans, shouts in Greek, and then the rattle of stones from the wall.

Suddenly her limbs were released from the icy grip that had held them and she dashed forward, hand pulling the grenade she had taken from the stores in the cave out of her pocket.

A figure reeled away from the wall on the northern side, upper body bent low. She thought it was her lover. He was followed by two more, and she recognised the voice of Manolis directing the chase. Without giving a second thought to what she was doing, she pulled the pin from the grenade.

'Here, Manoli,' she called, watching as he stopped about ten metres in front of her. 'This is for you.' She tossed the grenade between him and the men with him.

Then she ran after Tzortz, not looking back when she heard the muffled explosion. Perhaps her lover hadn't been wounded so badly – he was moving quickly, heading for their cave. She caught up with him and put her arm round his back. It was only when they reached their place and she lit the lamp that she realised there was blood all over both of them. Her lover sprawled on the blanket they had lain on earlier that evening, begging for morphine.

Then the walls had begun to shake. At first she'd thought her brother and his companions were throwing grenades at them, then she recognised the deep rumble of an earthquake. Gradually the movement and noise faded, the cave full of dust that almost obscured the lamp she had lit. And then, as her lover sank into a drugged doze, Maro saw the life-sized carved bodies laid out on the stony floor in a previously concealed space that had opened up in the cave wall. She remembered shapes that her primary school teacher had drawn on the blackboard, the shapes of ancient statues that had been found on the neighbouring islands. She rubbed her hand across the dusty stone and realised that the marble glistening in the lamplight was blue, not white. The pair of what must have been lovers had their arms wrapped around each other, their blank faces looking upwards. Lovers lying together for eternity, she thought, glancing at the now unconscious Tzortz.

Maro gave a start and came back to herself, back to the room in the *kastro*. Ach, Tzortz, she thought. That was the end of the good times for us. You were in a wretched state, there was great loss of blood. It was a miracle that the earthquake didn't bury us. I managed to clear a way to the cave entrance. There were more tremors later and I'm sure our secret place was lost after we left it for the last time, lost and destroyed along with the stone lovers who had watched over it for thousands of years. I kept you alive, gave you water and drugs from the emergency pack until the British *kaïki* came. The Trigoniotes and Theocharis's men, the murderers who attacked you and the other British, were looking for us but they didn't find the cave. I'll never know how I got you down to the landing point on the west coast. You'd managed to speak on the radio and tell your base to change the rendezvous from Vathy inlet. I half carried, half dragged you down the rocky slopes, stopping all the time to make sure we weren't seen. It seemed to take hours, but I did it. I got you on to the boat, kissed you – you were delirious. Again I wished you 'Safe return, my love'. And you said you would come back, you promised we would meet again. Then the boat backed away, engine thrashing the blue-black water into a frenzy of foam.

Maro tried to control her breathing, tried to stop the rush of her thoughts, but it was useless.

For years I didn't see you again, Tzortz. I thought you must have died. I was sure you would have come for me if you'd been able. Yes, I thought you'd died . . . until finally you did return and everything turned to dust and a lifetime of bitter tears.

The old woman slumped forward, the strength ebbing from her limbs, suddenly unsure after all the years about what she had done. Had it been worth blowing her brother Manolis's arm off and blinding her cousin in one eye for a lover who never returned? And what about Tasos, Tzortz's son? Manolis had beaten her remorselessly when she finally came down from the hills with her swollen belly. Beaten her so that Tasos was deformed and sentenced to a short, empty life. And the village had treated her like a pariah ever since. She should have left, gone to the big city, but she was afraid that Tzortz might return to the island. There was no one she could trust to tell him where she'd gone. And so, homeless, she had worked her fields and paid an extortionate rent for a hovel to a grasping islander. Could she justify what she had done? Now everything seemed like a cruel game, one she had played with all her heart when she was young, but had lost. So much for immortality, the love that doesn't die. It was a tale for children, a spell, a myth fashioned out of air by a deceitful god. Ach, Tzortz.

Then Maro thought of Panos Theocharis. He had known what Manolis and his men were going to do, he had gone along with it. Perhaps he'd even arranged it. Tzortz survived but the other two Englishmen were slaughtered like goats, their bodies chained to heavy stones and dropped overboard from a *trata* beyond the islets on the southern coast – she had watched from the hills above. Theocharis and her brothers were murderers – they deserved to be punished even though her lover didn't report them on the radio or afterwards. If he had done, they would surely have had to pay after the war.

'Ach, Tzortz,' she moaned. 'Why did you fail me? Why did you return, only to abandon me again in the cruellest way?'

Maro felt her eyes flicker. She found that she could no longer summon up the images of her loved ones. She tried in vain to call them to her. Tasos had gone, Tzortz had gone and she was alone, longing for the abyss.

Panos Theocharis put the phone down on the desk in his study and turned to his wife. 'How strange.'

'What is it?' Dhimitra asked, looking up from her magazine.

'That was the policeman in the village. He says that the body of an American tourist has been found in the hills south of the estate and that a women who was with him is missing. They're organising a search. He wanted to know if we'd seen any sign of her.'

'Who are they?' Dhimitra asked, standing up and walking to her husband.

'He was called Lance Leonard. No one seemed to know her name.'

She looked at him blankly. 'You told him you don't know them?' she asked. 'And haven't seen them?'

Theocharis nodded. 'Of course.' He glanced at his wife. '*You* don't know them, do you?'

Dhimitra turned away. 'I think I may have seen them in the bar, but I didn't speak to them.' She stepped towards the balcony. 'Ah, here's Aris.' She leaned forward to examine the Jeep more closely. 'And Mitsos. They have the investigator Mavros.'

'Good,' her husband said, an expression of relief on his face. 'I'll talk to him before we show the figurines to that snake of a dealer. How much longer do you need to prepare Eleni?'

'I think I've got through to her,' Dhimitra said with a tight smile. 'She's cleaning herself up now. That'll give her a chance to consider the advantages of remaining on our side – and the dangers of talking to Mavros or the ministry.' She swivelled round on her high heels and headed for the door. 'I'll go and make the point to her one last time.'

Theocharis nodded. 'After you've done that, go and entertain Roufos until we're ready to make the presentation in the gallery. If that's not too much to ask.'

Dhimitra smiled, this time showing her teeth. 'I think I can manage that, Pano.'

After the door closed behind her, Theocharis turned back to the high windows and took in the fields of the Kambos and the village beyond. God, this island, he thought. It was part of him, part of his family's history, he'd been associated with it all his life. But sometimes Trigono was too much to bear, the weight of the place crushed him.

The old man tried again to work out what had been going on recently. He felt tired, decrepit, unable to control events in the way he had done for so long. Everything started to go wrong with that girl Rosa Ozal, the one he suspected had been sent to spy on his collection and the dig. Dhimitra hadn't believed him, said she was just a tourist, but he wasn't convinced. Rosa Ozal, the one who'd left so suddenly. And just a few days ago there had been the double drowning from Lefteris's boat. He still wasn't sure if that had been an accident. But worst of all there had been Liz Clifton, the other woman who left before her time. She had been asking questions in the village about George Lawrence of all people. After all these years that English officer had come back to haunt him. Christ and the Holy Mother, the madman had seen himself as some kind of new Achilles. He was a typical public school and Oxbridge classicist who thought he knew everything about Greek civilisation, even thought he knew how to fight for the country's freedom. How naive the fool had been. But what would have happened to his own reputation if the woman had gone ahead and written the biography she was planning of the second-rate poet, using material from the diary she had located? The only thing to do had been to arrange for it and everything else of significance to be removed from her room. That must have made her see the light.

But Theocharis was still unable to stop himself going over what had happened on the ridge all those years ago, that night when the moonlight was bright one moment and obscured by clouds the next. There was no doubt in his mind that preventing Lawrence and his bloodthirsty men from doing more damage, bringing even more serious reprisals on the local population, had been the right thing to do. If only Manolis hadn't mistreated his sister, beaten her and destroyed her child, whipped up feelings against her in the village. That was cruel, but the war was to blame. The worst things happen in such times and people like Manolis who are vicious by nature have their characters ruined by war. At least that hadn't happened to him. Or had it? What he was considering for Alex Mavros was as callous as anything he'd done during the war. Was it really necessary? Oh God, was there no end to the guilt?

There was a heavy knock on the door. It was opened and Mavros was pushed through, Aris behind him.

'Please, sit down, Mr Mavros,' the museum benefactor said in Greek, indicating the sofa.

'What's this about my brother?' Mavros demanded, fixing him with wild eyes. 'You have news of him? What news?'

Theocharis glared at Aris. His son had a slack smile on his face. Could he do nothing right? The idiot had already told Mavros, leaving him no option but to proceed with the distasteful stratagem.

The old man nodded slowly, regaining his composure. The

investigator's agitation showed that the ploy was already having an effect. 'Yes, perhaps it's best if we dispense with pleasantries. I am rather busy. My proposition is very simple, Mr Mavros. I will give you information concerning the location of your brother after—'

'What kind of information?' Mavros interrupted. His voice was hoarse. 'Are you saying that Andonis is alive?'

Theocharis raised a hand. 'Please,' he said, giving the investigator a thin smile. 'You must agree to do this on my terms or not at all.' He looked at him, seeing the turmoil in his face. 'Do you agree?'

'Before I know what your terms are?' Mavros took a deep breath and eventually nodded. 'All right. Tell me how it's to be, Theocharis.'

'That's Mr Theocharis, you son of a bitch,' said Aris, shoving his elbow into Mavros's ribs.

'Enough,' Panos said, glaring at his son. 'Leave him alone.' He turned his eyes back to Mavros. 'I know this must be difficult for you after so many years, but you will understand that I have my own affairs to safeguard.' He smiled again, this time more expansively. 'These are the terms, which, as you have agreed, are non-negotiable. You will leave Trigono as soon as the wind allows. After you have been back in Athens for three days, I will arrange for a file containing material about your brother to be delivered to your home. The file will be in no way attributable to me and you would be extremely foolish to disclose the provenance of the information to anyone.' He opened his eyes wide. 'I retain the best legal advisers, as well as numerous operatives who act on my behalf in, shall we say, less overt ways.'

Aris let out a guffaw.

Theocharis continued talking without looking at his son. 'Mr Mavros, you are to ask no further questions about Rosa Ozal or about anything else concerning Trigono when you are back on the mainland. And there is to be no further communication between you and me, or between you and any of my family or staff. One more thing. Should you contravene any of these terms before you leave the island, our agreement will be terminated immediately and you will receive no information whatsoever about your brother.' He raised his shoulders. 'That is all.'

The investigator bowed his head and brought his hands to his forehead. For several anxious moments Theocharis thought he was going to decline the proposal.

'Very well,' said Mavros, looking up again. 'One question. Where did you get this material?'

'I have already referred to the people I employ to gather such data.' Theocharis turned towards the windows. 'If you need further convincing of its reliability, I will also say that I had certain dealings with the regime your brother was acting against. Not that you will ever be able to prove that. Goodbye, Mr Mavros.'

The tycoon watched as Mavros was led out of the tower to the Jeep. The man looked like he had been caught in an explosion, his head down and his shoulders slumped. The wind was flicking his long hair around like the mane of a horse. He wondered what it was about his eyes. There was something strange about them. But he was a beaten man now. Theocharis didn't think there would be any more problems from him. He felt a stab of remorse at what he had done but, whatever happened, family came first. That meant his own family, for all his son's manifest failings, and not the offspring of the communist Spyros Mavros.

'I am someone. You are someone. She is someone.'

The bound woman was fighting to bring up an image of who she was, but the words achieved nothing. I am someone. But who am I?

She stopped and tried to take a deep breath, to fill her lungs, but couldn't. She managed only short, gulping swallows of air, her throat wrenched in agony. Go on, she told herself. Continue the recital. We are someone. She broke off, a burst of hoarse laughter erupting from deep inside her, making her choke as the pain bit into her airway. We are someone, she whispered, blinking hard but not managing to squeeze a tear from her eyes. The royal we, the we that self-obsessed politicians sometimes used, the we that didn't mean more than one person at all, the we that meant I'm in charge and the rest of you are going to do what I say, the rich man's we.

Christ, woman, she thought. Get a grip. You can't even think straight any more. She pulled weakly at her bonds, the ropes no longer hurting her wrists and ankles. They'd been numb for a period of time that she couldn't determine. She wondered when the end was going to come, wished the last darkness would swallow her up. But it wouldn't, it refused to. She knew she was still in her place of captivity because, although it was dark, there was still the faint blur of light ahead that had been tantalising her, the blur that told her when the sun was up. But no water, no food. She was more convinced than ever that she'd been abandoned, left to rot away. At least she wasn't being filmed any more.

Jesus, she stank. The whole place stank. The smell had got worse recently, the dampness under her thighs rubbing her skin raw. But she knew that they weren't only coming from her, the waves of corruption. Deep in her consciousness was the glimpse she'd caught of the ravaged body when she was first brought to the place. She had tried to blot it out but it was still lurking inside her like a ghoul preparing to pounce.

Take me away, she pleaded silently, take me back to the real world. Is that the wind outside or the rush of blood in my veins? The blood that's keeping me alive pointlessly. Please, take me away.

And then her memory recovered something else and she slipped into another dimension, her nostrils suddenly clear of the cloying stench. She looked down and saw her body as it was that last evening, sheathed in the green dress that ended above her knees, her feet in the slingback shoes she'd paid far too much for. She raised her eyes and took in the mural in front of her. Faded colours, patches that had been replaced, but the scene was still vivid enough – the underworld river, the ferryman with his burning eyes, the souls on the banks with their hands outstretched, imploring the living to save them.

The old man with the sculpted beard and the stick was by her side, his lips moving but his words inaudible. All she could hear was the wind, loud in her ears now, a continuous flow of air over stalks of corn or the surface of the sea. Who was he? And then the others crowded round, the woman with the golden skin and hair, Aris, the overweight bald man, and the other woman with the dark curls and soft smile. What did they want from her?

Then, without warning, the noise in her ears stopped and she found herself in a large room, a study with a broad antique desk and high windows, distant lights twinkling through them. She was on her own with the old man and his name came back to her. Theocharis, Panos Theocharis. The wealthy businessman, the museum benefactor. They were sitting on a plush sofa and he was asking her questions, his head bent forward and his eyes focusing on hers.

'How do you know about George Lawrence? How do you know about his activities on Trigono? What is your interest in these matters?'

The questions went on, the next one posed as soon as she stuttered out her answer. She was nervous, intimidated by the tower and its owner, who had suddenly become very serious, almost hostile towards her. She didn't mean to mention the diary but Theocharis was a skilled interrogator; he'd quickly extracted the admission that she had obtained it in an auction of memorabilia in London.

'And does this diary mention me?' he asked, his eyes hooded and his expression stern. 'Does it mention the code-name Agamemnon?'

She prevaricated, mumbled something about Lawrence being unstable when he wrote the entries, but she could see the old man wasn't convinced.

'And does the great British hero George Lawrence describe the consequences of his actions?' Theocharis asked, his tone bitter. 'Does he express any regret for the people of this island who suffered as a result of his petty acts of sabotage?'

She told him that he did, that Lawrence had been plagued by doubts even though his commitment to the struggle prevailed.

She thought it would not be sensible to mention the local woman Maro. But why was the Greek so interested? Could he have had something to do with Lawrence's wounding and his sudden departure from Trigono? The official records were incomplete. It seemed he was incoherent for months after his evacuation by *kaïki*. The diary ended with the entry leading up to the Naxos mission.

'He was a coward, you know,' Theocharis said. 'He wrote feeble poetry after the war.'

She tried to defend Lawrence, saying that as far as she could tell the poems were accurate in their depiction of Trigono, even if they were melancholic and filled with obscure references to a tragic love affair. They were also dripping with regret, and the writer seemed to have experienced a terrible disillusion. She wished she had been able to talk to the woman Maro. Someone had told her she was still alive.

Her host had got to his feet unsteadily and loomed over her. 'The diary, my dear. I must have the diary. I will double what you paid for it.'

It was then that she knew she was on to something, when she knew she was on the brink of a breakthrough. The diary was the key. So she refused to sell it, shaking her head even when he offered ten times the price. He accepted this with surprising good grace, saying that he understood she had her book to write. It was only when the Jeep that was supposed to be taking her back to the village turned towards the dark mass of the southern hills that she realised the cost of her refusal. Although she had hidden her back-up diskette and a few photographs, the diary was easy enough to find.

And then everything turned to black.

The woman opened her eyes and took in the blurred line of light again, realising immediately that she was back in her own filth. There was still no release from the pain. But something had stayed with her from the scenes in the tower, something that made her shiver. The Jeep had been driven by a man. She couldn't bring his face back but she remembered the thick arms on the steering wheel. But the person in the other front seat was a woman, a voice that she'd heard before. She frowned, then felt tears finally flood her eyes. Could a woman really be involved in tying her up in this hole, in filming her and abusing her, in leaving her to die? Who was she? Why couldn't she summon up a face? Suddenly she remembered the animated conversation that had taken place when she was first in the cave, the hoarse voices. Her captors had been arguing and, yes, one of them was a woman.

A noise. She blinked, alert in a split second, trying to comprehend what was going on in front of her. The faint light had been obscured. There was a sound, a dragging sound, as if someone or something was scuffling along the rough rock walls and stony floor. Her heart leaped. Was this water, was this food? Oh God, was it freedom at last?

Then she was forced to blink as a bright light came on and was shone in her eyes. For a few moments she couldn't see anything. The noise she had heard continued, getting closer. The light moved erratically around what she could now see was a cave, stalactites hanging from the ceiling, the walls roughly formed. Glancing from side to side, she felt her heart stop. No, it couldn't be. A figure she was unable to make out in the flashes of light had dropped a naked female body near her and was busy attaching a rope to the wrists.

But that wasn't what made her shrink back against the jagged rock. A few seconds earlier the random movements of the torch had lit up another form at the far end of the cave. She saw the blackened, tattered corpse, teeth and bones glinting, that she had been fighting to keep out of her mind. And she saw the familiar ropes around the body's wrists and arms.

She let out a desperate, croaking cry. She had realised that she was only one of a growing collection of victims.

'This isn't a taxi,' Aris said, pulling up outside the Bar Astrapi. 'You can walk from here.'

Mavros opened the door, trying to ignore the mocking faces of the big man and the watchman Mitsos.

'You get the first ferry that leaves Trigono after the wind drops

or the deal's off, right?' Aris gave a hollow laugh. 'Safe journey,
wanker.'

Heading down the track past the spot where he'd been
attacked and blinking as the wind blew dust into his eyes,
Mavros thought about what he had done. Andonis. His brother
had been with him since he was a boy, had accompanied him
everywhere. Andonis was often invisible, always silent. When he
did appear it was only as flashes of memory, evanescent images
that had supplanted flesh and blood. But Andonis was still his
guardian spirit, the figure he always tried to take as an example
and measure up to. He couldn't ignore Andonis. He couldn't
consider prioritising the Ozal case and passing up a chance of
finding him. What if he were still alive? There was very little
hope after so long, but any hint was worth investigating.

Yes, he was doing the right thing. It went against the grain to
abandon a case, especially one that had developed in unexpected
directions and had led to him being attacked, but Andonis was
more important to him than Rosa Ozal. After all, her own brother
wasn't too concerned about her disappearance – he'd only called
Mavros once to find out how he was progressing. Maybe Rosa
was having a passionate affair with a Turkish waiter. As for the
dope dealer Rinus and the unfortunate American who'd fallen
from the ridge, they weren't his responsibility. And if Eleni the
archaeologist was right and Theocharis wanted to sell off the
Cycladic statues illicitly, so what? Greek tycoon breaks the law.
What else was new? No, Andonis was all that mattered. But guilt
gnawed at him, guilt concerning Aris Theocharis. He couldn't
forget the young couple that had drowned. Aris was involved
in their deaths in some way, as the damage to his boat and the
goatherd Dinos's testimony proved. What if it hadn't been an
accident? Could he really let the bastard walk away, even for
Andonis's sake?

Mavros turned into the paved street and stopped in his tracks.
There was a crowd of villagers blocking the road farther down,
their arms raised and their voices shrill. Most of them seemed to
be women. Moving forward, he realised they were outside Rena's

house. He started to run. As he got closer he made out the words
fonissa and *poutana* – murderess, whore.

'Let me pass!' he shouted in Greek. 'Let me pass. I have a room
in that house.'

Heads turned and voices began to drop.

'What's going on here?' he demanded. 'What are you doing?'

'Who's he?' he heard a woman ask.

'He's not from here,' another replied, staring at him.

'Rena?' he called. 'It's Alex. Let me in.'

There was pause, silence falling over the crowd.

'Rena?'

'Alex?' came a low voice from inside. 'I don't want to open the
door. They're going to hurt me.'

'Murderess!' screamed an elderly woman in black. 'She killed
her husband and now she's killed another man! Get her!'

Arms came up again and Mavros was jammed against the door.
His face was drizzled by spittle from the baying crowd, and for a
moment he thought he was going to be crushed. Then the noise
dropped as a pair of heavy bodies forced their way towards him.

'All right, mate?' the Englishman Roy asked, his shaven head
gleaming in the sun. 'What's this, then? A local custom?'

'Yeah,' said Norm, facing up to a pair of red-faced island
women. 'Burn the witch?'

'Not far off,' Mavros said, getting his breathing back under
control. 'You guys are making a habit of rescuing me.'

'Yeah, we're gonna start charging you for it,' Roy said, a grin
spreading across his face. 'Trace!' he shouted. 'Jane! Over here!
Our mate Alex has got himself in trouble again.'

Mavros watched as the two women pushed their way through
the islanders. The crowd had lost its impetus and people were
beginning to drift off. Trace didn't look too sure, but Jane was
holding her arm, a determined expression on her face.

'Rena?' he said at the door. 'It's okay now. The British are here.
You can let us in.' After a while he heard bolts being drawn. He
glanced down the street through the dispersing bodies and saw
the policeman Stamatis leaning against a wall and flicking a string

of worry beads. It was obvious that Rena wouldn't have got much protection from him. Farther down the road one-armed Manolis was staring at him, his face set hard.

'Quick!' the widow said when she opened up.

'Don't worry,' Norm said, taking a boxer's guard. 'We'll look after you.' He ushered Mavros and the others in. 'Got any beer?'

Rena closed the door behind them and bolted it, then smiled weakly. 'Yes, I have beer. Come and sit down.' She led them down the dark passage and pointed to the table under the pergola.

Mavros followed her into the kitchen, catching sight of the donkey Melpo munching hay at the end of the yard. 'What happened, Rena?' he asked.

She was still smiling, but he could tell her from the colour in her face and her breathing that she'd been badly frightened. 'They think I poisoned my husband, God rest his unclean soul, and now they think I killed the American.' She lifted cans of beer from the fridge, shaking her head. 'They are illiterates. They don't know any better.'

'The policeman didn't seem to care what they did.'

Rena gave a bitter laugh. 'He's in old Manolis's pocket. That family hates me because I look after poor Kyra Maro.'

'Where's the American's body?'

'I took it to the police station. That idiot Stamatis didn't want it in there so the doctor had it moved to the back of the medical centre.'

'Is a search being organised for the woman Gretchen?'

Rena bit her lip. 'Stamatis asked people, but they said it was too late in the day. I tried to get the men in the *kafeneion* to help, but they ignored me. They think she will be back soon.' She shrugged. 'Maybe she will. If she didn't slip like her man.'

Mavros looked into her eyes. 'Is that what you think happened to Lance?' He was remembering the look on his landlady's face when she'd been up on the ridge, the way she had stared at him as if he were a criminal – or an unwelcome witness. He only had her word that she was in the fields when the American fell.

Rena held his gaze and then lifted her chin. 'I don't know. But as soon as I've served the others, I'm going to look for the woman. Are you coming?'

Mavros dropped his head and didn't answer. He waited for her to walk into the yard. He couldn't risk going back out to the hills. What would Theocharis do about their agreement if he heard that he'd been snooping around in the vicinity of the dig? He thought of Andonis and wondered what his brother would have done in his place.

He went outside before Rena came back from the table. The British couples were drinking, their voices raised in excited chatter.

'Are you coming with us, then, Alex?' Norm said, pushing a chair in his direction. 'Your friend Rena's been telling us she's off to look for the American woman. Christ, what a thing to happen to her bloke.'

'You're going to join the search?' Mavros asked, declining the beer that he was offered.

'Yeah, we are,' said Jane, giving her companions an ironic look. 'Make a change from sitting around getting pissed all the time.'

'Not necessarily a change for the better,' Roy said.

'Oh, come on,' said Jane. 'We've got the hire car. That wreck'll take us as far as the road end. Then we can go on foot. It's about time we saw more of the island than the beaches.'

'You will come with us, Alex?' Rena said, her eyes on him.

Mavros closed his eyes and tried to make contact with his brother. Andoni, he pleaded, where are you? I can't decide on my own. What would you do if you were here? Gretchen is probably hurt and frightened. Would you help her? Yes, you would. You'd help her without hesitating.

Coming back to himself in the shaded yard, Mavros nodded and reached for the can of Amstel. 'Yes, okay,' he said in a low voice. He was trying to convince himself that Theocharis wouldn't see him and that, even if he did, he wouldn't necessarily take the search for the American woman as a breach of their arrangement – trying but not succeeding. 'Have you got a torch, Rena?' he asked. 'There are some caves we'll need to check.'

The widow nodded then turned to the kitchen, her head bowed like the condemned prisoner she'd been until the people round the table had come to her rescue.

21

'We'll never all fit in that,' Mavros said, his eyes on the ancient Renault Farma. It was a model he hadn't seen for a long time, the yellow bodywork pitted with dents.

'Course we will,' Roy said. 'You and Norm can stand up in the luggage compartment and lean on the canopy struts.' He grinned. 'Don't worry, the women will hang on to you from the back seat.'

Rena squeezed in beside Trace and wrapped an arm around Mavros's calves. When they were all on board, Roy started the engine and raced up the track past the Astrapi, narrowly missing the walls.

Mavros was trying to keep his head down. At least the wind was behind them, but it was still blasting as fiercely as before. The sky to the south was grey, the northerly having blown steely clouds over Trigono's hills. Although it was early in the autumn, he reckoned the first rains weren't far away. He glanced down at the widow. Her head was below his knees, her black hair in a tight knot under the habitual scarf. He was surprised at the softness of her hand on his legs. Despite the work she'd been doing in the fields, her skin was smooth. He wondered if she bathed it in some herbal concoction made from the dried leaves that festooned her kitchen. The light brown varnish on her nails was incongruous as well.

The overloaded vehicle crested the hill between the village and the central plain. Mavros felt the wind hit the back of his head even more violently, then they were over the brow and into a sheltered area. He looked ahead towards the great massif, the medieval tower and the rest of the Theocharis estate dwarfed by the louring hills. The rocks and scree glinted dully in the cloud-filtered light, the ridge hanging like the wall of a huge natural dam.

He tried to make sense of what had happened on the slopes of Vigla during the day. The American's death, the disappearance of his wife, partner, whatever Gretchen was – those events seemed to be the surface manifestations of something more complicated and sinister than he'd realised. What had happened in the cave? And where was Eleni? Why had she been so frightened of Aris? He had the feeling that it wasn't just disquiet at what Theocharis was planning to do with the ancient figurines – she seemed genuinely afraid. Then he remembered the blow he'd taken to the back of his head. Could he really have misjudged the location of the stone surface so badly? And if he had, why hadn't Eleni returned with help? Despite the flat tyres on her motorbike, which were another mystery, she should have been back by the time he was picked up by Aris and Mitsos.

They passed the farm buildings where he'd seen the donkey Melpo being mistreated by old Manolis's brother. He looked down at Rena's head again and ran through suspicions he couldn't ignore any longer. She'd been on the massif, she could have been near the American when he fell, and she'd given him a frightening look when he saw her on the ridge. Why? What if she really had done away with her husband, as the villagers thought? Could she have had something to do with Lance's death? But if that was the case, for whatever twisted reason, why would she be leading them back out there now? Then he remembered her fight with the Dutchman. Rinus had been up on the track too. Could he be involved? And why was there what looked like a genuine Cycladic figurine in a suitcase beneath her bed? He shook his head and cursed under his breath. Everyone on Trigono seemed to have something to hide. He wasn't much closer to finding out anything significant about Rosa Ozal, but he was sure she was connected to all this in some way.

Roy was driving at speed through the central part of the Kambos, the ruined windmills and the bullet-pocked church on their left. On their right the gate to the Theocharis estate was closed, a watchman patrolling behind it. Mavros felt an urge to burst in, find Eleni and ask her where she'd got to. Then it struck him that she might be in danger. No, he couldn't believe that. Aris was loudmouthed and hot tempered, but he didn't think the big man would harm the archaeologist. After all, she worked for his father.

'Shit!' Roy shouted, leaning forward. 'Who's that idiot?' He jammed his foot on the brake and swerved to the side of the asphalt.

A motorbike was moving quickly towards them in a cloud of dust, the rider apparently only seeing them at the last moment and skidding to a halt.

'Sorry,' came a male voice. The helmet visor was lifted. 'Where are all you people heading?'

'Could ask you the same question, Rinus,' Norm answered. 'What scared you? You were going like a rocket.'

The Dutchman pulled off his helmet and ran his eyes over the occupants of the car, passing over Rena quickly and acknowledging Mavros with what looked like relief. 'You're not going to believe this. I . . . I found two bodies.' He licked his lips and pointed up to the ridge. 'In an old herdsman's hut beyond the wall. I'm going to get help.'

Mavros jumped down and approached him. 'Who are they?' he asked, taking in Rinus's shallow breathing and nervous eyes. 'What happened to them?'

Rinus wiped his forearm across his forehead. 'It was terrible,' he said, the words rushed. 'A man and a woman, naked, blood all over their faces, their arms and legs tied.'

'What?' Rena gasped, the hostile glare she'd been directing at the Dutchman replaced by a frown. 'What do you mean? Are they alive?'

Mavros held up a hand. 'Did you recognise them, Rinus?' he asked. 'Who were they?'

'Yes,' he replied, his voice rising, 'yes, I recognised them.' His eyes were wide as he looked at Mavros. 'The woman was that crabby American who comes into the bar, Gretchen's her name. And the man . . . the man was Mikkel, as in Mikkel and Barbara. Oh Jesus, I don't know what could have happened to . . .'

'Are they alive?' Rena repeated, jumping down and gripping the Dutchman's arm.

Rinus took a step back as if he'd been slapped in the face. 'I don't think so. They're . . . they're in an awful state.'

Rena was staring at him. 'You fool,' she said. 'There are birds and dogs up there, they could—' She stopped when she saw the look Mavros was directing at her.

'You have to show us,' Mavros said. 'Now.'

Rinus shivered and then nodded. 'Yes, I have to show you,' he mumbled. 'But what about the doctor? The police?'

'I'll go,' Roy said. 'I'll take you lot to the end of the road then head back to the village.'

'You what?' Trace screamed. 'You can't leave us out here.'

'I'll be back as soon as I can,' he said. 'This should get the villagers out in force.'

Jane nudged her. 'Come on, Trace, it's an emergency. We have to do our bit. You were happy enough coming out to look for the woman.'

'Yeah,' Trace muttered. 'But we didn't know she was dead then, did we?'

'Turn your machine round,' Rena said to the Dutchman. 'You're coming with us.'

Mavros watched as Rinus pulled his helmet back on and started the BMW's engine. Then he revved hard and raised another cloud of dust as he burned off up the track. As he climbed back on to the Farma, Mavros wondered if he was even more anxious than he should have been. He clutched at the strut as Roy moved off with a jolt. But if Rinus had killed Gretchen and Mikkel, why was he volunteering information about them?

He had time to think about this as they walked up the steep track that led past the dig to the ridge. He caught sight of his mountain bike behind the bush where he'd left it in the morning. He'd forgotten about that. It seemed like days ago;

so much had happened since then. What did it all mean? Who had attacked the man and the woman? It was now looking possible that Lance's death wasn't an accident. There was someone violent and calculating out on the hills. He felt a tightness in his chest that was due not only to the hard climb. Then he remembered his brother Andonis, remembered the risk he was taking by being in the vicinity of the Theocharis estate. Jesus Christ, what was he doing?

They finally reached the ridge, Rena, Rinus and Mavros a long way ahead of Norm and the Englishwomen. Jane was holding Trace's arm and looking ahead with undisguised curiosity.

'They're over that way,' the Dutchman said, one arm raised beyond the wall towards a heap of ruins on the southern side.

'Keep going,' Rena said, her voice firm.

Mavros watched as Rinus moved off, his eyes restless, avoiding hers. The widow seemed to have a hold over the barman. As they approached the remains of the old hut, he wondered what it might be. Then he felt his heart begin to beat faster, his feet moving more rapidly across the bare, stony earth. The wind was still on the back of his head, blowing dust into the broken skin of his wounds.

And then Rinus was over the collapsed walls, his eyes bulging and his jaw slack.

'No,' he gasped. 'This can't be. It isn't possible.'

Mavros and Rena stepped over the unsteady pile and looked down into the hollowed space of what had once been the building's only room.

There was nothing to be seen but lichen-covered stones and the dry stalks of the previous spring's thistles.

Aris Theocharis closed the door of his father's underground gallery and walked up to the terrace. The wind was buffeting the tower, throwing leaves and dust into his eyes, but he didn't care. He went over to the wall beyond the pool and sat on it, facing the old stone building and trying to calm the raging in his head. The old bastard. What was he doing making his own son look like a fool in front of that asshole dealer Roufos? What was he doing throwing him out after the bitch Eleni had made the presentation about the Cycladic statuettes? Like he didn't know how to negotiate, like he didn't know how to behave himself during a deal. The old fucker. He leaned back into the wind, feeling the open space beneath him. As for that cow Dhimitra, she'd pay for the come-and-fuck-me grin she flashed him when the old man told him to leave them. She was nothing more than a street whore painted gold and stuffed with silicone, a street whore with a dope habit that she thought she could control. Yes, she'd pay for that, she'd pay for it in his bed later. Dhimitra liked to be tied up, liked to be splayed and mounted from behind. She'd get a surprise tonight.

Aris put his hand on his groin and kneaded it, his jaw loose. A Filipina maid came on to the terrace with a brush and he shot her a look, grunting as she hurried away with her head down. They were all bitches and he knew how to exact payment from them – yes, he knew. He'd learned how to handle women in the fuck-joints and the S and M clubs back in New York City. They needed a firm hand and a hard heart. He had those, he'd always been in charge, he hadn't just inherited money from the old bastard. But they bored him, the hookers and the pathetic amateurs who wanted to see how low they could sink. Since the beginning of the summer he'd felt the need for young flesh, new blood. Trigono was virgin territory.

That little slut Navsika had fitted the bill perfectly. He'd had his eye on her for years, looking out for her every September, watching as she grew taller and filled out, turned into a real looker. But he knew she was dirty inside, he could tell from the way she looked at men. She was hot for it even when she was a kid. Yes, Navsika. This year he'd decided to hunt her, make a move on her. Hell, if she didn't want to give it away, he could buy it from her – or beat it out of her. But the little bitch wouldn't even look at him, it was like he didn't exist. His family owned most of Trigono and he was just so much mule shit to her. That made him even more determined.

So he'd watched them, Navsika and that little shit Yiangos she hung around with, waited till Lefteris had gone to Syros. He knew they'd get up to something then, and he was right. They were off on the *trata* as soon as she got off work from the souvenir shop in the village. He'd prepared the *Artemis* earlier, was after them at a distance, keeping an eye on them with the powerful radar he'd had fitted last year. At first he wondered where they were going. He was sure they'd anchor somewhere so they could get down to it in peace – Yiangos was too scared of Lefteris to risk doing any damage to the boat by getting distracted when he was at sea. They went round the point of Oura at the island's south-eastern corner and headed for the islet of Eschati, and that was when he realised what they were planning. There was a beach he himself had taken an Italian tart to a couple of years back. She'd complained about getting sand up her, but he hadn't felt anything. Yes, that was where they were headed. He followed them, dropping back as soon as he rounded the cape, his heart beating fast. This was exciting, this was a lot of fun. He reckoned that if he caught them at it he'd be able to get himself into her too. Yiangos would be terrified of Lefteris finding out that he'd taken the *trata* all the way down there.

But then it had got weird. The *Sotiria* had disappeared behind the low rise of Eschati and he gunned his engine, felt the *kaïki* leap forward as the Volvo's thrust kicked in. His plan was to skirt the southern shore of the islet and come up on them unseen, catch them with their swimming costumes down. Just the thought of the bitch's triangle of hair above her thighs was making him hard. But as he approached Eschati, engine revs cut to dampen the sound, he caught sight of another craft coming fast at him on the port beam – a speedboat, with a couple of swarthy guys in it, one of them standing up and holding on to the safety rail as they got closer. They were carving out a great arc, swinging round from the islet as if they were changing course, and he felt their eyes as they scoped him then veered away at an even sharper angle and headed back towards Ios. Shit, there went his plan. The speed king had made so much noise that the pair of lovebirds would definitely have been interrupted. Still, he kept going, bringing the *Artemis* round carefully and inching towards the stern of the *trata*.

On the terrace in the wind, Aris wiped his brow as the recollection gripped him. The bright blue of the sea dancing around the small island had made him blink, struggle to focus, and then he'd seen them. But what the fuck was going on? Yiangos was up on a rock above the strip of sand, naked as the day he was born, looking out to the south with his hand shading his eyes. Aris saw the boy wave desperately at the speedboat, his face panic stricken. And Navsika? She was in nothing but her skin too, her amazing tits pointing straight at him.

She'd spotted him immediately and screamed words at Yiangos. '*Ela, to thirio ein'edho.*' Come, the beast is here. Reaching for her bikini bottom, pulling it on, one arm over her big brown nipples. Fuck. What did she mean calling him that? The beast? That was what the kids called him in the village when he caught them laughing. And Yiangos was scrambling down the cliff, heaving up his trunks when he hit the sand, glaring at him and shouting, something about how he'd scared them off – 'You fat bastard . . . they won't be back for days now . . . they'll probably never be back. Christ and the Holy Mother, what a disaster . . .'

Aris had opened up the engine – no need for stealth any more – held his position in the swell as the pair of them swam back to the *Sotiria* and scrambled on board. Yiangos was winching the anchor up, ignoring Navsika's insistent questions, pushing her away as he continued to shout at Aris, calling him every name he could think of, accusing him of ruining the business, didn't he realise what he'd done, dirty pervert who only wanted to screw all the village's girls . . . It went on, and Aris had felt the anger come down on him, the anger and the frustration. Christ, he'd seen the tart's honey pot but he hadn't got into it. The little bitch was staring at him like he was a pig wallowing in his own muck, and Yiangos was telling him what Lefteris would do to them all now – 'You fucking lazy, arse-fucking, useless fat beast . . .'

So he'd waited until they were under way, waited till he could target them clear of the rocks around Eschati, then put the Volvo into maximum revs and drove straight at them, only veering to port as the bow neared the *trata*. He was intending to scare them by going close, but he felt the shock as his centre planks hit them amidships, throwing the pair of them back on to the nets that were heaped on the stern in readiness for the new fishing season. And then his wave had rocked the *Sotiria* and they were both flipped overboard, their feet and hands caught in the nets, their wide eyes locked on his for long seconds before they were wrenched under the surface of the dazzling blue water and dragged away towards Vathy inlet and the islands that shielded it. By the time he caught up with the *trata* and got a line on to her, by the time he engaged the winches to haul up the net, Navsika and Yiangos were lifeless. But still he was raging, the veins in his neck knotted and his head pounding. So he'd pulled off their swimming costumes and gazed at the girl's secret place, taken in the boy's limp cock, till he felt the fever subside. Then he wrapped them up in the net and dropped them back in the water.

Aris had looked around and seen that the sea was empty in all directions. He steered east and headed away at full speed, leaving them to roll about in their underwater shroud. Good riddance. He felt no regret. The peasants, calling him 'the beast'. That would fucking teach them. It was only as he rounded Oura that he understood why Yiangos had been so enraged. Yes, now it all fell into place – the speedboat and the deserted island far from prying eyes. Christ, that was what Lefteris was up to – running the dope that Rinus supplied from the Bar Astrapi, the dope that Dhimitra and Christ knows how many others of Trigono's wealthy residents used. And the not-so-wealthy local kids, for all he knew. Yes, he'd seen the fisherman in the bar occasionally, as laconic and threatening as ever, but with a small smile at the corner of his mouth. He'd seen Yiangos talking to Rinus like they were conspirators. And all he'd wanted was some of Navsika's juice. Fuck the drugs, though. That was one business he'd never got involved in back in New York. He'd seen what it did to the guys who ran it. He knew he didn't have the balls for it, not even on Trigono – especially not if Lefteris was behind it.

He'd asked Dhimitra if she knew what the fisherman was up to, but she'd told him to keep out of it and concentrate on securing his inheritance. He sometimes wondered if there was something going on between his stepmother and Lefteris. She'd probably like a bit of island rough trade.

He stood up and stepped heavily across the tiles of the terrace. Lefteris. What was the psycho up to? He'd seen him up on the hills when he and Mitsos were bringing Eleni to the tower. Christ. Maybe he was in the dig. He'd been seen on the slopes above it more than once recently by the watchmen. Had he heard about the finds and decided to look for more pieces for himself? That fucker was capable of anything. He wasn't frightened of the old man. Aris was sure the fisherman suspected what had happened to Yiangos and was waiting to extract payment for his son's death. But if he could catch him trespassing, bring Lefteris back to his father as a trophy before he could make his move, then maybe, just maybe, he would be trusted again. That might stop the old man dragging him over the coals for what he'd done to the family fortune with his gambling, threatening to cut him off without a cent. Yes, it was worth a try, even though Lefteris wasn't a man to cross. But the gorilla Mitsos would help – Mitsos would put the squeeze on the fisherman.

He headed downstairs, noticing that the doors to the gallery were still closed. Mitsos was waiting at the bottom of the stairs and he told him to shift himself, they had work to do. A few minutes later the Jeep was on its way up the road towards the track leading to the dig.

Mavros glanced at Rinus and then at Rena. They looked like a ghost had risen up in front of them.

'What's going on?' he asked, turning as he heard a shout from Norm. He raised an arm to keep the rest of the party at the wall.

The Dutchman's mouth was still open, his face white. 'They were here,' he said haltingly. 'I . . . I swear they were. They were lying—'

'Lying like you?' Rena interrupted. 'Have you been taking that poison you sell?' The widow was clenching her fists. 'That poison you've ruined the village with?'

Rinus was shaking his head. 'No,' he said in a weak voice. He looked away. 'Yes.'

'Is that why you came up here?' Mavros asked quietly, stepping closer.

Rena laughed humourlessly. 'He doesn't only come here to get – how do you say it? – high? He has an arrangement with Dinos the goatherd.' She shook her head. 'I saw them once. Dinos was on top, Rinus was underneath like a she-goat.' She raised her shoulders. 'I don't care. If that's what makes them happy . . .' Her face hardened. 'But if you have given drugs to that poor boy, I will cut off your *archidhia*. If you have any balls.'

Mavros put a hand on her arm. 'We have other priorities now, Rena.' He looked back at the Dutchman. 'You definitely saw Gretchen and Mikkel here?'

He nodded, eyes still lowered.

'Okay,' Mavros said. 'I believe you. Either they came back from the dead and managed to untie themselves – in which case we would probably have met them coming down – or someone moved them.' He started walking quickly towards the wall. 'Come on,' he said over his shoulder. 'There are a lot of caves and mine workings to check.'

'What about down there?' Rinus asked, pointing towards the inlet of Vathy below.

'It's a long way to carry two bodies,' Mavros replied, vaulting the stone dyke. He had remembered where he'd been before he heard the scream from the ridge. 'We'll try the caves first. I found one earlier that didn't smell too healthy.' He glanced at Rena, but she kept her eyes off him as she cleared the wall. Did she know the place he meant?

After explaining to the British trio what had happened, Mavros led the group to the scree slope above the valley by the concealed cave.

'What, down there?' Trace said, her voice shrill. 'I'll break my ankles.'

'Come on, girl,' Jane encouraged. 'Think how many pounds you'll lose from this walk.'

Norm was nodding, his shaven head glistening with sweat despite the northerly wind. 'Yeah, and just think how good the beers'll taste when we get back to the village.'

Trace didn't look convinced, but she started down the slope after Rena, her arms extended. As he moved after them, Mavros caught the flash of a metallic surface to the east. He wasn't sure, but he reckoned it was the Theocharis Jeep. Who was inside it and where was it heading? To the dig? Perhaps Eleni had finally persuaded Aris to help her look for him. No, it was hours since he'd been knocked out in the cave. What had happened to her?

After an extended bout of slipping and squealing, they reached the enclosed ground where Lance had been found.

'What is this place we're going to?' Jane asked, panting for breath.

'A cave I found earlier,' Mavros said. 'You don't all have to come into it. In fact, it would be better if the rest of you looked inside any other openings near by.'

Rena frowned at him. 'I don't think so, Alex,' she said. 'It will be safer if we all keep together.'

Mavros tried to penetrate her thoughts but her face was giving nothing away. Could he trust her? He decided he could and nodded, moving towards the narrow entrance. He took the torch out of his bag and turned it on.

'There isn't much room,' he warned. 'I'll tell you when to follow.'

Rena stepped forward. 'I'm coming with you,' she said. She glanced at Rinus and then at Norm. 'Make sure this person does not run away.'

Mavros saw the Englishman nod, then he squeezed himself between the rocks and moved into the zigzag passage. Even before he entered the side of the hill, the smell made him gag.

'What is that?' he gasped.

'Dead meat,' Rena said from behind him.

'That's what I thought,' Mavros said.

Then they were into a larger space, the torch beam illuminating rough stone and a sandy floor. Sure enough, there was the splayed body of a goat against the far wall, its ribcage cracked apart and the cavity cleaned out.

Mavros squatted down. 'Someone cut this with a blade,' he said, nodding at the smooth surfaces where the pelt had been opened.

Rena was to his left, her head back, sniffing the rank air. 'There is more,' she said. 'Something worse.'

He stood next to her and shone the light in her face. 'Tell me the truth, Rena,' he said. 'Have you ever been in here before?'

She shook her head. 'Never,' she said, pushing the torch down. 'I told you. I don't like caves.'

He nodded. 'All right. Let's see over there. Some of these caves have hidden sections . . . yes, there's another passage here. It's low, keep your head down.' He dropped to his knees and moved through, suddenly feeling vulnerable – another blow to the head would probably finish him. But he managed to clear the passage and pull himself into an inner chamber, gagging as an even more miasmic stench hit his nostrils. Then he shone the torch back to help Rena. As she was pulling herself upright he swung the light round. And felt his eyelids shoot apart at the scene of horror.

'What the—' He broke off when he heard Rena's cry of disgust, then looked again, bracing himself as he ran his eyes across the wide cave. To his right a blackened corpse lay against the rock face, the teeth forming a ghastly smile in the beam. Despite the advanced state of decay it was instantly recognisable as human. Beyond it was a tripod supporting a video camera. Near by there was a pile of cardboard squares with large red letters. The top one said 'One week'. Looking to his left, Mavros saw two more bodies, one male and one female, both naked, their upper extremities drenched in blood and their wrists and ankles roped to rings in the wall. Gretchen and Mikkel. He bent his head, pinching his nose to get a few gulps of odourless air, but the mephitic stench had infected his taste buds. It was as he was about to go to the captives that he heard the noise, a faint, panting plea from the dark end of the cave. The hairs on his neck rose.

'What was that?' Rena asked hoarsely. 'What was that, Alex?'

Mavros picked his way over the floor, at first trying to avoid the bones and the damp patches, but giving up as he got closer and the torch revealed another naked form. This one was filthy, the limbs misshapen by the ropes that were confining them. It was a woman – he could see breasts beneath an arm placed over them in an incongruous attempt at modesty. She was gasping, the breath catching in her throat and her eyes wide in terror.

'It's all right,' he said, leaning over her and taking in pitifully shrunken limbs and loose skin. 'We'll help you. We're going to get you out.' He bent closer and realised that the sound he was now hearing was crazed laughter.

'Too . . . too . . . late,' he made out. 'Drink . . . water . . .'

He turned to Rena, noticing that her eyes were damp. 'She needs water,' he said. 'In my bag. I left it in the other cave.'

But the widow wasn't listening to him. She was already on her knees by the woman, hands scrabbling at the ropes on the deeply scored wrists. 'Liz?' she said. 'Is it you, Liz?'

'You know her?' Mavros asked, looking more closely and realising he had seen the captive woman before, in the photographs kept by Rena and Eleni. 'This is Liz? Elizabeth Clifton?'

Rena nodded, her eyes brimming with tears, as the bound woman mouthed a word of affirmation and made another choked demand.

'I'll get the water,' Mavros said, turning away. 'You keep the torch.' Bending over Gretchen and Mikkel, he felt for pulse and breath. Both were alive. He stepped carefully over them and slipped through into the outer chamber.

It was as he entered it that he heard the screams from outside. They quickly got louder, closer, and then, in the increasing gloom, he realised that other people had come into the cave.

'What's going on?' he shouted. 'Who's there?'

The screams were dampened and a cigarette lighter flared. In its faint glow he made out Rinus and the two Englishwomen, all three faces taut with terror.

'It's Lefteris,' Rinus said in an empty voice. 'Lefteris forced us in.'

There was a scraping noise in the narrow entrance tunnel, then a dull thud. It was followed by another one, farther out.

'It's Lefteris,' Rinus repeated. 'The madman's blocking the way out with boulders.' He shook his head then took his thumb off the lighter, plunging the cave into total darkness. The faint glow of daylight that Mavros had seen when he crawled through was now gone. 'This is where it ends,' the Dutchman said. Trace was on her knees, sobbing.

'Where's Norm?' Mavros asked in a low voice.

Jane looked up from where she was tending her friend. 'I can't believe it. Out of the blue the bastard attacked him, put him down. If I get my hands on him . . .'

'Lefteris hit him with a piece of metal,' Rinus said. 'A length of piping, I think.'

Mavros scrambled across the cave floor, his fingernails filling with grit. He pushed against the blockage in the entrance, feeling it move slightly before it knocked against the boulder behind. There was no further movement. He was aware of a light flow of air against his cheek, but it was doing nothing to improve the foul atmosphere.

He rocked back on his heels, thoughts cascading through his mind. Lefteris. The fisherman with the implacable stare, son of one-armed Manolis, father of the drowned Yiangos. What hell had he made for them, the living and the dead, in this stinking, secret cave?

Eleni stood in the centre of the subterranean gallery and tried to smile. Despite Theocharis's expectant look, she couldn't oblige him – couldn't congratulate the dealer Roufos, that sick, calculating bastard, on becoming Theocharis's sole agent for the sale of the figurines, couldn't share in the old man's satisfaction at the imminent increase of his riches. The only thing she could do was ignore his wife's jubilant smiles. At least the swaggering Aris wasn't there. He would have gloried in the arrangement more than anyone, even though he'd had nothing to do with it; and he'd have mocked her about the disposal of the pieces that she'd discovered.

My God, she thought, what have I done? Those beautiful creations, their sublime lines and the unique blue marble. Now they'll remain hidden from public view for ever, they'll rest in the secure vault of some billionaire collector-thief. She was swamped by a wave of revulsion at her complicity.

'Excuse me, Mr Theocharis,' she said quietly, walking away before he could question her. If she remained in the gallery any longer, she would empty her stomach over the nearest display case. Her employer wasn't quick enough to catch her, but Dhimitra was. Eleni heard the loud click of her stilettos on the flagstones behind her.

'Don't do anything foolish, Eleni,' the mistress of the tower hissed as Eleni opened the heavy door. 'You're implicated in this as much as anyone.' She smiled sardonically. 'Would you like to spend the rest of your working life in prison?' She laughed, the sound catching in her throat. 'Maybe that would suit you. There are plenty of dykes inside.'

Swallowing hard, Eleni kept her eyes off the tycoon's wife and turned towards the nearest bathroom.

'We'll see you at dinner, then,' Dhimitra said, taking cigarettes and a diamond-studded lighter from her bag. 'Dear Eleni.' She laughed again.

Eleni made it to the bathroom and threw up into the basin, making no effort to avoid the gold taps. 'Fuck it,' she said under her breath. 'What the hell am I doing here? These people are criminals, bandits, nothing better than common thieves – worse, because thieves have to eat. The rich steal because it's their birthright, because they enjoy it. What am I doing helping them?'

She sat down on the mahogany toilet seat and bent forward, burying her face in the silk skirt Theocharis had given her to wear for the presentation – the sales pitch, as Aris had put it. Christ, what was she doing here? And what about Alex Mavros? She'd just left him in the cave, told no one about him after he cracked his head on the rock. The poor guy was probably still concussed from the attack last night. She was sure that Theocharis had arranged that, put Lefteris or his watchmen on the job. The old man was terrified that Mavros was from the ministry. She didn't think so, he was only trying to find Rosa Ozal. Was he all right? God, she should have told someone. But who? No one here would have helped. They were already suspicious of her because she'd allowed him into the dig. She'd reckoned he was safer on his own, but what if the blow had been worse than it looked?

She stood up and dashed water over her face, staring at the dark rings under her eyes in the mirror. To think that bastard Roufos had already tried to hook her, asked her if she would like to visit him in his room later. She'd given him a frozen glare. And what about Aris? He'd been after her for years, found it exciting that she preferred women, the pervert. Where was he now? Shit, she didn't care about any of the Theocharis family. Was Alex Mavros lying bleeding on that cave floor, dying because she didn't have the guts to help him?

Eleni unlocked the door and glanced out. She could smell the heavy aroma of Dhimitra's tobacco, but she didn't seem to be near by. Slipping off her shoes, she ran across the hall and out of the tower. The straight road ahead was too obvious, so she turned right and made her way behind a line of orange trees, feeling the soil between her toes. If she was lucky, the idiot at the gate would be asleep in his hutch – he often was. She'd go home and change, then get out of the estate and back to the cave. That was what she had to do.

It was while she was waiting for a gardener working on a flower-bed near her house to turn his back that a scene she had witnessed flashed in front of Eleni again. Aris, it was Aris. He kept coming back to her. Aris and the Jeep, a week ago after dinner in the tower, the night before Liz Clifton left so suddenly. She'd been going back to her place and the Jeep had roared past, Aris at the wheel. And Liz was in the back seat, smiling at something the fat slob was saying, smiling and leaning forward to the woman who was sitting in the other front seat.

There had been an empty expression on Barbara Hoeg's face, a look that had seemed insignificant at the time but now struck Eleni as calculating and truly frightening. Barbara. Where was she? She never missed an evening at the Astrapi. Maybe Liz hadn't left suddenly of her own will. Could Barbara have had something to do with Liz's disappearance? She and Aris? And what about Rosa? Had she ever left the island?

Eleni was suddenly sure that Alex had been asking the right questions all along. But she was filled with quaking fear at what the answers might turn out to be.

22

Kyra Maro sat on her bed, the door to the cell-like room closed. Although she'd been feeling faint all day and her stomach was empty, she couldn't bring herself to eat or drink. But she was wondering what had happened to Rena. It was unlike her to miss delivering food. She extended a hand to the tin box that she'd lifted on to the bed with difficulty.

Ach, Taso, she said to herself, you are here as always, my faithful boy. You have always been close, from the cold night I forced your crumpled form into the world until your last smiling moments – and since the day I dug you up with my own hands from the graveyard at Myli. Your father, he is the one I have really lost.

The old woman raised her eyes to the photograph in the icon niche. The young soldier was looking down at her with the shy smile she had hardly ever seen. Because from their initial meeting Tzortz had not been shy – he had been filled with joy and love, for her and for Greece. Until the days when the war had closed its fist around them near the end of his time on the island. Maro bowed her head, one hand still on Tasos's box.

'Ach, Tzortz,' she mouthed. 'It was love that killed you, the love you felt for a ravaged country. If you hadn't tried to bring the fight to these islands, you might have survived longer than you did, survived the peace as well as the war. Was it guilt that destroyed you? Or shame? Why couldn't you tell me? I would have helped you. I would have washed away your pain.'

Suddenly images were cascading in front of Maro, images she had kept at bay for decades. There was her lover standing in the doorway of the hut outside the village, the hovel she'd been forced to rent so that the child was spared the islanders' taunts and abuse. It was a cold winter afternoon six years after the war, the sun already beginning to sink in the west. She had gone to Tzortz immediately, recognising his features despite the ragged beard and the filthy coat that covered his painfully thin form.

'My love,' she said, clutching his blackened hand, 'you have come for me after all these years.' She tried to draw him close, but he stepped back, his gaze fixed beyond her.

'So it's true what they say in the *kafeneion*,' Tzortz said hoarsely. 'It is true that you bore a . . . a monster.' There was a film of tears on his bloodshot eyes. 'Is it . . . is it mine?'

Maro had stepped back to Tasos, her arm around the seven-year-old and her face stinging as if it had been slapped. 'What . . . what has happened to you, Tzortz?' she stammered. 'This is your son. How can you listen to those cowards? Manolis and the others have poisoned the village with their lies.' She pushed Tasos gently forward. 'This is your son. He may not be able to speak, but he is happy and loving.'

But Tzortz had looked down and turned away, as if the boy's misshapen head and his trusting smile were too much to bear.

She called after him, begged him to stay, but he was stumbling down the road to the Kambos like a blind man, his back bent and his arms extended. She thought she heard a long, bitter cry above the gusts of wind. Leaning weakly against the door frame, her heart pounding, Maro tried to convince herself that she hadn't been dreaming, that her lover really had come back to Trigono. By the time she'd done that, Tzortz was over the ridge and out of sight. She flew about the hut, pulling a threadbare coat on to her son – she couldn't leave him on his own – and gathering up the donkey's harness. In a few minutes they were on the road, old Erato moving quickly in response to her commands and Tasos grinning widely at the unaccustomed afternoon excursion.

Another rapid cascade of images made the old woman blink. And then she made out her lover again, a sharp pain jabbing into her chest as she realised that she had to face the bitter final scene that she'd fended off for so long. She had lost her lover on the road towards the Theocharis estate, and by the time she picked him up again he was well ahead, ascending the steep path towards the saddle between Vigla and Profitis Ilias. The hills were grey and forbidding in the fading light. But Erato accepted the long pursuit without complaint, and they were only about a hundred metres behind when Tzortz disappeared over the ridge. Maro had been wondering if he was heading for the cave, their secret place, the place she had never been back to after his departure, but he had kept going. At last Maro had reached the wall that ran along the saddle, the donkey panting for breath and the wind rippling through Tasos's short hair. Her blood froze when she saw what her lover was doing on the rocks far below.

'No, Tzortz, no!' she screamed, her words snatched away by the gusts. 'No, wait for me!' Hands darting in a frenzy, she tethered Erato to the wall, then tied Tasos to the donkey, rubbing his cheeks and smiling to reassure him. Then she was running down the sheer slope, her ankles twisting on the uneven surface. 'Wait, Tzortz!' she was crying. 'I'm coming!'

But she was too late. By the time she reached the narrow line of flat rocks at the water's edge, her lover had finished loading his pockets with stones. The breath caught in her throat as she took in the rock, as large as a watermelon, that he'd lashed across his midriff.

'No!' she screeched. 'Why, Tzortz? Why?'

But the only man she'd ever loved made no reply. He looked at her once then shook his head before facing the windswept sea and the last of the light. The water closed over him with scarcely a sound.

Maro sank to her knees, her hands beating the pitted rock until the skin was torn away. She would have jumped in after him, tried to save him, but she knew the water was deep there and she had her son to think of. Pray God he hadn't understood what had happened. From that day since she'd never known why her lover had returned when he did, or why he had committed himself to the grey-blue element. Did he still hold himself responsible for what had happened to the villagers and his men during the war? Or was it because of poor, innocent Tasos? Was he so ashamed of his love for her and the child it had produced? He left all those questions unanswered, and they had tortured her even more than the hatred of the villagers. At least none of them had recognised the ragged figure that had appeared on Trigono but was not seen again.

The hardest thing to bear was that the place where he had chosen to leave the surface of the earth had been the very spot Maro had dragged him to when the *kaïki* came to pick him up during the war. She thought she had saved him, but all she had done was show him the way to the underworld.

Mavros shone the torch around the figures in the outer cave. Rinus and the Englishwomen, their heads down, were huddled by the blocked entrance as far as they could get from the decomposing goat. 'There are three people tied up in the next cave. Has anyone got a knife?' He directed the beam at his satchel and took out his water bottle.

Jane reached for the small backpack she'd been wearing on the hills. 'Here.' She gave him a Swiss Army knife. 'I always come prepared.' She swallowed a laugh. 'You'd better take this as well,' she added, handing over a bottle of water. 'Those poor people must need it more than we do. Anything I can do?'

Mavros shook his head. 'Not for the moment. Try to keep your friend's spirits up.' He went back into the inner chamber. Kneeling down by the woman at the far end, he cut the ropes and helped her to sit up.

Rena had taken off her black cardigan. 'Oh, Liz,' she said, 'what has happened to you? Who did this?' She put the garment around the woman's naked upper body.

Mavros cracked the seal on one of the bottles and put it to the woman's lips, letting her take no more than a few sips. He could hear the breath racking her lungs and catching in her throat. 'So this is the woman who stayed with you recently, Rena,' he said. 'The one who left unexpectedly.'

The widow nodded, her eyes locked on the weakened form beside her. 'Yes, this is Liz. Who could have done this to her?'

She stared into the gloom beyond the torch beam. 'What has been going on in here?' She turned to Mavros. 'What happened in the other cave?'

He pursed his lips, not wanting to frighten the woman he'd just freed. 'We're trapped,' he said in Greek.

'Is it Lefteris?' Rena asked.

Mavros's suspicions of Rena came back in a rush. 'How did you know?' he demanded.

She shrugged. 'Who else could it be? He's often out hunting in this area and he's the craziest person on Trigono.'

Mavros nodded. He ought to have paid more attention to the fisherman than to the foreign residents. 'Look after her,' he said. 'She shouldn't have much water.' He took the light and went over to the other bound figures. He leaned close to the battered faces. They were both breathing more regularly. He dribbled water from the second bottle into their mouths and then cut their bonds.

'Mikkel and the American woman,' Rena said. 'Why are they here? Did Lefteris bring them down from the hut on his own?'

'Two good questions,' Mavros said, putting his ear close to Mikkel's mouth. 'I think he's coming round.' He pulled the German's body up so that the grey-blond head was resting on his thigh. 'Mikkel?' he said. 'Mikkel? Can you hear me? It's Alex.'

There was a long silence then a faint croak came from the broken mouth. 'Barbara . . . Barbara . . .' He said nothing more.

Mavros eased his head back on to the cave floor and went back to Rena, having first shone the torch on the human remains at the other side of the chamber. 'Is that . . . do you think that's Rosa?' he asked.

Rena kept her eyes fixed on Liz. 'Christ and the Holy Mother, I hope not. I can't look.'

The woman in her arms shivered, the tip of her tongue moving over cracked lips.

Mavros drew closer. 'Did you see who brought you here, Liz?' he asked. 'Can you remember anything?'

Elizabeth Clifton raised an unsteady arm and pointed to the water bottle. Rena gave her a little more, then dabbed her mouth with a handkerchief.

'Not . . . not who brought me in here,' she whispered. 'I think . . . I think they gave me drugs . . . my memory's been playing . . . playing tricks. It still is. But I remember I was in a big car, a . . . four-by-four. Big man driving, bald, Aris . . .'

'Aris Theocharis?' Mavros said.

She nodded. 'Yes.' Her chin slumped on to her chest. 'And . . . and a woman.'

Mavros looked at Rena. 'Blonde hair, a lot of make-up, Greek?' He had a flash of Dhimitra sitting next to Aris in the Astrapi.

Liz shook her head feebly. 'No . . . not Greek . . . foreign . . . German, I think . . .'

There was an agonised gasp from the darkness. 'Barbara . . . oh God, Barbara . . . what have you done?'

Mavros kept his gaze on Liz. Her eyes had opened wide at Mikkel's words. 'Was that her name? Barbara?'

She blinked and nodded. 'Yes . . . yes, that was it. Barbara.'

'Barbara and Aris did this?' Rena said in disbelief. 'Barbara and Aris?'

'No!'

Mavros shone the light on Mikkel. He was trying to raise himself up from the floor.

'Not . . . not Barbara and Aris,' the German said, his eyes wide and his jaw loose, as if the terrible realisation had just struck him. 'Barbara and Lefteris.' He started to weep, a rasping, rending sound. 'Lefteris . . . Lefteris killed Barbara, the animal. He killed her in our pool.'

There was a rustle from the far wall and Rinus came into the triangle of light. 'What the hell's he talking about?' he demanded. 'Christ,' he said, peering down. 'That's Liz, isn't it?'

'Yes,' the widow replied, her tone harsh. 'This is Liz and she's been suffering from your filthy drugs. Admit it, you poisoner. You and Lefteris used Yiangos to pick up the drugs and now the poor boy's dead. Lefteris used drugs to keep Liz how he wanted her in

this . . . in this tomb.' She spat on the floor. 'I should have torn
you to pieces when I had the chance.'

Mikkel was still crying, words jumbled in the rush of air. 'Oh
God . . . oh God, Barbara, how could you do it? He told me . . .
Lefteris told me before he knocked me out in the ruined hut . . .
told me what the two of you had done to the poor women. Beaten
them and filmed them and . . .' He stopped and controlled his
breathing. 'No, Barbara,' he said, his voice weak. 'It wasn't your
fault. It was the addiction, the addiction drove you to it. You
would never have helped the madman otherwise, you were never
interested in dirty sex and sadism, you were never . . . oh God, but
you were. I could never satisfy you, you wanted to tie me up, you
wanted to beat me . . . oh, Jesus Christ . . .'

'Oh, Jesus Christ is right,' Mavros said, rocking back on his heels
and looking around the foul-smelling cave. 'But Christ isn't going
to let us out of here and I can't get a signal on my mobile phone.
All we can do is hope that someone works out where we are.'

He started running through their chances. Roy would be back
from the village with help soon, but the likelihood of anyone
finding their way to the blocked entrance wasn't great. From
what he could tell, not many locals knew about this place. And
Eleni? Would she be looking for him in the caves beyond the dig
that were separated by the rock wall? If she was, shouting would be
worth while. After all, he now realised, he had heard Liz Clifton's
scratching.

That was the best Mavros could come up with. At his instiga-
tion, those in the cave with functioning voices began to yell their
hearts out.

Aris ducked under the ancient lintel and moved into the passage with the grave chambers, the dull throb of the generator
in his ears. 'Come on, Mitso,' he shouted. He waited for the
watchman to join him, then headed towards the rock wall at
the far end.

'This place gives me the creeps, boss,' Mitsos said.

'Grow up,' Aris said over his shoulder. 'They're only skeletons.

We'll have a look in the tombs on the way back. I reckon that cow Eleni has been hiding things from us.'

'So what are we looking for?' Mitsos asked.

Aris stopped at the apparently solid wall. 'Not what, who. That lunatic Lefteris. I'm sure he's been snooping round the dig. Probably when you were playing with yourself in your tent.'

'Well, he's not in here now,' the watchman said, turning for the exit.

'Wait a minute,' Aris ordered. 'The archaeologist and that private dick bastard were in here earlier on and they disappeared. I want to have a closer . . . shit, do you believe this? How could I miss it?' He had run his thick fingers along the rough surface and located the gap at the edge in the gloom. 'This is where they went. Come on.' He squeezed his bulk round the blind corner and disappeared.

In the next cave he switched on the torch he'd brought from the Jeep. 'Right, Mitso, we're going to look everywhere in here. Who knows what we might find?' His voice was quivering with excitement.

But this soon vanished as they worked their way up the network and discovered nothing apart from scuffed footprints. Then they entered the last cave, crawling under the low wall to find the faint light of the sunset shining through the line of small apertures. They stood for a few moments, taking in the solid wall ahead.

'Looks like it's the end of the road, boss,' Mitsos said, trying to disguise his relief. 'Hey, what's that noise?' He cocked an ear. 'Can you hear it? Sounds like somebody shouting.'

Aris listened and then nodded. 'More than one person. On the other side of the rock.' He shrugged. 'Not much we can do from here. We'll have to go round on the surface.' He shouted back and heard the noise get louder. 'Who the fuck do you think it is?'

'Can't make the voices out.' Mitsos shrugged and moved to the far corner. 'What's this?' he asked. 'Looks like a tarpaulin. It is a tarpaulin.' He tugged the heavy canvas aside and stared down at green wooden crates.

Aris shouldered him out of the way. 'What have we here?' He

was fired up again, thinking of a priceless find, a treasure that would get him back in favour with his father. 'Something that the archaeologist has been hiding away?' He pulled up the lid of the top box and bent over the contents. 'Look at this.' He lifted up a criss-crossed metal ball, a ring on the top. 'It's a grenade, isn't it?'

Mitsos nodded, stepping back. 'Yes, it's a grenade. I think you'd better put it down.' He stretched out a hand. 'Carefully, boss. It looks pretty old. They can—'

The first explosion threw both men on to their backs. The subsequent, much louder blast buried them in stone fragments and dust as it brought down the rock wall. If either of them had been able to see, they could not have failed to notice the life-size marble statue on the floor of the hollow chamber that had just been revealed.

Mavros picked himself up gingerly, feeling his head for damage. To his amazement he found no more wounds, only a thick layer of grit in his hair. He stood up and retrieved the torch. By some miracle it had survived the explosion. Shining it around the cave, he saw that the other occupants were moving. Rena was holding a hand to her face where blood was welling from a cut and Liz was clutching her ears. Mikkel was wiping dust from his eyes while even the previously comatose Gretchen was showing signs of life, gasping and choking but able painfully to sit up.

Rinus stumbled into the outer chamber and returned quickly. 'Trace and Jane are all right,' he said, wiping blood from his forehead. 'What happened? Can we get out that way?'

Mavros nodded. 'The cave system leads to the dig. I found some explosives in—' He broke off as the torchlight fell on the sublime shape that was lying on the ground ahead. 'Oh my God,' he said, his eyes widening. 'Oh my God.'

He was dimly aware of the others gathering around him, staring silently at the piece. It was in the Cycladic style and, as far as he could tell, it was unique. There were the usual graceful lines and limbs, the arms folded beneath the woman's pointed breasts, her triangular head and nose raised upwards as if to the wide heavens. As in the smaller figurine Eleni had found, the marble was pale blue, its surface smooth, scarcely pitted by the passage of time or by the blast. But unlike the other piece, unlike any Cycladic work he'd ever seen before, this one was of two bodies, a male with braided hair alongside the woman, his arm round her back, the perfect, narrow fingers of one hand on the female's upper arm. It was a vision of love and serenity, of a prehistoric harmony that must once have prevailed on Trigono.

He stepped over the uneven surface and through the gaping hole in the cave wall, taking in the sprawled bodies on the other side. Both were motionless, dust-covered, but blood was welling up through the mineral layer. In the limited natural light from the apertures he caught sight of a tattered green sunshade on the far side. Aris. He was the nearer of the bodies, his head seriously damaged and the face shot with stone splinters. Moving to the other, he recognised the bulky frame of the watchman Mitsos. He must have been farther from the source of the blast and he looked less affected by it. His arms were twitching and his head rolling.

'Come on!' Mavros shouted to the others. 'The roof and walls may not be safe. We've got to get out.' He slipped back through the hole and ushered them out of the prison cave – Rena supporting Liz, Rinus helping Mikkel, and the two Englishwomen looking after Gretchen, whose head was lolling. He pointed them in the direction of the next exit hole and then pulled Mitsos to his feet. Aris was still out cold and he would have to take his chances till a rescue party arrived. They were also leaving the remains of what he feared was Rosa Ozal, but there was nothing that could be done for her now.

It was a struggle but the unscathed members of the group eventually got the injured through the caves, past the grave chambers and into the open air. The sun had sunk far into the west and twilight was well advanced, the north wind slightly less strong now that night was on its way.

'What shall we do?' Rinus asked, looking around the enclosed area of the dig nervously. 'Do you think Lefteris is still in the vicinity?'

'I'm certain he is,' Mavros said. 'But help should be on its way soon. Where the hell's Roy got to?' He checked his mobile and saw that it was still not picking up a signal. 'You stay here with the others. Get them back under cover in the trench. The generator will give light. If you feel like it, you can try to get your friend Aris out.'

The Dutchman looked very reluctant to re-enter the caves. 'Where are you going?'

'Down the track. I'll call for help from the Theocharis estate if I don't meet anyone on my way.'

Rinus nodded. 'Be careful, Alex.'

Mavros returned the nod and set off for the fence. This time he found the gate open. Presumably Aris hadn't thought he'd be gone for long. He went through it, glancing about in the gloom. If Lefteris was lurking out there, he was easy prey. He headed down the track past Eleni's useless motorbike, remembering that his mountain bike was at the bottom of the hill. He had only taken a few steps down the rutted path when he saw a shadowy figure ahead of him. He stopped moving, his heart pounding. Then he heard a familiar voice.

'Alex?'

'Eleni.' Relief flooded through him.

'Are you all right?' she asked, coming closer. 'I was on my way to find you. How's your head? That was quite a bang you gave yourself.'

'I survived it,' Mavros replied. 'You're a bit late. Where have you been?'

'Theocharis kept me in the tower.' Her voice was bitter. 'We've been busy impressing a dealer with the figurines I found. At least Aris and that wanker Mitsos didn't find the last one. I hid it under a bush. The bastards messed up my tyres.'

'I noticed.' Mavros gave her a résumé of what he and the others had been through, watching in the dying light as her face registered surprise and then horror at the discovery of Liz and the other victims. She didn't seem particularly interested in the double statue. When he'd finished, he started walking rapidly down the track again. 'I'm going to find a place with a signal to call for help,' he said over his shoulder.

'What shall I do?' Eleni called after him.

'Say goodbye,' said a deep voice in Greek to her left.

Mavros froze and jerked his head round. He made out a heavy form behind the archaeologist, one arm round her neck and the other holding a knife to her side.

'No!' he shouted. 'Don't, Lefteri, don't! It's finished. Too many people know what you've done. You can't kill everyone.' He started to move up the path cautiously.

'Can't I?' the fisherman asked with a hollow laugh. 'Can't I?'

'People know about what you've been doing,' Mavros said, trying to stop himself from gabbling. 'We all know about you. And I've told the police too.' He held up his mobile phone.

'Fuck you,' Lefteris said with a grunt. 'I'm not stupid. You can't get a signal out here, you Athenian pimp.'

'Barbara was your partner, wasn't she?' Mavros said, playing for time but standing still when Lefteris moved the knife closer to Eleni's side, making her gasp. 'Why did the two of you kidnap the women?'

The fisherman gazed at him in the gathering gloom, his eyes narrowed. 'Why do you think? I got to stick it in them, she got to film them. She hated that Rosa bitch because all the men in the Astrapi fancied her. Barbara was getting older and she couldn't take it. She liked seeing young women rot. And the other one? She was a real beauty. Barbara wanted her to pay too. Besides, she was asking too many questions about the past.' He glared at Mavros. 'Don't come any closer, you louse. My father and I would have crushed your head the other night if your friends hadn't saved you. You won't escape me again. But first you can watch this one die.'

Eleni's eyes were bulging, focused on Mavros.

'You killed Barbara, didn't you?' he said quickly, remembering Mikkel's words. 'Why?'

The islander grunted again. 'The bitch was losing control. She spent all her time playing the videos, watching the women suffer. She needed the dope too much and there hasn't been any since my fool of a son screwed up the delivery.' His eyes dropped for a moment. 'Besides, I can't get it up any more.' He pushed his groin against Eleni. 'Not even when I'm rubbing myself against a soft arse like this one.' He shook his head. 'Don't ask me why Barbara was doing it. She filmed them starving and dying of thirst, she even kept filming the first one on the same day every week after she was dead. She talked me into ramming a goat bone into the last one.' He gave a slack smile. 'Barbara was falling apart, she was crazy. If it had gone on much longer, she'd have landed me in trouble. I had enough of it. Killing her was easy.' Lefteris gave Mavros a bitter smile. 'Besides, you were turning up the heat with all your questions about Rosa. So you can take some of the blame, you piece of shit.' He cleared his throat. 'Don't worry, woman. It won't hurt for much longer.' He squeezed Eleni's neck then swore as she sank her teeth into his wrist.

Mavros stepped forward but he wasn't quick enough. The noise he'd been aware of behind him for a few seconds increased in volume and the three of them were caught in the glare of headlights on full beam. A vehicle was speeding up the slope, veering from side to side and, almost too late, Mavros realised it wasn't going to stop. He leaped out of the way, rolling over on the hard ground and watching it head straight at Lefteris and Eleni. At the last moment she managed to wrestle free of the fisherman's grip and dive away. There was a solid thud as the yellow hire car's front end ran into him, the blade of his knife glinting in the beam as it spiralled away through the air.

'Are you all right?' the driver asked, jumping down and running to Eleni.

'I think so,' she replied, standing up shakily.

Mavros joined them, his T-shirt studded with sharp burrs. 'Roy,' he said, taking in the Englishman. 'Christ, you took a chance there.'

Roy nodded. 'I saw the bastard was holding a knife to her

so I took him out.' He smiled loosely. 'Me and Norm were commandos. You learn moves that you never forget. Don't worry, love,' he said to Eleni. 'I'd have missed you even if you hadn't got out the way.' He looked ahead to the glow from the dig. 'Where's everyone else? Are they all okay?'

Mavros told him what had happened to Norm.

'I wouldn't worry about him too much,' Roy said. 'In the unit we used to say his head was made of concrete.' He glanced down. 'Is that bastard alive?'

Mavros had completely forgotten about Lefteris. He kneeled down by the islander's sprawled body and felt for a pulse. He didn't find one.

23

The island doctor arrived shortly afterwards. His breath smelled of ouzo, but he seemed to know what he was doing. He paid most attention to Liz Clifton and then to Aris after a group of locals had carried him out of the cave. As soon as the wind dropped, they would be taken to Athens by helicopter. The less seriously injured – Mikkel, Gretchen and Mitsos – were to be moved to the village for treatment in the pick-ups and vans that had belatedly followed Roy out to the southern massif. Before the American woman was driven from the dig plateau she asked after her man. Mavros had to tell her that Lance was dead.

'The idiot.' Although Gretchen's voice was weak, her tone was as irritated as ever. 'I told him to keep back from the edge. The fisherman told me he thought we were spying on him. Lance never had a chance.' She paused to take a breath. 'That crazy guy threw him over the edge before he could move. I went to look for him and got caught. I . . . I only managed to scream once before I was knocked out. I woke up in some ruined building with the Greek standing over me . . . God, he was frightening . . . I've never seen anyone so angry. He hit me again and I came round in that stinking cave. How did I get there?'

Mavros shrugged. 'He must have carried you and Mikkel down. He was as strong as an ox.'

'What a waste,' Gretchen said, her eyes dampening at last. 'It's my fault that we were out there. I was trying to find another way into the dig. I was only doing my job. I wanted to compare funerary customs.' She gave a crooked smile. 'I suppose the killer's behaviour will be a good source for my study of anger.'

Mavros looked to the sky in distaste and let a pair of villagers carry her away. He felt eyes on him and looked down the slope. One-armed Manolis was standing in a van's headlights. For a moment he thought the old man was going to approach him and berate him for what had happened to his son, but he didn't. He just turned away and melted into the night with his head down. Rena watched him go, a bloodstained dressing held to her face. She smiled shyly at Mavros then climbed into a pick-up.

Roy came out of the darkness to the west. Norm was walking behind him, one hand on his head. The Englishwomen ran to their men with shrieks of delight.

'Told you he'd be all right,' Roy said with a grin. 'The lead piping's had it, though.'

Norm gave a hollow laugh. 'Very funny, mate. At least I haven't run into anyone recently.'

'You'd better drive back, then,' Roy said, punching his shoulder.

Jane shook her head in despair. 'You guys,' she said. 'You're like kids. We could have been killed.'

'Nah,' Norm said, putting his arm around her. 'We had all the angles covered.'

Jane didn't look convinced, but her expression lightened as she nudged him in the ribs.

'See you in the bar later, Alex?' Trace asked.

He shrugged. 'I don't think Rinus will be opening. He's going to be helping the police with their enquiries pretty soon if Rena and Mikkel get their way.'

Norm shook his head and winced. 'No worries. I know where his spare key is.'

Mavros watched as they got into the Farma. To his amazement it started, despite the badly damaged front end.

After the injured had gone, Eleni insisted that Mavros accompany her to Paliopyrgos. While the convoy of vehicles had been loading up, she'd gone back into the cave system to make a preliminary examination of the entwined prehistoric figures. This had made her look even more determined. They got a lift down from the hillside in a pick-up. On the way into the tower, Mavros caught a glimpse of the dealer, Tryfon Roufos, through a doorway. Now he knew that Eleni was right – Theocharis had been going to dispose of the pieces she'd found.

In the study, after Mavros had told Theocharis and Dhimitra what had happened, Eleni stepped forward. 'You cannot sell the figurines,' she said to the museum benefactor. 'If you proceed, I'll go to the press. Alex will help me.' She shrugged. 'I don't care if you implicate me. Do you want to tell Roufos or shall I?'

The old man looked at her briefly then shook his head. 'I will tell him.' He glanced at Mavros and then at his wife. 'You are right, Eleni. All the finds must go to the museum.'

The archaeologist nodded, saying nothing about the largest and potentially most significant piece.

'The doctor told me that Aris might lose his sight,' Theocharis continued. 'The fool. What did he think he was doing?' He suddenly sank back on to the sofa. 'My God, what will become of us now? The family is falling apart.'

Dhimitra stubbed out her cigarette and went to him, but he pushed her away with surprising force. The gilded ex-singer gave him a look of undisguised loathing then walked out of the room.

Mavros and Eleni turned to follow but they stopped when they heard Theocharis's voice. It was now querulous.

'Mr Mavros,' he said. 'Look in the right-hand drawer of the desk. You will find an old diary. I had it taken from Elizabeth Clifton's room along with everything else my people could find pertaining to . . . pertaining to the war. I swear that I didn't know anything about what happened to her subsequently. Aris must have been talked into taking her up the track by the German woman. She could be very persuasive when she wanted to be. But believe me, my son was unaware of the horrors perpetrated by Lefteris and Barbara Hoeg in the cave.' He shook his head. 'I have been told by my sources in New York how low he has sunk, but he has never been able to keep his mouth shut. He would have let something slip, if not to me then to Dhimitra or to the others he thinks are his friends.'

Mavros went to the desk and took out the battered leather book, opening it to see tiny, almost illegible writing.

'There is much about the war in Trigono in there,' Theocharis said, 'not all of it flattering to me. Perhaps it will help you to understand the island and its people a little better.' He shook his head. 'I must apologise for the injuries that Manolis and Lefteris inflicted on you after you left the bar. I wanted them to find out about you, but they let their innate savagery get the better of them. Lefteris later removed your identification card and authorisation. He put them back during the night. He retained a key to the widow's house from the time when they had an affair.'

Mavros closed the book and stepped back towards the sofa. 'And Andonis?' he asked, his heartbeat quickening. 'My brother Andonis? Do you really have any information about him?'

The old man glanced up at him, his face gaunt beneath the tapered beard and his eyes cloudy. 'I'm sorry,' he said, his voice even fainter. 'That was nothing more than a device to get you off Trigono.'

Mavros felt his stomach somersault. After clenching and unclenching his fists several times he managed to convince himself that he'd never really believed Theocharis knew anything about Andonis. He had gone along with it because he had to, because love of his brother and the bonds of family duty required him to.

Eleni took his arm and led him away, leaving Trigono's leading citizen alone in his soulless mausoleum.

Mavros didn't leave Trigono immediately. He was exhausted, his head throbbing from the blows he'd taken. Army helicopters flew the badly injured away on the first day, the wind having dropped and been replaced, with typical Aegean unpredictability, by a southerly. He had slept badly and got up early in the morning, the events on the southern hills still troubling him.

Because of the complexity of the case and the fact that both Greek and foreign natives were among the dead and the suspects, a police unit was sent from Athens. They arrived at midday and took statements from everyone with painstaking attention to detail. Mavros managed to get them off his back by calling his high-ranking contact Kriaras and promising to make himself available as soon as he was back in Athens. Roy was questioned about Lefteris's death but he wasn't arrested and it didn't seem likely that he'd face charges.

Eleni, accompanied by a pair of policemen, was to take the smaller Cycladic pieces, including the one she'd retrieved from the bush where she'd hidden it, to the Culture Ministry's experts. She would also report the find of the life-size statue – it hadn't yet been removed from the unsafe cave. She was hopeful that she would be assigned a team of assistants to recover the latest find and to continue the dig, given its increased significance.

'Thank you for everything you've done, Alex,' she said after she had knocked on Rena's door. She declined to enter the widow's house. 'You're a duplicitous bastard, but your heart's in the right place.' Her expression darkened. 'I only wish I had been as questioning as you about Rosa's unexpected departure, the departure that never was. And about Liz.'

'People change their plans, leave early all the time,' Mavros said. 'It's the nature of the islands in the summer. Don't blame yourself.' He touched her arm. 'Who took the photos of you with Rosa and Liz. Was it Rinus?'

The archaeologist frowned and then nodded. 'Don't you ever give up? Yes, it was the Dutchman. He likes to think he's a woman-chaser, but mostly we laughed at him. He spent his spare time with porn videos. Or with poor Dinos. At least he never hurt him.'

'But he hit Rosa, didn't he?' Mavros said.

'Tapped her, more like. She slapped him so hard in return that his cheek glowed for a week. He didn't bother her again.'

'But he told people he'd seen Rosa leave,' he mused. 'Barbara put him up to that. Maybe he got some kind of kick out of the lie.' He met Eleni's eyes. 'Do you think he suspected what she and Lefteris were doing?'

She bit her lip and then shrugged. 'Who knows? I doubt it. We'll probably never find out.'

Rinus had been arrested for drug possession after the police searched his flat and found small amounts of grass and Ecstasy. Dealing would be a tougher charge to make stick. If he was lucky he'd serve a short sentence and be deported. Whatever happened, he wouldn't be coming back to Trigono.

'Good luck at the ministry.' Mavros smiled and touched her arm. 'No hard feelings?'

Eleni shook her head. 'No, Alex. I don't know why I tried to seduce you. I was under pressure, I was looking for a way to get back at Theocharis. I thought that if you were a dealer or a thief, you might—' She broke off and laughed. 'No, that's not it. You're a good-looking man. I just wanted you, that's all.' She leaned forward and kissed him on the cheek. 'You look terrible now, though. Get some sleep.' She turned and walked quickly down the street.

When Mavros surfaced in the late afternoon, he sat down at the table under the pergola in the yard and went through the diary that Theocharis had given him, deciphering the handwriting with difficulty. Then he told Rena about what old Maro had been through during the war.

'Christ and the Holy Mother,' Rena said when he finished. She was dabbing her eyes around the dressing on her cheek. 'She never told me. The poor woman. So it was true that she loved a foreign man in the war. My worthless husband told me she did and that she was responsible for her brother Manolis losing his arm. I thought he was just peddling gossip. But what happened to Kyra Maro's officer? For all his promises he never came back.' She looked across the yard at Melpo. The donkey had taken up residence there since the villagers' siege of the house and was chewing hay contentedly, her black eyes gleaming. 'Women are nothing but beasts of burden,' Rena said bitterly. 'They whip us, they crush us, and for what? Love? Children? That's all shit!'

Mavros nodded slowly, flicking his worry beads. Having to keep his hands off them when he was pretending to be a tourist had almost driven him back to cigarettes. 'By "they" you mean men?'

'Who else?' the widow replied, glaring at him. 'Don't tell me you treat women any differently.'

He froze, remembering Niki. She'd left a message on his mobile for him to call her that morning.

Rena was nodding, aware that she'd struck a nerve. 'Exactly. And what about Rinus? And Aris? I'm not even talking about that bastard Lefteris.' She shook her head. 'The only men who come out of this series of horrors with any dignity are the weak ones – Mikkel, the American who died . . .'

'Come on, Rena,' Mavros said. 'You're being unfair. Surely you don't think the Englishmen Roy and Norm were weak. As for George Lawrence, maybe he didn't even survive the war. Liz will probably know about that. I'll see if I can visit her in hospital when I get back to Athens.'

'Hmm.' Rena concentrated on searching for grit in a bowl of dry rice. 'I pray to God that she recovers.'

Mavros went into his room and called Niki. He was connected to her message service. It was only when it ran on beyond the usual instructions that he realised there was a new response.

'If Alex Mavros, private investigator and professional shit, is calling, let him stay on Trigono and copulate with the goats. Andhroniki Glezou doesn't need him. Go to hell, liar.'

He held the phone away from his ear and stared at it. He wasn't sure if Niki was serious, but he felt bad about telling her he'd been on Zakynthos. Hearing his name all over the TV and the radio when news of the case broke couldn't have been pleasant. He'd already had to make reassuring calls to his mother and sister, as well as promise his friend the reporter Lambis Bitsos an exclusive interview.

Sitting down on the bed, he went over the other things that had happened earlier in the day. Barbara's body had been removed from the freezer in her home that morning, following Mikkel's admission that he'd put it there for safe-keeping. The German was in a terrible state. Mavros thought about what he'd been through. Not only had he found his woman dead in the pool, but he'd been savagely attacked by Lefteris. The fisherman had

put the unconscious Mikkel and Gretchen next to the stoned
barman and then removed them, presumably to terrify Rinus
into silence about the drug trafficking. Dinos the goatherd had
seen Lefteris carrying the unconscious bodies. He appeared from
a hiding place on Profitis Ilias at dawn, his eyes wide. The city
policemen hadn't been able to make much sense of what he was
saying and Mavros had helped to calm the frightened young man
down. Dinos's mother came to meet him at the police station and
gave him an unsympathetic glare. No wonder he spent his time
on the hills with the goats.

Mavros went back outside and stood across the table from
the widow. 'Why were you so hostile to the Dutchman, Rena?'
he asked.

She looked up at him and shook her head. 'I told you I
was involved with Lefteris until I understood what a madman he
was.'

He nodded.

'His son Yiangos helped me, distracted his father from me when
he started beating me. I . . . I loved that boy.' Her eyes flashed. 'I
never had sex with him, despite what the idiot villagers think. But
I did love him, the wretched soul. When he told me what Lefteris
and Rinus were making him do, transporting and selling the drugs
in the village, I hated them for it. But I couldn't do anything about
it. Yiangos made me promise not to talk. He was very frightened
of Lefteris.'

Mavros sat down. 'Rena, why did you look at me like you
wanted to kill me when I saw you on the ridge above Lance's
body?'

The widow nodded. 'It was strange,' she said slowly. 'I'd been
working in the fields and my mind must have been wandering.
The wind was enough to drive anyone crazy. I looked down and
thought I saw my husband Argyris standing over his own corpse.'
She twitched her head. 'Ridiculous. You don't resemble him in
any way.' She gave an embarrassed smile. 'There was something
else.' She dropped her gaze. 'Your eyes, Alex. One of them is
different, the bright blue marked with brown. It fascinated me

and worried me at the same time. The old traditions are foolish, I know, but I couldn't stop myself thinking of the evil eye. There were times I thought you were the bringer of bad fortune.' She looked up at him and laughed lightly. 'If you are born a peasant, you can never shake off the beliefs you grow up with.'

Mavros felt uncomfortable. He had been vain enough to imagine that Rena fancied him and in fact she'd thought he was an emissary of the Devil. Then he remembered another occasion when the widow had scared him. 'I saw you out here in the early morning with a knife in your hand.' He was thinking about the absence of photos on her walls and the crumpled image of her husband under her pillow. 'Argyris . . . he wasn't good to you?'

Rena gave a sharp laugh. 'You could say that. He was weak compared with Lefteris, but he knew how to hurt me, especially after he'd been drinking.' She shook her head. 'Not that I knew anything different. My parents treated me harshly when I was a child. They wanted a son but I was all that arrived. I left my own island to get away from them.' She laughed again, this time bitterly. 'I didn't realise that Trigono was hell on earth. Sometimes I wish they were all dead, the islanders who hate Kyra Maro and me.'

Mavros held his eyes on her, steeling himself to ask the questions that still plagued him. 'Rena, I need to know,' he said slowly. 'I found some things I don't understand in your bedroom. A copy of a book about Trigono during the war – you know the one, written by the Paros historian Vlastos – and an ancient figurine.'

The widow's face was a study in melancholy. 'You are good at your job, Alex.' She shook her head. 'But the way you do it is wrong, the lying about who you are and the searching without permission.' She swallowed a sudden sob. 'Even if you did find poor Rosa.'

Mavros handed her a tissue and waited for her to dry her eyes. He heard the donkey's regular chewing from the corner of the yard above the chirping of the birds in the bougainvillaea. He could feel guilt gnawing at him, but he didn't know how else he could have broken the case.

'Oh, Alex,' Rena said with a sigh. 'Let it go. It's finished now.' She shook her head at him again. 'I took the book from the library the day before old Theocharis came to remove all the copies. I didn't want him to have his way, even though I didn't understand what he was doing. I was going to put it back in the library later. And the marble figure, that beautiful thing? I found it in Kyra Maro's field a few weeks ago. I was going to hand it over to the archaeologist, but as she'd tried to steal Rosa and Liz from me I thought again.' She looked away. 'If you must know, I want to give it to poor Maro. Especially now I know how she has suffered in her life.'

Mavros nodded. 'Don't worry, I won't tell anyone. But, Rena, why didn't you report the disappearances of Rosa and Liz?'

She looked at him as if he were a child. 'Have you any idea how many tourists visit this island in the summer, Alex? Have you any idea how many of them leave before they said they would? Why do you think I ask people to pay in advance?' She shrugged. 'I was upset because I thought they were my friends . . . my lovers.' She bent her head as another sob convulsed her. 'Oh God, how could they do that to Rosa? How could they leave her to rot? Oh God . . .'

Mavros felt a flood of compassion and he leaned forward, putting his hand on the widow's. He looked at her, with her dark hair drawn back under the scarf and the sleeves of her black blouse rolled up over her smooth arms. She had her forbidding side, but she was as fine a human being as he'd ever met – gentle, caring and selfless. He was ashamed that he had harboured suspicions about her. 'To think that the villagers say you poisoned your husband,' he said, taking his hand from hers and getting to his feet. 'The morons.' He turned away.

Her voice followed him across the yard. 'Are you completely sure I didn't, Alex?'

He stopped for a moment but didn't look back.

In the evening Mavros went out to the hill above the enclosed cemetery and looked away across the darkening waves to the western islands. The sun was low, the clouds in the pale blue sky suffused with a bright pink radiance. He was trying to get the case out of his mind, trying to lose himself in the beauty of the Aegean, but his experiences on Trigono were too vivid. In practical terms, the case had been a success – he had found Rosa Ozal, even though part of him wished he'd never seen her ravaged form. Indirectly, he had saved some precious artworks for Greece and the rest of humankind, as well as putting the screws on a rich man who had been corrupted by his wealth and power. And there would be fewer illicit drugs on the island, at least for a while.

But he still felt dispirited. If he had concentrated on Lefteris earlier, if he had followed up the signs he'd seen of the killer's violent nature, perhaps Barbara and Lance wouldn't have died and perhaps Gretchen and Mikkel would have escaped the physical and mental trauma they'd been subjected to. As it was, as the fisherman had pointed out, his questions had only brought about more senseless crimes.

He looked at the sea, following a white *trata* as it headed for the fishing grounds, gulls already above its stern. There was nothing he could have done for the young couple who had drowned, nothing he could have done to save Rosa Ozal from the savagery Lefteris had inherited from his father Manolis and turned into something worse. As he'd learned from Lawrence's diary, the old man had always been hard, his character forged by the island's harsh demands and by the war. That cruelty had been magnified as it moved down the generations. As for Barbara, he didn't have the courage to imagine how her mind had worked.

But then, as he became aware of the first stars in the sky's canopy, Mavros saw the other side of Trigono, its softer, more human dimension. The Cycladic figures rose up before him, the smooth lines of their unseeing faces and marble bodies, the entwined limbs of the ageless lovers that had been revealed by the explosion. George Lawrence and Maro had sustained themselves by love during the war, for all the lieutenant's poetic fantasies about Greece. Perhaps the doomed young couple, Yiangos and Navsika, had been passionate about each other too.

Suddenly he thought of his parents. Spyros and Dorothy had survived the war and the civil strife that followed it by loving each other without restraint. He considered his relationship with Niki and felt unworthy. But perhaps, like all the other romantic episodes in his life, this one was condemned to failure because of Andonis. Perhaps he loved his lost brother too much – the memory rather than the reality of him – to admit anyone else to his heart.

Mavros closed his eyes to shut out the shore and the running waves, the graveyard with its glowing white headstones and the islands fading into dusk.

It was time to leave Trigono and get back to the big city.

Kyra Maro left Tasos's bones in the box under her bed. This time she didn't feel the need to take them out – he was already so close. There was a pain in her chest that made breathing difficult but she wasn't concerned by it. She leaned back on the pillows, letting her thoughts drift.

'Ach, Rena,' she said quietly. 'You're a good woman. You brought me food this evening even though I didn't want it. And there was a strange look on your face, a sweet sadness in the way you smiled at me that for a moment made me wonder if you'd found something out about my life. I never told you about Tzortz or Tasos. It was better that way. You were already too close to me and the villagers hate you for it. Yes, you're a good woman, but even now I am keeping my counsel, keeping my beloved to myself. But where are they? Often they have risen up before me as they used to be, firm fleshed and joyful, only for me to wrap my arms around them and discover that they were phantoms, shadows without substance. Now it seems that I do not even have that consolation. Where are they? What remains of Tasos is beside me, but Tzortz; you are deep in the chill salt water. Was it for this emptiness that I fought across the years to have your name inscribed on the war memorial? Was it for this that I crept out in the night and wrote your name on the stone when Theocharis had it removed? Ach, Tzortz, I loved you for so little time on the surface of the earth and for so long in spirit. When will the torment end?'

In an instant Maro was back on the hills of the southern massif, the sun sinking in a blast of red over Andiparos. In her pocket was a handful of pomegranate seeds, an offering to the goddess of the underworld. She was running down the hillside with all her youthful vigour, the broom and thistles catching at her bare legs, but Tzortz was already on the flat rock by the water's edge. She kept screaming her lover's name, screaming it above the mocking cries of the gulls, begging him to wait.

And then, to her amazement, the story of her life was changed. Tzortz beckoned to her, his coat and torso no longer weighed down by stones. He smiled, and behind him she saw a boat approach, a shrouded figure at the helm. The water was slapping against the hull as it bobbed on the darkening surface. Maro was at the shore, the skin on the soles of her feet being scraped by the rock's sharp surface.

'Come, my love,' she heard her lover call. 'We must go now.'

He jumped into the water, but his head came back above the surface immediately. Without hesitating she followed him, pulling herself forward with her arms, surprised that the sea was not cold. When she reached the boat, Tzortz was already on board. He bent down and took her in his arms, lifting her on to the deck. Her heart soared as she saw Tasos beside them, their small son smiling, his head smooth and undamaged.

And as the sunlight died, the three of them sailed away together.

Into a deeper shade of blue.

24

Mavros watched as Deniz Ozal walked listlessly across the yard of the Fat Man's café and slumped on to a chair. Above them the blue-grey sky was choked with fumes, the noise of traffic throbbing in the distance. Grapes that had dropped from the vines lay uncollected on the gravel and the enclosed space smelled of fermenting juice. The improvised wasp traps hanging from the pergola were full of insects, a dull buzz emanating from the few that were still alive.

'Would you like a cup of coffee?' he asked the Turkish-American. 'You take *varyglyko*, don't you?'

Ozal waved a hand weakly. 'No coffee.' His face was pale and sweaty. 'I can't keep anything down.'

Mavros shook his head to keep the Fat Man at bay, not that he'd shown much inclination to take an order. 'I'm very sorry about your sister,' he said, feeling the inadequacy of the words.

His client was nodding slowly. 'Yeah, well, you did a hell of a job.' He looked up briefly. 'Except I kinda wish you'd never found poor Rosa.' He swallowed hard and brought a handkerchief to his face. 'They wanted me to look at her remains, you know. What could I tell them? They already knew it was her from the dental records.' He clenched his face. 'Those fucking bastards, why did they do that to her?' He stared into Mavros's eyes as if he expected an answer. When one failed to come, he bowed his head again. 'She was on holiday, for Chrissakes, all she wanted was sun and sand, maybe a bit of sex, how the fuck would I know?' His words tailed away into a groan.

Mavros's curiosity got the better of him. 'She wasn't checking the place out for you, was she? Trying to get a look at Theocharis's private collection?' His client gave him an agonised look. 'I saw you meet Tryfon Roufos after you came here. He has a reputation. I want a straight answer. Were you going to bid for antiquities from Trigono?'

'What?' Deniz Ozal's expression was incredulous. 'Is that what you think? I sent my sister into that nest of vipers? Fuck you, dick.' He pulled an envelope from his jacket pocket and unfolded documents. 'It's none of your business, but take a look if you want. Imperial Turkish coins. That's what I'm buying from Roufos. If the asshole ever shows up at his office.'

Mavros pushed the papers away. Ozal's indignation had already convinced him. Rosa had simply been unlucky in her choice of holiday island.

'One thing puzzles me,' his client said, standing up unsteadily. 'That postcard we got from Rosa in Turkey after she had supposedly left Trigono.'

Mavros nodded. He'd been thinking about that himself. 'Barbara Hoeg must have forged her writing – they were capital letters – or got someone else to do it. She was a designer, remember. She'd have known plenty of draughtsmen. I guess she sent it to some contact in Turkey to post.'

Ozal was fumbling in his pockets again. 'If the postcard Rosa sent from Trigono hadn't turned up after all that time, I'd never have sent you down there.' He shrugged. 'Like I say, I almost wish I hadn't.'

Mavros nodded. He felt the same way. But at least he'd managed to save Liz Clifton from sharing Rosa's fate.

'Here,' the Turkish-American said. 'A bonus for your trouble. You look like you took a major beating.'

Mavros glanced at the wad of notes and handed it back. Standing up and reaching into his own pocket, he took out the plastic bag containing Rosa's postcards and photographs. 'You'll want these back. Use the money for flowers. Your mother will need comforting.'

Deniz Ozal looked at him in amazement then pocketed the cash.

'Hell of a lot of flowers, dick,' he said, and turned away. 'See you around.'

Mavros watched him go, shaking his head. He wished he could believe that the antiquities dealer would give some relief to his mother, but he didn't think the Turkish-American was capable of it.

The Fat Man lumbered up. 'Did I see correctly just now?' he demanded. 'Did you turn down money?' He didn't wait for a reply. 'Are you out of your mind?'

'Come on, Yiorgo, I don't want his blood money.'

The café owner grunted. 'So suddenly now you're the class warrior, refusing the rich man's loot? Didn't your father teach you anything? First you take their capital, then you stage the revolution.'

Mavros sat down wearily. 'Go away, Fat Man,' he said.

'I was going to ask you if you'd like the last piece of *galaktoboureko*. I kept it specially.' Yiorgos turned towards the bar. 'But if you don't want—'

'I want it,' Mavros interrupted. 'Bring it over here and I'll tell you about the case.'

A wide grin spread across the Fat Man's face. 'That's better. Just a minute while I close up.' Despite the way he disparaged Mavros's career, he was always keen to hear the details of his investigations.

Mavros waited till his friend had barricaded them from the outside world and returned with the pastry. The Fat Man put it on the table and then sank on to the chair opposite. For a moment Mavros thought it was going to collapse under the weight, but it held.

'Aach!' he said as he tasted the *galaktoboureko*. 'Better than ever.' Then he started the story. He was breaking every rule of client confidentiality, but he didn't care. The Fat Man was his confessor, as far as the atheist son of a leading communist could have such a figure. Besides, if he couldn't trust Yiorgos Pandazopoulos, the world and everything in it was lost.

*　　*　　*

'May the bastards rot in hell,' the Fat Man cursed when Mavros finished speaking an hour later. 'All of them. The murderers, the rich man who tried to sell his country's heritage to that shit Roufos, the British officer who seduced the island girl—'

Mavros raised a hand. 'No, Yiorgo. George Lawrence wasn't a bad man. I spoke to the writer Liz Clifton in the hospital yesterday. She almost died from the effects of prolonged dehydration, but she's improving now.' He ran his thumb over his worry beads. 'By the way, in case you were wondering, she was the one who put the disk and the photos in the chimney. The one of George Lawrence was hers, but the other two were Rosa's. Liz found them in a gap beside the fireplace. They must have been holiday snaps Rosa had taken that weren't found by Lefteris when he took the rest of her possessions, or by Rena when she was cleaning. Anyway, she told me that Lawrence's poems show that he was tortured by guilt about his conduct. And the diary proves how much in love he was with Maro.'

'Love!' scoffed the Fat Man. 'There are more important things in the world than love.'

Mavros lowered his gaze. Maybe Yiorgos was right. His own love life had never been very successful. He hadn't even been able to track down Niki since his return. She hadn't left any nasty surprises for him at his flat, but she wasn't answering any of her phones. Maybe she had found someone more reliable.

'Ah,' said the Fat Man. 'You agree.'

'No, I don't,' Mavros said, shaking his head and dropping the beads on to the table. 'I had a call from the widow Rena. Old Maro died in her sleep last night. A photo of George Lawrence was in her arms and . . . and she was smiling.' He felt his eyes sting as his brother Andonis's face suddenly rose up. As ever, there was a smile on his lips too.

'Christ and the Holy Mother,' Yiorgos said anxiously. 'Don't tell me you're turning into a romantic. Surely private investigators can't afford to have too many emotions. You have to nail the bad guys like Theocharis and Roufos.'

'Don't worry. I'll get Roufos the next time, Yiorgo.' Mavros looked at him quizzically. 'But you're wrong. Private investigators can't afford to do *without* their emotions.'

The Fat Man heaved himself to his feet. 'See, what do I always tell you, Alex? You're a freak with an alien's eye, a half-breed. You keep letting your passionate Scottish side overrule your natural Greek coldness.' His lips formed into a crooked smile.

Mavros looked at him seriously. 'That's right,' he said in a level voice. 'I'm a permanent stranger. I don't fit in anywhere.' Then he laughed. 'Now get your hundred per cent Greek carcass over to the stove and make me a coffee. At the double, comrade.'

The Fat Man obliged.

WIN

A DREAM HOLIDAY FOR TWO ON A GREEK ISLAND

Win a two-week self-catering holiday on a Greek Island
including flights, accommodation and transfers for two people,
courtesy of Advantage Travel Centres and Argo Holidays.

Advantage Travel Centres is the UK's largest group of
independent travel agents, offering unparalleled choice,
professional advice and competitively priced holidays.

Argo Holidays is a specialist in holidays to Greece and Cyprus
and has been providing high quality service since 1994. Argo's
portfolio includes a superb range of locations featuring 19 Greek
Islands and 7 mainland resorts with departures from most major
UK airports.

For more information on Advantage Travel Centres visit
www.advantage4travel.com

To enter the competition
simply answer the following question:

What nationality is private investigator Alex Mavros?

Then send your answer on a postcard with
your name, address and a daytime telephone number to:

A DEEPER SHADE OF BLUE holiday competition
Marketing Department
Hodder & Stoughton Publishers
338 Euston Road, London, NW1 3BH

Closing date for entries: 30 June 2003

See over for terms and conditions

TERMS AND CONDITIONS

1   The competition is open to residents of the UK and Ireland only excluding employees of Hodder Headline, Advantage Travel Centres and Argo Holidays, their families, agents and anyone connected with the promotion of the competition. Entrants must be aged 18 years or over and hold a valid 10-year passport.

2   Closing date for receipt of entries is 30 June 2003.

3   The first entry drawn on 4 July 2003 will be declared the winner and notified by post.

4   The decision of the judges is final. No correspondence will be entered into.

5   No purchase necessary. Number of entries restricted to one per household.

6   The prize consists of a two-week holiday for two people to a Greek island served by Argo Holidays, in self-catering accommodation. It includes standard class return flights from the UK to the destination Greek airport, transport between the arrival airport and the holiday accommodation, and 14-nights' accommodation including service charges. Not included in the prize: travel and other insurance, optional excursions, gratuities, food, drinks, laundry and any other items of a personal nature.

7   All holidays are subject to availability and tour operator's terms and conditions apply.

8   The prize is non-transferable and non-refundable and no alternatives can be substituted.

9   Hodder Headline reserves the right at any time to amend or terminate any part of the promotion without prior notice.

10   Hodder Headline cannot accept responsibility for the service provided by Argo Holidays.

11   Applicants must send their applications by registered post to ensure delivery. Responsibility cannot be accepted for damaged, illegible, or incomplete entries, or those arriving after the closing date.

12   The winner's name will be available from the above address from 4 July 2003.

13   Winners may be required to participate in publicity events.

14   Competition closes 30 June 2003 and the holiday must be taken by end of October 2004.

Promoter: Hodder Headline, 338 Euston Road, London, NW1 3BH